D1030879

THE BODLEY HEAD
SCOTT FITZGERALD
VOLUME 5

THE BODLEY HEAD

SCOTT FITZGERALD

VOLUME 5

SHORT STORIES

SELECTED AND INTRODUCED BY

MALCOLM COWLEY

THE BODLEY HEAD

LONDON SYDNEY TORONTO

The publishers are indebted to Charles Scribner's Sons, New York, for permission to reprint, in an expanded and adapted form, Malcolm Cowley's introduction to *The Stories of F. Scott Fitzgerald* (1951)

SBN 370 00565 1
This selection © The Bodley Head Ltd 1963

Printed and bound in Great Britain for
The Bodley Head Ltd
9 Bow Street, London WC2
by William Clowes & Sons Ltd, Beccles
Set in Plantin
First published 1963
Reprinted 1968

CONTENTS

INTRODUCTION

THOSE Americans who were lucky enough to be born a little before the end of the old century, in any of the years from 1895 to 1900, went through much of their lives with a feeling that the new century had been placed in their charge; it was like a business in financial straits that could be rescued by a timely change in management. Optimists as they were by nationality, they believed that the business was fundamentally sound. They identified themselves with the century; its teens were their teens, troubled but confident; its world war was theirs to fight on the winning side; its reckless twenties were their twenties. As they launched into their careers they looked about them for spokesmen, and the first one they found was F. Scott Fitzgerald.

Among his qualifications for the role was the sort of background that his generation regarded as typical. Scott was a mid-Western boy, born in St Paul on September 24, 1896, to a family of Irish descent that had some social standing and a very small fortune inherited by the mother. The father was not a business success, and the fortune diminished year by year, so that the Fitzgeralds, like all people in their situation, had to think a lot about money. It was help from a maiden aunt that enabled Scott to fulfil his early dream of going to an Eastern preparatory school and then going to Princeton.

He liked to imagine himself as the hero of romantic dramas and worked in bursts to cut a figure among his classmates. At the Newman School—which was Catholic, as the name suggests—he went through a period of being the most unpopular boy, then redeemed himself by making the football team and winning first prize in the senior field day. At Princeton he was too light for football and took no interest in less heroic sports, but he showed some talent as a campus politician. He was taken into what he

7

regarded as the best of the eating clubs, the Cottage—
which he would describe in his first novel as 'an impressive mélange of brilliant adventurers and well-dressed
philanderers'—and he also wrote a large part of two
musical comedies produced with success by the Triangle
Club. The second of these was *The Evil Eye*, with lyrics
by Fitzgerald and a libretto by his friend Edmund Wilson.
The *Princetonian* reported on January 7, 1916, that when
it was played in Chicago 'Three hundred young ladies
occupied the front rows of the house and following the
show, they stood up, gave the Princeton locomotive and
tossed their bouquets at cast and chorus.'

They were among the first of Fitzgerald's flappers and
he would have loved them, all three hundred, but he
didn't make the tour with the Triangle show. At the
end of November he had withdrawn from college, partly
because of illness, but also because his marks had fallen
so low that there was every chance of his being suspended
after the midyear examinations. He had to abandon his
hope of being president of the Triangle Club and a big
man in his class. 'A year of terrible disappointments and
the end of all college dreams,' he wrote in the big ledger
that served as a bookkeeping record of his triumphs and
disasters. 'Everything bad in it was my own fault.' The
next year, 1916–17, he described in the ledger as 'A
pregnant year of endeavour. Outwardly a failure with
moments of danger but the foundation of my literary life.'
Fitzgerald was back at Princeton and was paying somewhat more attention to his studies, now that he had failed
to make his mark in football or campus politics, but
chiefly he was writing funny pieces for the *Tiger* and
serious prose and verse for the *Nassau Literary Magazine*.
He also managed to put together the first draft of a novel.
under the accurate title of *The Romantic Egotist*.

In the autumn of 1917, after passing a special examination, he received a provisional commission as second
lieutenant in the Regular Army. He went off to training
camp, where he finished most of the novel during week-

ends, and then served in Alabama as aide-de-camp to Major General J. A. Ryan. It was at a dance in Montgomery that he fell in love with a judge's daughter, Zelda Sayre, whom he described to his friends as 'the most beautiful girl in Alabama *and* Georgia'; one state wasn't big enough to encompass his admiration. 'I didn't have the two top things: great animal magnetism or money,' he wrote years afterwards in his notebook. 'I had the two second things, though: good looks and intelligence. So I always got the top girl.'

He was engaged to the judge's daughter, but they couldn't marry until he was able to support her. After being discharged from the Army without getting overseas, Fitzgerald went to New York and looked for a job. *The Romantic Egotist* had been rejected by Scribner's, with letters from Maxwell Perkins—not yet a famous editor—that showed a real interest in Fitzgerald's future work. His stories were coming back from the magazines, and at one time he had 122 rejection slips pinned in a frieze around his cheap bedroom on Morningside Heights. The job he found was with an advertising agency, and his pay started at ninety dollars a month, with not much chance of rapid advancement; the only praise he received was for a slogan written for a steam laundry in Muscatine, Iowa: 'We Keep You Clean in Muscatine.' He was trying to save money, but the girl in Alabama saw that the effort was hopeless and broke off the engagement on the score of common sense. Fitzgerald borrowed from his classmates, stayed drunk for three weeks, and then went home to St Paul to rewrite his novel under a new title. This time Scribner's accepted it, and the book was published at the end of March, 1920.

This Side of Paradise was a very young man's novel and memory book. The author put into it samples of everything he had written until that time: short stories, poems, essays, fragments of autobiography, sketches, and dialogues. Some of the material had already been printed in the *Nassau Lit*, so that his friends described the book

1*

as the collected works of F. Scott Fitzgerald. It also had suggestions of being the rejected works of Compton Mackenzie and H. G. Wells, with more than a hint of *Stover at Yale*; but for all its faults and borrowings it was held together by its energy, honesty, self-confidence, and it spoke in the voice of a new generation. His contemporaries recognized the voice as their own and his elders listened.

Suddenly the magazines were eager to print Fitzgerald's stories and willing to pay high prices for them. The result shows in his big ledger: in 1919 he earned $879 by his writing; in 1920 he earned—and spent—$18,850. Early success had been added to everything else that made him stand out as a representative of his generation, and Fitzgerald himself was beginning to believe in his representative quality. He was learning that when he wrote truly about his dreams and misadventures and discoveries, other people recognized themselves in the picture.

The point has to be made that Fitzgerald was not 'typical' of his own age or any other. He lived harder than most people have ever lived and acted out his dreams with an extraordinary intensity of emotion. The dreams themselves were not at all unusual; in the beginning they were dreams of becoming a football star and a big man in college, of being a hero on the battlefield, of winning through to financial success, and of getting the top girl; they were the commonplace aspirations shared by almost all the young men of his time and social class. It was the emotion he put into them, and the honesty with which he expressed the emotion, that made them seem distinguished. By feeling intensely he made his readers believe in the unique value of the world in which they lived. Years afterwards he would say, writing in the third person, that he continued to feel grateful to the Jazz Age because 'It bore him up, flattered him and gave him more money than he had dreamed of, simply for telling people that he felt as they did.'

At the beginning of April, 1920, Zelda came to New York and they were married in the rectory of St Patrick's Cathedral—although Zelda's family was Episcopalian and Scott had ceased to be a good Catholic. To their bewilderment they found themselves adopted not as a Southerner and a mid-Westerner respectively, not even as detached observers, but—Scott afterwards wrote—'as the arch type of what New York wanted.' A new age was beginning, and Scott and Zelda were venturing into it innocently, hand in hand. Zelda said, 'It was always tea-time or late at night.' Scott said, 'We felt like small children in a great bright unexplored barn.'

Scott also said, 'America was going on the greatest, gaudiest spree in history and there was going to be plenty to tell about it.' There is still plenty to tell about it, in the light of a new age that is curious about the 1920's and persistently misjudges them. The gaudiest spree in history was also a moral revolt, and beneath the revolt were social transformations. The American 1920's were the age when Puritanism was under attack, with the Protestant churches losing their dominant position. They were the age when the country ceased to be English and Scottish and when the children of later migrations moved forward to take their places in the national life. Theodore Dreiser, whom Fitzgerald regarded as the greatest living American writer, was German Catholic by descent, H. L. Mencken was North German Protestant, and Fitzgerald did not forget for a moment that one side of his own family was 'straight potato-famine Irish.' Most of his heroes had Irish names and all except Gatsby were city bred, thus reflecting another social change. The 1920's were the age when American culture became urban instead of rural and when New York set the social and intellectual standards for the country, while its own standards were being set by transplanted Southerners and mid-Westerners like Zelda and Scott.

More essentially the 1920's were the age when a *production* ethic—of saving and self-denial in order to accumulate capital for new enterprises—gave way to a *consumption* ethic that was needed to provide markets for the new commodities endlessly streaming from the production lines. Instead of being exhorted to save money, more and more of it, people were being instructed in a thousand ways to buy, enjoy, use once and throw away, in order to buy a later and more expensive model. They followed the instructions, with the result that more goods were produced and consumed or wasted and money was easier to earn than ever in the past. Foresight went out of fashion. 'The Jazz Age,' Fitzgerald would say, 'now raced along under its own power, served by great filling stations full of money. . . . Even when you were broke you didn't worry about money, because it was in such profusion around you.'

Young men and women in the 1920's had a sense of reckless confidence not only about money but about life in general. It was part of their background: they had grown up in the years when middle-class Americans read Herbert Spencer and believed in the doctrine of automatic social evolution. No matter how rebellious and cynical the youngsters thought of themselves as being, they clung to their childhood notion that the world would improve without their help; therefore most of them felt excused from seeking the common good. Plunging into their personal adventures, they took risks that didn't impress them as being risks because, in their hearts, they believed in the happy ending.

They were truly rebellious, however, and were determined to make an absolute break with the standards of the pre-war generation. The distinction between highbrow and lowbrow (or liberal and conservative) was not yet sharp enough to divide American society; the real gulf was between the young and the old. The younger set paid few visits to their parents' homes, and some of them hardly exchanged a social word with men or women over forty. The elders were suspected of being stuffy, and besides they had made a mess of the world; they were

discredited in younger eyes by the war and the Treaty
of Versailles, by Prohibition, by the Red scare of 1919–20,
and by the scandals that clustered round Teapot Dome
and the little green house on K Street, in Washington,
where members of President Harding's Cabinet and
sometimes the President himself played poker with the
oil barons. So let the discredited elders keep to themselves; the youngsters would then have a free field in
which to test their own standards of the good life.

Those standards were elementary and close to being
savage. Rejecting almost everything else, the spokesmen
for the new generation celebrated the value of simple
experiences like love, foreign travel, good food, drunkenness, and personal talent freely expressed. They also
recognized the value of patient craftsmanship when they
had time for it, and the value of being truthful, even if
it hurt their families or friends and most of all if it
hurt themselves; almost any action seemed excusable and
even admirable in those days if one simply told the truth
about it, without boasting, without shame. They liked
to say yes to every proposal that suggested excitement.
Will you take a new job, throw up the job, go to Paris
and starve, travel round the world in a freighter? Will
you get married, leave your husband, spend a week-end
for two in Biarritz? Will you ride through Manhattan
on the roof of a taxi and then go bathing in the Plaza
fountain? 'WYBMADIITY?' read a sign on the mirror
behind the bar of a popular speakeasy, the Dizzy Club.
Late at night one asked the bartender what it meant, and
he answered, 'Will You Buy Me a Drink If I Tell You?'
The answer was yes, always yes, and the fictional heroine
of the 1920's was Serena Blandish, the girl who couldn't
say no. Or the heroine was Joyce's Molly Bloom as she
dreamed about the days when she was being courted:
'. . . and I thought as well him as another and then I
asked him with my eyes to ask again yes and then he
asked me would I yes to say yes my mountain flower
and first I put my arms around him yes and drew him

down to me so he could feel my breasts all perfume yes and his heart was going like mad and yes I said yes I will Yes.'

The masculine ideal of the 1920's was what Fitzgerald called 'the old dream of being an entire man in the Goethe–Byron–Shaw tradition, with an opulent American touch, a sort of combination of J. P. Morgan, Topham Beauclerk and St Francis of Assisi.' The entire man would be one who 'did everything,' good and bad, who realized all the potentialities of his nature and thereby acquired wisdom. The entire man, in the 1920's, was one who followed the Rule of the Thelemites as revealed by Rabelais: *Fais ce qu vouldras*, 'Do what you will!' But that rule implied a second imperative like an echo: 'Will!' To be admired by the 1920's young men had to *will* all sorts of actions and had to possess enough energy and boldness to carry out even momentary wishes. They lived in the moment with what they liked to call 'an utter disregard of consequences.' In spirit they all made pilgrimages to the abbey of the Thelemites, where they consulted the Oracle of the Divine Bottle and received for answer the one word *Trinch*. They obeyed the oracle and drank, in those days of the Volstead Act when drinking was a rite of comradeship and an act of rebellion. As Fitzgerald said at the time, they drank 'cocktails before meals like Americans, wines and brandies like Frenchmen, beer like Germans, whiskey-and-soda like the English . . . this preposterous mélange that was like a gigantic cocktail in a nightmare.'

But the 1920's were not so much a drinking as a dancing age—the Jazz Age, as Fitzgerald liked to call it. In those days one heard jazz everywhere—from orchestras in ballrooms, from wind-up phonographs in the parlours, from loudspeakers blaring in dime stores, lunch wagons, even machine shops, repeating the same tunes time and again: 'Organ Grinder,' 'Limehouse Blues,' 'Empty Bed Blues,' 'Vagabond Lover,' 'Broadway Melody'—and jazz wasn't regarded as something to listen to and be cool about, without even tapping one's foot; jazz was music with a useful purpose, *Gebrauchsmusik,* to use a once popular German word; it was music to which one danced:

I met her in Chicago and she was married—
dance all day,
leave your man, Sweet Mamma, and come away;
pink nails and permanent kisses, to dance all day, all day—·
how it was sad.

Please, Mr Orchestra, play us another tune.

My daddy went and left me and left the cupboard bare;
who will pay the butcher bill now Daddy isn't there?
Shuffle your feet.

Found another daddy and he taught me not to care
and how to care;
found another daddy that I'll follow anywhere.
Shuffle your feet, dance,

dance among the tables, dance across the floor,
slip your arms around me, we'll go dancing out the door,
Sweet Mamma, anywhere, through any door;
wherever the banjos play is Tennessee.

Jazz carried with it a constant message of change, excitement, violent escape, with an undertone of sadness, but also with a promise of enjoyment somewhere around the corner of next week, perhaps at midnight in a distant country. The young men heard the message and followed it anywhere, through any door, even the one that led into what was then, for Americans, the new world of difficult art. They danced too much, they drank too much, but they also worked, with something of the same desperation; they worked to rise, to earn social rank, to sell, to advertise, to organize, to invent gadgets, and to create enduring works of literature. In ten years, before losing their first vitality, they gave a new tempo to American life.

The 1920's were a good age for works of art, and in some ways they were a bad age for artists as persons.

The works of art have come down to us, and we are now finding again how honest and impressive they were in their often fragmentary fashion. Many of the artists failed to survive; in general the age did not encourage them to develop steadily or to achieve unified careers. The age has been blamed for the relative failures of Fitzgerald and others like him, but a great deal of this talk was sentimental. They did not fail as artists, or we should not be rereading their works. If they failed in their personal lives it was not because they were victims of the historical environment; it was—among other reasons —because they acted on dangerous principles which happened to be those of the age, but which they also took into themselves and accepted as their own. In that sense they succumbed like the age itself, not so much to the pressure of exterior forces as by inner necessity.

Fitzgerald not only represented the age but came to suspect that he had helped to create it, by setting the pattern of conduct that would be followed by persons a little younger than himself. 'If I had anything to do with creating the manners of the contemporary American girl I certainly made a botch of the job,' he said in a 1925 letter. In his notebook he observed that one of his relatives was still a flapper in the 1930's. 'There is no doubt,' he added, 'that she originally patterned herself upon certain immature and unfortunate writings of mine, so that I have a special fondness for —— as for one who has lost an arm or a leg in one's service.' A drunken young man teetered up to his door and said, 'I had to see you. I feel I owe you more than I can say. I feel that you formed my life.' It was not the young man—later a widely read novelist and an alcoholic—but Fitzgerald himself who was the principal victim of his capacity for creating fictional types in life. 'Sometimes,' he told another visitor late at night, 'I don't know whether Zelda and I are real or whether we are characters in one of my novels.'

That was in the spring of 1933, a few weeks after the

banks had closed all over the country. The Fitzgeralds were living at La Paix, a brown wooden late-Victorian lodge on a thirty-acre estate near Baltimore—'La Paix (my God!),' Scott wrote at the head of a letter. In the afternoon the house had been filled with little sounds of life—the coloured cook and her relatives arguing in the kitchen, Zelda talking to her nurse or rustling about the studio as she painted furiously, Scott somewhere in a back room dictating to his secretary, then their daughter coming home from school and playing under the big oak trees on the lawn. Zelda wasn't well enough to come down to dinner, but the visitor was taken to see her afterwards; her face was emaciated, and she had raked her fingers down one cheek, leaving four parallel red stripes. After dinner the sounds of life died away from the house. Little Scottie was put to bed, the cook and her friends went home, Zelda had to rest, and big Scott wandered from room to room with a glass in his hand, explaining that it was water; then, as he started another trip to refill the glass in the kitchen, he confessed that it was gin. There was not enough furniture, there were no carpets to absorb the inhuman noises of the night. Everything creaked and echoed. The visitor sat alone in the one big chair in the almost empty living-room and thought that the house was the perfect setting for a ghost story, with Scott and Zelda as ghosts, the golden boy of 1920 and the belle of two states. Their generation had been defeated by life—so it seemed at the time—and yet in their own defeat they were still its representative figures.

II

In victory and defeat Fitzgerald retained a quality that very few writers are able to acquire: a sense of living in history. Manners and morals were changing all through his life and he set himself the task of recording the changes. They were revealed to him, not by statistics or news reports, but in terms of living characters, and the characters were revealed by gestures, each appropriate to a certain year. He wrote: 'One day in 1926 we'—meaning the members of his generation—'looked down and found we had flabby arms and a fat pot and we couldn't say boop-boop-a-doop to a Sicilian. . . . By 1927 a widespread neurosis began to be evident, faintly signalled, like a nervous beating of the feet, by the popularity of cross-word puzzles. . . . By this time'—also in 1927—'contemporaries of mine had begun to disappear into the dark maw of violence. . . . By 1928 Paris had grown suffocating. With each new shipment of Americans spewed up by the boom the quality fell off, until towards the end there was something sinister about the crazy boatloads.'

He tried to find the visible act that revealed a moral quality inherent in a certain moment of time. He was haunted by time, as if he wrote in a room full of clocks and calendars. He made lists by the hundred, including lists of the popular songs, the football players, the top débutantes (with the types of beauty they cultivated), the hobbies and the slang expressions of a given year; he felt that all these names and phrases belonged to the year and helped to reveal its momentary colour. 'After all,' he said in an otherwise undistinguished magazine story, 'any given moment has its value; it can be questioned in the light of after-events, but the moment remains. The young prince in velvet gathered in lovely domesticity around the queen amid the hush of rich draperies may presently grow up to be Pedro the Cruel or Charles the Mad, but the moment of beauty was there.'

Fitzgerald lived in his great moments, and lived in them again when he remembered their drama; but he also stood apart from them and coldly reckoned their causes and consequences. That is his doubleness or irony, and it is one of his distinguishing marks as a writer. He took part in the ritual orgies of his time, but he also kept a secretly detached position, regarding himself as a pauper living among millionaires, a Celt among Sassenachs, and a sullen peasant among the nobility; he said that his point of vantage 'was the dividing line between two generations,' pre-war and post-war. Always he cultivated a double vision. In his novels and stories he was trying to present the glitter of life in the Princeton eating clubs, on the North Shore of Long Island, in Hollywood, and on the French Riviera; he surrounded his characters with a mist of admiration, and at the same time he kept driving the mist away. He liked to know 'where the milk is watered and the sugar sanded, the rhinestone passed for the diamond and the stucco for stone.' It was as if all his stories described a big dance to which he had taken, as he once wrote, the prettiest girl:

> There was an orchestra—Bingo-Bango
> Playing for us to dance the tango
> And the people all clapped as we arose
> For her sweet face and my new clothes—

and as if he stood at the same time outside the ballroom, a little mid-Western boy with his nose to the glass, wondering how much the tickets cost and who paid for the music. But it was not a dance he was watching so much as it was a drama of conflicting manners and aspirations in which he was both the audience and the leading actor. As audience he kept a cold eye on the actor's performance. He wrote of himself when he was twenty, 'I knew that at bottom I lacked the essentials. At the last crisis, I knew I had no real courage, perseverance or self-respect.' Sixteen years later he was just as critical, if in a more discriminating fashion, and he said to the visitor at La Paix, 'I've got a very limited talent. I'm a workman of letters, a professional. I know when to write and when to stop writing.' It was the maximum of critical detachment, but it was combined with the maximum of immersion in the drama. He said in his notebook, and without the least exaggeration, 'Taking things hard, from Ginevra to Joe Mankiewicz,' mentioning the names of his first unhappy love and of a Hollywood producer who, so he thought, had ruined one of his best scripts: 'That's the stamp that goes into my books so that people read it blind like Braille.'

The drama he watched and in which he played—and overplayed—a leading part was a moral drama leading to rewards and punishments. 'Sometimes I wish I had gone along with that gang,' he said in a letter that discussed musical comedies and mentioned Cole Porter and Rogers and Hart; 'but I guess I am too much a moralist at heart and want to preach at people in some acceptable form, rather than to entertain them.' The morality he wanted to preach was a simple one, in the midst of the prevailing confusion. Its four cardinal virtues were Industry, Discipline, Responsibility (in the sense of meeting one's social and financial obligations) and Maturity (in the sense of learning to expect little from life while making one's best effort always). The good people in his stories had these virtues and the bad ones had the corresponding vices. 'All I believe in in life,' he wrote to his daughter, 'is the rewards for virtue (according to your talents) and the *punishments* for not fulfilling your duties, which are doubly costly.'

The handle by which he took hold of his characters was their dreams. These, as I said, might be commonplace or even cheap, but almost always Fitzgerald managed to surround them with an atmosphere of the mysterious and illimitable or of the pitifully doomed. His great scenes were, so to speak, played to music: sometimes the music from a distant ballroom, sometimes that of a phonograph braying out a German tango, sometimes the wind in the leaves, sometimes the stark music of the heart. When there was no music at least there were pounding rhythms: 'The city's quick metropolitan rhythm of love and birth and death that supplied dreams to the unimaginative'; 'The rhythm of the week-end, with its birth, its planned gaieties and its announced end'; 'New York's flashing, dynamic good looks, its tall man's quick-step.' Fitzgerald's dream of his mature years, after he had outgrown the

notion of becoming a big man in college, was also set
to a sort of music, perhaps that of the *Unfinished Sym-
phony*; it was the dream of becoming a great writer,
specifically a great novelist who would do for American
society in our time what Turgenev, for example, had
done for the old régime in Russia.

It was not his dream to be a poet, yet that was how
he started and in some ways he remained a poet primarily.
He said of himself, 'The talent that matures early is
usually of the poetic type, which mine was in large part.'
His favourite author was Keats, not Turgenev or Flau-
bert. 'I suppose I've read it a hundred times,' he said about
the 'Ode on a Grecian Urn.' 'About the tenth time I
began to know what it was about, and caught the chime
in it and the exquisite inner mechanics. Likewise with
the "Nightingale," which I can never read without tears
in my eyes; likewise "The Pot of Basil," with its great
stanzas about the two brothers. . . . Knowing these things
very young and granted an ear, one could scarcely ever
afterwards be unable to distinguish between gold and
dross in what one read.' When his daughter was learning
to be a writer he advised her to read Keats and Browning
and try her hand at a sonnet in iambic pentameter. He
added, 'The only thing that will help you is poetry, which
is the most concentrated form of style.'

Fitzgerald himself was a poet who never learned some
of the elementary rules for writing prose. His grammar
was shaky and his spelling definitely bad; for example
he wrote 'ect.' more often than 'etc.' and misspelled the
name of his friend Monsignor Fay on the dedication
page of *This Side of Paradise*. In his letters he always
misspelled the given names of his first and last loves.
He was not a student, for all the books he read; not a
theoretician and perhaps one should flatly say, not a
thinker. He counted on his friends to do much of his
thinking for him; at Princeton it was John Peale Bishop
who, he said, 'made me see, in the course of a couple of
months, the difference between poetry and non-poetry.'

Twenty years later, at the time of his crack-up, he re-examined his scale of values and found thinking incredibly difficult; he compared it to 'the moving about of great secret trunks.' He was then forced to the conclusion 'That I had done very little thinking, save within the problems of my craft. For twenty years a certain man had been my intellectual conscience. That man was Edmund Wilson.' Another contemporary, Ernest Hemingway, 'had been an artistic consience to me. I had not imitated his infectious style, because my own style, such as it is, was formed before he published anything, but there was an awful pull towards him when I was on the spot.'

Fitzgerald was making the confession in order to keep straight with himself, not to forestall any revelation that might have been made by his critics. The critics would have said that there was little of Wilson's influence perceptible in his work and still less of Hemingway's, although he once wrote a story about two dogs, 'Shaggy's Morning,' that is a delicate and deliberate burlesque of the Hemingway manner. By listening hard one can over-hear a few, a very few suggestions of Hemingway in the dialogue of other stories, especially the later ones, but Fitzgerald was faithful to his own vision of the world and his own way of expressing it. His debt to Wilson and Hemingway is real, but hard to define. In spite of what he said, they didn't supply him with an artistic or intellectual conscience, since he had always possessed a lively conscience of his own; but they did serve as models of literary conduct by which he tested his moral attitude towards the problems of his craft.

To satisfy his conscience he kept trying to write not merely as well as he could, like an honest literary crafts-man, but somehow better than he was able. There was more than one occasion when he actually surpassed him-self—that is, when he so immersed himself in a subject that it carried him beyond his usual or natural capacities as demonstrated in the past. The writing of *The Great Gatsby* was among the first of these occasions. There are

scenes in the novel—like Nick's first conversation with
Daisy, like the party at Gatsby's, like Nick's farewell
to Gatsby, and like his final meditations on the story—
that are not only better than anything Fitzgerald had
previously written but are not even foreshadowed in his
earlier work. 'I can never remember the times when I
wrote anything,' he said in his notebook—'*This Side of
Paradise* time or *Beautiful and Damned* or *Gatsby* time,
for instance. Lived in story.' By living in the story he
became wiser, so it seemed, than he was in ordinary life.
He said that sometimes he went back and read his own
books for advice on his problems: 'How much I know
sometimes—how little at others,' he added.

By choice and fate he wrote what might be called the
novel of centrality, that is, the novel dealing with representative young men and women in what seemed to be
a central situation. The characters would not be hopeless
people chained by their prejudices and at the mercy of
social and economic forces—'creatures of the environment,' in a favourite phrase of the naturalistic writers. Instead they would have talent and opportunities and at
least an apparent freedom of movement, so that the decisions they made would have an effect not only on their
own careers but on the lives of others, by giving examples
to be shunned or followed: like himself his heroes would
be exemplary. The story, of whatever length, would be
concerned with how they prospered in the world, how
they fell in love, and how they made or failed to make
an adjustment with life. It is the story that Stendhal
told in *The Red and the Black* and Dickens told in *David
Copperfield*: given a society with many false standards,
how will a young man rise in it, by what advantages, what
stratagems? Fitzgerald laid the story in his own time and
his social observation was not much inferior to that of
the masters.

I do not find it a serious flaw in his work that the
heroes ended by resembling himself or that he gave most
of them Irish names or at least (to Dick Diver, of *Tender*

Is the Night) a 'faint Irish melody' in the voice in order to make the identification stronger. Sometimes the heroes started as very different persons and were transformed imperceptibly, as he worked over them, into an image of the author. When his friend Bishop wrote him a critical letter about *The Great Gatsby*, Fitzgerald answered, 'Also you are right about Gatsby being blurred and patchy. I never at any one time saw him clear myself—for he started out as one man I knew and then changed into myself—the amalgam was never clear in my mind.' Actually the book gains as well as loses by the blurredness of Gatsby; it gains in mystery what it loses in definition. Dick Diver also started out as one man Fitzgerald knew —Gerald Murphy—'and then changed into myself,' changed so completely that Dick's fate was a prophecy of what would happen to the author; but again the change adds a new quality to the novel. Fitzgerald's personal life, enlarged as it was by his sympathies and his gift for putting himself in others' places, was more interesting than any lives he might have invented or merely observed; he had every reason for writing disguised autobiographies, as authors have done from the beginning. 'There never was a good biography of a good novelist,' he said in his notebook. 'There couldn't be. He is too many people, if he's any good.' What he meant was that the heroes of his stories were never himself as he was in life, but himself as projected into different situations, such as might have been encountered by members of his spiritual family. 'Books are like brothers,' he said. 'I am an only child. Gatsby my imaginary eldest brother, Amory'—in *This Side of Paradise*—'my younger, Anthony'—in *The Beautiful and Damned*—'my worry, Dick my comparatively good brother, but all of them far from home.'

In life and art Fitzgerald set a high value on persistent effort. 'After all, Max, I am a plodder,' he said in one of his letters to Maxwell Perkins. 'One time I had a talk with Ernest Hemingway, and I told him, against all logic that was then current, that I was the tortoise and he was the hare, and that's the truth of the matter, that everything I have ever attained has been through long and persistent struggle while it is Ernest who has a touch of genius which enables him to bring off extraordinary things with facility. I have no facility. I have a faculty for being cheap, if I want to indulge that . . . but when I decided to be a serious man, I tried to struggle over every point until I have made myself into a slow-moving Behemoth.' Moving slowly with *Tender Is the Night,* he produced a very long manuscript and put aside most of it, including a number of scenes that were as good as any in the finished novel. After the book was published and was apparently forgotten, he started revising it again, for a new edition that might some day appear. *The Last Tycoon* was planned as a short novel of fifty thousand words and it was only half-finished at his death, but his notes and drafts and synopses and character sketches are valuable in themselves. There are three drafts of the first chapter and the third one is an effective piece of writing that struck into new territory for Fitzgerald. But he scrawled at the head of the chapter, 'Rewrite from mood. Has become stilted with rewriting. Don't look [at previous draft]. Rewrite from mood.' On the fourth and tenth revision he still would have been unsatisfied, unless the chapter fitted the outlines of his dream.

He devoted less care to his stories than to his novels, since he regarded himself as a novelist primarily. 'Stories are best written in either one jump or three, according to length,' he told his daughter. 'The three-jump story should be done on three successive days, then a day or so for revise and off she goes. This of course is an ideal—' and in his later years Fitzgerald seldom achieved it. There were stories that he kept revising for months or even years, but he never regarded them as his best. Writing stories paid him better than any other literary work. In 1929, one of his best years, he earned $27,000 by his stories and only $5,450 from all other sources, including $31.77 described as 'royalty from book.' Books were his first interest, however, and it was the novel, not the short story, that he described as 'the strongest and supplest medium for conveying thought and emotion from one human being to another.'

His publishers used to bring out a collection of Fitzgerald's stories one or two seasons after each of his novels. It was a logical practice because, in a way, the stories clustered round the novel that was written during the same period. Most of the early ones, for example, might have dealt with the further adventures of Amory and Isabelle and Rosalind, the three so-wicked youngsters who had appeared in *This Side of Paradise*. They appeared once more in 'May Day' (1920), which was in some respects a preliminary sketch for his second novel, *The Beautiful and Damned*. Fitzgerald said that 'Winter Dreams' (1922) was a first version of *The Great Gatsby*, and 'Absolution' (1924) was originally intended as a prologue to *Gatsby*. During the next seven years he wrote many stories about Americans in Paris, on the Riviera, and in Switzerland— the backgrounds he would use in *Tender Is the Night*— and among the stories is 'One Trip Abroad' (1930), which, though it is not the strongest story in the group, would serve as a preview of the finished novel.

The stories contributed to the novels in still another fashion. On the magazine clip sheets of a very early one, 'The Smilers,' Fitzgerald wrote in a bold hand, 'This story has been stripped of any phrases of interest and is positively not to be republished in any form.' The 'phrases of interest' were copied in his notebook, where they were classified alphabetically under various headings—A for Anecdotes, B for Bright Clippings, C for Conversation and Things Overheard—and were thus kept in dead storage, but readily available, until the day when he might be able to incorporate them into a novel. The clip sheets were then consigned to a big folder marked "Junked and Dismantled Stories." Not only the failed stories but many that deserved better treatment were stripped of their useful parts like a worn-out motor car. He was willing to sacrifice a whole story, sometimes a good one, for the sake of a sentence or two that might strengthen a scene in *Tender Is the Night* or *The Last Tycoon*.

But that wasn't Fitzgerald's final judgment on the stories as a group. Like other serious writers he had the old and usually unsatisfied ambition to leave behind him a definitive body of work. There would be, so he hoped and planned, a uniform edition of his writings, and in it the stories would occupy almost as much space as the novels. He said in his notebook that The Collected Works of F. Scott Fitzgerald would fill seventeen volumes. There would be seven novels, including three still to be written, and one of these, tentatively called *In the Darkest Hour*, would be in two volumes. Besides the novels there would be seven volumes of stories, one volume of poetry and plays, and a final volume of essays. Nor was this all: at fifty-five or sixty, if he reached that age, Fitzgerald hoped to prepare a Revised Edition in twelve volumes—probably in dull, rich bindings like the New York Edition of Henry James—and once again the stories would be given their full place. He must have felt as we do to-day, that many of them are as good in their impulsive fashion as the novels he rewrote so often. They are like the sketches of a gifted artist, sharp and immediate in their perceptions, so that they bring us face to face with the artist's world. Even the worst of the stories have sudden insights that are like flinging back curtain from windows hidden in what had seemed to be flimsily decorated walls, while the best are suffused with emotion and their insights are everywhere.

' I have asked a lot of my emotions—one hundred and twenty stories,' Fitzgerald said in a prose poem that he wrote two years before leaving for Hollywood. 'The price was high, right up with Kipling, because there was one little drop of something—not blood, not a tear, not my seed, but me more intimately than these, in every story, it was the extra I had.' And he added, because he was then in a state of physical illness and nervous exhaustion, 'Now it has gone and I am just like you now.'

III

During the years 1935 and 1936 he suffered from a complete physical and emotional breakdown. It was never a secret from his friends, and Fitzgerald soon told the world about it, in 'The Crack-Up' and two other articles printed by *Esquire* in the spring of 1936. The articles revealed the intimate worries of an author who had come to regard himself 'as a cracked plate, the kind that one wonders whether it is worth preserving. . . . It can never again be warmed on the stove nor shuffled with the other plates in the dishpan; it will not be brought out for company, but it will do to hold crackers late at night or to go into the ice box under left-overs.'

The causes of his breakdown are not mysterious, and they have been described with understanding by Arthur Mizener and Andrew Turnbull, his two biographers. Fitzgerald himself described the symptoms, which were excruciatingly painful, but by no means unusual. By now the case records of brilliant men, thousands of them who have gone to pieces, are available to physicians, and there is nothing suffered by Fitzgerald that has not been Greek-named and catalogued in the medical textbooks. There are, however, two features of his experience that make it something more than a commonplace case history. The first is the unusual candour with which he wrote about it. He was, it is true, a little less than completely honest about his alcoholism, but that is a symptom of the disease itself and one he tried hard to overcome. He revealed everything else, on condition that it did not hurt others but only himself.

I do not think it is fair to use the cant word 'exhibition-ism' in connection with the three articles he wrote for *Esquire*. They contain no hint that he was deriving a twisted pleasure from torturing himself in public. What they do suggest is a sense of duty. It is as if he were saying, 'When I undertook to be a certain type of writer, I also undertook to tell the essential truth about my world and myself. The task has been pleasant at moments in the past, and now that it is supremely painful I still must tell the truth at the cost of losing my self-respect if I fail to do so.' Without much bravado and with fewer excuses than he might well have offered, he simply told the story. Writers have done that before, but usually they have waited until long afterwards, when the story was no longer painful and they could even boast of having found a path back to health. They have offered all sorts of self-degrading confessions, but on one point they have remained silent; they have admitted everything except the possibility of having lost their talent. Fitzgerald told the story in the midst of his crack-up, with no cure for it in sight, and he truly shocked his literary colleagues, including Hemingway, by suggesting that his talent might have vanished with his emotional vitality.

In a memorial poem to Fitzgerald, his Princeton class-mate John Peale Bishop set down a memory of those tortured years:

> I have lived with you the hour of your humiliation.
> I have seen you turn upon the others in the night
> And of sad self-loathing
> Concealing nothing
> Heard you cry: *I am lost. But you are lower!*
> And you had that right.
> The damned do not so own to their damnation.

Fitzgerald for all his tortures was still in purgatory and not in those colder circles of hell where the heart congeals. Because he clung to his honesty and his sense of values, he suffered more than the truly damned. 'It was despair, despair, despair—despair day and night,' said a nurse who cared for him in 1936. He spent his nights brooding over what he had failed to accomplish. About three o'clock, he said, the real horror 'would develop over the roof-tops, and in the strident horns of night-owl taxis and the shrill monody of revellers' arrival over the way. Horror and waste—

'—Waste and horror—what I might have been and done that is lost, spent, gone, dissipated, unrecapturable.' 'In a real dark night of the soul it is always three o'clock in the morning, day after day.' At times like these a man keeps his sanity by force of will or loses it by what amounts to a deliberate decision. Fitzgerald did not retreat into delusions or trances or any other substitutes for the womb. There was a hard core in his character—call it mid-Western Puritanism if you will, or middle-class Irish Catholicism, or simple obstinacy—and it kept him from evading his obligations to his family and his creditors and his talent as an artist. He met the obligations, and that is the second truly remarkable feature of Fitzgerald's case: not his symptoms or his sufferings, but his sense of duty and his will to survive.

He had suffered a permanent defeat and he did not try to hide its consequences from himself or the world. 'A man does not recover from such jolts,' he said in one of the articles for *Esquire*—'he becomes a different person and, eventually, the new person finds new things to care about.' In the summer of 1937 the new person was strong enough to make a trip to Hollywood. Fitzgerald had been given a six-months' contract by Metro-Goldwyn-Mayer, and when the contract expired in January, 1938, it was renewed for a year at an increased salary. With hope abandoned for Zelda's recovery, he had fallen in love with Sheilah Graham, a movie columnist, and—except when he was drinking—he lived with or near her in excessively quiet domesticity. He was drinking very little at the time and proved to be a capable screen craftsman, although his best scenarios were not produced in the form in which he wrote them. During his first eighteen months in Hollywood he earned $88,391, paid off most of his debts, and put his insurance policies in order.

The story is not a simple one of moral redemption and qualified success in another field. At the beginning of February, 1939, a week after the MGM contract ran out, Fitzgerald was sent east by another producer, Walter

Wanger; with the help of young Budd Schulberg he was to write a film about the Dartmouth Winter Carnival. He began drinking on the eastbound plane, got into a violent dispute with Wanger, and continued drinking at Dartmouth and in New York; it was his biggest, saddest, most desperate spree, But that wasn't his end, even though it was the end of the principal character in Schulberg's novel about the trip, *The Disenchanted*; Fitzgerald's story went on.

It went on through a period—as Andrew Turnbull describes it—'of hospitals, nurses, night sweats, sedatives,' and renewed despair. For three months he was confined to bed. It was a recurrence of tuberculosis, he told his friends truly, though they had reason to suspect that it was complicated by a recurrence of alcoholism. During the autumn he was strong enough to lay plans for *The Last Tycoon* and also to look for another studio job, but unsuccessfully; he came to believe that the producers had put his name on an informal blacklist. All through the winter of 1939–40 he suffered from what he called 'the awful lapses and sudden reverses and apparent cures and thorough poisoning effect of lung trouble. Suffice to say there were months with a high of 99·8, months at 99·6 and then up and down and a stabilization at 99·2 every afternoon when I could write in bed.' He was grey-faced and emaciated and seldom left his room, but he was writing again—if only for a few hours each day—and that was the important news. Although most of his books were still in print, nobody was reading them and his name was almost forgotten; now he was setting out to regain his place in literature.

His record of production for the last year of his life would have been remarkable for a man in perfect health. While continuing work on the novel, he wrote twenty stories for *Esquire*, including seventeen in the Pat Hobby series. Most of the Hobby stories weren't good by his own standards, but at least they caught the Hollywood atmosphere and they also made fun of the author's weaknesses, thereby proving that Fitzgerald hadn't lost his ironic attitude towards himself or his gift of double vision. Suddenly he resumed his interrupted correspondence with his friends, and he sent his daughter an extraordinary series of letters that continued through the year; perhaps they were too urgent and full of tired wisdom for a girl in college, but then Fitzgerald was writing them as a sort of personal and literary testament.

In the spring he wrote—and twice rewrote from the beginning—a scenario based on his story 'Babylon Revisited'; it was the best of his scenarios and, according to the producer who ordered it, the best he ever read. Shirley Temple wasn't available for the part of Honoria, and the story has never been filmed. Again Fitzgerald began drinking, but then he sobered up and went to work for a studio in September, earning enough, he thought, to carry him through the writing of *The Last Tycoon*. Work on it was delayed by a serious heart attack in November, but for most of the month he was writing steadily. He had said in a letter to his daughter, 'I wish now I'd *never* relaxed or looked back—but said at the end of *The Great Gatsby*: "I've found my line—from now on this comes first. This is my immediate duty—without this I am nothing." ' In the year 1940 he had found his line again, and had found something more than that, since he now possessed a deeper sense of the complexities of life than he had when writing *Gatsby*. He was doing his best work of the year in December. He had been sober for a long time and seemed to be less worried about illness, when suddenly, a few days before Christmas, there was another series of coronary attacks and he died—not like a strayed reveller but like a partner of the elder J. P. Morgan, working too hard until his heart gave out.

At the time of his death Fitzgerald had written about a hundred and sixty stories in all; the exact number would be hard to determine because some of his work was on the borderline between fiction and the informal essay or 'magazine piece.' The forty-six stories that had gone into his four published collections had included most of the best ones, but not all, with some of the not-so-good; Fitzgerald was always a shrewd but erratic judge of his own work. The last collection that he made himself, *Taps at Reveille*, had appeared in 1935, and the stories of his last years had not been reprinted.

Even with the extraordinary revival of interest in Fitzgerald that started a few years after he died, the stories were still scattered and some of them were hard to find. In 1950 Charles Scribner's Sons, his publishers, asked me to make a selection from the stories of all periods, including those of his Hollywood years. I had the sympathetic advice of his daughter, Frances Scott Fitzgerald Lanahan, of his literary agent, the late Harold Ober, and of his first biographer, Arthur Mizener, among others, and *The Stories of F. Scott Fitzgerald*—twenty-eight of them —was as good a volume as I could put together. It had the great fault, however, of being one volume only. Among the stories that should be preserved, a dozen or so had to be omitted for want of space. Later some of these—but for reasons of copyright, not all—appeared in Arthur Mizener's collection of stories and autobiographical pieces, *Afternoon of an Author*. *The Pat Hobby Stories*, all seventeen, were assembled by Arnold Gingrich, editor of *Esquire*, and published as a book in 1962.

That explains the background of the present selection. Through the generosity of The Bodley Head—the first publisher to issue a collected Fitzgerald and thus to fulfil his lifetime dream—I have been allowed two volumes instead of one for the best of Fitzgerald's stories. As in the one-volume selection that I edited for Scribner's, I have devoted most of the space to the work of his middle period, 1926–31, when he was giving his time chiefly to shorter fiction. His first two books of stories, *Flappers and Philosophers* (1920) and *Tales of the Jazz Age* (1922), received full attention in their own day, and from these I have taken only five stories in all (after hesitating over the

longest of the five, 'May Day,' which is not my favourite).
From *All the Sad Young Men* I have taken another five,
or a little more than half the book. From *Taps at Reveille*
(1935), by far his best collection, I have taken thirteen,
and to these I have added seven other stories written at
the same period as those in *Taps* but omitted from that
volume, I think mistakenly. One of them, 'The Bowl,' is
reprinted here for the first time. The selection ends with
ten of the shorter pieces that Fitzgerald wrote after his
crack-up.

Taken together the forty stories compose an informal
history of two decades in American life, or rather of one
decade with its long aftermath. The history is more intimate than anything in the textbooks and in some ways
more vivid than the picture of the time that we find in
Fitzgerald's novels, where the material was composed and
recomposed; the stories were written closer to the scene
and retain the emotion of the moment. But they do more
than merely speak for the time, since they also speak for
the author; and taken together they form a sort of journal
of his whole career. It was a different career from the one
we had expected to find after reading his first books and
hearing about his decline. What seems important in it
now is not the early success and not the neglect and
heartbreak of his later years, and not even the contrast
between them that lends an easy point to other men's
novels; it is above all the struggle against defeat and the
sort of qualified triumph he earned by the struggle. Fitzgerald remains an exemplar and an archetype, but not of
the 1920's alone; in the end he represents the human
spirit in one of its permanent forms.

MALCOLM COWLEY

I
EARLY
SUCCESS

EDITOR'S NOTE

THE eight stories in this first group belong to the period of Fitzgerald's early success and have as background his first loves, his marriage to Zelda Sayre (after their engagement had been broken because of his poverty), and the glitter of their new life among the rich. The stories were written between the autumn of 1919, when he was twenty-three and heard the great news that his novel had been accepted, and the spring of 1924, when the Fitzgeralds decided to live in Europe. Two of them were reprinted in *Flappers and Philosophers* (1920), three in *Tales of the Jazz Age* (1922), and the last three in *All the Sad Young Men* (1926).

The book starts with the best of Fitzgerald's fantasies, 'The Diamond as Big as the Ritz.' Although it was written in the winter of 1921–22, it is printed out of its chronological order because it states a theme that would often recur in his work. A middle-class boy falls in love with the heiress to a great fortune and she returns his love, but the boy is murdered by her family or destroyed by her wealth. 'The Diamond as Big as the Ritz' can have a happy ending—at least for the lovers—because it is a fantasy; but the fable would reappear in *The Great Gatsby* and there it would be carried to its tragic conclusion. Having fallen in love with the rich Mrs Buchanan, Gatsby would be murdered as efficiently as were the visitors to Braddock Washington's diamond mountain.

The other stories in the group are reprinted in the order of their magazine publication. 'Bernice Bobs Her Hair' is the best of the flapper stories that made Fitzgerald's reputation as a popular writer. When it was published in the spring of 1920, bobbed hair was a national issue like the Volstead Act, and the young author received hundreds of letters from excited readers of the *Saturday Evening*

Post. Many were shocked by the 'line' that Marjorie invented to make her cousin popular. It was copied from life, or at least from the remarks that Fitzgerald had composed for his pretty young sister Annabel when she was going to her first big dances.... 'The Ice Palace' (1920) grew out of his worries in the autumn before his marriage, when he was living at home in St Paul and was making frantic visits to Zelda in Alabama. The contrast between North and South was one of his favourite themes; he would return to it in 'The Jelly-Bean,' 'The Last of the Belles,' and in several uncollected pieces.... 'May Day' (1920) is the longest and most ambitious of his early stories. It catches the spirit of the crazy spring when we were all coming back from the wars and when Fitzgerald, besides looking for a job, was drinking too much with his classmates at the Knickerbocker bar; he projected his sense of failure into the character of Gordon Sterrett. More than that, he interwove two other plots into that of Sterrett's failure with greater skill than he had shown before and would usually show in the future; he never learned to be a good engineer of plots. Soon, however, he became a better judge of persons and situations than he was when writing 'May Day.'

Fitzgerald says of 'The Jelly-Bean' (1920), 'It was the first story in which I had a collaborator. For, finding that I was unable to manage the crap-shooting episode, I turned it over to my wife, who, as a Southern girl, was presumably an expert on the technique and terminology of that great sectional pastime.'... There is more depth of feeling in the last three stories. 'Winter Dreams' (1922) was suggested by an earlier episode in the writer's life: at Princeton he had been in love with a debutante who was something like Judy Jones in the story (later she would reappear as the heroine of the Josephine series). In other respects 'Winter Dreams' is not at all a copy of Fitzgerald's life, but it offers a revealing summary of his early feelings about love and money and social position.... 'The Sensible Thing' (1924) is autobiographical in the strict sense; it is the story of his broken and renewed engagement to Zelda Sayre. . . . 'Absolution' (1924) is rich in memories of his Catholic boyhood and his propensity for living in an imaginary world. At first it was intended as a prologue to *The Great Gatsby*; then Fitzgerald decided that he would be wiser to leave Gatsby's background wrapped in mist. But the story retains its connection with the novel, which was a turning point in his career. He was working on a deeper level of experience than he had attempted to reach in the past, and he continued to work on it in the best of the stories that followed.

The date given for each story—I should say to prevent misunderstanding—is that of its first appearance in a magazine.

THE DIAMOND
AS BIG AS THE RITZ
[1922]

JOHN T. UNGER came from a family that had been well known in Hades—a small town on the Mississippi River—for several generations. John's father had held the amateur golf championship through many a heated contest; Mrs Unger was known 'from hot-box to hot-bed,' as the local phrase went, for her political addresses; and young John T. Unger, who had just turned sixteen, had danced all the latest dances from New York before he put on long trousers. And now, for a certain time, he was to be away from home. That respect for a New England education which is the bane of all provincial places, which drains them yearly of their most promising young men, had seized upon his parents. Nothing would suit them but that he should go to St Midas' School near Boston—Hades was too small to hold their darling and gifted son.

Now in Hades—as you know if you ever have been there —the names of the more fashionable preparatory schools and colleges mean very little. The inhabitants have been so long out of the world that, though they make a show of keeping up to date in dress and manners and literature, they depend to a great extent on hearsay, and a function that in Hades would be considered elaborate would doubtless be hailed by a Chicago beef-princess as 'perhaps a little tacky.'

John T. Unger was on the eve of departure. Mrs Unger, with maternal fatuity, packed his trunks full of linen suits and electric fans, and Mr Unger presented his son with an asbestos pocket-book stuffed with money.

'Remember, you are always welcome here,' he said. 'You can be sure, boy, that we'll keep the home fires burning.'

'I know,' answered John huskily.

'Don't forget who you are and where you come from,' continued his father proudly, 'and you can do nothing to harm you. You are an Unger—from Hades.'

So the old man and the young shook hands and John walked away with tears streaming from his eyes. Ten minutes later he had passed outside the city limits, and he stopped to glance back for the last time. Over the gates the old-fashioned Victorian motto seemed strangely attractive to him. His father had tried time and time again to have it changed to something with a little more push and verve about it, such as 'Hades—Your Opportunity,' or else a plain 'Welcome' sign set over a hearty handshake pricked out in electric lights. The old motto was a little depressing, Mr Unger had thought—but now . . .

So John took his look and then set his face resolutely towards his destination. And, as he turned away, the lights of Hades against the sky seemed full of a warm and passionate beauty.

St Midas' School is half an hour from Boston in a Rolls-Pierce motor-car. The actual distance will never be known, for no one, except John T. Unger, had ever arrived there save in a Rolls-Pierce and probably no one ever will again. St Midas' is the most expensive and the most exclusive boys' preparatory school in the world.

John's first two years there passed pleasantly. The fathers of all the boys were money-kings and John spent his summers visiting at fashionable resorts. While he was very fond of all the boys he visited, their fathers struck him as being much of a piece, and in his boyish way he often wondered at their exceeding sameness. When he told them where his home was they would ask jovially, 'Pretty hot down there?' and John would muster a faint smile and answer, 'It certainly is.' His response would have been

2*

heartier had they not all made this joke—at best varying it with, 'Is it hot enough for you down there?' which he hated just as much.

In the middle of his second year at school, a quiet, handsome boy named Percy Washington had been put in John's form. The newcomer was pleasant in his manner and exceedingly well dressed even for St Midas', but for some reason he kept aloof from the other boys. The only person with whom he was intimate was John T. Unger, but even to John he was entirely uncommunicative concerning his home or his family. That he was wealthy went without saying, but beyond a few such deductions John knew little of his friend, so it promised rich confectionery for his curiosity when Percy invited him to spend the summer at his home 'in the West.' He accepted, without hesitation.

It was only when they were in the train that Percy became, for the first time, rather communicative. One day while they were eating lunch in the dining-car and discussing the imperfect characters of several of the boys at school, Percy suddenly changed his tone and made an abrupt remark.

'My father,' he said, 'is by far the richest man in the world.'

'Oh,' said John, politely. He could think of no answer to make to this confidence. He considered 'That's very nice,' but it sounded hollow and was on the point of saying, 'Really?' but refrained since it would seem to question Percy's statement. And such an astounding statement could scarcely be questioned.

'By far the richest,' repeated Percy.

'I was reading in the *World Almanack*,' began John, 'that there was one man in America with an income of over five million a year and four men with incomes of over three million a year, and——'

'Oh, they're nothing,' Percy's mouth was a half-moon of scorn. 'Catch-penny capitalists, financial small-fry, petty merchants and money-lenders. My father could buy them out and not know he'd done it.'

'But how does he——'

'Why haven't they put down *his* income tax? Because he doesn't pay any. At least he pays a little one—but he doesn't pay any on his *real* income.'

'He must be very rich,' said John simply. 'I'm glad. I like very rich people.'

'The richer a fella is, the better I like him.' There was a look of passionate frankness upon his dark face. 'I visited the Schnlitzer-Murphys last Easter. Vivian Schnlitzer-Murphy had rubies as big as hen's eggs, and sapphires that were like globes with lights inside them——'

'I love jewels,' agreed Percy enthusiastically. 'Of course I wouldn't want anyone at school to know about it, but I've got quite a collection myself. I used to collect them instead of stamps.'

'And diamonds,' continued John eagerly. 'The Schnlitzer-Murphys had diamonds as big as walnuts——'

'That's nothing.' Percy had leaned forward and dropped his voice to a low whisper. 'That's nothing at all. My father has a diamond bigger than the Ritz-Carlton Hotel.'

II

The Montana sunset lay between two mountains like a gigantic bruise from which dark arteries spread themselves over a poisoned sky. An immense distance under the sky crouched the village of Fish, minute, dismal, and forgotten. There were twelve men, so it was said, in the village of Fish, twelve sombre and inexplicable souls who sucked a lean milk from the almost literally bare rock upon which a mysterious populatory force had begotten them. They had become a race apart, these twelve men of Fish, like some species developed by an early whim of nature, which on second thought had abandoned them to struggle and extermination.

Out of the blue-black bruise in the distance crept a long line of moving lights upon the desolation of the land, and the twelve men of Fish gathered like ghosts at the shanty depot to watch the passing of the seven o'clock train, the

Transcontinental Express from Chicago. Six times or so a year the Transcontinental Express, through some inconceivable jurisdiction, stopped at the village of Fish, and when this occurred a figure or so would disembark, mount into a buggy that always appeared from out of the dusk, and drive off towards the bruised sunset. The observation of this pointless and preposterous phenomenon had become a sort of cult among the men of Fish. To observe, that was all; there remained in them none of the vital quality of illusion which would make them wonder or speculate, else a religion might have grown up around these mysterious visitations. But the men of Fish were beyond all religion—the barest and most savage tenets of even Christianity could gain no foothold on that barren rock—so there was no altar, no priest, no sacrifice; only each night at seven the silent concourse by the shanty depot, a congregation who lifted up a prayer of dim, anaemic wonder.

On this June night, the Great Brakeman, whom, had they deified anyone, they might well have chosen as their celestial protagonist, had ordained that the seven o'clock train should leave its human (or inhuman) deposit at Fish. At two minutes after seven Percy Washington and John T. Unger disembarked, hurried past the spellbound, the agape, the fearsome eyes of the twelve men of Fish, mounted into a buggy which had obviously appeared from nowhere, and drove away.

After half an hour, when the twilight had coagulated into dark, the silent negro who was driving the buggy hailed an opaque body somewhere ahead of them in the gloom. In response to his cry, it turned upon them a luminous disk which regarded them like a malignant eye out of the unfathomable night. As they came closer, John saw that it was the tail-light of an immense automobile, larger and more magnificent than any he had ever seen. Its body was of gleaming metal richer than nickel and lighter than silver, and the hubs of the wheels were studded with iridescent geometric figures of green and yellow—John did not dare to guess whether they were glass or jewel.

Two negroes, dressed in glittering livery such as one sees in pictures of royal processions in London, were standing at attention beside the car and as the two young men dismounted from the buggy they were greeted in some language which the guest could not understand, but which seemed to be an extreme form of the Southern negro's dialect.

'Get in,' said Percy to his friend, as their trunks were tossed to the ebony roof of the limousine. 'Sorry we had to bring you this far in that buggy, but of course it wouldn't do for the people on the train or those Godforsaken fellas in Fish to see this automobile.'

'Gosh! What a car!' This ejaculation was provoked by its interior. John saw that the upholstery consisted of a thousand minute and exquisite tapestries of silk, woven with jewels and embroideries, and set upon a background of cloth of gold. The two armchair seats in which the boys luxuriated were covered with stuff that resembled duvetyn, but seemed woven in numberless colours of the ends of ostrich feathers.

'What a car!' cried John again, in amazement.

'This thing?' Percy laughed. 'Why, it's just an old junk we use for a station wagon.'

By this time they were gliding along through the darkness towards the break between the two mountains.

'We'll be there in an hour and a half,' said Percy, looking at the clock. 'I may as well tell you it's not going to be like anything you ever saw before.'

If the car was any indication of what John would see, he was prepared to be astonished indeed. The simple piety prevalent in Hades has the earnest worship of and respect for riches as the first article of its creed—had John felt otherwise than radiantly humble before them, his parents would have turned away in horror at the blasphemy.

They had now reached and were entering the break between the two mountains and almost immediately the way became much rougher.

'If the moon shone down here, you'd see that we're in a

big gulch,' said Percy, trying to peer out of the window. He spoke a few words into the mouthpiece and immediately the footman turned on a searchlight and swept the hillsides with an immense beam.

'Rocky, you see. An ordinary car would be knocked to pieces in half an hour. In fact it'd take a tank to navigate it unless you knew the way. You notice we're going uphill now.'

They were obviously ascending, and within a few minutes the car was crossing a high rise, where they caught a glimpse of a pale moon newly risen in the distance. The car stopped suddenly and several figures took shape out of the dark beside it—these were negroes also. Again the two young men were saluted in the same dimly recognizable dialect; then the negroes set to work and four immense cables dangling from overhead were attached with hooks to the hubs of the great jewelled wheels. At a resounding 'Hey-yah!' John felt the car being lifted slowly from the ground—up and up—clear of the tallest rocks on both sides—then higher, until he could see a wavy, moonlit valley stretched out before him in sharp contrast to the quagmire of rocks that they had just left. Only on one side was there still rock— and then suddenly there was no rock beside them or any-where around.

It was apparent that they had surmounted some immense knife-blade of stone, projecting perpendicularly into the air. In a moment they were going down again, and finally with a soft bump they were landed upon the smooth earth.

'The worst is over,' said Percy, squinting out the window. 'It's only five miles from here, and our own road—tapestry brick—all the way. This belongs to us. This is where the United States ends, father says.'

'Are we in Canada?'

'We are not. We're in the middle of the Montana Rockies. But you are now on the only five square miles of land in the country that's never been surveyed.'

'Why hasn't it? Did they forget it?'

'No,' said Percy, grinning, 'they tried to do it three

times. The first time my grandfather corrupted a whole department of the State survey; the second time he had the official maps of the United States tinkered with—that held them for fifteen years. The last time was harder. My father fixed it so that their compasses were in the strongest magnetic field ever artificially set up. He had a whole set of surveying instruments made with a slight defection that would allow for this territory not to appear, and he substituted them for the ones that were to be used. Then he had a river deflected and he had what looked like a village built up on its banks—so that they'd see it, and think it was a town ten miles farther up the valley. There's only one thing my father's afraid of,' he concluded, 'only one thing in the world that could be used to find us out.'

'What's that?'

Percy sank his voice to a whisper.

'Aeroplanes,' he breathed. 'We've got half-a-dozen anti-aircraft guns and we've arranged it so far—but there've been a few deaths and a great many prisoners. Not that we mind *that*, you know, father and I, but it upsets mother and the girls, and there's always the chance that some time we won't be able to arrange it.'

Shreds and tatters of chinchilla, courtesy clouds in the green moon's heaven, were passing the green moon like precious Eastern stuffs paraded for the inspection of some Tartar Khan. It seemed to John that it was day, and that he was looking at some lads sailing above him in the air, showering down tracts and patent medicine circulars, with their messages of hope for despairing, rockbound hamlets. It seemed to him that he could see them look down out of the clouds and stare—and stare at whatever there was to stare at in this place whither he was bound—What then? Were they induced to land by some insidious device there to be immured far from patent medicines and from tracts until the judgment day—or, should they fail to fall into the trap, did a quick puff of smoke and the sharp round of a splitting shell bring them drooping to earth—and 'upset' Percy's mother and sisters. John shook his head and the wraith of a hollow laugh issued silently from his parted lips. What desperate transaction lay hidden here? What a moral expedient of a bizarre Crœsus? What terrible and golden mystery? . . .

The chinchilla clouds had drifted past now and outside the Montana night was bright as day. The tapestry brick of the road was smooth to the tread of the great tyres as they rounded a still, moonlit lake; they passed into darkness for a moment, a pine grove, pungent and cool, then they came out into a broad avenue of lawn and John's exclamation of pleasure was simultaneous with Percy's taciturn 'We're home.'

Full in the light of the stars, an exquisite château rose from the borders of the lake, climbed in marble radiance half the height of an adjoining mountain, then melted in grace, in perfect symmetry, in translucent feminine languor, into the massed darkness of a forest of pine. The many towers, the slender tracery of the sloping parapets, the chiselled wonder of a thousand yellow windows with their oblongs and hectagons and triangles of golden light, the shattered softness of the intersecting planes of star-shine and blue shade, all trembled on John's spirit like a chord of music. On one of the towers, the tallest, the blackest at its base, an arrangement of exterior lights at the top made a sort of floating fairyland—and as John gazed up in warm enchantment the faint acciaccare sound of violins drifted down in a rococo harmony that was like nothing he had ever heard before. Then in a moment the car stopped before wide, high marble steps around which the night air was fragrant with a host of flowers. At the top of the steps two great doors swung silently open and amber light flooded out upon the darkness, silhouetting the figure of an exquisite lady with black, high-piled hair, who held out her arms towards them.

'Mother,' Percy was saying, 'this is my friend, John Unger, from Hades.'

Afterwards John remembered that first night as a daze of many colours, of quick sensory impressions, of music soft as a voice in love, and of the beauty of things, lights and shadows, and motions and faces. There was a white-haired man who stood drinking a many-hued cordial from a crystal thimble set on a golden stem. There was a girl with a flowery face, dressed like Titania with braided sapphires in her hair. There was a room where the solid, soft gold of the walls yielded to the pressure of his hand, and a room that was like a platonic conception of the ultimate prison—ceiling, floor, and all, it was lined with an unbroken mass of diamonds, diamonds of every size and shape, until, lit with tall violet lamps in the corners, it dazzled the eyes with a whiteness that could be compared only with itself, beyond human wish or dream.

Through a maze of these rooms the two boys wandered. Sometimes the floor under their feet would flame in brilliant patterns from lighting below, patterns of barbaric clashing colours, of pastel delicacy, of sheer whiteness, or of subtle and intricate mosaic, surely from some mosque on the Adriatic Sea. Sometimes beneath layers of thick crystal he would see blue or green water swirling, inhabited by vivid fish and growths of rainbow foliage. Then they would be treading on furs of every texture and colour or along corridors of palest ivory, unbroken as though carved complete from the gigantic tusks of dinosaurs extinct before the age of man. . . .

Then a hazily remembered transition, and they were at dinner—where each plate was of two almost imperceptible layers of solid diamond between which was curiously worked a filigree of emerald design, a shaving sliced from green air. Music, plangent and unobtrusive, drifted down through far corridors—his chair, feathered and curved insidiously to his back, seemed to engulf and overpower him as he drank his first glass of port. He tried drowsily to answer a question that had been asked him, but the honeyed luxury that clasped his body added to the illusion of sleep—jewels, fabrics, wines, and metals blurred before his eyes into a sweet mist. . . .

'Yes,' he replied with a polite effort, 'it certainly is hot enough for me down there.'

He managed to add a ghostly laugh; then, without movement, without resistance, he seemed to float off and away, leaving an iced dessert that was pink as a dream. . . . He fell asleep.

When he awoke he knew that several hours had passed. He was in a great quiet room with ebony walls and a dull illumination that was too faint, too subtle, to be called a light. His young host was standing over him.

'You fell asleep at dinner,' Percy was saying. 'I nearly did, too—it was such a treat to be comfortable again after this year of school. Servants undressed and bathed you while you were sleeping.'

'Is this a bed or a cloud?' sighed John. 'Percy, Percy—before you go, I want to apologize.'

'For what?'

'For doubting you when you said you had a diamond as big as the Ritz-Carlton hotel.'

Percy smiled.

'I thought you didn't believe me. It's that mountain you know.'

'What mountain?'

'The mountain the château rests on. It's not very big for a mountain. But except about fifty feet of sod and gravel on top it's solid diamond. *One* diamond, one cubic mile without a flaw. Aren't you listening? Say——'

But John T. Unger had again fallen asleep.

III

Morning. As he awoke he perceived drowsily that the room had at the same moment become dense with sunlight. The ebony panels of one wall had slid aside on a sort of track, leaving his chamber half open to the day. A large negro in a white uniform stood beside his bed.

'Good evening,' muttered John, summoning his brains from the wild places.

'Good morning, sir. Are you ready for your bath, sir?

Oh, don't get up—I'll put you in, if you'll just unbutton your pyjamas—there. Thank you, sir.'

John lay quietly as his pyjamas were removed—he was amused and delighted; he expected to be lifted like a child by this black Gargantua who was tending him, but nothing of the sort happened; instead he felt the bed tilt up slowly on its side—he began to roll, startled at first, in the direction of the wall, but when he reached the wall its drapery gave way, and sliding two yards farther down a fleecy incline he plumped gently into water the same temperature as his body.

He looked about him. The runway or rollway on which he had arrived had folded gently back into place. He had been projected into another chamber and was sitting in a sunken bath with his head just above the level of the floor. All about him, lining the walls of the room and the sides and bottom of the bath itself, was a blue aquarium, and gazing through the crystal surface on which he sat, he could see fish swimming among amber lights and even gliding without curiosity past his outstretched toes, which were separated from them only by the thickness of the crystal. From overhead, sunlight came down through sea-green glass.

'I suppose, sir, that you'd like hot rosewater and soapsuds this morning, sir—and perhaps cold salt water to finish.'

The negro was standing beside him.

'Yes,' agreed John, smiling inanely, 'as you please.' Any idea of ordering this bath according to his own meagre standards of living would have been priggish and not a little wicked.

The negro pressed a button and a warm rain began to fall, apparently from overhead, but really, so John discovered after a moment, from a fountain arrangement near by. The water turned to a pale rose colour and jets of liquid soap spurted into it from four miniature walrus heads at the corners of the bath. In a moment a dozen little paddle-wheels, fixed to the sides, had churned the mixture into a

radiant rainbow of pink foam which enveloped him softly
with its delicious lightness, and burst in shining, rosy
bubbles here and there about him.

'Shall I turn on the moving-picture machine, sir?'
suggested the negro deferentially. 'There's a good one-reel
comedy in this machine to-day, or I can put in a serious
piece in a moment, if you prefer it.'

'No, thanks,' answered John, politely but firmly. He was
enjoying his bath too much to desire any distraction. But
distraction came. In a moment he was listening intently to the
sound of flutes from just outside, flutes dripping a melody
that was like a waterfall, cool and green as the room itself,
accompanying a frothy piccolo, in play more fragile than
the lace of suds that covered and charmed him.

After a cold salt-water bracer and a cold fresh finish, he
stepped out and into a fleecy robe, and upon a couch covered
with the same material he was rubbed with oil, alcohol, and
spice. Later he sat in a voluptuous chair while he was shaved
and his hair was trimmed.

'Mr Percy is waiting in your sitting-room,' said the
negro, when these operations were finished. 'My name is
Gygsum, Mr Unger, sir. I am to see to Mr Unger every
morning.'

John walked out into the brisk sunshine of his living-
room, where he found breakfast waiting for him and Percy,
gorgeous in white kid knickerbockers, smoking in an easy
chair.

IV

This is a story of the Washington family as Percy sketched
it for John during breakfast.

The father of the present Mr Washington had been a
Virginian, a direct descendant of George Washington, and
Lord Baltimore. At the close of the Civil War he was a
twenty-five-year-old Colonel with a played-out plantation
and about a thousand dollars in gold.

Fitz-Norman Culpepper Washington, for that was the

young Colonel's name, decided to present the Virginia estate to his younger brother and go West. He selected two dozen of the most faithful blacks, who, of course, worshipped him, and bought twenty-five tickets to the West, where he intended to take out land in their names and start a sheep and cattle ranch.

When he had been in Montana for less than a month and things were going very poorly indeed, he stumbled on his great discovery. He had lost his way when riding in the hills, and after a day without food he began to grow hungry. As he was without his rifle, he was forced to pursue a squirrel, and in the course of the pursuit he noticed that it was carrying something shiny in its mouth. Just before it vanished into its hole—for Providence did not intend that this squirrel should alleviate his hunger—it dropped its burden. Sitting down to consider the situation Fitz-Norman's eye was caught by a gleam in the grass beside him. In ten seconds he had completely lost his appetite and gained one hundred thousand dollars. The squirrel which had refused with annoying persistence to become food, had made him a present of a large and perfect diamond.

Late that night he found his way to camp and twelve hours later all the males among his darkies were back by the squirrel hole digging furiously at the side of the mountain. He told them he had discovered a rhinestone mine, and, as only one or two of them had ever seen even a small diamond before, they believed him, without question. When the magnitude of his discovery became apparent to him, he found himself in a quandary. The mountain was a diamond —it was literally nothing else but solid diamond. He filled four saddle bags full of glittering samples and started on horseback for St Paul. There he managed to dispose of half a dozen small stones—when he tried a larger one a storekeeper fainted and Fitz-Norman was arrested as a public disturber. He escaped from jail and caught the train for New York, where he sold a few medium-sized diamonds and received in exchange about two hundred thousand dollars in gold. But he did not dare to produce any exceptional gems—in fact, he left New York just in time. Tremendous excitement had been created in jewellery circles, not so much by the size of his diamonds as by their appearance in the city from mysterious sources. Wild rumours became current that a diamond mine had been discovered in the Catskills, on the Jersey coast, on Long Island, beneath Washington Square. Excursion trains, packed with men carrying picks and shovels, began to leave New York hourly, bound for various neighbouring El Dorados. But by that time young Fitz-Norman was on his way back to Montana.

By the end of a fortnight he had estimated that the diamond in the mountain was approximately equal in quantity to all the rest of the diamonds known to exist in the world. There was no valuing it by any regular computation, however, for it was *one solid diamond*—and if it were offered for sale not only would the bottom fall out of the market, but also, if the value should vary with its size in the usual arithmetical progression, there would not be enough gold in the world to buy a tenth part of it. And what could anyone do with a diamond that size?

It was an amazing predicament. He was, in one sense, the richest man that ever lived—and yet was he worth anything at all? If his secret should transpire there was no telling to what measures the Government might resort in order to prevent a panic, in gold as well as in jewels. They might take over the claim immediately and institute a monopoly.

There was no alternative—he must market his mountain in secret. He sent South for his younger brother and put him in charge of his coloured following—darkies who had never realized that slavery was abolished. To make sure of this, he read them a proclamation that he had composed, which announced that General Forrest had reorganized the shattered Southern armies and defeated the North in one pitched battle. The negroes believed him implicitly. They passed a vote declaring it a good thing and held revival services immediately.

Fitz-Norman himself set out for foreign parts with one

hundred thousand dollars and two trunks filled with rough diamonds of all sizes. He sailed for Russia in a Chinese junk and six months after his departure from Montana he was in St Petersburg. He took obscure lodgings and called immediately upon the court jeweller, announcing that he had a diamond for the Czar. He remained in St Petersburg for two weeks, in constant danger of being murdered, living from lodging to lodging, and afraid to visit his trunks more than three or four times during the whole fortnight.

On his promise to return in a year with larger and finer stones, he was allowed to leave for India. Before he left, however, the Court Treasurers had deposited to his credit, in American banks, the sum of fifteen million dollars—under four different aliases.

He returned to America in 1868, having been gone a little over two years. He had visited the capitals of twenty-two countries and talked with five emperors, eleven kings, three princes, a shah, a khan, and a sultan. At that time, Fitz-Norman estimated his own wealth at one billion dollars. One fact worked consistently against the disclosure of his secret. No one of his larger diamonds remained in the public eye for a week before being invested with a history of enough fatalities, amours, revolutions and wars to have occupied it from the days of the first Babylonian Empire.

From 1870 until his death in 1900, the history of Fitz-Norman Washington was a long epic in gold. There were side issues, of course—he evaded the surveys, he married a Virginia lady, by whom he had a single son, and he was compelled, due to a series of unfortunate complications, to murder his brother, whose unfortunate habit of drinking himself into an indiscreet stupor had several times endangered their safety. But very few other murders stained these happy years of progress and expansion.

Just before he died he changed his policy, and with all but a few million dollars of his outside wealth bought up rare minerals in bulk, which he deposited in the safety vaults of banks all over the world, marked as bric-a-brac. His son, Braddock Tarleton Washington, followed this policy on an even more intensive scale. The minerals were converted into the rarest of all elements—radium—so that the equivalent of a billion dollars in gold could be placed in a receptacle no bigger than a cigar box.

When Fitz-Norman had been dead three years his son, Braddock, decided that the business had gone far enough. The amount of wealth that he and his father had taken out of the mountain was beyond all exact computation. He kept a note-book in cipher in which he set down the approximate quantity of radium in each of the thousand banks he patronized, and recorded the alias under which it was held. Then he did a very simple thing—he sealed up the mine.

He sealed up the mine. What had been taken out of it would support all the Washingtons yet to be born in un-paralleled luxury for generations. His one care must be the protection of his secret, lest in the possible panic attendant on its discovery he should be reduced with all the property-holders in the world to utter poverty.

This was the family among whom John T. Unger was staying. This was the story he heard in his silver-walled living-room the morning after his arrival.

V

After breakfast, John found his way out the great marble entrance, and looked curiously at the scene before him. The whole valley, from the diamond mountain to the steep granite cliff five miles away, still gave off a breath of golden haze which hovered idly above the fine sweep of lawns and lakes and gardens. Here and there clusters of elms made delicate groves of shade, contrasting strangely with the tough masses of pine forest that held the hills in a grip of dark-blue green. Even as John looked he saw three fawns in single file patter out from one clump about a half mile away and disappear with awkward gaiety into the black-ribbed half-light of another. John would not have been surprised to see a goat foot-piping his way among the trees or to catch a glimpse of pink nymph-skin and flying yellow hair between the greenest of the green leaves.

In some such cool hope he descended the marble steps, disturbing faintly the sleep of two silky Russian wolfhounds at the bottom, and set off along a walk of white and blue brick that seemed to lead in no particular direction.

He was enjoying himself as much as he was able. It is youth's felicity as well as its insufficiency that it can never live in the present, but must always be measuring up the day against its own radiantly imagined future—flowers and gold, girls and stars, they are only pre-figurations and prophecies of that incomparable, unattainable young dream.

John rounded a soft corner where the massed rosebushes filled the air with heavy scent, and struck off across a park towards a patch of moss under some trees. He had never lain upon moss, and he wanted to see whether it was really soft enough to justify the use of its name as an adjective. Then he saw a girl coming towards him over the grass. She was the most beautiful person he had ever seen.

She was dressed in a white little gown that came just below her knees, and a wreath of mignonettes clasped with blue slices of sapphire bound up her hair. Her pink bare feet scattered the dew before them as she came. She was younger than John—not more than sixteen.

'Hello,' she cried softly, 'I'm Kismine.'

She was much more than that to John already. He advanced towards her, scarcely moving as he drew near lest he should tread on her bare toes.

'You haven't met me,' said her soft voice. Her blue eyes added, 'Oh, but you've missed a great deal!' . . . 'You met my sister, Jasmine, last night. I was sick with lettuce poisoning,' went on her soft voice, and her eyes continued, 'and when I'm sick I'm sweet—and when I'm well.'

'You have made an enormous impression on me,' said John's eyes, 'and I'm not so slow myself'—'How do you do?' said his voice. 'I hope you're better this morning.' 'You darling,' added his eyes tremulously.

John observed that they had been walking along the path.

On her suggestion they sat down together upon the moss, the softness of which he failed to determine.

He was critical about women. A single defect—a thick ankle, a hoarse voice, a glass eye—was enough to make him utterly indifferent. And here for the first time in his life he was beside a girl who seemed to him the incarnation of physical perfection.

'Are you from the East?' asked Kismine with charming interest.

'No,' answered John simply. 'I'm from Hades.'

Either she had never heard of Hades, or she could think of no pleasant comment to make upon it, for she did not discuss it further.

'I'm going East to school this fall,' she said. 'D'you think I'll like it? I'm going to New York to Miss Bulge's. It's very strict, but you see over the weekends I'm going to live at home with the family in our New York house, because father heard that the girls had to go walking two by two.'

'Your father wants you to be proud,' observed John.

'We are,' she answered, her eyes shining with dignity. 'None of us has ever been punished. Father said we never should be. Once when my sister Jasmine was a little girl she pushed him downstairs and he just got up and limped away.

'Mother was—well, a little startled,' continued Kismine, 'when she heard that you were from—from where you *are* from, you know. She said that when she was a young girl— but then, you see, she's a Spaniard and old-fashioned.'

'Do you spend much time out here?' asked John, to conceal the fact that he was somewhat hurt by this remark. It seemed an unkind allusion to his provincialism.

'Percy and Jasmine and I are here every summer, but next summer Jasmine is going to Newport. She's coming out in London a year from this fall. She'll be presented at Court.'

'Do you know,' began John hesitantly, 'you're much more sophisticated than I thought you were when I first saw you?'

'Oh, no, I'm not,' she exclaimed hurriedly. 'Oh, I

wouldn't think of being. I think that sophisticated young people are *terribly* common, don't you? I'm not at all, really. If you say I am, I'm going to cry.'

She was so distressed that her lip was trembling. John was impelled to protest:

'I didn't mean that; I only said it to tease you.'

'Because I wouldn't mind if I *were*,' she persisted, 'but I'm *not*. I'm very innocent and girlish. I never smoke, or drink, or read anything except poetry. I know scarcely any mathematics or chemistry. I dress *very* simply—in fact, I scarcely dress at all. I think sophisticated is the last thing you can say about me. I believe that girls ought to enjoy their youths in a wholesome way.'

'I do too,' said John heartily.

Kismine was cheerful again. She smiled at him, and a still-born tear dripped from the corner of one blue eye.

'I like you,' she whispered, intimately. 'Are you going to spend all your time with Percy while you're here, or will you be nice to me? Just think—I'm absolutely fresh ground. I've never had a boy in love with me in all my life. I've never been allowed even to *see* boys alone—except Percy. I came all the way out here into this grove hoping to run into you, where the family wouldn't be around.'

Deeply flattered, John bowed from the hips as he had been taught at dancing school in Hades.

'We'd better go now,' said Kismine sweetly. 'I have to be with mother at eleven. You haven't asked me to kiss you once. I thought boys always did that nowadays.'

John drew himself up proudly.

'Some of them do,' he answered, 'but not me. Girls don't do that sort of thing—in Hades.'

Side by side they walked back towards the house.

VI

John stood facing Mr Braddock Washington in the full sunlight. The elder man was about forty with a proud, vacuous face, intelligent eyes, and a robust figure. In the mornings he smelt of horses—the best horses. He carried a plain walking-stick of grey birch with a single large opal for a grip. He and Percy were showing John around.

'The slaves' quarters are there.' His walking-stick indicated a cloister of marble on their left that ran in graceful Gothic along the side of the mountain. 'In my youth I was distracted for a while from the business of life by a period of absurd idealism. During that time they lived in luxury. For instance, I equipped every one of their rooms with a tile bath.'

'I suppose,' ventured John, with an ingratiating laugh, 'that they used the bathtubs to keep coal in. Mr Schnlitzer-Murphy told me that once he——'

'The opinions of Mr Schnlitzer-Murphy are of little importance, I should imagine,' interrupted Braddock Washington, coldly. 'My slaves did not keep coal in their bathtubs. They had orders to bathe every day, and they did. If they hadn't I might have ordered a sulphuric acid shampoo. I discontinued the baths for quite another reason. Several of them caught cold and died. Water is not good for certain races—except as a beverage.'

John laughed, and then decided to nod his head in sober agreement. Braddock Washington made him uncomfortable.

'All these negroes are descendants of the ones my father brought North with him. There are about two hundred and fifty now. You notice that they've lived so long apart from the world that their original dialect has become an almost indistinguishable patois. We bring a few of them up to speak English—my secretary and two or three of the house servants.

'This is the golf course,' he continued, as they strolled along the velvet winter grass. 'It's all a green, you see—no fairway, no rough, no hazards.'

He smiled pleasantly at John.

'Many men in the cage, father?' asked Percy suddenly.

Braddock Washington stumbled, and let forth an involuntary curse.

'One less than there should be,' he ejaculated darkly—

and then added after a moment, 'We've had difficulties.'

'Mother was telling me,' exclaimed Percy, 'that Italian teacher——'

'A ghastly error,' said Braddock Washington angrily. 'But of course there's a good chance that we may have got him. Perhaps he fell somewhere in the woods or stumbled over a cliff. And then there's always the probability that if he did get away his story wouldn't be believed. Nevertheless, I've had two dozen men looking for him in different towns around here.'

'And no luck?'

'Some. Fourteen of them reported to my agent that they'd each killed a man answering to that description, but of course it was probably only the reward they were after——'

He broke off. They had come to a large cavity in the earth about the circumference of a merry-go-round and covered by a strong iron grating. Braddock Washington beckoned to John, and pointed his cane down through the grating. John stepped to the edge and gazed. Immediately his ears were assailed by a wild clamour from below.

'Come on down to Hell!'

'Hello, kiddo, how's the air up there?'

'Hey! Throw us a rope!'

'Got an old doughnut, Buddy, or a couple of second-hand sandwiches?'

'Say, fella, if you'll push down that guy you're with, we'll show you a quick disappearance scene.'

'Paste him one for me, will you?'

It was too dark to see clearly into the pit below, but John could tell from the coarse optimism and rugged vitality of the remarks and voices that they proceeded from middle-class Americans of the more spirited type. Then Mr Washington put out his cane and touched a button in the grass, and the scene below sprang into light.

'These are some adventurous mariners who had the misfortune to discover El Dorado,' he remarked.

Below them there had appeared a large hollow in the earth shaped like the interior of a bowl. The sides were

steep and apparently of polished glass, and on its slightly
concave surface stood about two dozen men clad in the half
costume, half uniform, of aviators. Their upturned faces,
lit with wrath, with malice, with despair, with cynical
humour, were covered by long growths of beard, but with
the exception of a few who had pined perceptibly away,
they seemed to be a well-fed, healthy lot.

Braddock Washington drew a garden chair to the edge of
the pit and sat down.

'Well, how are you, boys?' he inquired genially.

A chorus of execration in which all joined except a few
too dispirited to cry out, rose up into the sunny air, but
Braddock Washington heard it with unruffled composure.
When its last echo had died away he spoke again.

'Have you thought up a way out of your difficulty?'

From here and there among them a remark floated up.

'We decided to stay here for love!'

'Bring us up there and we'll find us a way!'

Braddock Washington waited until they were again
quiet. Then he said:

'I've told you the situation. I don't want you here. I wish
to heaven I'd never seen you. Your own curiosity got you
here, and any time that you can think of a way out which
protects me and my interests I'll be glad to consider it.
But so long as you confine your efforts to digging tunnels—
yes, I know about the new one you've started—you won't
get very far. This isn't as hard on you as you make it out,
with all your howling for the loved ones at home. If you
were the type who worried much about the loved ones at
home, you'd never have taken up aviation.'

A tall man moved apart from the others, and held up his
hand to call his captor's attention to what he was about to
say.

'Let me ask you a few questions!' he cried. 'You pretend to be a fair-minded man.'

'How absurd. How could a man of *my* position be fair-
minded towards *you*? You might as well speak of a Spaniard
being fair-minded towards a piece of steak.'

At this harsh observation the faces of the two dozen steaks fell, but the tall man continued:

'All right!' he cried. 'We've argued this out before. You're not a humanitarian and you're not fair-minded, but you're human—at least you say you are—and you ought to be able to put yourself in our place for long enough to think how—how—how——'

'How what?' demanded Washington, coldly.

'—how unnecessary——'

'Not to me.'

'Well,—how cruel——'

'We've covered that. Cruelty doesn't exist where self-preservation is involved. You've been soldiers: you know that. Try another.'

'Well, then, how stupid.'

'There,' admitted Washington, 'I grant you that. But try to think of an alternative. I've offered to have all or any of you painlessly executed if you wish. I've offered to have your wives, sweethearts, children, and mothers kidnapped and brought out here. I'll enlarge your place down there and feed and clothe you the rest of your lives. If there was some method of producing permanent amnesia I'd have all of you operated on and released immediately, somewhere outside of my preserves. But that's as far as my ideas go.'

'How about trusting us not to peach on you?' cried some-one.

'You don't proffer that suggestion seriously,' said Washington, with an expression of scorn. 'I did take out one man to teach my daughter Italian. Last week he got away.'

A wild yell of jubilation went up suddenly from two dozen throats and a pandemonium of joy ensued. The prisoners clog-danced and cheered and yodelled and wrestled with one another in a sudden uprush of animal spirits. They even ran up the glass sides of the bowl as far as they could, and slid back to the bottom upon the natural cushions of their bodies. The tall man started a song in which they all joined——

> '*Oh, we'll hang the kaiser*
> *On a sour apple tree——*'

Braddock Washington sat in inscrutable silence until the song was over.

'You see,' he remarked, when he could gain a modicum of attention. 'I bear you no ill-will. I like to see you enjoying yourselves. That's why I didn't tell you the whole story at once. The man—what was his name? Critchtichiello?—was shot by some of my agents in fourteen different places.'

Not guessing that the places referred to were cities, the tumult of rejoicing subsided immediately.

'Nevertheless,' cried Washington with a touch of anger, 'he tried to run away. Do you expect me to take chances with any of you after an experience like that?'

Again a series of ejaculations went up.

'Sure!'

'Would your daughter like to learn Chinese?'

'Hey, I can speak Italian! My mother was a wop.'

'Maybe she'd like t'learna speak N'Yawk!'

'If she's the little one with the big blue eyes I can teach her a lot of things better than Italian.'

'I know some Irish songs—and I could hammer brass once't.'

Mr Washington reached forward suddenly with his cane and pushed the button in the grass so that the picture below went out instantly, and there remained only that great dark mouth covered dismally with the black teeth of the grating.

'Hey!' called a single voice from below, 'you ain't goin' away without givin' us your blessing?'

But Mr Washington, followed by the two boys, was already strolling on towards the ninth hole of the golf course, as though the pit and its contents were no more than a hazard over which his facile iron had triumphed with ease.

VII

July under the lee of the diamond mountain was a month of blanket nights and of warm, glowing days. John and Kismine were in love. He did not know that the little gold football (inscribed with the legend *Pro deo et patria et St*

Mida) which he had given her rested on a platinum chain next to her bosom. But it did. And she for her part was not aware that a large sapphire which had dropped one day from her simple coiffure was stowed away tenderly in John's jewel box.

Late one afternoon when the ruby and ermine music room was quiet, they spent an hour there together. He held her hand and she gave him such a look that he whispered her name aloud. She bent towards him—then hesitated.

'Did you say "Kismine"?' she asked softly, 'or——'

She had wanted to be sure. She thought she might have misunderstood.

Neither of them had ever kissed before, but in the course of an hour it seemed to make little difference.

The afternoon drifted away. That night when a last breath of music drifted down from the highest tower, they each lay awake, happily dreaming over the separate minutes of the day. They had decided to be married as soon as possible.

VIII

Every day Mr Washington and the two young men went hunting or fishing in the deep forests or played golf around the somnolent course—games which John diplomatically allowed his host to win—or swam in the mountain coolness of the lake. John found Mr Washington a somewhat exacting personality—utterly uninterested in any ideas or opinions except his own. Mrs Washington was aloof and reserved at all times. She was apparently indifferent to her two daughters, and entirely absorbed in her son Percy, with whom she held interminable conversations in rapid Spanish at dinner.

Jasmine, the elder daughter, resembled Kismine in appearance—except that she was somewhat bow-legged, and terminated in large hands and feet—but was utterly unlike her in temperament. Her favourite books had to do with poor girls who kept house for widowed fathers. John learned from Kismine that Jasmine had never recovered

3+S.F.

from the shock and disappointment caused her by the termination of the World War, just as she was about to start for Europe as a canteen expert. She had even pined away for a time, and Braddock Washington had taken steps to promote a new war in the Balkans—but she had seen a photograph of some wounded Serbian soldiers and lost interest in the whole proceedings. But Percy and Kismine seemed to have inherited the arrogant attitude in all its harsh magnificence from their father. A chaste and consistent selfishness ran like a pattern through their every idea.

John was enchanted by the wonders of the château and the valley. Braddock Washington, so Percy told him, had caused to be kidnapped a landscape gardener, an architect, a designer of stage settings, and a French decadent poet left over from the last century. He had put his entire force of negroes at their disposal, guaranteed to supply them with any materials that the world could offer, and left them to work out some ideas of their own. But one by one they had shown their uselessness. The decadent poet had at once begun bewailing his separation from the boulevards in spring—he made some vague remarks about spices, apes, and ivories, but said nothing that was of any practical value. The stage designer on his part wanted to make the whole valley a series of tricks and sensational effects—a state of things that the Washingtons would soon have grown tired of. And as for the architect and the landscape gardener, they thought only in terms of convention. They must make this like this and that like that.

But they had, at least, solved the problem of what was to be done with them—they all went mad early one morning after spending the night in a single room trying to agree upon the location of a fountain, and were now confined comfortably in an insane asylum at Westport, Connecticut.

'But,' inquired John curiously, 'who did plan all your wonderful reception rooms and halls, and approaches and bathrooms——?'

'Well,' answered Percy, 'I blush to tell you, but it was a moving-picture fella. He was the only man we found who was used to playing with an unlimited amount of money, though he did tuck his napkin in his collar and couldn't read or write.'

As August drew to a close John began to regret that he must soon go back to school. He and Kismine had decided to elope the following June.

'It would be nicer to be married here,' Kismine confessed, 'but of course I could never get father's permission to marry you at all. Next to that I'd rather elope. It's terrible for wealthy people to be married in America at present—they always have to send out bulletins to the press saying that they're going to be married in remnants, when what they mean is just a peck of old second-hand pearls and some used lace worn once by the Empress Eugénie.'

'I know,' agreed John fervently. 'When I was visiting the Schnlitzer-Murphys, the eldest daughter, Gwendolyn, married a man whose father owns half of West Virginia. She wrote home saying what a tough struggle she was carrying on on his salary as a bank clerk—and then she ended up by saying that "Thank God, I have four good maids anynow, and that helps a little."'

'It's absurd,' commented Kismine. 'Think of the millions and millions of people in the world, labourers and all, who get along with only two maids.'

One afternoon late in August a chance remark of Kismine's changed the face of the entire situation, and threw John into a state of terror.

They were in their favourite grove, and between kisses John was indulging in some romantic forebodings which he fancied added poignancy to their relations.

'Sometimes I think we'll never marry,' he said sadly. 'You're too wealthy, too magnificent. No one as rich as you are can be like other girls. I should marry the daughter of some well-to-do wholesale hardware man from Omaha or Sioux City, and be content with her half-million.'

'I knew the daughter of a wholesale hardware man once,' remarked Kismine. 'I don't think you'd have been contented with her. She was a friend of my sister's. She visited here.'

'Oh, then you've had other guests?' exclaimed John in surprise.

Kismine seemed to regret her words.

'Oh, yes,' she said hurriedly, 'we've had a few.'

'But aren't you—wasn't your father afraid they'd talk outside?'

'Oh, to some extent, to some extent,' she answered. 'Let's talk about something pleasanter.'

But John's curiosity was aroused.

'Something pleasanter!' he demanded. 'What's unpleasant about that? Weren't they nice girls?'

To his great surprise Kismine began to weep.

'Yes—th—that's the—the whole t-trouble. I grew qu-quite attached to some of them. So did Jasmine, but she kept inv-viting them anyway. I couldn't under*stand* it.'

A dark suspicion was born in John's heart.

'Do you mean that they *told*, and your father had them —removed?'

'Worse than that,' she muttered brokenly. 'Father took no chances—and Jasmine kept writing them to come, and they had *such* a good time!'

She was overcome by a paroxysm of grief.

Stunned with the horror of this revelation, John sat there open-mouthed, feeling the nerves of his body twitter like so many sparrows perched upon his spinal column.

'Now, I've told you, and I shouldn't have,' she said, calming suddenly and drying her dark blue eyes.

'Do you mean to say that your father had them *murdered* before they left?'

She nodded.

'In August usually—or early in September. It's only natural for us to get all the pleasure out of them that we can first.'

'How abominable! How—why, I must be going crazy! Did you really admit that——'

'I did,' interrupted Kismine, shrugging her shoulders.

'We can't very well imprison them like those aviators, where they'd be a continual reproach to us every day. And it's always been made easier for Jasmine and me, because father had it done sooner than we expected. In that way we avoided any farewell scene——'

'So you murdered them! Uh!' cried John.

'It was done very nicely. They were drugged while they were asleep—and their families were always told that they died of scarlet fever in Butte.'

'But—I fail to understand why you kept on inviting them!'

'I didn't,' burst out Kismine. 'I never invited one. Jasmine did. And they always had a very good time. She'd give them the nicest presents towards the last. I shall probably have visitors too—I'll harden up to it. We can't let such an inevitable thing as death stand in the way of enjoying life while we have it. Think how lonesome it'd be out here if we never had *any* one. Why, father and mother have sacrificed some of their best friends just as we have.'

'And so,' cried John accusingly, 'and so you were letting me make love to you and pretending to return it, and talking about marriage, all the time knowing perfectly well that I'd never get out of here alive——'

'No,' she protested passionately. 'Not any more. I did at first. You were here. I couldn't help that, and I thought your last days might as well be pleasant for both of us. But then I fell in love with you, and—and I'm honestly sorry you're going to—going to be put away—though I'd rather you'd be put away than ever kiss another girl.'

'Oh, you would, would you?' cried John ferociously.

'Much rather. Besides, I've always heard that a girl can have more fun with a man whom she knows she can never marry. Oh, why did I tell you? I've probably spoiled your whole good time now, and we were really enjoying things when you didn't know it. I knew it would make things sort of depressing for you.'

'Oh, you did, did you?' John's voice trembled with anger. 'I've heard about enough of this. If you haven't any more pride and decency than to have an affair with a fellow that you know isn't much better than a corpse, I don't want to have any more to do with you!'

'You're not a corpse!' she protested in horror. 'You're not a corpse! I won't have you saying that I kissed a corpse!'

'I said nothing of the sort!'

'You did! You said I kissed a corpse!'

'I didn't!'

Their voices had risen, but upon a sudden interruption they both subsided into immediate silence. Footsteps were coming along the path in their direction, and a moment later the rose bushes were parted displaying Braddock Washington, whose intelligent eyes set in his good-looking vacuous face were peering in at them.

'Who kissed a corpse?' he demanded in obvious disapproval.

'Nobody,' answered Kismine quickly. 'We were just joking.'

'What are you two doing here, anyhow?' he demanded gruffly. 'Kismine, you ought to be—to be reading or playing golf with your sister. Go read! Go play golf! Don't let me find you here when I come back!'

Then he bowed at John and went up the path.

'See?' said Kismine crossly, when he was out of hearing. 'You've spoiled it all. We can never meet any more. He won't let me meet you. He'd have you poisoned if he thought we were in love.'

'We're not, any more!' cried John fiercely, 'so he can set his mind at rest upon that. Moreover, don't fool yourself that I'm going to stay around here. Inside of six hours I'll be over those mountains, if I have to gnaw a passage through them, and on my way East.'

They had both got to their feet, and at this remark Kismine came close and put her arm through his.

'I'm going, too.'

'You must be crazy——'

'Of course I'm going,' she interrupted patiently.

'You most certainly are not. You——'

'Very well,' she said quietly, 'we'll catch up with father now and talk it over with him.'

Defeated, John mustered a sickly smile.

'Very well, dearest,' he agreed, with pale and unconvincing affection, 'we'll go together.'

His love for her returned and settled placidly on his heart. She was his—she would go with him to share his dangers. He put his arms about her and kissed her fervently. After all she loved him; she had saved him, in fact.

Discussing the matter, they walked slowly back towards the château. They decided that since Braddock Washington had seen them together they had best depart the next night. Nevertheless, John's lips were unusually dry at dinner, and he nervously emptied a great spoonful of peacock soup into his left lung. He had to be carried into the turquoise and sable card-room and pounded on the back by one of the under-butlers, which Percy considered a great joke.

IX

Long after midnight John's body gave a nervous jerk, and he sat suddenly upright, staring into the veils of somnolence that draped the room. Through the squares of blue darkness that were his open windows, he had heard a faint faraway sound that died upon a bed of wind before identifying itself on his memory, clouded with uneasy dreams. But the sharp noise that had succeeded it was nearer, was just outside the room—the click of a turned knob, a footstep, a whisper, he could not tell; a hard lump gathered in the pit of his stomach, and his whole body ached in the moment that he strained agonizingly to hear. Then one of the veils seemed to dissolve, and he saw a vague figure standing by the door, a figure only faintly limned and blocked in upon the darkness, mingled so with the folds of the drapery as to seem distorted, like a reflection seen in a dirty pane of glass.

With a sudden movement of fright or resolution John

pressed the button by his bedside, and the next moment he was sitting in the green sunken bath of the adjoining room, waked into alertness by the shock of the cold water which half filled it.

He sprang out, and, his wet pyjamas scattering a heavy trickle of water behind him, ran for the aquamarine door which he knew led out onto the ivory landing of the second floor. The door opened noiselessly. A single crimson lamp burning in a great dome above lit the magnificent sweep of the carved stairways with a poignant beauty. For a moment John hesitated, appalled by the silent splendour massed about him, seeming to envelop in its gigantic folds and contours the solitary drenched little figure shivering upon the ivory landing. Then simultaneously two things happened. The door of his own sitting-room swung open, precipitating three naked negroes into the hall—and, as John swayed in wild terror towards the stairway, another door slid back in the wall on the other side of the corridor, and John saw Braddock Washington standing in the lighted lift, wearing a fur coat and a pair of riding boots which reached to his knees and displayed, above, the glow of his rose-coloured pyjamas.

On the instant the three negroes—John had never seen any of them before, and it flashed through his mind that they must be the professional executioners—paused in their movement towards John, and turned expectantly to the man in the lift, who burst out with an imperious command:

'Get in here! All three of you! Quick as hell!'

Then, within the instant, the three negroes darted into the cage, the oblong of light was blotted out as the lift door slid shut, and John was again alone in the hall. He slumped weakly down against an ivory stair.

It was apparent that something portentous had occurred, something which, for the moment at least, had postponed his own petty disaster. What was it? Had the negroes risen in revolt? Had the aviators forced aside the iron bars of the grating? Or had the men of Fish stumbled blindly through the hills and gazed with bleak, joyless eyes upon the gaudy

valley? John did not know. He heard a faint whir of air as
the lift whizzed up again, and then, a moment later, as it
descended. It was probable that Percy was hurrying to his
father's assistance, and it occurred to John that this was
his opportunity to join Kismine and plan an immediate
escape. He waited until the lift had been silent for several
minutes; shivering a little with the night cool that whipped
in through his wet pyjamas, he returned to his room and
dressed himself quickly. Then he mounted a long flight of
stairs and turned down the corridor carpeted with Russian
sable which led to Kismine's suite.

The door of her sitting-room was open and the lamps were
lighted. Kismine, in an angora kimono, stood near the
window of the room in a listening attitude, and as John
entered noiselessly, she turned towards him.

'Oh, it's you!' she whispered, crossing the room to him.
'Did you hear them?'

'I heard your father's slaves in my——'

'No,' she interrupted excitedly. 'Aeroplanes!'

'Aeroplanes? Perhaps that was the sound that woke me.'

'There're at least a dozen. I saw one a few moments ago
dead against the moon. The guard back by the cliff fired
his rifle and that's what roused father. We're going to open
on them right away.'

'Are they here on purpose?'

'Yes—it's that Italian who got away——'

Simultaneously with her last word, a succession of sharp
cracks tumbled in through the open window. Kismine
uttered a little cry, took a penny with fumbling fingers from
a box on her dresser, and ran to one of the electric lights.
In an instant the entire château was in darkness—she had
blown out the fuse.

'Come on!' she cried to him. 'We'll go up to the roof
garden, and watch it from there!'

Drawing a cape about her, she took his hand, and they
found their way out the door. It was only a step to the tower
-lift, and as she pressed the button that shot them upward he
put his arms around her in the darkness and kissed her

3*

mouth. Romance had come to John Unger at last. A minute later they had stepped out upon the star-white platform. Above, under the misty moon, sliding in and out of the patches of cloud that eddied below it, floated a dozen dark-winged bodies in a constant circling course. From here and there in the valley flashes of fire leaped towards them, followed by sharp detonations. Kismine clapped her hands with pleasure, which a moment later, turned to dismay as the aeroplanes at some prearranged signal, began to release their bombs and the whole of the valley became a panorama of deep reverberant sound and lurid light.

Before long the aim of the attackers became concentrated upon the points where the anti-aircraft guns were situated, and one of them was almost immediately reduced to a giant cinder to lie smouldering in a park of rose bushes.

'Kismine,' begged John, 'you'll be glad when I tell you that this attack came on the eve of my murder. If I hadn't heard that guard shoot off his gun back by the pass I should now be stone dead——'

'I can't hear you!' cried Kismine, intent on the scene before her. 'You'll have to talk louder!'

'I simply said,' shouted John, 'that we'd better get out before they begin to shell the Château!'

Suddenly the whole portico of the negro quarters cracked asunder, a geyser of flame shot up from under the colonnades, and great fragments of jagged marble were hurled as far as the borders of the lake.

'There go fifty thousand dollars' worth of slaves,' cried Kismine, 'at pre-war prices. So few Americans have any respect for property.'

John renewed his efforts to compel her to leave. The aim of the aeroplanes was becoming more precise minute by minute, and only two of the anti-aircraft guns were still retaliating. It was obvious that the garrison, encircled with fire, could not hold out much longer.

'Come on!' cried John, pulling Kismine's arm, 'we've got to go. Do you realize that those aviators will kill you without question if they find you?'

She consented reluctantly.

'We'll have to wake Jasmine!' she said, as they hurried towards the lift. Then she added in a sort of childish delight: 'We'll be poor, won't we? Like people in books. And I'll be an orphan and utterly free. Free and poor! What fun!' She stopped and raised her lips to him in a delighted kiss.

'It's impossible to be both together,' said John grimly. 'People have found that out. And I should choose to be free as preferable of the two. As an extra caution you'd better dump the contents of your jewel box into your pockets.'

Ten minutes later the two girls met John in the dark corridor and they descended to the main floor of the château. Passing for the last time through the magnificence of the splendid halls, they stood for a moment out on the terrace, watching the burning negro quarters and the flaming embers of two planes which had fallen on the other side of the lake. A solitary gun was still keeping up a sturdy popping, and the attackers seemed timorous about descending lower, but sent their thunderous fireworks in a circle around it, until any chance shot might annihilate its Ethiopian crew.

John and the two sisters passed down the marble steps, turned sharply to the left, and began to ascend a narrow path that wound like a garter about the diamond mountain. Kismine knew a heavily wooded spot half-way up where they could lie concealed and yet be able to observe the wild night in the valley—finally to make an escape, when it should be necessary, along a secret path laid in a rocky gully.

X

It was three o'clock when they attained their destination. The obliging and phlegmatic Jasmine fell off to sleep immediately, leaning against the trunk of a large tree, while John and Kismine sat, his arm around her, and watched the desperate ebb and flow of the dying battle among the ruins of a vista that had been a garden spot that morning. Shortly after four o'clock the last remaining gun gave out a clanging sound and went out of action in a swift tongue of red smoke. Though the moon was down, they saw that the flying bodies were circling closer to the earth. When the planes had made certain that the beleaguered possessed no further resources, they would land and the dark and glittering reign of the Washingtons would be over.

With the cessation of the firing the valley grew quiet. The embers of the two aeroplanes glowed like the eyes of some monster crouching in the grass. The château stood dark and silent, beautiful without light as it had been beautiful in the sun, while the woody rattles of Nemesis filled the air above with a growing and receding complaint. Then John perceived that Kismine, like her sister, had fallen sound asleep.

It was long after four when he became aware of footsteps along the path they had lately followed, and he waited in breathless silence until the persons to whom they belonged had passed the vantage-point he occupied. There was a faint stir in the air now that was not of human origin, and the dew was cold; he knew that the dawn would break soon. John waited until the steps had gone a safe distance up the mountain and were inaudible. Then he followed. About half-way to the steep summit the trees fell away and a hard saddle of rock spread itself over the diamond beneath. Just before he reached this point he slowed down his pace, warned by an animal sense that there was life just ahead of him. Coming to a high boulder, he lifted his head gradually above its edge. His curiosity was rewarded; this is what he saw:

Braddock Washington was standing there motionless, silhouetted against the grey sky without sound or sign of life. As the dawn came up out of the east, lending a cold green colour to the earth, it brought the solitary figure into insignificant contrast with the new day.

While John watched, his host remained for a few moments absorbed in some inscrutable contemplation; then he signalled to the two negroes who crouched at his feet to lift the burden which lay between them. As they struggled upright, the first yellow beam of the sun struck through the innumerable prisms of an immense and exquisitely chiselled diamond—and a white radiance was kindled that glowed upon the air like a fragment of the morning star. The bearers staggered beneath its weight for a moment—then their rippling muscles caught and hardened under the wet shine of the skins and the three figures were again motionless in their defiant impotency before the heavens.

After a while the white man lifted his head and slowly raised his arms in a gesture of attention, as one who would call a great crowd to hear—but there was no crowd, only the vast silence of the mountain and the sky, broken by faint bird voices down among the trees. The figure on the saddle of rock began to speak ponderously and with an inextinguishable pride.

'You out there—' he cried in a trembling voice. 'You—there—!' He paused, his arms still uplifted, his head held attentively as though he were expecting an answer. John strained his eyes to see whether there might be men coming down the mountain, but the mountain was bare of human life. There was only sky and a mocking flute of wind along the tree-tops. Could Washington be praying? For a moment John wondered. Then the illusion passed—there was something in the man's whole attitude antithetical to prayer.

'Oh, you above there!'

The voice was become strong and confident. This was no forlorn supplication. If anything, there was in it a quality of monstrous condescension.

'You there——'

Words, too quickly uttered to be understood, flowing one into the other. . . . John listened breathlessly, catching a phrase here and there, while the voice broke off, resumed, broke off again—now strong and argumentative, now coloured with a slow, puzzled impatience. Then a conviction commenced to dawn on the single listener, and as realization crept over him a spray of quick blood rushed through his arteries. Braddock Washington was offering a bribe to God!

That was it—there was no doubt. The diamond in the arms of his slaves was some advance sample, a promise of more to follow.

That, John perceived after a time, was the thread running through his sentences. Prometheus Enriched was calling to witness forgotten sacrifices, forgotten rituals, prayers obsolete before the birth of Christ. For a while his discourse took the form of reminding God of this gift or that which Divinity had deigned to accept from men—great churches if he would rescue cities from the plague, gifts of myrrh and gold, of human lives and beautiful women and captive armies, of children and queens, of beasts of the forest and field, sheep and goats, harvests and cities, whole conquered lands that had been offered up in lust or blood for His appeasal, buying a meed's worth of alleviation from the Divine wrath—and now he, Braddock Washington, Emperor of Diamonds, king and priest of the age of gold, arbiter of splendour and luxury, would offer up a treasure such as princes before him had never dreamed of, offer it up not in suppliance, but in pride.

He would give to God, he continued, getting down to specifications, the greatest diamond in the world. This diamond would be cut with many more thousand facets than there were leaves on a tree, and yet the whole diamond would be shaped with the perfection of a stone no bigger than a fly. Many men would work upon it for many years. It would be set in a great dome of beaten gold, wonderfully carved and equipped with gates of opal and crusted sapphire. In the middle would be hollowed out a chapel presided over by an altar of iridescent, decomposing, ever-changing radium which would burn out the eyes of any worshipper who lifted up his head from prayer—and on this altar there would be slain for the amusement of the Divine Benefactor any victim He should choose, even though it should be the greatest and most powerful man alive.

In return he asked only a simple thing, a thing that for God would be absurdly easy—only that matters should be as they were yesterday at this hour and that they should so remain. So very simple! Let but the heavens open, swallowing these men and their aeroplanes—and then close again. Let him have his slaves once more, restored to life and well.

There was no one else with whom he had ever needed to treat or bargain.

He doubted only whether he had made his bribe big enough. God had His price, of course. God was made in man's image, so it had been said: He must have His price. And the price would be rare—no cathedral whose building consumed many years, no pyramid constructed by ten thousand workmen, would be like this cathedral, this pyramid.

He paused here. That was his proposition. Everything would be up to specifications and there was nothing vulgar in his assertion that it would be cheap at the price. He implied that Providence could take it or leave it.

As he approached the end his sentences became broken, became short and uncertain, and his body seemed tense, seemed strained to catch the slightest pressure or whisper of life in the spaces around him. His hair had turned gradually white as he talked, and now he lifted his head high to the heavens like a prophet of old—magnificently mad.

Then, as John stared in giddy fascination, it seemed to him that a curious phenomenon took place somewhere around him. It was as though the sky had darkened for an instant, as though there had been a sudden murmur in a gust of wind, a sound of far-away trumpets, a sighing like the rustle of a great silken robe—for a time the whole of nature round about partook of this darkness: the birds' song ceased; the trees were still, and far over the mountain there was a mutter of dull, menacing thunder.

That was all. The wind died along the tall grasses of the valley. The dawn and the day resumed their place in a time, and the risen sun sent hot waves of yellow mist that made its path bright before it. The leaves laughed in the sun, and their laughter shook the trees until each bough was like a girls' school in fairyland. God had refused to accept the bribe.

For another moment John watched the triumph of the

day. Then, turning, he saw a flutter of brown down by the lake, then another flutter, then another, like the dance of golden angels alighting from the clouds. The aeroplanes had come to earth.

John slid off the boulder and ran down the side of the mountain to the clump of trees, where the two girls were awake and waiting for him. Kismine sprang to her feet, the jewels in her pockets jingling, a question on her parted lips, but instinct told John that there was no time for words. They must get off the mountain without losing a moment. He seized a hand of each, and in silence they threaded the tree-trunks, washed with light now and with the rising mist. Behind them from the valley came no sound at all, except the complaint of the peacocks far away and the pleasant undertone of morning.

When they had gone about a half a mile, they avoided the park land and entered a narrow path that led over the next rise of ground. At the highest point of this they paused and turned around. Their eyes rested upon the mountainside they had just left—oppressed by some dark sense of tragic impendency.

Clear against the sky a broken, white-haired man was slowly descending the steep slope, followed by two gigantic and emotionless negroes, who carried a burden between them which still flashed and glittered in the sun. Half-way down two other figures joined them—John could see that they were Mrs Washington and her son, upon whose arm she leaned. The aviators had clambered from their machines to the sweeping lawn in front of the château, and with rifles in hand were starting up the diamond mountain in skirmishing formation.

But the little group of five which had formed farther up and was engrossing all the watchers' attention had stopped upon a ledge of rock. The negroes stooped and pulled up what appeared to be a trapdoor in the side of the mountain. Into this they all disappeared, the white-haired man first, then his wife and son, finally the two negroes, the glittering tips of whose jewelled head-dresses caught the sun for a moment before the trap-door descended and engulfed them all.

Kismine clutched John's arm.

'Oh,' she cried wildly, 'where are they going? What are they going to do?'

'It must be some underground way of escape——'

A little scream from the two girls interrupted his sentence.

'Don't you see?' sobbed Kismine hysterically. 'The mountain is wired!'

Even as she spoke John put up his hands to shield his sight. Before their eyes the whole surface of the mountain had changed suddenly to a dazzling burning yellow, which showed up through the jacket of turf as light shows through a human hand. For a moment the intolerable glow continued, and then like an extinguished filament it disappeared, revealing a black waste from which blue smoke arose slowly, carrying off with it what remained of vegetation and of human flesh. Of the aviators there was left neither blood nor bone—they were consumed as completely as the five souls who had gone inside.

Simultaneously, and with an immense concussion, the château literally threw itself into the air, bursting into flaming fragments as it rose, and then tumbling back upon itself in a smoking pile that lay projecting half into the water of the lake. There was no fire—what smoke there was drifted off mingling with the sunshine, and for a few minutes longer a powdery dust of marble drifted from the great featureless pile that had once been the house of jewels. There was no more sound and the three people were alone in the valley.

XI

At sunset John and his two companions reached the high cliff which had marked the boundaries of the Washingtons' dominion, and looking back found the valley tranquil and lovely in the dusk. They sat down to finish the food which Jasmine had brought with her in a basket.

'There!' she said, as she spread the tablecloth and put

the sandwiches in a neat pile upon it. 'Don't they look tempting? I always think that food tastes better out-doors.'

'With that remark,' remarked Kismine, 'Jasmine enters the middle class.'

'Now,' said John eagerly, 'turn out your pockets and let's see what jewels you brought along. If you made a good selection we three ought to live comfortably all the rest of our lives.'

Obediently Kismine put her hand in her pocket and tossed two handfuls of glittering stones before him.

'Not so bad,' cried John, enthusiastically. 'They aren't very big, but—Hello!' His expression changed as he held one of them up to the declining sun. 'Why, these aren't diamonds! There's something the matter!'

'By golly!' exclaimed Kismine, with a startled look. 'What an idiot I am!'

'Why, these are rhinestones!' cried John.

'I know.' She broke into a laugh. 'I opened the wrong drawer. They belonged on the dress of a girl who visited Jasmine. I got her to give them to me in exchange for diamonds. I'd never seen anything but precious stones before.'

'And this is what you brought?'

'I'm afraid so.' She fingered the brilliants wistfully. 'I think I like these better. I'm a little tired of diamonds.'

'Very well,' said John gloomily. 'We'll have to live in Hades. And you will grow old telling incredulous women that you got the wrong drawer. Unfortunately your father's bank-books were consumed with him.'

'Well, what's the matter with Hades?'

'If I come home with a wife at my age my father is just as liable as not to cut me off with a hot coal, as they say down there.'

Jasmine spoke up.

'I love washing,' she said quietly. 'I have always washed my own handkerchiefs. I'll take in laundry and support you both.'

'Do they have washwomen in Hades?' asked Kismine innocently.

'Of course,' answered John. 'It's just like anywhere else.'

'I thought—perhaps it was too hot to wear any clothes.' John laughed.

'Just try it!' he suggested. 'They'll run you out before you're half started.'

'Will father be there?' she asked.

John turned to her in astonishment.

'Your father is dead,' he replied sombrely. 'Why should he go to Hades? You have it confused with another place that was abolished long ago.'

After supper they folded up the table-cloth and spread their blankets for the night.

'What a dream it was,' Kismine sighed, gazing up at the stars. 'How strange it seems to be here with one dress and a penniless fiancé!

'Under the stars,' she repeated. 'I never noticed the stars before. I always thought of them as great big diamonds that belonged to someone. Now they frighten me. They make me feel that it was all a dream, all my youth.'

'It *was* a dream,' said John quietly. 'Everybody's youth is a dream, a form of chemical madness.'

'How pleasant then to be insane!'

'So I'm told,' said John gloomily. 'I don't know any longer. At any rate, let us love for a while, for a year or so, you and me. That's a form of divine drunkenness that we can all try. There are only diamonds in the whole world, diamonds and perhaps the shabby gift of disillusion. Well, I have that last and I will make the usual nothing of it.' He shivered. 'Turn up your coat collar, little girl, the night's full of chill and you'll get pneumonia. His was a great sin who first invented consciousness. Let us lose it for a few hours.'

So wrapping himself in his blanket he fell off to sleep.

BERNICE BOBS HER HAIR

[1920]

AFTER dark on Saturday night one could stand on the first tee of the golf-course and see the country-club windows as a yellow expanse over a very black and wavy ocean. The waves of this ocean, so to speak, were the heads of many curious caddies, a few of the more ingenious chauffeurs, the golf professional's deaf sister—and there were usually several stray, diffident waves who might have rolled inside had they so desired. This was the gallery.

The balcony was inside. It consisted of the circle of wicker chairs that lined the wall of the combination clubroom and ballroom. At these Saturday-night dances it was largely feminine; a great babel of middle-aged ladies with sharp eyes and icy hearts behind lorgnettes and large bosoms. The main function of the balcony was critical. It occasionally showed grudging admiration, but never approval, for it is well known among ladies over thirty-five that when the younger set dance in the summer-time it is with the very worst intentions in the world, and if they are not bombarded with stony eyes stray couples will dance weird barbaric interludes in the corners, and the more popular, more dangerous, girls will sometimes be kissed in the parked limousines of unsuspecting dowagers.

But, after all, this critical circle is not close enough to the stage to see the actors' faces and catch the subtler byplay. It can only frown and lean, ask questions and make satisfactory deductions from its set of postulates, such as the one which states that every young man with a large income leads the life of a hunted partridge. It

84

never really appreciates the drama of the shifting, semi-cruel world of adolescence. No; boxes, orchestra-circle, principals, and chorus are represented by the medley of faces and voices that sway to the plaintive African rhythm of Dyer's dance orchestra.

From sixteen-year-old Otis Ormonde, who has two more years at Hill School, to G. Reece Stoddard, over whose bureau at home hangs a Harvard law diploma; from little Madeleine Hogue, whose hair still feels strange and uncomfortable on top of her head, to Bessie MacRae, who has been the life of the party a little too long—more than ten years—the medley is not only the centre of the stage but contains the only people capable of getting an unobstructed view of it.

With a flourish and a bang the music stops. The couples exchange artificial, effortless smiles, facetiously repeat '*la-de-da-da* dum-*dum*,' and then the clatter of young feminine voices soars over the burst of clapping.

A few disappointed stags caught in midfloor as they had been about to cut in subsided listlessly back to the walls, because this was not like the riotous Christmas dances—these summer hops were considered just pleasantly warm and exciting, where even the younger marrieds rose and performed ancient waltzes and terrifying fox trots to the tolerant amusement of their younger brothers and sisters.

Warren McIntyre, who casually attended Yale, being one of the unfortunate stags, felt in his dinner-coat pocket for a cigarette and strolled out onto the wide, semidark veranda, where couples were scattered at tables, filling the lantern-hung night with vague words and hazy laughter. He nodded here and there at the less absorbed and as he passed each couple some half-forgotten fragment of a story played in his mind, for it was not a large city and every one was Who's Who to every one else's past. There, for example, were Jim Strain and Ethel Demorest, who had been privately engaged for three years. Every one knew that as soon as Jim managed to hold a job for more than two months she would marry him. Yet how bored they both looked, and how wearily Ethel regarded Jim sometimes, as if she wondered why she had trained the vines of her affection on such a wind-shaken poplar.

Warren was nineteen and rather pitying with those of his friends who hadn't gone East to college. But, like most boys, he bragged tremendously about the girls of his city when he was away from it. There was Genevieve Ormonde, who regularly made the rounds of dances, house-parties, and football games at Princeton, Yale, Williams, and Cornell; there was black-eyed Roberta Dillon, who was quite as famous to her own generation as Hiram Johnson or Ty Cobb; and, of course, there was Marjorie Harvey, who besides having a fairylike face and a dazzling, bewildering tongue was already justly celebrated for having turned five cart-wheels in succession during the past pump-and-slipper dance at New Haven.

Warren, who had grown up across the street from Marjorie, had long been 'crazy about her.' Sometimes she seemed to reciprocate his feeling with a faint gratitude, but she had tried him by her infallible test and informed him gravely that she did not love him. Her test was that when she was away from him she forgot him and had affairs with other boys. Warren found this discouraging, especially as Marjorie had been making little trips all summer, and for the first two or three days after each arrival home he saw great heaps of mail on the Harveys' hall table addressed to her in various masculine handwritings. To make matters worse, all during the month of August she had been visited by her cousin Bernice from Eau Claire, and it seemed impossible to see her alone. It was always necessary to hunt round and find some one to take care of Bernice. As August waned this was becoming more and more difficult.

Much as Warren worshipped Marjorie, he had to admit that Cousin Bernice was sorta dopeless. She was pretty, with dark hair and high colour, but she was no fun on a

party. Every Saturday night he danced a long arduous
duty dance with her to please Marjorie, but he had never
been anything but bored in her company.

'Warren'—a soft voice at his elbow broke in upon his
thoughts, and he turned to see Marjorie, flushed and
radiant as usual. She laid a hand on his shoulder and a
glow settled almost imperceptibly over him.

'Warren,' she whispered, 'do something for me—dance
with Bernice. She's been stuck with little Otis Ormonde
for almost an hour.'

Warren's glow faded.

'Why—sure,' he answered half-heartedly.

'You don't mind, do you? I'll see that you don't get
stuck.'

' 'Sall right.'

Marjorie smiled—that smile that was thanks enough.

'You're an angel, and I'm obliged loads.'

With a sigh the angel glanced round the veranda, but
Bernice and Otis were not in sight. He wandered back
inside, and there in front of the women's dressing-
room he found Otis in the centre of a group of young
men who were convulsed with laughter. Otis was brandish-
ing a piece of timber he had picked up, and discoursing
volubly.

'She's gone in to fix her hair,' he announced wildly.
'I'm waiting to dance another hour with her.'

Their laughter was renewed.

'Why don't some of you cut in?' cried Otis resentfully.
'She likes more variety.'

'Why, Otis,' suggested a friend, 'you've just barely got
used to her.'

'Why the two-by-four, Otis?' inquired Warren, smiling.

'The two-by-four? Oh, this? This is a club. When she
comes out I'll hit her on the head and knock her in
again.'

Warren collapsed on a settee and howled with glee.

'Never mind, Otis,' he articulated finally. 'I'm relieving
you this time.'

Otis simulated a sudden fainting attack and handed the stick to Warren.

'If you need it, old man,' he said hoarsely.

No matter how beautiful or brilliant a girl may be, the reputation of not being frequently cut in on makes her position at a dance unfortunate. Perhaps boys prefer her company to that of the butterflies with whom they dance a dozen times an evening, but youth in this jazz-nourished generation is temperamentally restless, and the idea of fox-trotting more than one full fox trot with the same girl is distasteful, not to say odious. When it comes to several dances and the intermissions between she can be quite sure that a young man, once relieved, will never tread on her wayward toes again.

Warren danced the next full dance with Bernice, and finally, thankful for the intermission, he led her to a table on the veranda. There was a moment's silence while she did unimpressive things with her fan.

'It's hotter here than in Eau Claire,' she said.

Warren stifled a sigh and nodded. It might be for all he knew or cared. He wondered idly whether she was a poor conversationalist because she got no attention or got no attention because she was a poor conversationalist.

'You going to be here much longer?' he asked, and then turned rather red. She might suspect his reasons for asking.

'Another week,' she answered, and stared at him as if to lunge at his next remark when it left his lips.

Warren fidgeted. Then with a sudden charitable impulse he decided to try part of his line on her. He turned and looked at her eyes.

'You've got an awfully kissable mouth,' he began quietly.

This was a remark that he sometimes made to girls at college proms when they were talking in just such half dark as this. Bernice distinctly jumped. She turned an ungraceful red and became clumsy with her fan. No one had ever made such a remark to her before.

'Fresh!'—the word had slipped out before she realized

it, and she bit her lip. Too late she decided to be amused, and offered him a flustered smile.

Warren was annoyed. Though not accustomed to have that remark taken seriously, still it usually provoked a laugh or a paragraph of sentimental banter. And he hated to be called fresh, except in a joking way. His charitable impulse died and he switched the topic.

'Jim Strain and Ethel Demorest sitting out as usual,' he commented.

This was more in Bernice's line, but a faint regret mingled with her relief as the subject changed. Men did not talk to her about kissable mouths, but she knew that they talked in some such way to other girls.

'Oh, yes,' she said, and laughed. 'I hear they've been mooning round for years without a red penny. Isn't it silly?'

Warren's disgust increased. Jim Strain was a close friend of his brother's, and anyway he considered it bad form to sneer at people for not having money. But Bernice had had no intention of sneering. She was merely nervous.

II

When Marjorie and Bernice reached home at half after midnight they said good night at the top of the stairs. Though cousins, they were not intimates. As a matter of fact Marjorie had no female intimates—she considered girls stupid. Bernice on the contrary all through this parent-arranged visit had rather longed to exchange those confidences flavoured with giggles and tears that she considered an indispensable factor in all feminine intercourse. But in this respect she found Marjorie rather cold; felt somehow the same difficulty in talking to her that she had in talking to men. Marjorie never giggled, was never frightened, seldom embarrassed, and in fact had very few of the qualities which Bernice considered appropriately and blessedly feminine.

As Bernice busied herself with tooth-brush and paste

this night she wondered for the hundredth time why she never had any attention when she was away from home. That her family were the wealthiest in Eau Claire; that her mother entertained tremendously, gave little dinners for her daughter before all dances and bought her a car of her own to drive round in, never occurred to her as factors in her home-town social success. Like most girls she had been brought up on the warm milk prepared by Annie Fellows Johnston and on novels in which the female was beloved because of certain mysterious womanly qualities, always mentioned but never displayed.

Bernice felt a vague pain that she was not at present engaged in being popular. She did not know that had it not been for Marjorie's campaigning she would have danced the entire evening with one man; but she knew that even in Eau Claire other girls with less position and less pulchritude were given a much bigger rush. She attributed this to something subtly unscrupulous in those girls. It had never worried her, and if it had her mother would have assured her that the other girls cheapened themselves and that men really respected girls like Bernice.

She turned out the light in her bathroom, and on an impulse decided to go in and chat for a moment with her aunt Josephine, whose light was still on. Her soft slippers bore her noiselessly down the carpeted hall, but hearing voices inside she stopped near the partly opened door. Then she caught her own name, and without any definite intention of eavesdropping lingered—and the thread of the conversation going on inside pierced her consciousness sharply as if it had been drawn through with a needle.

'She's absolutely hopeless!' It was Marjorie's voice. 'Oh, I know what you're going to say! So many people have told you how pretty and sweet she is, and how she can cook! What of it? She has a bum time. Men don't like her.'

'What's a little cheap popularity?'

Mrs Harvey sounded annoyed.

'It's everything when you're eighteen,' said Marjorie emphatically. 'I've done my best. I've been polite and I've made men dance with her, but they just won't stand being bored. When I think of that gorgeous colouring wasted on such a ninny, and think what Martha Carey could do with it—oh!'

'There's no courtesy these days.'

Mrs Harvey's voice implied that modern situations were too much for her. When she was a girl all young ladies who belonged to nice families had glorious times.

'Well,' said Marjorie, 'no girl can permanently bolster up a lame-duck visitor, because these days it's every girl for herself. I've even tried to drop her hints about clothes and things, and she's been furious—given me the funniest looks. She's sensitive enough to know she's not getting away with much, but I'll bet she consoles herself by thinking that she's very virtuous and that I'm too gay and fickle and will come to a bad end. All unpopular girls think that way. Sour grapes! Sarah Hopkins refers to Genevieve and Roberta and me as gardenia girls! I'll bet she'd give ten years of her life and her European education to be a gardenia girl and have three or four men in love with her and be cut in on every few feet at dances.'

'It seems to me,' interrupted Mrs Harvey rather wearily, 'that you ought to be able to do something for Bernice. I know she's not very vivacious.'

Marjorie groaned.

'Vivacious! Good grief! I've never heard her say anything to a boy except that it's hot or the floor's crowded or that she's going to school in New York next year. Sometimes she asks them what kind of car they have and tells them the kind she has. Thrilling!'

There was a short silence, and then Mrs Harvey took up her refrain:

'All I know is that other girls not half so sweet and attractive get partners. Martha Carey, for instance, is stout and loud, and her mother is distinctly common. Roberta Dillon is so thin this year that she looks as though Arizona were the place for her. She's dancing herself to death.'

'But, mother,' objected Marjorie impatiently, 'Martha is cheerful and awfully witty and an awfully slick girl, and Roberta's a marvellous dancer. She's been popular for ages!'

Mrs Harvey yawned.

'I think it's that crazy Indian blood in Bernice,' continued Marjorie. 'Maybe she's a reversion to type. Indian women all just sat round and never said anything.'

'Go to bed, you silly child,' laughed Mrs Harvey. 'I wouldn't have told you that if I'd thought you were going to remember it. And I think most of your ideas are perfectly idiotic,' she finished sleepily.

There was another silence, while Marjorie considered whether or not convincing her mother was worth the trouble. People over forty can seldom be permanently convinced of anything. At eighteen our convictions are hills from which we look; at forty-five they are caves in which we hide.

Having decided this, Marjorie said good night. When she came out into the hall it was quite empty.

III

While Marjorie was breakfasting late next day Bernice came into the room with a rather formal good morning, sat down opposite, stared intently over and slightly moistened her lips.

'What's on your mind?' inquired Marjorie, rather puzzled.

Bernice paused before she threw her hand-grenade.

'I heard what you said about me to your mother last night.'

Marjorie was startled, but she showed only a faintly heightened colour and her voice was quite even when she spoke.

'Where were you?'

'In the hall. I didn't mean to listen—at first.'

After an involuntary look of contempt Marjorie dropped her eyes and became very interested in balancing a stray corn-flake on her finger.

'I guess I'd better go back to Eau Claire—if I'm such a nuisance.' Bernice's lower lip was trembling violently and she continued on a wavering note: 'I've tried to be nice, and—and I've been first neglected and then insulted. No one ever visited me and got such treatment.'

Marjorie was silent.

'But I'm in the way, I see. I'm a drag on you. Your friends don't like me.' She paused, and then remembered another one of her grievances. 'Of course I was furious last week when you tried to hint to me that that dress was unbecoming. Don't you think I know how to dress myself?'

'No,' murmured Marjorie less than half-aloud.

'What?'

'I didn't hint anything,' said Marjorie succinctly. 'I said, as I remember, that it was better to wear a becoming dress three times straight than to alternate it with two frights.'

'Do you think that was a very nice thing to say?'

'I wasn't trying to be nice.' Then after a pause: 'When do you want to go?'

Bernice drew in her breath sharply.

'Oh!' It was a little half-cry.

Marjorie looked up in surprise.

'Didn't you say you were going?'

'Yes, but——'

'Oh, you were only bluffing!'

They stared at each other across the breakfast-table for a moment. Misty waves were passing before Bernice's eyes, while Marjorie's face wore that rather hard expression that she used when slightly intoxicated undergraduates were making love to her.

'So you were bluffing,' she repeated as if it were what she might have expected.

Bernice admitted it by bursting into tears. Marjorie's eyes showed boredom.

'You're my cousin,' sobbed Bernice. 'I'm v-v-visiting you. I was to stay a month, and if I go home my mother will know and she'll wah-wonder——'

Marjorie waited until the shower of broken words collapsed into little sniffles.

'I'll give you my month's allowance,' she said coldly, 'and you can spend this last week anywhere you want. There's a very nice hotel——'

Bernice's sobs rose to a flute note, and rising of a sudden she fled from the room.

An hour later, while Marjorie was in the library absorbed in composing one of those non-committal, marvellously elusive letters that only a young girl can write, Bernice reappeared, very red-eyed and consciously calm. She cast no glance at Marjorie but took a book at random from the shelf and sat down as if to read. Marjorie seemed absorbed in her letter and continued writing. When the clock showed noon Bernice closed her book with a snap.

'I suppose I'd better get my railroad ticket.'

This was not the beginning of the speech she had rehearsed upstairs, but as Marjorie was not getting her cues—wasn't urging her to be reasonable; it's all a mistake —it was the best opening she could muster.

'Just wait till I finish this letter,' said Marjorie without looking round. 'I want to get it off in the next mail.'

After another minute, during which her pen scratched busily, she turned round and relaxed with an air of 'at your service.' Again Bernice had to speak.

'Do you want me to go home?'

'Well,' said Marjorie, considering, 'I suppose if you're not having a good time you'd better go. No use being miserable.'

'Don't you think common kindness——'

'Oh, please don't quote "Little Women"!' cried Marjorie impatiently. 'That's out of style.'

'You think so?'

'Heavens, yes! What modern girl could live like those inane females?'

'They were the models for our mothers.'

Marjorie laughed.

'Yes, they were—not! Besides, our mothers were all very well in their way, but they know very little about their daughters' problems.'

Bernice drew herself up.

'Please don't talk about my mother.'

Marjorie laughed.

'I don't think I mentioned her.'

Bernice felt that she was being led away from her subject.

'Do you think you've treated me very well?'

'I've done my best. You're rather hard material to work with.'

The lids of Bernice's eyes reddened.

'I think you're hard and selfish, and you haven't a feminine quality in you.'

'Oh, my Lord!' cried Marjorie in desperation. 'You little nut! Girls like you are responsible for all the tiresome colourless marriages; all those ghastly inefficiencies that pass as feminine qualities. What a blow it must be when a man with imagination marries the beautiful bundle of clothes that he's been building ideals round, and finds that she's just a weak, whining, cowardly mass of affectations!'

Bernice's mouth had slipped half open.

'The womanly woman!' continued Marjorie. 'Her whole early life is occupied in whining criticisms of girls like me who really do have a good time.'

Bernice's jaw descended farther as Marjorie's voice rose.

'There's some excuse for an ugly girl whining. If I'd been irretrievably ugly I'd never have forgiven my parents for bringing me into the world. But you're starting life without any handicap—' Marjorie's little fist clinched. 'If you expect me to weep with you you'll be disappointed.

Go or stay, just as you like.' And picking up her letters she left the room.

Bernice claimed a headache and failed to apppear at luncheon. They had a matinée date for the afternoon, but the headache persisting, Marjorie made explanations to a not very downcast boy. But when she returned late in the afternoon she found Bernice with a strangely set face waiting for her in her bedroom.

'I've decided,' began Bernice without preliminaries, 'that maybe you're right about things—possibly not. But if you'll tell me why your friends aren't—aren't interested in me I'll see if I can do what you want me to.'

Marjorie was at the mirror shaking down her hair.

'Do you mean it?'

'Yes.'

'Without reservations? Will you do exactly what I say?'

'Well, I——'

'Well nothing! Will you do exactly as I say?'

'If they're sensible things.'

'They're not! You're no case for sensible things.'

'Are you going to make—to recommend——'

'Yes, everything. If I tell you to take boxing lessons you'll have to do it. Write home and tell your mother you're going to stay another two weeks.'

'If you'll tell me——'

'All right—I'll just give you a few examples now. First, you have no ease of manner. Why? Because you're never sure about your personal appearance. When a girl feels that she's perfectly groomed and dressed she can forget that part of her. That's charm. The more parts of yourself you can afford to forget the more charm you have.'

'Don't I look all right?'

'No; for instance, you never take care of your eyebrows. They're black and lustrous, but by leaving them straggly they're a blemish. They'd be beautiful if you'd take care of them in one-tenth the time you take doing nothing. You're going to brush them so that they'll grow straight.'

Bernice raised the brows in question.

'Do you mean to say that men notice eyebrows?'

'Yes—subconsciously. And when you go home you ought to have your teeth straightened a little. It's almost imperceptible, still——'

'But I thought,' interrupted Bernice in bewilderment, 'that you despised little dainty feminine things like that.'

'I hate dainty minds,' answered Marjorie. 'But a girl has to be dainty in person. If she looks like a million dollars she can talk about Russia, ping-pong, or the League of Nations and get away with it.'

'What else?'

'Oh, I'm just beginning! There's your dancing.'

'Don't I dance all right?'

'No, you don't—you lean on a man; yes, you do—ever so slightly. I noticed it when we were dancing together yesterday. And you dance standing up straight instead of bending over a little. Probably some old lady on the side-line once told you that you looked so dignified that way. But except with a very small girl it's much harder on the man, and he's the one that counts.'

'Go on.' Bernice's brain was reeling.

'Well, you've got to learn to be nice to men who are sad birds. You look as if you'd been insulted whenever you're thrown with any except the most popular boys. Why, Bernice, I'm cut in on every few feet—and who does most of it? Why, those very sad birds. No girl can afford to neglect them. They're the big part of any crowd. Young boys too shy to talk are the very best conversational practice. Clumsy boys are the best dancing practice. If you can follow them and yet look graceful you can follow a baby tank across a barb-wire sky-scraper.'

Bernice sighed profoundly, but Marjorie was not through.

'If you go to a dance and really amuse, say, three sad birds that dance with you; if you talk so well to them that they forget they're stuck with you, you've done something. They'll come back next time, and gradually so many sad birds will dance with you that the attractive boys will see there's no danger of being stuck—then they'll dance with you.'

'Yes,' agreed Bernice faintly. 'I think I begin to see.'

'And finally,' concluded Marjorie, 'poise and charm will just come. You'll wake up some morning knowing you've attained it, and men will know it too.'

Bernice rose.

'It's been awfully kind of you—but nobody's ever talked to me like this before, and I feel sort of startled.'

Marjorie made no answer but gazed pensively at her own image in the mirror.

'You're a peach to help me,' continued Bernice.

Still Marjorie did not answer, and Bernice thought she had seemed too grateful.

'I know you don't like sentiment,' she said timidly.

Marjorie turned to her quickly.

'Oh, I wasn't thinking about that. I was considering whether we hadn't better bob your hair.'

Bernice collapsed backward upon the bed.

IV

On the following Wednesday evening there was a dinner-dance at the country club. When the guests strolled in Bernice found her place-card with a slight feeling of irritation. Though at her right sat G. Reece Stoddard, a most desirable and distinguished young bachelor, the all-important left held only Charley Paulson. Charley lacked height, beauty, and social shrewdness, and in her new enlightenment Bernice decided that his only qualification to be her partner was that he had never been stuck with her. But this feeling of irritation left with the last of the soup-plates, and Marjorie's specific instruction came to her. Swallowing her pride she turned to Charley Paulson and plunged.

'Do you think I ought to bob my hair, Mr Charley Paulson?'

Charley looked up in surprise.

'Why?'

'Because I'm considering it. It's such a sure and easy way of attracting attention.'

Charley smiled pleasantly. He could not know this had been rehearsed. He replied that he didn't know much about bobbed hair. But Bernice was there to tell him.

'I want to be a society vampire, you see,' she announced coolly, and went on to inform him that bobbed hair was the necessary prelude. She added that she wanted to ask his advice, because she had heard he was so critical about girls.

Charley, who knew as much about the psychology of women as he did of the mental states of Buddhist contemplatives, felt vaguely flattered.

'So I've decided,' she continued, her voice rising slightly, 'that early next week I'm going down to the Sevier Hotel barber-shop, sit in the first chair, and get my hair bobbed.' She faltered, noticing that the people near her had paused in their conversation and were listening; but after a confused second Marjorie's coaching told, and she finished her paragraph to the vicinity at large. 'Of course I'm charging admission, but if you'll all come down and encourage me I'll issue passes for the inside seats.'

There was a ripple of appreciative laughter, and under cover of it G. Reece Stoddard leaned over quickly and said to her ear: 'I'll take a box right now.'

She met his eyes and smiled as if he had said something surpassingly brilliant.

'Do you believe in bobbed hair?' asked G. Reece in the same undertone.

'I think it's unmoral,' affirmed Bernice gravely. 'But, of course, you've either got to amuse people or feed 'em' or shock 'em.' Marjorie had culled this from Oscar Wilde. It was greeted with a ripple of laughter from the men and a series of quick, intent looks from the girls. And then as though she had said nothing of wit or moment Bernice turned again to Charley and spoke confidentially in his ear.

'I want to ask you your opinion of several people. I imagine you're a wonderful judge of character.'

Charley thrilled faintly—paid her a subtle compliment by overturning her water.

Two hours later, while Warren McIntyre was standing passively in the stag line abstractedly watching the dancers and wondering whither and with whom Marjorie had disappeared, an unrelated perception began to creep slowly upon him—a perception that Bernice, cousin to Marjorie, had been cut in on several times in the past five minutes. He closed his eyes, opened them and looked again. Several minutes back she had been dancing with a visiting boy, a matter easily accounted for; a visiting boy would know no better. But now she was dancing with some one else, and there was Charley Paulson headed for her with enthusiastic determination in his eye. Funny—Charley seldom danced with more than three girls an evening.

Warren was distinctly surprised when—the exchange having been effected—the man relieved proved to be none other than G. Reece Stoddard himself. And G. Reece seemed not at all jubilant at being relieved. Next time Bernice danced near, Warren regarded her intently. Yes, she was pretty, distinctly pretty; and to-night her face seemed really vivacious. She had that look that no woman, however histrionically proficient, can successfully counterfeit—she looked as if she were having a good time. He liked the way she had her hair arranged, wondering if it was brilliantine that made it glisten so. And that dress was becoming—a dark red that set off her shadowy eyes and high colouring. He remembered that he had thought her pretty when she first came to town, before he had realized that she was dull. Too bad she was dull—dull girls unbearable—certainly pretty though.

His thoughts zigzagged back to Marjorie. This disappearance would be like other disappearances. When she reappeared he would demand where she had been—would be told emphatically that it was none of his business. What a pity she was so sure of him! She basked in the knowledge that no other girl in town interested him; she defied him to fall in love with Genevieve or Roberta.

Warren sighed. The way to Marjorie's affections was a labyrinth indeed. He looked up. Bernice was again dancing with the visiting boy. Half unconsciously he took a step out from the stag line in her direction, and hesitated. Then he said to himself that it was charity. He walked towards her—collided suddenly with G. Reece Stoddard.

'Pardon me,' said Warren.

But G. Reece had not stopped to apologize. He had again cut in on Bernice.

That night at one o'clock Marjorie, with one hand on the electric-light switch in the hall, turned to take a last look at Bernice's sparkling eyes.

'So it worked?'

'Oh, Marjorie, yes!' cried Bernice.

'I saw you were having a gay time.'

'I did! The only trouble was that about midnight I ran short of talk. I had to repeat myself—with different men of course. I hope they won't compare notes.'

'Men don't,' said Marjorie, yawning, 'and it wouldn't matter if they did—they'd think you were even trickier.'

She snapped out the light, and as they started up the stairs Bernice grasped the banister thankfully. For the first time in her life she had been danced tired.

'You see,' said Marjorie at the top of the stairs, 'one man sees another man cut in and he thinks there must be something there. Well, we'll fix up some new stuff to-morrow. Good night.'

'Good night.'

As Bernice took down her hair she passed the evening before her in review. She had followed instructions exactly. Even when Charley Paulson cut in for the eighth time she had simulated delight and had apparently been both interested and flattered. She had not talked about the weather or Eau Claire or automobiles or her school, but had confined her conversation to me, you, and us.

But a few minutes before she fell asleep a rebellious thought was churning drowsily in her brain—after all, it was she who had done it. Marjorie, to be sure, had given her her conversation, but then Marjorie got much of her conversation out of things she read. Bernice had bought the red dress, though she had never valued it highly before Marjorie dug it out of her trunk—and her own voice had said the words, her own lips had smiled, her own feet had danced. Marjorie nice girl—vain, though—nice evening —nice boys—like Warren—Warren—Warren—what's-his-name—Warren——

She fell asleep.

V

To Bernice the next week was a revelation. With the feeling that people really enjoyed looking at her and listening to her came the foundation of self-confidence. Of course there were numerous mistakes at first. She did not know, for instance, that Draycott Deyo was studying for the ministry; she was unaware that he had cut in on her because he thought she was a quiet, reserved girl. Had she known these things she would not have treated him to the line which began 'Hello, Shell Shock!' and continued with the bathtub story—'It takes a frightful lot of energy to fix my hair in the summer—there's so much of it—so I always fix it first and powder my face and put on my hat; then I get into the bathtub, and dress afterwards. Don't you think that's the best plan?'

Though Draycott Deyo was in the throes of difficulties concerning baptism by immersion and might possibly have seen a connection, it must be admitted that he did not. He considered feminine bathing an immoral subject, and gave her some of his ideas on the depravity of modern society.

But to offset that unfortunate occurrence Bernice had several signal successes to her credit. Little Otis Ormonde pleaded off from a trip East and elected instead to follow her with a puppylike devotion, to the amusement of his crowd and to the irritation of G. Reece Stoddard, several of whose afternoon calls Otis completely ruined by the disgusting tenderness of the glances he bent on Bernice. He even told her the story of the two-by-four and the dressing-room to show her how frightfully mistaken he and every one else had been in their first judgment of her. Bernice laughed off that incident with a slight sinking sensation.

Of all Bernice's conversation perhaps the best known and most universally approved was the line about the bobbing of her hair.

'Oh, Bernice, when you goin' to get the hair bobbed?'

'Day after to-morrow maybe,' she would reply, laughing. 'Will you come and see me? Because I'm counting on you, you know.'

'Will we? You know! But you better hurry up.'

Bernice, whose tonsorial intentions were strictly dishonourable, would laugh again.

'Pretty soon now. You'd be surprised.'

But perhaps the most significant symbol of her success was the grey car of the hypercritical Warren McIntyre, parked daily in front of the Harvey house. At first the parlourmaid was distinctly startled when he asked for Bernice instead of Marjorie; after a week of it she told the cook that Miss Bernice had gotta hold Miss Marjorie's best fella.

And Miss Bernice had. Perhaps it began with Warren's desire to rouse jealousy in Marjorie; perhaps it was the familiar though unrecognized strain of Marjorie in Bernice's conversation; perhaps it was both of these and something of sincere attraction besides. But somehow the collective mind of the younger set knew within a week that Marjorie's most reliable beau had made an amazing face-about and was giving an indisputable rush to Marjorie's guest. The question of the moment was how Marjorie would take it. Warren called Bernice on the 'phone twice a day, sent her notes, and they were frequently seen together in his roadster, obviously engrossed in one of those tense, significant conversations as to whether or not he was sincere.

Marjorie on being twitted only laughed. She said she was mighty glad that Warren had at last found some one who appreciated him. So the younger set laughed, too, and guessed that Marjorie didn't care and let it go at that.

One afternoon when there were only three days left of her visit Bernice was waiting in the hall for Warren, with whom she was going to a bridge party. She was in rather a blissful mood, and when Marjorie—also bound for the party—appeared beside her and began casually to adjust her hat in the mirror, Bernice was utterly unprepared for anything in the nature of a clash. Marjorie did her work very coldly and succinctly in three sentences.

'You may as well get Warren out of your head,' she said coldly.

'What?' Bernice was utterly astounded.

'You may as well stop making a fool of yourself over Warren McIntyre. He doesn't care a snap of his fingers about you.'

For a tense moment they regarded each other—Marjorie scornful, aloof; Bernice astounded, half-angry, half-afraid. Then two cars drove up in front of the house and there was a riotous honking. Both of them gasped faintly, turned, and side by side hurried out.

All through the bridge party Bernice strove in vain to master a rising uneasiness. She had offended Marjorie, the sphinx of sphinxes. With the most wholesome and innocent intentions in the world she had stolen Marjorie's property. She felt suddenly and horribly guilty. After the bridge game, when they sat in an informal circle and the conversation became general, the storm gradually broke. Little Otis Ormonde inadvertently precipitated it.

'When you going back to kindergarten, Otis?' some one had asked.

'Me? Day Bernice gets her hair bobbed.'

'Then your education's over,' said Marjorie quickly.

'That's only a bluff of hers. I should think you'd have realized.'

'That a fact?' demanded Otis, giving Bernice a reproachful glance.

Bernice's ears burned as she tried to think up an effectual comeback. In the face of this direct attack her imagination was paralysed.

'There's a lot of bluffs in the world,' continued Marjorie quite pleasantly. 'I should think you'd be young enough to know that, Otis.'

'Well,' said Otis, 'maybe so. But gee! With a line like Bernice's——'

'Really?' yawned Marjorie. 'What's her latest bon mot?'

No one seemed to know. In fact, Bernice, having trifled with her muse's beau, had said nothing memorable of late.

'Was that really all a line?' asked Roberta curiously.

Bernice hesitated. She felt that wit in some form was demanded of her, but under her cousin's suddenly frigid eyes she was completely incapacitated.

'I don't know,' she stalled.

'Splush!' said Marjorie. 'Admit it!'

Bernice saw that Warren's eyes had left a ukulele he had been tinkering with and were fixed on her questioningly.

'Oh, I don't know!' she repeated steadily. Her cheeks were glowing.

'Splush!' remarked Marjorie again.

'Come through, Bernice,' urged Otis. 'Tell her where to get off.'

Bernice looked round again—she seemed unable to get away from Warren's eyes.

'I like bobbed hair,' she said hurriedly, as if he had asked her a question, 'and I intend to bob mine.'

'When?' demanded Marjorie.

'Any time.'

'No time like the present,' suggested Roberta.

Otis jumped to his feet.

4*

'Good stuff!' he cried. 'We'll have a summer bobbing party. Sevier Hotel barber-shop, I think you said.'

In an instant all were on their feet. Bernice's heart throbbed violently.

'What?' she gasped.

Out of the group came Marjorie's voice, very clear and contemptuous.

'Don't worry—she'll back out!'

'Come on, Bernice!' cried Otis, starting towards the door.

Four eyes—Warren's and Marjorie's—stared at her, challenged her, defied her. For another second she wavered wildly.

'All right,' she said swiftly, 'I don't care if I do.'

An eternity of minutes later, riding down-town through the late afternoon beside Warren, the others following in Roberta's car close behind, Bernice had all the sensations of Marie Antoinette bound for the guillotine in a tumbrel. Vaguely she wondered why she did not cry out that it was all a mistake. It was all she could do to keep from clutching her hair with both hands to protect it from the suddenly hostile world. Yet she did neither. Even the thought of her mother was no deterrent now. This was the test supreme of her sportsmanship; her right to walk unchallenged in the starry heaven of popular girls.

Warren was moodily silent, and when they came to the hotel he drew up at the curb and nodded to Bernice to precede him out. Roberta's car emptied a laughing crowd into the shop, which presented two bold plate-glass windows to the street.

Bernice stood on the curb and looked at the sign, Sevier Barber-Ship. It was a guillotine indeed, and the hangman was the first barber, who, attired in a white coat and smoking a cigarette, leaned nonchalantly against the first chair. He must have heard of her; he must have been waiting all week, smoking eternal cigarettes beside that portentous, too-often-mentioned first chair. Would they blindfold her? No, but they would tie a white cloth round her neck lest any of her blood—nonsense—hair—should get on her clothes.

'All right, Bernice,' said Warren quickly.

With her chin in the air she crossed the sidewalk, pushed open the swinging screen-door, and giving not a glance to the uproarious, riotous row that occupied the waiting bench, went up to the first barber.

'I want you to bob my hair.'

The first barber's mouth slid somewhat open. His cigarette dropped to the floor.

'Huh?'

'My hair—bob it!'

Refusing further preliminaries, Bernice took her seat on high. A man in the chair next to her turned on his side and gave her a glance, half lather, half amazement. One barber started and spoiled little Willy Schuneman's monthly haircut. Mr O'Reilly in the last chair grunted and swore musically in ancient Gaelic as a razor bit into his cheek. Two bootblacks became wide-eyed and rushed for her feet. No, Bernice didn't care for a shine.

Outside a passer-by stopped and stared; a couple joined him; half a dozen small boys' noses sprang into life, flattened against the glass; and snatches of conversation borne on the summer breeze drifted in through the screen-door.

'Lookada long hair on a kid!'

'Where'd yuh get 'at stuff? 'At's a bearded lady he just finished shavin'.'

But Bernice saw nothing, heard nothing. Her only living sense told her that this man in the white coat had removed one tortoiseshell comb and then another; that his fingers were fumbling clumsily with unfamiliar hairpins; that this hair, this wonderful hair of hers, was going—she would never again feel its long voluptuous pull as it hung in a dark-brown glory down her back. For a second she was near breaking down, and then the picture before her swam mechanically into her vision—Marjorie's mouth curling in a faint ironic smile as if to say:

'Give up and get down! You tried to buck me and I called your bluff. You see you haven't got a prayer.'

And some last energy rose up in Bernice, for she clenched her hands under the white cloth, and there was a curious narrowing of her eyes that Marjorie remarked on to some one long afterward.

Twenty minutes later the barber swung her round to face the mirror, and she flinched at the full extent of the damage that had been wrought. Her hair was not curly, and now it lay in lank lifeless blocks on both sides of her suddenly pale face. It was ugly as sin—she had known it would be ugly as sin. Her face's chief charm had been a Madonna-like simplicity. Now that was gone and she was —well, frightfully mediocre—not stagy; only ridiculous, like a Greenwich Villager who had left her spectacles at home.

As she climbed down from the chair she tried to smile —failed miserably. She saw two of the girls exchange glances; noticed Marjorie's mouth curved in attenuated mockery—and that Warren's eyes were suddenly very cold.

'You see'—her words fell into an awkward pause—'I've done it.'

'Yes, you've—done it,' admitted Warren.

'Do you like it?'

There was a half-hearted 'Sure' from two or three voices, another awkward pause, and then Marjorie turned swiftly and with serpent-like intensity to Warren.

'Would you mind running me down to the cleaners?' she asked. 'I've simply got to get a dress there before supper. Roberta's driving right home and she can take the others.'

Warren stared abstractedly at some infinite speck out the window. Then for an instant his eyes rested coldly on Bernice before they turned to Marjorie.

'Be glad to,' he said slowly.

VI

Bernice did not fully realize the outrageous trap that had been set for her until she met her aunt's amazed glance just before dinner.

'Why, Bernice!'

'I've bobbed it, Aunt Josephine.'

'Why, child!'

'Do you like it?'

'Why, Ber-nice!'

'I suppose I've shocked you.'

'No, but what'll Mrs Deyo think to-morrow night? Bernice, you should have waited until after the Deyos' dance —you should have waited if you wanted to do that.'

'It was sudden, Aunt Josephine. Anyway, why does it matter to Mrs Deyo particularly?'

'Why, child,' cried Mrs Harvey, 'in her paper on "The Foibles of the Younger Generation" that she read at the last meeting of the Thursday Club she devoted fifteen minutes to bobbed hair. It's her pet abomination. And the dance is for you and Marjorie!'

'I'm sorry.'

'Oh, Bernice, what'll your mother say? She'll think I let you do it.'

'I'm sorry.'

Dinner was an agony. She had made a hasty attempt with a curling-iron, and burned her finger and much hair. She could see that her aunt was both worried and grieved, and her uncle kept saying, 'Well, I'll be darned!' over and over in a hurt and faintly hostile tone. And Marjorie sat very quietly, entrenched behind a faint smile, a faintly mocking smile.

Somehow she got through the evening. Three boys called; Marjorie disappeared with one of them, and Bernice made a listless unsuccessful attempt to entertain the two others—sighed thankfully as she climbed the stairs to her room at half past ten. What a day!

When she had undressed for the night the door opened and Marjorie came in.

'Bernice,' she said, 'I'm awfully sorry about the Deyo dance. I'll give you my word of honour I'd forgotten all about it.'

' 'Sall right,' said Bernice shortly. Standing before the mirror she passed her comb slowly through her short hair.

'I'll take you down-town to-morrow,' continued Marjorie, 'and the hairdresser'll fix it so you'll look slick. I didn't imagine you'd go through with it. I'm really mighty sorry.'

'Oh, 'sall right!'

'Still it's your last night, so I suppose it won't matter much.'

Then Bernice winced as Marjorie tossed her own hair over her shoulders and began to twist it slowly into two long blond braids until in her cream-coloured négligé she looked like a delicate painting of some Saxon princess. Fascinated, Bernice watched the braids grow. Heavy and luxurious they were, moving under the supple fingers like restive snakes—and to Bernice remained this relic and the curling-iron and a to-morrow full of eyes. She could see G. Reece Stoddard, who liked her, assuming his Harvard manner and telling his dinner partner that Bernice shouldn't have been allowed to go to the movies so much; she could see Draycott Deyo exchanging glances with his mother and then being conscientiously charitable to her. But then perhaps by to-morrow Mrs Deyo would have heard the news; would send round an icy little note requesting that she fail to appear—and behind her back they would all laugh and know that Marjorie had made a fool of her; that her chance at beauty had been sacrificed to the jealous whim of a selfish girl. She sat down suddenly before the mirror, biting the inside of her cheek.

'I like it,' she said with an effort. 'I think it will be becoming.'

Marjorie smiled.

'It looks all right. For heaven's sake, don't let it worry you!'

'I won't.'

'Good night, Bernice.'

But as the door closed something snapped within Bernice. She sprang dynamically to her feet, clenching her hands, then swiftly and noiselessly crossed over to her bed and from underneath it dragged out her suitcase. Into it she tossed toilet articles and a change of clothing. Then she turned to her trunk and quickly dumped in two drawer-fuls of lingerie and summer dresses. She moved quietly, but with deadly efficiency, and in three-quarters of an hour her trunk was locked and strapped and she was fully dressed in a becoming new travelling suit that Marjorie had helped her pick out.

Sitting down at her desk she wrote a short note to Mrs Harvey, in which she briefly outlined her reasons for going. She sealed it, addressed it, and laid it on her pillow. She glanced at her watch. The train left at one, and she knew that if she walked down to the Marborough Hotel two blocks away she could easily get a taxicab.

Suddenly she drew in her breath sharply and an expression flashed into her eyes that a practised character reader might have connected vaguely with the set look she had worn in the barber's chair—somehow a development of it. It was quite a new look for Bernice—and it carried conse-quences.

She went stealthily to the bureau, picked up an article that lay there, and turning out all the lights stood quietly until her eyes became accustomed to the darkness. Softly she pushed open the door to Marjorie's room. She heard the quiet, even breathing of an untroubled conscience asleep.

She was by the bedside now, very deliberate and calm. She acted swiftly. Bending over she found one of the braids of Marjorie's hair, followed it up with her hand to the point nearest the head, and then holding it a little slack so that the sleeper would feel no pull, she reached down with the shears and severed it. With the pigtail in her hand she held her breath. Marjorie had muttered something in her sleep. Bernice deftly amputated the other braid, paused for an instant, and then flitted swiftly and silently back to her own room.

Downstairs she opened the big front door, closed it carefully behind her, and feeling oddly happy and exuberant stepped off the porch into the moonlight, swinging her heavy grip like a shopping-bag. After a minute's brisk walk she discovered that her left hand still held the two blond braids. She laughed unexpectedly—had to shut her mouth hard to keep from emitting an absolute peal. She was passing Warren's house now, and on the impulse she set down her baggage, and swinging the braids like pieces of rope flung them at the wooden porch, where they landed with a slight thud. She laughed again, no longer restraining herself.

'Huh!' she giggled wildly. 'Scalp the selfish thing!'

Then picking up her suitcase she set off at a half-run down the moonlit street.

THE ICE PALACE

[1920]

THE sunlight dripped over the house like golden paint
over an art jar, and the freckling shadows here and there
only intensified the rigour of the bath of light. The Butterworth and Larkin houses flanking were intrenched behind
great stodgy trees; only the Happer house took the full
sun, and all day long faced the dusty road-street with a
tolerant kindly patience. This was the city of Tarleton
in southernmost Georgia, September afternoon.

Up in her bedroom window Sally Carrol Happer rested
her nineteen-year-old chin on a fifty-two-year-old sill and
watched Clark Darrow's ancient Ford turn the corner.
The car was hot—being partly metallic it retained all the
heat it absorbed or evolved—and Clark Darrow sitting
bolt upright at the wheel wore a pained, strained expression as though he considered himself a spare part, and
rather like to break. He laboriously crossed two dust
ruts, the wheels squeaking indignantly at the encounter,
and then with a terrifying expression he gave the steering-
gear a final wrench and deposited self and car approximately in front of the Happer steps. There was a plaintive
heaving sound, a death-rattle, followed by a short silence;
and then the air was rent by a startling whistle.

Sally Carrol gazed down sleepily. She started to yawn,
but finding this quite impossible unless she raised her chin
from the window-sill, changed her mind and continued
silently to regard the car, whose owner sat brilliantly if
perfunctorily at attention as he waited for an answer to
his signal. After a moment the whistle once more split the
dusty air.

'Good mawnin'.'

With difficulty Clark twisted his tall body round and bent a distorted glance on the window.

' 'Tain't mawnin', Sally Carrol.'

'Isn't it, sure enough?'

'What you doin'?'

'Eatin' 'n apple.'

'Come on go swimmin'—want to?'

'Reckon so.'

'How 'bout hurryin' up?'

'Sure enough.'

Sally Carrol sighed voluminously and raised herself with profound inertia from the floor, where she had been occupied in alternately destroying parts of a green apple and painting paper dolls for her younger sister. She approached a mirror, regarded her expression with a pleased and pleasant languor, dabbed two spots of rouge on her lips and a grain of powder on her nose, and covered her bobbed corn-coloured hair with a rose-littered sunbonnet. Then she kicked over the painting water, said, 'Oh, damn!'—but it lay—and left the room.

'How you, Clark?' she inquired a minute later as she slipped nimbly over the side of the car.

'Mighty fine, Sally Carrol.'

'Where we go swimmin'?'

'Out to Walley's Pool. Told Marylyn we'd call by an' get her an' Joe Ewing.'

Clark was dark and lean, and when on foot was rather inclined to stoop. His eyes were ominous and his expression somewhat petulant except when startlingly illuminated by one of his frequent smiles. Clark had 'a income' —just enough to keep himself in ease and his car in gasoline—and he had spent the two years since he graduated from Georgia Tech in dozing round the lazy streets of his home town, discussing how he could best invest his capital for an immediate fortune.

Hanging round he found not at all difficult; a crowd of little girls had grown up beautifully, the amazing Sally Carrol foremost among them; and they enjoyed being swum with and danced with and made love to in the flower-filled summery evenings—and they all liked Clark immensely. When feminine company palled there were half a dozen other youths who were always just about to do something, and meanwhile were quite willing to join him in a few holes of golf, or a game of billiards, or the consumption of a quart of 'hard yella licker.' Every once in a while one of these contemporaries made a farewell round of calls before going up to New York or Philadelphia or Pittsburgh to go into business, but mostly they just stayed round in this languid paradise of dreamy skies and firefly evenings and noisy niggery street fairs—and especially of gracious, soft-voiced girls, who were brought up on memories instead of money.

The Ford having been excited into a sort of restless resentful life Clark and Sally Carrol rolled and rattled down Valley Avenue into Jefferson Street, where the dust road became a pavement; along opiate Millicent Place, where there were half a dozen prosperous, substantial mansions; and on into the down-town section. Driving was perilous here, for it was shopping time; the population idled casually across the streets and a drove of low-moaning oxen were being urged along in front of a placid street-car; even the shops seemed only yawning their doors and blinking their windows in the sunshine before retiring into a state of utter and finite coma.

'Sally Carrol,' said Clark suddenly, 'it a fact that you're engaged?'

She looked at him quickly.

'Where'd you hear that?'

'Sure enough, you engaged?'

' 'At's a nice question!'

'Girl told me you were engaged to a Yankee you met up in Ashville last summer.'

Sally Carrol sighed.

'Never saw such an old town for rumours.'

'Don't marry a Yankee, Sally Carrol. We need you round here.' Sally Carrol was silent a moment.

'Clark,' she demanded suddenly, 'who on earth shall I marry?'

'I offer my services.'

'Honey, you couldn't support a wife,' she answered cheerfully. 'Anyway, I know you too well to fall in love with you.'

' 'At doesn't mean you ought to marry a Yankee,' he persisted.

'Suppose I love him?'

He shook his head.

'You couldn't. He'd be a lot different from us, every way.'

He broke off as he halted the car in front of a rambling, dilapidated house. Marylyn Wade and Joe Ewing appeared in the doorway.

' 'Lo, Sally Carrol.'

'Hi!'

'How you-all?'

'Sally Carrol,' demanded Marylyn as they started off again, 'you engaged?'

'Lawdy, where'd all this start? Can't I look at a man 'thout everybody in town engagin' me to him?'

Clark stared straight in front of him at a bolt on the clattering wind-shield.

'Sally Carrol,' he said with a curious intensity, 'don't you like us?'

'What?'

'Us down here?'

'Why, Clark, you know I do. I adore all you boys.'

'Then why you gettin' engaged to a Yankee?'

'Clark, I don't know. I'm not sure what I'll do, but—well, I want to go places and see people. I want my mind to grow. I want to live where things happen on a big scale.'

'What you mean?'

'Oh, Clark, I love you, and I love Joe here, and Ben Arrot, and you-all, but you'll—you'll——'

'We'll all be failures?'

'Yes. I don't mean only money failures, but just sort of—of ineffectual and sad, and—oh, how can I tell you?'

'You mean because we stay here in Tarleton?'

'Yes, Clark; and because you like it and never want to change things or think or go ahead.'

He nodded and she reached over and pressed his hand.

'Clark,' she said softly, 'I wouldn't change you for the world. You're sweet the way you are. The things that'll make you fail I'll love always—the living in the past, the lazy days and nights you have, and all your carelessness and generosity.'

'But you're goin' away?'

'Yes—because I couldn't ever marry you. You've a place in my heart no one else ever could have, but tied down here I'd get restless. I'd feel I was—wastin' myself. There's two sides to me, you see. There's the sleepy old side you love; an' there's a sort of energy—the feelin' that makes me do wild things. That's the part of me that may be useful somewhere, that'll last when I'm not beautiful any more.'

She broke off with characteristic suddenness and sighed, Oh, sweet cooky!' as her mood changed.

Half closing her eyes and tipping back her head till it rested on the seat-back she let the savoury breeze fan her eyes and ripple the fluffy curls of her bobbed hair. They were in the country now, hurrying between tangled growths of bright-green coppice and grass and tall trees that sent sprays of foliage to hang a cool welcome over the road. Here and there they passed a battered Negro cabin, its oldest white-haired inhabitant smoking a corncob pipe beside the door, and half a dozen scantily clothed pickaninnies parading tattered dolls on the wild-grown grass in front. Farther out were lazy cotton-fields, where even the workers seemed intangible shadows lent by the sun to the earth, not for toil, but to while away some age-old tradition in the golden September fields. And round the drowsy picturesqueness, over the trees and shacks and muddy rivers, flowed the heat, never hostile, only comforting, like a great warm nourishing bosom for the infant earth.

'Sally Carrol, we're here!'

'Poor chile's soun' asleep.'

'Honey, you dead at last outa sheer laziness?'

'Water, Sally Carrol! Cool water waitin' for you!'

Her eyes opened sleepily.

'Hi! she murmured, smiling.

II

In November Harry Bellamy, tall, broad, and brisk, came down from his Northern city to spend four days. His intention was to settle a matter that had been hanging fire since he and Sally Carrol had met in Asheville, North Carolina, in midsummer. The settlement took only a quiet afternoon and an evening in front of a glowing open fire, for Harry Bellamy had everything she wanted; and, besides, she loved him—loved him with that side of her she kept especially for loving. Sally Carrol had several rather clearly defined sides.

On his last afternoon they walked, and she found their steps tending half-unconsciously towards one of her favourite haunts, the cemetery. When it came in sight, grey-white and golden-green under the cheerful late sun, she paused, irresolute, by the iron gate.

'Are you mournful by nature, Harry?' she asked with a faint smile.

'Mournful? Not I.'

'Then let's go in here. It depresses some folks, but I like it.'

They passed through the gateway and followed a path that led through a wavy valley of graves—dusty-grey and mouldy for the fifties; quaintly carved with flowers and jars for the seventies; ornate and hideous for the nineties, with fat marble cherubs lying in sodden sleep on stone pillows, and great impossible growths of nameless granite flowers. Occasionally they saw a kneeling figure with tributary flowers, but over most of the graves lay silence and withered leaves with only the fragrance that their own shadowy memories could waken in living minds.

They reached the top of a hill where they were fronted by a tall, round head-stone, freckled with dark spots of damp and half grown over with vines.

'Margery Lee,' she read; '1844–1873. Wasn't she nice? She died when she was twenty-nine. Dear Margery Lee,' she added softly. 'Can't you see her, Harry?'

'Yes, Sally Carrol.'

He felt a little hand insert itself into his.

'She was dark, I think; and she always wore her hair with a ribbon in it, and gorgeous hoop-skirts of alice blue and old rose.'

'Yes.'

'Oh, she was sweet, Harry! And she was the sort of girl born to stand on a wide, pillared porch and welcome folks in. I think perhaps a lot of men went away to war meanin' to come back to her; but maybe none of 'em ever did.'

He stooped down close to the stone, hunting for any record of marriage.

'There's nothing here to show.'

'Of course not. How could there be anything there better than just "Margery Lee," and that eloquent date?'

She drew close to him and an unexpected lump came into his throat as her yellow hair brushed his cheek.

'You see how she was, don't you, Harry?'

'I see,' he agreed gently. 'I see through your precious eyes. You're beautiful now, so I know she must have been.'

Silent and close they stood, and he could feel her shoulders trembling a little. An ambling breeze swept up the hill and stirred the brim of her floppidy hat.

'Let's go down there!'

She was pointing to a flat stretch on the other side of the hill where along the green turf were a thousand greyish-white crosses stretching in endless, ordered rows like the stacked arms of a battalion.

'Those are the Confederate dead,' said Sally Carrol simply.

They walked along and read the inscriptions, always only a name and a date, sometimes quite indecipherable.

'The last row is the saddest—see, 'way over there. Every cross has just a date on it, and the word "Unknown." '

She looked at him and her eyes brimmed with tears.

'I can't tell you how real it is to me, darling—if you don't know.'

'How you feel about it is beautiful to me.'

'No, no, it's not me, it's them—that old time that I've tried to have live in me. These were just men, unimportant evidently or they wouldn't have been "unknown"; but they died for the most beautiful thing in the world —the dead South. You see,' she continued, her voice still husky, her eyes glistening with tears, 'people have these dreams they fasten onto things, and I've always grown up with that dream. It was so easy because it was all dead and there weren't any disillusions comin' to me. I've tried in a way to live up to those past standards of noblesse oblige—there's just the last remnants of it, you know, like the roses of an old garden dying all round us—streaks of strange courtliness and chivalry in some of these boys an' stories I used to hear from a Confederate soldier who lived next door, and a few old darkies. Oh, Harry, there was something, there was something! I couldn't ever make you understand, but it was there.'

'I understand,' he assured her again quietly.

Sally Carrol smiled and dried her eyes on the tip of a handkerchief protruding from his breast pocket.

'You don't feel depressed, do you, lover? Even when I cry I'm happy here, and I get a sort of strength from it.'

Hand in hand they turned and walked slowly away. Finding soft grass she drew him down to a seat beside her with their backs against the remnants of a low broken wall.

'Wish those three old women would clear out,' he complained. 'I want to kiss you, Sally Carrol.'

'Me, too.'

They waited impatiently for the three bent figures to move off, and then she kissed him until the sky seemed to fade out and all her smiles and tears to vanish in an ecstasy of eternal seconds.

Afterwards they walked slowly back together, while on the corners twilight played at somnolent black-and-white checkers with the end of day.

'You'll be up about mid-January,' he said, 'and you've got to stay a month at least. It'll be slick. There's a winter carnival on, and if you've never really seen snow it'll be like fairy-land to you. There'll be skating and skiing and tobogganing and sleigh-riding, and all sorts of torchlight parades on snow-shoes. They haven't had one for years, so they're going to make it a knock-out.'

'Will I be cold, Harry?' she asked suddenly.

'You certainly won't. You may freeze your nose, but you won't be shivery cold. It's hard and dry, you know.'

'I guess I'm a summer child. I don't like any cold I've ever seen.'

She broke off and they were both silent for a minute.

'Sally Carrol,' he said very slowly, 'what do you say to—March?'

'I say I love you.'

'March?'

'March, Harry.'

III

All night in the Pullman it was very cold. She rang for the porter to ask for another blanket, and when he couldn't give her one she tried vainly, by squeezing down into the bottom of her berth and doubling back the bedclothes, to snatch a few hours' sleep. She wanted to look her best in the morning.

She rose at six and sliding uncomfortably into her

clothes stumbled up to the diner for a cup of coffee. The
snow had filtered into the vestibules and covered the
floor with a slippery coating. It was intriguing, this cold,
it crept in everywhere. Her breath was quite visible and
she blew into the air with a naïve enjoyment. Seated in
the diner she stared out the window at white hills and
valleys and scattered pines whose every branch was a
green platter for a cold feast of snow. Sometimes a solitary
farmhouse would fly by, ugly and bleak and lone on the
white waste; and with each one she had an instant of chill
compassion for the souls shut in there waiting for spring.

As she left the diner and swayed back into the Pullman
she experienced a surging rush of energy and wondered
if she was feeling the bracing air of which Harry had
spoken. This was the North, the North—her land now!

> 'Then blow, ye winds, heigho!
> A-roving I will go,'

she chanted exultantly to herself.

'What's 'at?' inquired the porter politely.

'I said: "Brush me off." '

The long wires of the telegraph-poles doubled; two
tracks ran up beside the train—three—four; came a succession of white-roofed houses, a glimpse of a trolley-car
with frosted windows, streets—more streets—the city.

She stood for a dazed moment in the frosty station
before she saw three fur-bundled figures descending upon
her.

'There she is!'

'Oh, Sally Carrol!'

Sally Carrol dropped her bag.

'Hi!'

A faintly familiar icy-cold face kissed her, and then she
was in a group of faces all apparently emitting great clouds
of heavy smoke; she was shaking hands. There were
Gordon, a short, eager man of thirty who looked like an
amateur knocked-about model for Harry, and his wife,
Myra, a listless lady with flaxen hair under a fur auto-

mobile cap. Almost immediately Sally Carrol thought of her as vaguely Scandinavian. A cheerful chauffeur adopted her bag, and amid ricochets of half-phrases, exclamations, and perfunctory listless 'my dears' from Myra, they swept each other from the station.

Then they were in a sedan bound through a crooked succession of snowy streets where dozens of little boys were hitching sleds behind grocery wagons and automobiles.

'Oh,' cried Sally Carrol, 'I want to do that! Can we, Harry?'

'That's for kids. But we might——'

'It looks like such a circus!' she said regretfully.

Home was a rambling frame house set on a white lap of snow, and there she met a big, grey-haired man of whom she approved, and a lady who was like an egg, and who kissed her—these were Harry's parents. There was a breathless indescribable hour crammed full of half-sentences, hot water, bacon and eggs and confusion; and after that she was alone with Harry in the library, asking him if she dared smoke.

It was a large room with a Madonna over the fireplace and rows upon rows of books in covers of light gold and dark gold and shiny red. All the chairs had little lace squares where one's head should rest, the couch was just comfortable, the books looked as if they had been read —some—and Sally Carrol had an instantaneous vision of the battered old library at home, with her father's huge medical books, and the oil-paintings of her three great-uncles, and the old couch that had been mended up for forty-five years and was still luxurious to dream in. This room struck her as being neither attractive nor particularly otherwise. It was simply a room with a lot of fairly expensive things in it that all looked about fifteen years old.

'What do you think of it up here?' demanded Harry eagerly. 'Does it surprise you? Is it what you expected, I mean?'

'You are, Harry,' she said quietly, and reached out her arms to him.

But after a brief kiss he seemed anxious to extort enthusiasm from her.

'The town, I mean. Do you like it? Can you feel the pep in the air?'

'Oh, Harry,' she laughed, 'you'll have to give me time. You can't just fling questions at me.'

She puffed at her cigarette with a sigh of contentment.

'One thing I want to ask you,' he began rather apologetically; 'you Southerners put quite an emphasis on family, and all that—not that it isn't quite all right, but you'll find it a little different here. I mean—you'll notice a lot of things that'll seem to you sort of vulgar display at first, Sally Carrol; but just remember that this is a three-generation town. Everybody has a father, and about half of us have grandfathers. Back of that we don't go.'

'Of course,' she murmured.

'Our grandfathers, you see, founded the place, and a lot of them had to take some pretty queer jobs while they were doing the founding. For instance, there's one woman who at present is about the social model for the town; well, her father was the first public ash man— things like that.'

'Why,' said Sally Carrol, puzzled, 'did you s'pose I was goin' to make remarks about people?'

'Not at all,' interrupted Harry; 'and I'm not apologizing for any one either. It's just that—well, a Southern girl came up here last summer and said some unfortunate things, and—oh, I just thought I'd tell you.'

Sally Carrol felt suddenly indignant—as though she had been unjustly spanked—but Harry evidently considered the subject closed, for he went on with a great surge of enthusiasm.

'It's carnival time, you know. First in ten years. And there's an ice palace they're building now that's the first they've had since eighty-five. Built out of blocks of the clearest ice they could find—on a tremendous scale.'

She rose and walking to the window pushed aside the heavy Turkish portières and looked out.

'Oh!' she cried suddenly. 'There's two little boys makin' a snow man! Harry, do you reckon I can go out an' help 'em?'

'You dream! Come here and kiss me.'

She left the window rather reluctantly.

'I don't guess this is a very kissable climate, is it? I mean, it makes you so you don't want to sit round, doesn't it?'

'We're not going to. I've got a vacation for the first week you're here, and there's a dinner-dance to-night.'

'Oh, Harry,' she confessed, subsiding in a heap, half in his lap, half in the pillows, 'I sure do feel confused. I haven't got an idea whether I'll like it or not, an' I don't know what people expect, or anythin'. You'll have to tell me, honey.'

'I'll tell you,' he said softly, 'if you'll just tell me you're glad to be here.'

'Glad—just awful glad!' she whispered, insinuating herself into his arms in her own peculiar way. 'Where you are is home for me, Harry.'

And as she said this she had the feeling for almost the first time in her life that she was acting a part.

That night, amid the gleaming candles of a dinner-party, where the men seemed to do most of the talking while the girls sat in a haughty and expensive aloofness, even Harry's presence on her left failed to make her feel at home.

'They're a good-looking crowd, don't you think?' he demanded. 'Just look round. There's Spud Hubbard, tackle at Princeton last year, and Junie Morton—he and the red-haired fellow next to him were both Yale hockey captains; Junie was in my class. Why, the best athletes in the world come from these States round here. This is a man's country, I tell you. Look at John J. Fishburn!'

'Who's he?' asked Sally Carrol innocently.

'Don't you know?'

'I've heard the name.'

'Greatest wheat man in the Northwest, and one of the greatest financiers in the country.'

She turned suddenly to a voice on her right.

'I guess they forgot to introduce us. My name's Roger Patton.'

'My name is Sally Carrol Happer,' she said graciously.

'Yes, I know. Harry told me you were coming.'

'You a relative?'

'No, I'm a professor.'

'Oh,' she laughed.

'At the university. You're from the South, aren't you?'

'Yes; Tarleton, Georgia.'

She liked him immediately—a reddish-brown moustache under watery blue eyes that had something in them that these other eyes lacked, some quality of appreciation. They exchanged stray sentences through dinner, and she made up her mind to see him again.

After coffee she was introduced to numerous good-looking young men who danced with conscious precision and seemed to take it for granted that she wanted to talk about nothing except Harry.

'Heavens,' she thought, 'they talk as if my being engaged made me older than they are—as if I'd tell their mothers on them!'

In the South an engaged girl, even a young married woman, expected the same amount of half-affectionate badinage and flattery that would be accorded a débutante, but here all that seemed banned. One young man, after getting well started on the subject of Sally Carrol's eyes, and how they had allured him ever since she entered the room, went into a violent confusion when he found she was visiting the Bellamys—was Harry's fiancée. He seemed to feel as though he had made some risqué and inexcusable blunder, became immediately formal, and left her at the first opportunity.

She was rather glad when Roger Patton cut in on her and suggested that they sit out a while.

'Well,' he inquired, blinking cheerily, 'how's Carmen from the South?'

'Mighty fine. How's—how's Dangerous Dan McGrew? Sorry, but he's the only Northerner I know much about.'

He seemed to enjoy that.

'Of course,' he confessed, 'as a professor of literature I'm not supposed to have read Dangerous Dan McGrew.'

'Are you a native?'

'No, I'm a Philadelphian. Imported from Harvard to teach French. But I've been here ten years.'

'Nine years, three hundred an' sixty-four days longer than me.'

'Like it here?'

'Uh-huh. Sure do!'

'Really?'

'Well, why not? Don't I look as if I were havin' a good time?'

'I saw you look out the window a minute ago—and shiver.'

'Just my imagination,' laughed Sally Carrol. 'I'm used to havin' everythin' quiet outside, an' sometimes I look out an' see a flurry of snow, an' it's just as if somethin' dead was movin'.'

He nodded appreciatively.

'Ever been North before?'

'Spent two Julys in Asheville, North Carolina.'

'Nice-looking crowd, aren't they?' suggested Patton, indicating the swirling floor.

Sally Carrol started. This had been Harry's remark.

'Sure are! They're—canine.'

'What?'

She flushed.

'I'm sorry; that sounded worse than I meant it. You see I always think of people as feline or canine, irrespective of sex.'

'Which are you?'

'I'm feline. So are you. So are most Southern men an' most of these girls here.'

'What's Harry?'

'Harry's canine distinctly. All the men I've met to-night seem to be canine.'

'What does "canine" imply? A certain conscious masculinity as opposed to subtlety?'

'Reckon so. I never analysed it—only I just look at people an' say 'canine' or 'feline' right off. It's right absurd, I guess.'

'Not at all. I'm interested. I used to have a theory about these people. I think they're freezing up.'

'What?'

'I think they're growing like Swedes—Ibsenesque, you know. Very gradually getting gloomy and melancholy. It's these long winters. Ever read any Ibsen?'

She shook her head.

'Well, you find in his characters a certain brooding rigidity. They're righteous, narrow, and cheerless, without infinite possibilities for great sorrow or joy.'

'Without smiles or tears?'

'Exactly. That's my theory. You see there are thousands of Swedes up here. They come, I imagine, because the climate is very much like their own, and there's been a gradual mingling. There're probably not half a dozen here to-night, but—we've had four Swedish governors. Am I boring you?'

'I'm mighty interested.'

'Your future sister-in-law is half Swedish. Personally I like her, but my theory is that Swedes react rather badly on us as a whole. Scandinavians, you know, have the largest suicide rate in the world.'

'Why do you live here if it's so depressing?'

'Oh, it doesn't get me. I'm pretty well cloistered, and I suppose books mean more than people to me anyway.'

'But writers all speak about the South being tragic. You know—Spanish señoritas, black hair and daggers an' haunting music.'

He shook his head.

'No, the Northern races are the tragic races—they don't indulge in the cheering luxury of tears.'

Sally Carrol thought of her graveyard. She supposed that that was vaguely what she had meant when she said it didn't depress her.

'The Italians are about the gayest people in the world—but it's a dull subject,' he broke off. 'Anyway, I want to tell you you're marrying a pretty fine man.'

Sally Carol was moved by an impulse of confidence.

'I know. I'm the sort of person who wants to be taken care of after a certain point, and I feel sure I will be.'

'Shall we dance? You know,' he continued as they rose, 'it's encouraging to find a girl who knows what she's marrying for. Nine-tenths of them think of it as a sort of walking into a moving-picture sunset.'

She laughed, and liked him immensely.

Two hours later on the way home she nestled near Harry in the back seat.

'Oh, Harry,' she whispered, 'it's so co-old!'

'But it's warm in here, darling girl.'

'But outside it's cold; and oh, that howling wind!'

She buried her face deep in his fur coat and trembled involuntarily as his cold lips kissed the tip of her ear.

IV

The first week of her visit passed in a whirl. She had her promised toboggan-ride at the back of an automobile through a chill January twilight. Swathed in furs she put in a morning tobogganing on the country-club hill; even tried skiing, to sail through the air for a glorious moment and then land in a tangled laughing bundle on a soft snow-drift. She liked all the winter sports, except an afternoon spent snow-shoeing over a glaring plain under pale yellow sunshine, but she soon realized that these things were for children—that she was being humoured and that the enjoyment round her was only a reflection of her own.

At first the Bellamy family puzzled her. The men were

5+s.f.

reliable and she liked them; to Mr Bellamy especially, with his iron-grey hair and energetic dignity, she took an immediate fancy, once she found that he was born in Kentucky; this made him a link between the old life and the new. But towards the women she felt a definite hostility. Myra, her future sister-in-law, seemed the essence of spiritless conventionality. Her conversation was so utterly devoid of personality that Sally Carrol, who came from a country where a certain amount of charm and assurance could be taken for granted in the women, was inclined to despise her.

'If those women aren't beautiful,' she thought, 'they're nothing. They just fade out when you look at them. They're glorified domestics. Men are the centre of every mixed group.'

Lastly there was Mrs Bellamy, whom Sally Carrol detested. The first day's impression of an egg had been confirmed—an egg with a cracked, veiny voice and such an ungracious dumpiness of carriage that Sally Carrol felt that if she once fell she would surely scramble. In addition, Mrs Bellamy seemed to typify the town in being innately hostile to strangers. She called Sally Carrol 'Sally,' and could not be persuaded that the double name was anything more than a tedious ridiculous nickname. To Sally Carrol this shortening of her name was like presenting her to the public half clothed. She loved 'Sally Carrol'; she loathed 'Sally.' She knew also that Harry's mother disapproved of her bobbed hair; and she had never dared smoke downstairs after that first day when Mrs Bellamy had come into the library sniffing violently.

Of all the men she met she preferred Roger Patton, who was a frequent visitor at the house. He never again alluded to the Ibsenesque tendency of the populace, but when he came in one day and found her curled upon the sofa bent over 'Peer Gynt' he laughed and told her to forget what he'd said—that it was all rot.

And then one afternoon in her second week she and Harry hovered on the edge of a dangerously steep quarrel.

She considered that he precipitated it entirely, though the Serbia in the case was an unknown man who had not had his trousers pressed.

They had been walking homeward between mounds of high-piled snow and under a sun which Sally Carrol scarcely recognized. They passed a little girl done up in grey wool until she resembled a small Teddy bear, and Sally Carrol could not resist a gasp of maternal appreciation.

'Look! Harry!'

'What?'

'That little girl—did you see her face?'

'Yes, why?'

'It was red as a little strawberry. Oh, she was cute!'

'Why, your own face is almost as red as that already! Everybody's healthy here. We're out in the cold as soon as we're old enough to walk. Wonderful climate!'

She looked at him and had to agree. He was mighty healthy-looking; so was his brother. And she had noticed the new red in her own cheeks that very morning.

Suddenly their glances were caught and held, and they stared for a moment at the street-corner ahead of them. A man was standing there, his knees bent, his eyes gazing upward with a tense expression as though he were about to make a leap towards the chilly sky. And then they both exploded into a shout of laughter, for coming closer they discovered it had been a ludicrous momentary illusion produced by the extreme bagginess of the man's trousers.

'Reckon that's one on us,' she laughed.

'He must be a Southerner, judging by those trousers,' suggested Harry mischievously.

'Why, Harry!'

Her surprised look must have irritated him.

'Those damn Southerners!'

Sally Carrol's eyes flashed.

'Don't call 'em that!'

'I'm sorry, dear,' said Harry, malignantly apologetic, 'but you know what I think of them. They're sort of—

sort of degenerates—not at all like the old Southerners. They've lived so long down there with all the coloured people that they've gotten lazy and shiftless.'

'Hush your mouth, Harry!' she cried angrily. 'They're not! They may be lazy—anybody would be in that climate —but they're my best friends, an' I don't want to hear 'em criticised in any such sweepin' way. Some of 'em are the finest men in the world.'

'Oh, I know. They're all right when they come North to college, but of all the hangdog, ill-dressed, slovenly lot I ever saw, a bunch of small-town Southerners are the worst!'

Sally Carrol was clenching her gloved hands and biting her lip furiously.

'Why,' continued Harry, 'there was one in my class at New Haven, and we all thought that at last we'd found the true type of Southern aristocrat, but it turned out that he wasn't an aristocrat at all—just the son of a Northern carpetbagger, who owned about all the cotton round Mobile.'

'A Southerner wouldn't talk the way you're talking now,' she said evenly.

'They haven't the energy!'

'Or the somethin' else.'

'I'm sorry, Sally Carrol, but I've heard you say yourself that you'd never marry——'

'That's quite different. I told you I wouldn't want to tie my life to any of the boys that are round Tarleton now, but I never made any sweepin' generalities.'

They walked along in silence.

'I probably spread it on a bit thick, Sally Carrol. I'm sorry.'

She nodded but made no answer. Five minutes later as they stood in the hallway she suddenly threw her arms round him.

'Oh, Harry,' she cried, her eyes brimming with tears, 'let's get married next week. I'm afraid of having fusses like that. I'm afraid, Harry. It wouldn't be that way if we were married.'

But Harry, being in the wrong, was still irritated.

'That'd be idiotic. We decided on March.'

The tears in Sally Carrol's eyes faded; her expression hardened slightly.

'Very well—I suppose I shouldn't have said that.'

Harry melted.

'Dear little nut!' he cried. 'Come and kiss me and let's forget.'

That very night at the end of a vaudeville performance the orchestra played 'Dixie' and Sally Carrol felt something stronger and more enduring than tears and smiles of the day brim up inside her. She leaned forward gripping the arms of her chair until her face grew crimson.

'Sort of get you, dear?' whispered Harry.

But she did not hear him. To the spirited throb of the violins and the inspiring beat of the kettledrums her own old ghosts were marching by and on into the darkness, and as fifes whistled and sighed in the low encore they seemed so nearly out of sight that she could have waved good-bye.

> 'Away, away,
>   Away down South in Dixie!
> Away, away,
>   Away down South in Dixie!'

V

It was a particularly cold night. A sudden thaw had nearly cleared the streets the day before, but now they were traversed again with a powdery wraith of loose snow that travelled in wavy lines before the feet of the wind, and filled the lower air with a fine-particled mist. There was no sky—only a dark, ominous tent that draped in the tops of the streets and was in reality a vast approaching army of snowflakes—while over it all, chilling away the comfort from the brown-and-green glow of lighted windows and muffling the steady trot of the horse pulling their sleigh, interminably washed the north wind. It was a dismal town after all, she thought—dismal.

Sometimes at night it had seemed to her as though no one lived here—they had all gone long ago—leaving lighted houses to be covered in time by tombing heaps of sleet. Oh, if there should be snow on her grave! To be beneath great piles of it all winter long, where even her headstone would be a light shadow against light shadows. Her grave—a grave that should be flower-strewn and washed with sun and rain.

She thought again of those isolated country houses that her train had passed, and of the life there the long winter through—the ceaseless glare through the windows, the crust forming on the soft drifts of snow, finally the slow, cheerless melting, and the harsh spring of which Roger Patton had told her. Her spring—to lose it for ever—with its lilacs and the lazy sweetness it stirred in her heart. She was laying away that spring—afterwards she would lay away that sweetness.

With a gradual insistence the storm broke. Sally Carrol felt a film of flakes melt quickly on her eyelashes, and Harry reached over a furry arm and drew down her complicated flannel cap. Then the small flakes came in skirmish-line, and the horse bent his neck patiently as a transparency of white appeared momentarily on his coat.

'Oh, he's cold, Harry,' she said quickly.

'Who? The horse? Oh, no, he isn't. He likes it!'

After another ten minutes they turned a corner and came in sight of their destination. On a tall hill outlined in vivid glaring green against the wintry sky stood the ice palace. It was three stories in the air, with battlements and embrasures and narrow icicled windows, and the innumerable electric lights inside made a gorgeous transparency of the great central hall. Sally Carrol clutched Harry's hand under the fur robe.

'It's beautiful!' he cried excitedly. 'My golly, it's beautiful, isn't it! They haven't had one here since eighty-five!'

Somehow the notion of there not having been one since eighty-five oppressed her. Ice was a ghost, and this mansion of it was surely peopled by those shades of the eighties, with pale faces and blurred snow-filled hair.

'Come on, dear,' said Harry.

She followed him out of the sleigh and waited while he hitched the horse. A party of four—Gordon, Myra, Roger Patton, and another girl—drew up beside them with a mighty jingle of bells. There were quite a crowd already, bundled in fur or sheepskin, shouting and calling to each other as they moved through the snow, which was now so thick that people could scarcely be distinguished a few yards away.

'It's a hundred and seventy feet tall,' Harry was saying to a muffled figure beside him as they trudged towards the entrance; 'covers six thousand square yards.'

She caught snatches of conversation: 'One main hall'—'walls twenty to forty inches thick'—'and the ice cave has almost a mile of—'—'this Canuck who built it——'

They found their way inside, and dazed by the magic of the great crystal walls Sally Carrol found herself repeating over and over two lines from 'Kubla Khan':

> 'It was a miracle of rare device,
>   A sunny pleasure-dome with caves of ice!'

In the great glittering cavern with the dark shut out she took a seat on a wooden bench, and the evening's oppression lifted. Harry was right—it was beautiful; and her gaze travelled the smooth surface of the walls, the blocks for which had been selected for their purity and clearness to obtain this opalescent, translucent effect.

'Look! Here we go—oh, boy!' cried Harry.

A band in a far corner struck up: 'Hail, Hail, the Gang's All Here!' which echoed over to them in wild muddled acoustics, and then the lights suddenly went out; silence seemed to flow down the icy sides and sweep over them. Sally Carrol could still see her white breath in the darkness, and a dim row of pale faces over the other side.

The music eased to a sighing complaint, and from outside drifted in the full-throated resonant chant of the marching clubs. It grew louder like some pæan of a viking tribe traversing an ancient wild; it swelled—they were coming nearer; then a row of torches appeared, and another and another, and keeping time with their moccasined feet a long column of grey-mackinawed figures swept in, snowshoes slung at their shoulders, torches soaring and flickering as their voices rose along the great walls.

The grey column ended and another followed, the light streaming luridly this time over red toboggan caps and flaming crimson mackinaws, and as they entered they took up the refrain; then came a long platoon of blue and white, of green, of white, of brown and yellow.

'Those white ones are the Wacouta Club,' whispered Harry eagerly. 'Those are the men you've met round at dances.'

The volume of the voices grew; the great cavern was a phantasmagoria of torches waving in great banks of fire, of colours and the rhythm of soft-leather steps. The leading column turned and halted, platoon deployed in front of platoon until the whole procession made a solid flag of flame, and then from thousands of voices burst a mighty shout that filled the air like a crash of thunder, and sent the torches wavering. It was magnificent, it was tremendous! To Sally Carrol it was the North offering sacrifice on some mighty altar to the grey pagan God of Snow. As the shout died the band struck up again and there came more singing, and then long reverberating cheers by each club. She sat very quiet listening while the staccato cries rent the stillness; and then she started, for there was a volley of explosion, and great clouds of smoke went up here and there through the cavern—the flashlight photographers at work—and the council was over. With the band at their head the clubs formed in column once more, took up their chant, and began to march out.

'Come on!' shouted Harry. 'We want to see the labyrinths downstairs before they turn the lights off!'

They all rose and started towards the chute—Harry and Sally Carrol in the lead, her little mitten buried in his big fur gauntlet. At the bottom of the chute was a long empty room of ice, with the ceiling so low that they had to stoop —and their hands were parted. Before she realized what he intended Harry had darted down one of the half-dozen glittering passages that opened into the room and was only a vague receding blot against the green shimmer.

'Harry!' she called.

'Come on!' he cried back.

She looked round the empty chamber; the rest of the party had evidently decided to go home, were already outside somewhere in the blundering snow. She hesitated and then darted in after Harry.

'Harry!' she shouted.

She had reached a turning-point thirty feet down; she heard a faint muffled answer far to the left, and with a touch of panic fled towards it. She passed another turning, two more yawning alleys.

'Harry!'

No answer. She started to run straight forward, and then turned like lightning and sped back the way she had come, enveloped in a sudden icy terror.

She reached a turn—was it here?—took the left and came to what should have been the outlet into the long, low room, but it was only another glittering passage with darkness at the end. She called again but the walls gave back a flat, lifeless echo with reverberations. Retracing her steps she turned another corner, this time following a wide passage. It was like the green lane between the parted waters of the Red Sea, like a damp vault connecting empty tombs.

She slipped a little now as she walked, for ice had formed on the bottom of her overshoes; she had to run her gloves along the half-slippery, half-sticky walls to keep her balance.

'Harry!'

5*

Still no answer. The sound she made bounced mockingly down to the end of the passage.

Then on an instant the lights went out, and she was in complete darkness. She gave a small, frightened cry, and sank down into a cold little heap on the ice. She felt her left knee do something as she fell, but she scarcely noticed it as some deep terror far greater than any fear of being lost settled upon her. She was alone with this presence that came out of the North, the dreary loneliness that rose from ice-bound whalers in the Arctic seas, from smokeless, trackless wastes where were strewn the whitened bones of adventure. It was an icy breath of death; it was rolling down low across the land to clutch at her.

With a furious, despairing energy she rose again and started blindly down the darkness. She must get out. She might be lost in here for days, freeze to death and lie embedded in the ice like corpses she had read of, kept perfectly preserved until the melting of a glacier. Harry probably thought she had left with the others—he had gone by now; no one would know until late next day. She reached pitifully for the wall. Forty inches thick, they had said—forty inches thick!

'Oh!'

On both sides of her along the walls she felt things creeping, damp souls that haunted this palace, this town, this North.

'Oh, send somebody—send somebody!' she cried aloud.

Clark Darrow—he would understand; or Joe Ewing; she couldn't be left here to wander for ever—to be frozen, heart, body, and soul. This her—this Sally Carrol! Why, she was a happy thing. She was a happy little girl. She liked warmth and summer and Dixie. These things were foreign—foreign.

'You're not crying,' something said aloud. 'You'll never cry any more. Your tears would just freeze; all tears freeze up here!'

She sprawled full length on the ice.

'Oh, God!' she faltered.

A long single file of minutes went by, and with a great weariness she felt her eyes closing. Then some one seemed to sit down near her and take her face in warm, soft hands. She looked up gratefully.

'Why, it's Margery Lee,' she crooned softly to herself. 'I knew you'd come.' It really was Margery Lee, and she was just as Sally Carrol had known she would be, with a young, white brow, and wide, welcoming eyes, and a hoop-skirt of some soft material that was quite comforting to rest on.

'Margery Lee.'

It was getting darker now and darker—all those tomb-stones ought to be repainted, sure enough, only that would spoil 'em, of course. Still, you ought to be able to see 'em.

Then after a succession of moments that went fast and then slow, but seemed to be ultimately resolving them-selves into a multitude of blurred rays converging towards a pale-yellow sun, she heard a great cracking noise break her new-found stillness.

It was the sun, it was a light; a torch, and a torch beyond that, and another one, and voices; a face took flesh below the torch, heavy arms raised her, and she felt something on her cheek—it felt wet. Some one had seized her and was rubbing her face with snow. How ridiculous—with snow!

'Sally Carrol! Sally Carrol!'

It was Dangerous Dan McGrew; and two other faces she didn't know.

'Child, child! We've been looking for you two hours! Harry's half-crazy!'

Things came rushing back into place—the singing, the torches, the great shout of the marching clubs. She squirmed in Patton's arms and gave a long low cry.

'Oh, I want to get out of here! I'm going back home. Take me home'—her voice rose to a scream that sent a chill to Harry's heart as he came racing down the next passage—'to-morrow!' she cried with delirious, unre-strained passion—'To-morrow! To-morrow! To-morrow!'

VI

The wealth of golden sunlight poured a quite enervating yet oddly comforting heat over the house where day long it faced the dusty stretch of road. Two birds were making a great to-do in a cool spot found among the branches of a tree next door, and down the street a coloured woman was announcing herself melodiously as a purveyor of strawberries. It was April afternoon.

Sally Carol Happer, resting her chin on her arm, and her arm on an old window-seat gazed sleepily down over the spangled dust whence the heat waves were rising for the first time this spring. She was watching a very ancient Ford turn a perilous corner and rattle and groan to a jolting stop at the end of the walk. She made no sound, and in a minute a strident familiar whistle rent the air. Sally Carrol smiled and blinked.

'Good mawnin'.'

A head appeared tortuously from under the car-top below.

' 'Tain't mawnin', Sally Carrol.'

'Sure enough!' she said in affected surprise. 'I guess maybe not.'

'What you doin'?'

'Eatin' green peach. 'Spect to die any minute.'

Clark twisted himself a last impossible notch to get a view of her face.

'Water's warm as a kettla steam, Sally Carroll. Wanta go swimmin'?'

'Hate to move,' sighed Sally Carrol lazily, 'but I reckon so.'

MAY DAY

[1920]

THERE had been a war fought and won and the great city of the conquering people was crossed with triumphal arches and vivid with thrown flowers of white, red, and rose. All through the long spring days the returning soldiers marched up the chief highway behind the strump of drums and the joyous, resonant wind of the brasses, while merchants and clerks left their bickerings and figurings and, crowding to the windows, turned their white-bunched faces gravely upon the passing battalions.

Never had there been such splendour in the great city, for the victorious war had brought plenty in its train, and the merchants had flocked thither from the South and West with their households to taste of all the luscious feasts and witness the lavish entertainments prepared—and to buy for their women furs against the next winter and bags of golden mesh and varicoloured slippers of silk and silver and rose satin and cloth of gold.

So gaily and noisily were the peace and prosperity impending hymned by the scribes and poets of the conquering people that more and more spenders had gathered from the provinces to drink the wine of excitement, and faster and faster did the merchants dispose of their trinkets and slippers until they sent up a mighty cry for more trinkets and more slippers in order that they might give in barter what was demanded of them. Some even of them flung up their hands helplessly, shouting:

'Alas! I have no more slippers! and alas! I have no more

trinkets! May Heaven help me, for I know not what I shall do!'

But no one listened to their great outcry, for the throngs were far too busy—day by day, the foot-soldiers trod jauntily the highway and all exulted because the young men returning were pure and brave, sound of tooth and pink of cheek, and the young women of the land were virgins and comely both of face and of figure.

So during all this time there were many adventures that happened in the great city, and, of these, several—or perhaps one—are here set down.

I

At nine o'clock on the morning of the first of May, 1919, a young man spoke to the room clerk at the Biltmore Hotel, asking if Mr Philip Dean were registered there, and if so, could he be connected with Mr Dean's rooms. The inquirer was dressed in a well-cut shabby suit. He was small, slender, and darkly handsome; his eyes were framed above with unusually long eyelashes and below with the blue semi-circle of ill health, this latter effect heightened by an unnatural glow which coloured his face like a low, incessant fever.

Mr Dean was staying there. The young man was directed to a telephone at the side.

After a second his connection was made; a sleepy voice hello'd from somewhere above.

'Mr Dean?'—this very eagerly—'it's Gordon, Phil. It's Gordon Sterrett. I'm downstairs. I heard you were in New York and I had a hunch you'd be here.'

The sleepy voice became gradually enthusiastic. Well, how was Gordy, old boy! Well, he certainly was surprised and tickled! Would Gordy come right up, for Pete's sake!

A few minutes later Philip Dean, dressed in blue silk pyjamas, opened his door and the two young men greeted each other with a half-embarrassed exuberance. They were both about twenty-four, Yale graduates of the year before the war; but there the resemblance stopped abruptly. Dean was blond, ruddy, and rugged under his thin pyjamas. Everything about him radiated fitness and bodily comfort. He smiled frequently, showing large and prominent teeth.

'I was going to look you up,' he cried enthusiastically. 'I'm taking a couple of weeks off. If you'll sit down a sec I'll be right with you. Going to take a shower.'

As he vanished into the bathroom his visitor's dark eyes roved nervously around the room, resting for a moment on a great English travelling bag in the corner and on a family of thick silk shirts littered on the chairs amid impressive neckties and soft woollen socks.

Gordon rose and, picking up one of the shirts, gave it a minute examination. It was of very heavy silk, yellow with a pale blue stripe—and there were nearly a dozen of them. He stared involuntarily at his own shirt-cuffs—they were ragged and linty at the edges and soiled to a faint grey. Dropping the silk shirt, he held his coat-sleeves down and worked the frayed shirt-cuffs up till they were out of sight. Then he went to the mirror and looked at himself with listless, unhappy interest. His tie, of former glory, was faded and thumb-creased—it served no longer to hide the jagged buttonholes of his collar. He thought, quite without amusement, that only three years before he had received a scattering vote in the senior elections at college for being the best-dressed man in his class.

Dean emerged from the bathroom polishing his body.

'Saw an old friend of yours last night,' he remarked.

'Passed her in the lobby and couldn't think of her name to save my neck. That girl you brought up to New Haven senior year.'

Gordon started.

'Edith Bradin? That whom you mean?'

''At's the one. Damn good looking. She's still sort of a pretty doll—you know what I mean: as if you touched her she'd smear.'

He surveyed his shining self complacently in the mirror, smiled faintly, exposing a section of teeth.

'She must be twenty-three anyway,' he continued.

'Twenty-two last month,' said Gordon absently.

'What? Oh, last month. Well, I imagine she's down for the Gamma Psi dance. Did you know we're having a Yale Gamma Psi dance tonight at Delmonico's? You better come up, Gordy. Half of New Haven'll probably be there. I can get you an invitation.'

Draping himself reluctantly in fresh underwear, Dean lit a cigarette and sat down by the open window, inspecting his calves and knees under the morning sunshine which poured into the room.

'Sit down, Gordy,' he suggested, 'and tell me all about what you've been doing and what you're doing now and everything.'

Gordon collapsed unexpectedly upon the bed; lay there inert and spiritless. His mouth, which habitually dropped a little open when his face was in repose, became suddenly helpless and pathetic.

'What's the matter?' asked Dean quickly.

'Oh, God!'

'What's the matter?'

'Every God damn thing in the world,' he said miserably. 'I've absolutely gone to pieces, Phil. I'm all in.'

'Huh?'

'I'm all in.' His voice was shaking.

Dean scrutinized him more closely with appraising blue eyes.

'You certainly look all shot.'

'I am. I've made a hell of mess of everything.' He paused. 'I'd better start at the beginning—or will it bore you?'

'Not at all; go on.' There was, however, a hesitant note in Dean's voice. This trip East had been planned for a holiday—to find Gordon Sterrett in trouble exasperated him a little.

'Go on,' he repeated, and then added half under his breath, 'Get it over with.'

'Well,' began Gordon unsteadily, 'I got back from France in February, went home to Harrisburg for a month, and then came down to New York to get a job—one with an export company. They fired me yesterday.'

'Fired you?'

'I'm coming to that, Phil. I want to tell you frankly. You're about the only man I can turn to in a matter like this. You won't mind if I just tell you frankly, will you, Phil?'

Dean stiffened a bit more. The pats he was bestowing on his knees grew perfunctory. He felt vaguely that he was being unfairly saddled with responsibility; he was not even sure he wanted to be told. Though never surprised at finding Gordon Sterrett in mild difficulty, there was something in this present misery that repelled him and hardened him, even though it excited his curiosity.

'Go on.'

'It's a girl.'

'Hm.' Dean resolved that nothing was going to spoil his trip. If Gordon was going to be depressing, then he'd have to see less of Gordon.

'Her name is Jewel Hudson,' went on the distressed voice from the bed. 'She used to be "pure", I guess, up to about a year ago. Lived here in New York—poor family. Her people are dead now and she lives with an old aunt. You see it was just about the time I met her that everybody began to come back from France in droves—and all I did was to welcome the newly arrived and go on parties with 'em. That's the way it started, Phil, just from being glad to see everybody and having them glad to see me.'

'You ought to've had more sense.'

'I know,' Gordon paused, and then continued listlessly. 'I'm on my own now, you know, and Phil, I can't stand being poor. Then came this darn girl. She sort of fell in love with me for a while and, though I never intended to get so involved, I'd always seem to run into her somewhere. You can imagine the sort of work I was doing for those exporting people—of course, I always intended to draw; do illustrating magazines; there's a pile of money in it.'

'Why didn't you? You've got to buckle down if you want to make good,' suggested Dean with cold formalism.

'I tried, a little, but my stuff's crude. I've got talent,
Phil; I can draw—but I just don't know how. I ought to go
to art school and I can't afford it. Well, things came to a
crisis about a week ago. Just as I was down to about my last
dollar this girl began bothering me. She wants some money;
claims she can make trouble for me if she doesn't get it.'

'Can she?'

'I'm afraid she can. That's one reason I lost my job—
she kept calling up the office all the time, and that was sort
of the last straw down there. She's got a letter all written to
send to my family. Oh, she's got me, all right. I've got to
have some money for her.'

There was an awkward pause. Gordon lay very still, his
hands clenched by his side.

'I'm all in,' he continued, his voice trembling. 'I'm half
crazy, Phil. If I hadn't known you were coming East, I think
I'd have killed myself. I want you to lend me three hundred
dollars.'

Dean's hands, which had been patting his bare ankles,
were suddenly quiet—and the curious uncertainty playing
between the two became taut and strained.

After a second Gordon continued:

'I've bled the family until I'm ashamed to ask for another
nickel.'

Still Dean made no answer.

'Jewel says she's got to have two hundred dollars.'

'Tell her where she can go.'

'Yes, that sounds easy, but she's got a couple of drunken
letters I wrote her. Unfortunately she's not at all the flabby
sort of person you'd expect.'

Dean made an expression of distaste.

'I can't stand that sort of woman. You ought to have kept
away.'

'I know,' admitted Gordon wearily.

'You've got to look at things as they are. If you haven't
got money you've got to work and stay away from women.'

'That's easy for you to say,' began Gordon, his eyes
narrowing. 'You've got all the money in the world.'

'I most certainly have not. My family keep darn close tab on what I spend. Just because I have a little leeway I have to be extra careful not to abuse it.'

He raised the blind and let in a further flood of sunshine.

'I'm no prig, Lord knows,' he went on deliberately. 'I like pleasure—and I like a lot of it on a vacation like this, but you're—you're in awful shape. I never heard you talk just this way before. You seem to be sort of bankrupt—morally as well as financially.'

'Don't they usually go together?'

Dean shook his head impatiently.

'There's a regular aura about you that I don't understand. It's a sort of evil.'

'It's an air of worry and poverty and sleepless nights,' said Gordon, rather defiantly.

'I don't know.'

'Oh, I admit I'm depressing. I depress myself. But, my God, Phil, a week's rest and a new suit and some ready money and I'd be like—like I was. Phil, I can draw like a streak, and you know it. But half the time I haven't had the money to buy decent drawing materials—and I can't draw when I'm tired and discouraged and all in. With a little ready money I can take a few weeks off and get started.'

'How do I know you wouldn't use it on some other woman?'

'Why rub it in?' said Gordon quietly.

'I'm not rubbing it in. I hate to see you this way.'

'Will you lend me the money, Phil?'

'I can't decide right off. That's a lot of money and it'll be darn inconvenient for me.'

'It'll be hell for me if you can't—I know I'm whining, and it's all my own fault but—that doesn't change it.'

'When could you pay it back?'

This was encouraging. Gordon considered. It was probably wisest to be frank.

'Of course, I could promise to send it back next month, but—I'd better say three months. Just as soon as I start to sell drawings.'

'How do I know you'll sell any drawings?'

A new hardness in Dean's voice sent a faint chill of doubt over Gordon. Was it possible that he wouldn't get the money?

'I supposed you had a little confidence in me.'

'I did have—but when I see you like this I begin to wonder.'

'Do you suppose if I wasn't at the end of my rope I'd come to you like this? Do you think I'm enjoying it?' He broke off and bit his lip, feeling that he had better subdue the rising anger in his voice. After all, he was the suppliant.

'You seem to manage it pretty easily,' said Dean angrily. 'You put me in the position where, if I don't lend it to you, I'm a sucker—oh, yes, you do. And let me tell you it's no easy thing for me to get hold of three hundred dollars. My income isn't so big but that a slice like that won't play the deuce with it.'

He left his chair and began to dress, choosing his clothes carefully. Gordon stretched out his arms and clenched the edges of the bed, fighting back a desire to cry out. His head was splitting and whirring, his mouth was dry and bitter and he could feel the fever in his blood resolving itself into innumerable regular counts like a slow dripping from a roof.

Dean tied his tie precisely, brushed his eyebrows, and removed a piece of tobacco from his teeth with solemnity. Next he filled his cigarette case, tossed the empty box thoughtfully into the waste basket, and settled the case in his vest pocket.

'Had breakfast?' he demanded.

'No; I don't eat it any more.'

'Well, we'll go out and have some. We'll decide about that money later. I'm sick of the subject. I came East to have a good time.

'Let's go over to the Yale Club,' he continued moodily, and then added with an implied reproof: 'You've given up your job. You've got nothing else to do.'

'I'd have a lot to do if I had a little money,' said Gordon pointedly.

'Oh, for Heaven's sake drop the subject for a while! No point in glooming on my whole trip. Here, here's some money.'

He took a five-dollar bill from his wallet and tossed it over to Gordon, who folded it carefully and put it in his pocket. There was an added spot of colour in his cheeks, an added glow that was not fever. For an instant before they turned to go out their eyes met and in that instant each found something that made him lower his own glance quickly. For in that instant they quite suddenly and definitely hated each other.

II

Fifth Avenue and Forty-fourth Street swarmed with the noon crowd. The wealthy, happy sun glittered in transient gold through the thick windows of the smart shops, lighting upon mesh bags and purses and strings of pearls in grey velvet cases; upon gaudy feather fans of many colours; upon the laces and silks of expensive dresses; upon the bad paintings and the fine period furniture in the elaborate show rooms of interior decorators.

Working-girls, in pairs and groups and swarms, loitered by the windows, choosing their future boudoirs from some resplendent display which included even a man's silk pyjamas laid domestically across the bed. They stood in front of the jewellery stores and picked out their engagement rings, and their wedding rings and their platinum wrist watches, and then drifted on to inspect the feather fans and opera cloaks; meanwhile digesting the sandwiches and sundaes they had eaten for lunch.

All through the crowd were men in uniform, sailors from the great fleet anchored in the Hudson, soldiers with divisional insignia from Massachusetts to California wanting fearfully to be noticed, and finding the great city thoroughly fed up with soldiers unless they were nicely massed into pretty formations and uncomfortable under the weight of a pack and rifle.

Through this medley Dean and Gordon wandered; the

former interested, made alert by the display of humanity at its frothiest and gaudiest; the latter reminded of how often he had been one of the crowd, tired, casually fed, over-worked, and dissipated. To Dean the struggle was significant, young, cheerful; to Gordon it was dismal, meaningless, endless.

In the Yale Club they met a group of their former classmates who greeted the visiting Dean vociferously. Sitting in a semicircle of lounges and great chairs, they had a highball all around.

Gordon found the conversation tiresome and interminable. They lunched together *en masse*, warmed with liquor as the afternoon began. They were all going to the Gamma Psi dance that night—it promised to be the best party since the war.

'Edith Bradin's coming,' said someone to Gordon. 'Didn't she used to be an old flame of yours? Aren't you both from Harrisburg?'

'Yes.' He tried to change the subject. 'I see her brother occasionally. He's sort of a socialistic nut. Runs a paper or something here in New York.'

'Not like his gay sister, eh?' continued his eager informant. 'Well, she's coming tonight with a junior named Peter Himmell.'

Gordon was to meet Jewel Hudson at eight o'clock—he had promised to have some money for her. Several times he glanced nervously at his wrist-watch. At four to his relief, Dean rose and announced that he was going over to Rivers Brothers to buy some collars and ties. But as they left the Club another of the party joined them, to Gordon's great dismay. Dean was in a jovial mood now, happy, expectant of the evening's party, faintly hilarious. Over in Rivers he chose a dozen neckties, selecting each one after long consultations with the other man. Did he think narrow ties were coming back? And wasn't it a shame that Rivers couldn't get any more Welsh Margotson collars? There never was a collar like the 'Covington.'

Gordon was in something of a panic. He wanted the

money immediately. And he was now inspired also with a vague idea of attending the Gamma Psi dance. He wanted to see Edith—Edith whom he hadn't met since one romantic night at the Harrisburg Country Club just before he went to France. The affair had died, drowned in the turmoil of the war and quite forgotten in the arabesque of these three months, but a picture of her, poignant, debonair, immersed in her own inconsequential chatter, recurred to him unexpectedly and brought a hundred memories with it. It was Edith's face that he had cherished through college with a sort of detached yet affectionate admiration. He had loved to draw her—around his room had been a dozen sketches of her—playing golf, swimming—he could drew her pert, arresting profile with his eyes shut.

They left Rivers at five-thirty and paused for a moment on the sidewalk.

'Well,' said Dean genially, 'I'm all set now. Think I'll go back to the hotel and get a shave, haircut, and massage.'

'Good enough,' said the other man, 'I think I'll join you.'

Gordon wondered if he was to be beaten after all. With difficulty he restrained himself from turning to the man and snarling out, 'Go on away, damn you!' In despair he suspected that perhaps Dean had spoken to him, was keeping him along in order to avoid a dispute about the money.

They went into the Biltmore—a Biltmore alive with girls —mostly from the West and South, the stellar débutantes of many cities gathered for the dance of a famous fraternity of a famous university. But to Gordon they were faces in a dream. He gathered together his forces for a last appeal, was about to come out with he knew not what, when Dean suddenly excused himself to the other man and taking Gordon's arm led him aside.

'Gordy,' he said quickly, 'I've thought the whole thing over carefully and I've decided that I can't lend you that money. I'd like to oblige you, but I don't feel I ought to— it'd put a crimp in me for a month.'

Gordon, watching him dully, wondered why he had never before noticed how much those upper teeth projected.

'—I'm mighty sorry, Gordon,' continued Dean, 'but that's the way it is.'

He took out his wallet and deliberately counted out seventy-five dollars in bills.

'Here,' he said, holding them out, 'here's seventy-five; that makes eighty altogether. That's all the actual cash I have with me, besides what I'll actually spend on the trip.'

Gordon raised his clenched hand automatically, opened it as though it were a tongs he was holding, and clenched it again on the money.

'I'll see you at the dance,' continued Dean. 'I've got to get along to the barber shop.'

'So-long,' said Gordon in a strained and husky voice. 'So-long.'

Dean began to smile, but seemed to change his mind. He nodded briskly and disappeared.

But Gordon stood there, his handsome face awry with distress, the roll of bills clenched tightly in his hand. Then, blinded by sudden tears, he stumbled clumsily down the Biltmore steps.

III

About nine o'clock of the same night two human beings came out of a cheap restaurant in Sixth Avenue. They were ugly, ill-nourished, devoid of all except the very lowest form of intelligence, and without even that animal exuberance that in itself brings colour into life; they were lately vermin-ridden, cold, and hungry in a dirty town of a strange land; they were poor, friendless; tossed as driftwood from their births, they would be tossed as driftwood to their deaths. They were dressed in the uniform of the United States Army, and on the shoulder of each was the insignia of a drafted division from New Jersey, landed three days before.

The taller of the two was named Carrol Key, a name hinting that in his veins, however thinly diluted by genera-tions of degeneration, ran blood of some potentiality. But one could stare endlessly at the long, chinless face, the dull, watery eyes, and high cheek-bones, without finding a suggestion of either ancestral worth or native resourcefulness.

His companion was swart and bandy-legged, with rat-eyes and a much-broken hooked nose. His defiant air was obviously a pretence, a weapon of protection borrowed from that world of snarl and snap, of physical bluff and physical menace, in which he had always lived. His name was Gus Rose.

Leaving the café they sauntered down Sixth Avenue, wielding toothpicks with great gusto and complete detachment.

'Where to?' asked Rose, in a tone which implied that he would not be surprised if Key suggested the South Sea Islands.

'What you say we see if we can getta holda some liquor?' Prohibition was not yet. The ginger in the suggestion was caused by the law forbidding the selling of liquor to soldiers.

Rose agreed enthusiastically.

'I got an idea,' continued Key, after a moment's thought, 'I got a brother somewhere.'

'In New York?'

'Yeah. He's an old fella.' He meant that he was an elder brother. 'He's a waiter in a hash joint.'

'Maybe he can get us some.'

'I'll say he can!'

'B'lieve me, I'm goin' to get this darn uniform off me to-morra. Never get me in it again, neither. I'm goin' to get me some regular clothes.'

'Say, maybe I'm not.'

As their combined finances were something less than five dollars, this intention can be taken largely as a pleasant game of words, harmless and consoling. It seemed to please both of them, however, for they reinforced it with chuckling and mention of personages high in biblical circles, adding such further emphasis as 'Oh, boy!' 'You know!' and 'I'll say so!' repeated many times over.

The entire mental pabulum of these two men consisted of an offended nasal comment extended through the years upon the institution—army, business, or poorhouse—which kept them alive, and toward their immediate superior in that institution. Until that very morning the institution had been the 'government' and the immediate superior had been the 'Cap'n'—from these two they had glided out and were now in the vaguely uncomfortable state before they should adopt their next bondage. They were uncertain, resentful, and somewhat ill at ease. This they hid by pretending an elaborate relief at being out of the army, and by assuring each other that military discipline should never again rule their stubborn, liberty-loving wills. Yet, as a matter of fact, they would have felt more at home in a prison than in this new-found and unquestionable freedom.

Suddenly Key increased his gait. Rose, looking up and following his glance, discovered a crowd that was collecting fifty yards down the street. Key chuckled and began to run in the direction of the crowd; Rose thereupon also chuckled and his short bandy legs twinkled beside the long, awkward strides of his companion.

Reaching the outskirts of the crowd they immediately became an indistinguishable part of it. It was composed of ragged civilians somewhat the worse for liquor, and of soldiers representing many divisions and many stages of sobriety, all clustered around a gesticulating little Jew with long black whiskers, who was waving his arms and delivering an excited but succinct harangue. Key and Rose, having wedged themselves into the approximate parquet, scrutinized him with acute suspicion, as his words penetrated their common consciousness.

'—What have you got outa the war?' he was crying fiercely. 'Look arounja, look arounja! Are you rich? Have you got a lot of money offered you?—no; you're lucky if you're alive and got both your legs; you're lucky if you came back an' find your wife ain't gone off with some other fella that had the money to buy himself out of the war! That's when you're lucky! Who got anything out of it except J. P. Morgan an' John D. Rockerfeller?'

At this point the little Jew's oration was interrupted by

the hostile impact of a fist upon the point of his bearded chin and he toppled backward to a sprawl on the pavement.

'God damn Bolsheviki!' cried the big soldier-blacksmith who had delivered the blow. There was a rumble of approval, the crowd closed in nearer.

The Jew staggered to his feet, and immediately went down again before a half-dozen reaching-in fists. This time he stayed down, breathing heavily, blood oozing from his lip where it was cut within and without.

There was a riot of voices, and in a minute Rose and Key found themselves flowing with the jumbled crowd down Sixth Avenue under the leadership of a thin civilian in a slouch hat and the brawny soldier who had summarily ended the oration. The crowd had marvellously swollen to formidable proportions and a stream of more non-committal citizens followed it along the sidewalks lending their moral support by intermittent huzzas.

'Where we goin'?' yelled Key to the man nearest him.

His neighbour pointed up to the leader in the slouch hat.

'That guy knows where there's a lot of 'em! We're goin' to show 'em!'

'We're goin' to show 'em!' whispered Key delightedly to Rose, who repeated the phrase rapturously to a man on the other side.

Down Sixth Avenue swept the procession, joined here and there by soldiers and marines, and now and then by civilians, who came up with the inevitable cry that they were just out of the army themselves, as if presenting it as a card of admission to a newly formed Sporting and Amusement Club.

Then the procession swerved down a cross street and headed for Fifth Avenue and the word filtered here and there that they were bound for a Red meeting at Tolliver Hall.

'Where is it?'

The question went up the line and a moment later the answer floated back. Tolliver Hall was down on Tenth Street. There was a bunch of other sojers who was goin' to break it up and was down there now!

But Tenth Street had a faraway sound and at the word a general groan went up and a score of the procession dropped out. Among these were Rose and Key, who slowed down to a saunter and let the more enthusiastic sweep on by.

'I'd rather get some liquor,' said Key, as they halted and made their way to the sidewalk amid cries of 'Shell hole!' and 'Quitters!'

'Does your brother work around here?' asked Rose, assuming the air of one passing from the superficial to the eternal.

'He oughta,' replied Key. 'I ain't seen him for a coupla years. I been out to Pennsylvania since. Maybe he don't work at night anyhow. It's right along here. He can get us some o'right if he ain't gone.'

They found the place after a few minutes' patrol of the street—a shoddy tablecloth restaurant between Fifth Avenue and Broadway. Here Kay went inside to inquire for his brother, George, while Rose waited on the sidewalk.

'He ain't here no more,' said Key emerging. 'He's a waiter up to Delmonico's.'

Rose nodded wisely, as if he'd expected as much. One should not be surprised at a capable man changing jobs occasionally. He knew a waiter once—there ensued a long conversation as they walked as to whether waiters made more in actual wages than in tips—it was decided that it depended on the social tone of the joint wherein the waiter laboured. After having given each other vivid pictures of millionaires dining at Delmonico's and throwing away fifty-dollar bills after their first quart of champagne, both men thought privately of becoming waiters. In fact, Key's narrow brow was secreting a resolution to ask his brother to get him a job.

'A waiter can drink up all the champagne those fellas leave in bottles,' suggested Rose with some relish, and then added as an afterthought, 'Oh, boy!'

By the time they reached Delmonico's it was half past ten, and they were surprised to see a stream of taxis driving up to the door one after the other and emitting marvellous, hatless young ladies, each one attended by a stiff young gentleman in evening clothes.

'It's a party,' said Rose with some awe. 'Maybe we better not go in. He'll be busy.'

'No, he won't. He'll be o'right.'

After some hesitation they entered what appeared to them to be the least elaborate door and, indecision falling upon them immediately, stationed themselves nervously in an inconspicuous corner of the small dining-room in which they found themselves. They took off their caps and held them in their hands. A cloud of gloom fell upon them and both started when a door at one end of the room crashed open, emitting a comet-like waiter who streaked across the floor and vanished through another door on the other side.

There had been three of these lightning passages before the seekers mustered the acumen to hail a waiter. He turned, looked at them suspiciously, and then approached with soft, catlike steps, as if prepared at any moment to turn and flee.

'Say,' began Key, 'say, do you know my brother? He's a waiter here.'

'His name is Key,' annotated Rose.

Yes, the waiter knew Key. He was upstairs, he thought. There was a big dance going on in the main ballroom. He'd tell him.

Ten minutes later George Key appeared and greeted his brother with the utmost suspicion; his first and most natural thought being that he was going to be asked for money.

George was tall and weak chinned, but there his resemblance to his brother ceased. The waiter's eyes were not dull, they were alert and twinkling, and his manner was suave, indoor, and faintly superior. They exchanged formalities. George was married and had three children. He seemed fairly interested, but not impressed by the news that Carrol had been abroad in the army. This disappointed Carrol.

'George,' said the younger brother, these amenities having been disposed of, 'we want to get some booze, and they won't sell us none. Can you get us some?'

George considered.

'Sure. Maybe I can. It may be half an hour, though.'

'All right,' agreed Carrol, 'we'll wait.'

At this Rose started to sit down in a convenient chair, but was hailed to his feet by the indignant George.

'Hey! Watch out, you! Can't sit down here! This room's all set for a twelve o'clock banquet.'

'I ain't going to hurt it,' said Rose resentfully. 'I been through the delouser.'

'Never mind,' said George sternly, 'if the head waiter seen me here talkin' he'd romp all over me.'

'Oh.'

The mention of the head waiter was full explanation to the other two; they fingered their overseas caps nervously and waited for a suggestion.

'I tell you,' said George, after a pause, 'I got a place you can wait; you just come here with me.'

They followed him out the far door, through a deserted pantry and up a pair of dark winding stairs, emerging finally into a small room chiefly furnished by piles of pails and stacks of scrubbing brushes, and illuminated by a single dim electric light. There he left them, after soliciting two dollars and agreeing to return in half an hour with a quart of whiskey.

'George is makin' money, I bet,' said Key gloomily as he seated himself on an inverted pail. 'I bet he's making fifty dollars a week.'

Rose nodded his head and spat.

'I bet he is, too.'

'What'd he say the dance was of?'

'A lot of college fellas. Yale College.'

They both nodded solemnly at each other.

'Wonder where that crowda sojers is now?'

'I don't know. I know that's too damn long to walk for me.'

'Me too. You don't catch me walkin' that far.'

Ten minutes later restlessness seized them.

'I'm goin' to see what's out here,' said Rose, stepping cautiously towards the other door.

It was a swinging door of green baize and he pushed it open a cautious inch.

'See anything?'

For answer Rose drew in his breath sharply.

'Doggone! Here's some liquor I'll say!'

'Liquor?'

Key joined Rose at the door, and looked eagerly.

'I'll tell the world that's liquor,' he said, after a moment of concentrated gazing.

It was a room about twice as large as the one they were in —and in it was prepared a radiant feast of spirits. There were long walls of alternating bottles set along two white covered tables; whiskey, gin, brandy, French and Italian vermouths, and orange juice, not to mention an array of syphons and two great empty punch bowls. The room was as yet un-inhabited.

'It's for this dance they're just starting,' whispered Key; 'hear the violins playin'? Say, boy, I wouldn't mind havin' a dance.'

They closed the door softly and exchanged a glance of mutual comprehension. There was no need of feeling each other out.

'I'd like to get my hands on a coupla those bottles,' said Rose emphatically.

'Me too.'

'Do you suppose we'd get seen?'

Key considered.

'Maybe we better wait till they start drinkin' 'em. They got 'em all laid out now, and they know how many of them there are.'

They debated this point for several minutes. Rose was all for getting his hands on a bottle now and tucking it under his coat before anyone came into the room. Key, however, advocated caution. He was afraid he might get his brother in trouble. If they waited till some of the bottles were opened it'd be all right to take one, and everybody'd think it was one of the college fellas.

While they were still engaged in argument George Key

hurried through the room and, barely grunting at them, disappeared by way of the green baize door. A minute later they heard several corks pop, and then the sound of crackling ice and splashing liquid. George was mixing the punch.

The soldiers exchanged delighted grins.

'Oh, boy!' whispered Rose.

George reappeared.

'Just keep low, boys,' he said quickly. 'I'll have your stuff for you in five minutes.'

He disappeared through the door by which he had come.

As soon as his footsteps receded down the stairs, Rose, after a cautious look, darted into the room of delights and reappeared with a bottle in his hand.

'Here's what I say,' he said, as they sat radiantly digesting their first drink. 'We'll wait till he comes up, and we'll ask him if we can't just stay here and drink what he brings us—see. We'll tell him we haven't got any place to drink it —see. Then we can sneak in there whenever there ain't nobody in that there room and tuck a bottle under our coats We'll have enough to last us a coupla days—see?'

'Sure,' agreed Rose enthusiastically. 'Oh, boy! And if we want to we can sell it to sojers any time we want to.'

They were silent for a moment thinking rosily of this idea. Then Key reached up and unhooked the collar of his O.D. coat.

'It's hot in here, ain't it?'

Rose agreed earnestly.

'Hot as hell.'

IV

She was still quite angry when she came out of the dressing-room and crossed the intervening parlour of politeness that opened onto the hall—angry not so much at the actual happening which was, after all, the merest commonplace of her social existence, but because it had occurred on this particular night. She had no quarrel with herself. She had acted with that correct mixture of dignity and reticent pity which she always employed. She had succinctly and deftly snubbed him.

It had happened when their taxi was leaving the Biltmore —hadn't gone half a block. He had lifted his right arm awkwardly—she was on his right side—and attempted to settle it snugly around the crimson fur-trimmed opera cloak she wore. This in itself had been a mistake. It was inevitably more graceful for a young man attempting to embrace a young lady of whose acquiescence he was not certain, to first put his far arm around her. It avoided that awkward movement of raising the near arm.

His second *faux pas* was unconscious. She had spent the afternoon at the hairdresser's; the idea of any calamity overtaking her hair was extremely repugnant—yet as Peter made his unfortunate attempt the point of his elbow had just faintly brushed it. That was his second *faux pas*. Two were quite enough.

He had begun to murmur. At the first murmur she had decided that he was nothing but a college boy—Edith was twenty-two, and anyhow, this dance, first of its kind since the war, was reminding her, with the accelerating rhythm of its associations, of something else—of another dance and another man, a man for whom her feelings had been little more than a sad-eyed, adolescent mooniness. Edith Bradin was falling in love with her recollection of Gordon Sterrett.

So she came out of the dressing-room at Delmonico's and stood for a second in the doorway looking over the shoulders of a black dress in front of her at the groups of Yale men who flitted like dignified black moths around the head of the stairs. From the room she had left drifted out the heavy fragrance left by the passage to and fro of many scented young beauties—rich perfumes and the fragile memory-laden dust of fragrant powders. This odour drifting out acquired the tang of cigarette smoke in the hall, and then settled sensuously down the stairs and permeated the ballroom where the Gamma Psi dance was to be held. It was an odour she knew well, exciting, stimulating, restlessly sweet—the odour of a fashionable dance.

She thought of her own appearance. Her bare arms and shoulders were powdered to a creamy white. She knew they looked very soft and would gleam like milk against the black backs that were to silhouette them to-night. The hairdressing had been a success; her reddish mass of hair was piled and crushed and creased to an arrogant marvel of mobile curves. Her lips were finely made of deep carmine; the irises of her eyes were delicate, breakable blue, like china eyes. She was a complete, infinitely delicate, quite perfect thing of beauty, flowing in an even line from a complex coiffure to two small slim feet.

She thought of what she would say to-night at this revel, faintly presaged already by the sounds of high and low laughter and slippered footsteps, and movements of couples up and down the stairs. She would talk the language she had talked for many years—her line—made up of the current expressions, bits of journalese and college slang strung together into an intrinsic whole, careless, faintly provocative, delicately sentimental. She smiled faintly as she heard a girl sitting on the stairs near her say: 'You don't know the half of it, dearie!'

And as she smiled her anger melted for a moment, and closing her eyes she drew in a deep breath of pleasure. She dropped her arms to her sides until they were faintly touching the sleek sheath that covered and suggested her figure. She had never felt her own softness so much nor so enjoyed the whiteness of her own arms.

'I smell sweet,' she said to herself simply, and then came another thought—'I'm made for love.'

She liked the sound of this and thought it again; then in inevitable succession came her new-born riot of dreams about Gordon. The twist of her imagination which, two months before, had disclosed to her her unguessed desire to see him again, seemed now to have been leading up to this dance, this hour.

For all her sleek beauty, Edith was a grave, slow-thinking girl. There was a streak in her of that same desire to ponder, of that adolescent idealism that had turned her brother socialist and pacifist. Henry Bradin had left Cornell, where he had been an instructor in economics, and had come to New York to pour the latest cures for incurable evils into the columns of a radical weekly newspaper.

Edith, less fatuously, would have been content to cure Gordon Sterrett. There was a quality of weakness in Gordon that she wanted to take care of; there was a helplessness in him that she wanted to protect. And she wanted someone she had known a long while, someone who had loved her a long while. She was a little tired; she wanted to get married. Out of a pile of letters, half a dozen pictures and as many memories, and this weariness, she had decided that next time she saw Gordon their relations were going to be changed. She would say something that would change them. There was this evening. This was her evening. All evenings were her evenings.

Then her thoughts were interrupted by a solemn undergraduate with a hurt look and an air of strained formality who presented himself before her and bowed unusually low. It was the man she had come with, Peter Himmel. He was tall and humorous, with horned-rimmed glasses and an air of attractive whimsicality. She suddenly rather disliked him—probably because he had not succeeded in kissing her.

'Well,' she began, 'are you still furious at me?'

'Not at all.'

She stepped forward and took his arm.

'I'm sorry,' she said softly. 'I don't know why I snapped out that way. I'm in a bum humour to-night for some strange reason. I'm sorry.'

'S'all right,' he mumbled, 'don't mention it.'

He felt disagreeably embarrassed. Was she rubbing in the fact of his late failure?

'It was a mistake,' she continued, on the same consciously gentle key. 'We'll both forget it.' For this he hated her.

A few minutes later they drifted out on the floor while the dozen swaying, sighing members of the specially hired jazz orchestra informed the crowded ballroom that 'if a

saxophone and me are left alone why then two is com-
pan-ee!'

A man with a moustache cut in.

'Hello,' he began reprovingly. 'You don't remember me.'

'I can't just think of your name,' she said lightly—'and
I know you so well.'

'I met you up at—' His voice trailed disconsolately off
as a man with very fair hair cut in. Edith murmured a
conventional 'Thanks, loads—cut in later,' to the *inconnu*.

The very fair man insisted on shaking hands enthusiastically. She placed him as one of the numerous Jims
of her acquaintance—last name a mystery. She remembered
even that he had a peculiar rhythm in dancing and found
as they started that she was right.

'Going to be here long?' he breathed confidentially.

She leaned back and looked up at him.

'Couple of weeks.'

'Where are you?'

'Biltmore. Call me up some day.'

'I mean it,' he assured her. 'I will. We'll go to tea.'

'So do I—Do.'

A dark man cut in with intense formality.

'You don't remember me, do you?' he said gravely.

'I should say I do. Your name's Harlan.'

'No-ope. Barlow.'

'Well, I knew there were two syllables anyway. You're
the boy that played the ukulele so well up at Howard
Marshall's house party.'

'I played—but not——'

A man with prominent teeth cut in. Edith inhaled a slight
cloud of whiskey. She liked men to have had something to
drink; they were so much more cheerful, and appreciative
and complimentary—much easier to talk to.

'My name's Dean, Philip Dean,' he said cheerfully. 'You
don't remember me, I know, but you used to come up to
New Haven with a fellow I roomed with senior year,
Gordon Sterrett.'

Edith looked up quickly.

'Yes, I went up with him twice—to the Pump and Slipper and the Junior prom.'

'You've seen him, of course,' said Dean carelessly. 'He's here to-night. I saw him just a minute ago.'

Edith started. Yet she had felt quite sure he would be here.

'Why, no, I haven't——'

A fat man with red hair cut in.

'Hello, Edith,' he began.

'Why—hello there——'

She slipped, stumbled lightly.

'I'm sorry, dear,' she murmured mechanically.

She had seen Gordon—Gordon very white and listless, leaning against the side of a doorway, smoking and looking into the ballroom. Edith could see that his face was thin and wan—that the hand he raised to his lips with a cigarette was trembling. They were dancing quite close to him now.

'—They invite so darn many extra fellas that you—' the short man was saying.

'Hello, Gordon,' called Edith over her partner's shoulder. Her heart was pounding wildly.

His large dark eyes were fixed on her. He took a step in her direction. Her partner turned her away—she heard his voice bleating——

'—but half the stags get lit and leave before long, so——'

Then a low tone at her side.

'May I, please?'

She was dancing suddenly with Gordon; one of his arms was around her; she felt it tighten spasmodically; felt his hand on her back with the fingers spread. Her hand holding the little lace handkerchief was crushed in his.

'Why Gordon,' she began breathlessly.

'Hello, Edith.'

She slipped again—was tossed forward by her recovery until her face touched the black cloth of his dinner coat. She loved him—she knew she loved him—then for a minute there was silence while a strange feeling of uneasiness crept over her. Something was wrong.

Of a sudden her heart wrenched, and turned over as she
realized what it was. He was pitiful and wretched, a little
drunk, and miserably tired.

'Oh—' she cried involuntarily.

His eyes looked down at her. She saw suddenly that they
were blood-streaked and rolling uncontrollably.

'Gordon,' she murmured, 'we'll sit down, I want to sit
down.'

They were nearly in mid-floor, but she had seen two men
start toward her from opposite sides of the room, so she
halted, seized Gordon's limp hand and led him bumping
through the crowd, her mouth tight shut, her face a little
pale under her rouge, her eyes trembling with tears.

She found a place high up on the soft-carpeted stairs,
and he sat down heavily beside her.

'Well,' he began, staring at her unsteadily, 'I certainly
am glad to see you, Edith.'

She looked at him without answering. The effect of this
on her was immeasurable. For years she had seen men in
various stages of intoxication, from uncles all the way down
to chauffeurs, and her feelings had varied from amusement
to disgust, but here for the first time she was seized with a
new feeling—an unutterable horror.

'Gordon,' she said accusingly and almost crying, 'you
look like the devil.'

He nodded. 'I've had trouble, Edith.'

'Trouble?'

'All sorts of trouble. Don't you say anything to the family,
but I'm all gone to pieces. I'm a mess, Edith.'

His lower lip was sagging. He seemed scarcely to see
her.

'Can't you—can't you,' she hesitated, 'can't you tell me
about it, Gordon? You know I'm always interested in you.'

She bit her lip—she had intended to say something
stronger, but found at the end that she couldn't bring it out.

Gordon shook his head dully. 'I can't tell you. You're a
good woman. I can't tell a good woman the story.'

'Rot,' she said, defiantly. 'I think it's a perfect insult to call any one a good woman in that way. It's a slam. You've been drinking, Gordon.'

'Thanks.' He inclined his head gravely 'Thanks for the information.'

'Why do you drink?'

'Because I'm so damn miserable.'

'Do you think drinking's going to make it any better?'

'What you doing—trying to reform me?'

'No; I'm trying to help you, Gordon. Can't you tell me about it?'

'I'm in an awful mess. Best thing you can do is to pretend not to know me.'

'Why, Gordon?'

'I'm sorry I cut in on you—it's unfair to you. You're a pure woman—and all that sort of thing. Here, I'll get someone else to dance with you.'

He rose clumsily to his feet, but she reached up and pulled him down beside her on the stairs.

'Here, Gordon. You're ridiculous. You're hurting me. You're acting like a—like a crazy man——'

'I admit it. I'm a little crazy. Something's wrong with me, Edith. There's something left me. It doesn't matter.'

'It does, tell me.'

'Just that. I was always queer—little bit different from other boys. All right in college, but now it's all wrong. Things have been snapping inside me for four months like little hooks on a dress, and it's about to come off when a few more hooks go. I'm very gradually going loony.'

He turned his eyes full on her and began to laugh, and she shrank away from him.

'What *is* the matter?'

'Just me,' he repeated. 'I'm going loony. This whole place is like a dream to me—this Delmonico's——'

As he talked she saw he had changed utterly. He wasn't at all light and gay and careless—a great lethargy and discouragement had come over him. Revulsion seized her, followed by a faint, surprising boredom. His voice seemed to come out of a great void.

'Edith,' he said, 'I used to think I was clever, talented, an artist. Now I know I'm nothing. Can't draw, Edith. Don't know why I'm telling you this.'

She nodded absently.

'I can't draw, I can't do anything. I'm poor as a church mouse.' He laughed, bitterly and rather too loud. 'I've become a damn beggar, a leech on my friends. I'm a failure. I'm poor as hell.'

Her distaste was growing. She barely nodded this time, waiting for her first possible cue to rise.

Suddenly Gordon's eyes filled with tears.

'Edith,' he said, turning to her with what was evidently a strong effort at self-control, 'I can't tell you what it means to me to know there's one person left who's interested in me.'

He reached out and patted her hand, and involuntarily she drew it away.

'It's mighty fine of you,' he repeated.

'Well,' she said slowly, looking him in the eye, 'anyone's always glad to see an old friend—but I'm sorry to see you like this, Gordon.'

There was a pause while they looked at each other, and the momentary eagerness in his eyes wavered. She rose and stood looking at him, her face quite expressionless.

'Shall we dance?' she suggested, coolly.

—Love is fragile—she was thinking—but perhaps the pieces are saved, the things that hovered on lips, that might have been said. The new love words, the tenderness learned, are treasured up for the next lover.

V

Peter Himmel, escort to the lovely Edith, was unaccustomed to being snubbed; having been snubbed, he was hurt and embarrassed, and ashamed of himself. For a matter of two months he had been on special delivery terms with Edith Bradin and knowing that the one excuse and explanation of the special delivery letter is its value in sentimental correspondence, he had believed himself quite sure of his ground. He searched in vain for any reason why she should have taken this attitude in the matter of a simple kiss.

Therefore when he was cut in on by the man with the moustache he went out into the hall and, making up a sentence, said it over to himself several times. Considerably deleted, this was it:

'Well, if any girl ever led a man on and then jolted him, she did—and she has no kick coming if I go out and get beautifully boiled.'

So he walked through the supper room into a small room adjoining it, which he had located earlier in the evening. It was a room in which there were several large bowls of punch flanked by many bottles. He took a seat beside the table which held the bottles.

At the second highball, boredom, disgust, the monotony of time, the turbidity of events, sank into a vague background before which glittering cobwebs formed. Things became reconciled to themselves, things lay quietly on their shelves; the troubles of the day arranged themselves in trim formation and at his curt wish of dismissal, marched off and disappeared. And with the departure of worry came brilliant, permeating symbolism. Edith became a flighty, negligible girl, not to be worried over; rather to be laughed at. She fitted like a figure of his own dream into the surface world forming about him. He himself became in a measure symbolic, a type of the continent bacchanal, the brilliant dreamer at play.

Then the symbolic mood faded and as he sipped his third highball his imagination yielded to the warm glow and he lapsed into a state similar to floating on his back in pleasant water. It was at this point that he noticed that a green baize door near him was open about two inches, and that through the aperture a pair of eyes were watching him intently.

'Hm,' murmured Peter calmly.

The green door closed—and then opened again—a bare half inch this time.

'Peek-a-boo,' murmured Peter.

6*

The door remained stationary and then he became aware of a series of tense intermittent whispers.

'One guy.'

'What's he doin'?'

'He's sittin' lookin'.'

'He better beat it off. We gotta get another li'l' bottle.'

Peter listened while the words filtered into his consciousness.

'Now this,' he thought, 'is most remarkable.'

He was excited. He was jubilant. He felt that he had stumbled upon a mystery. Affecting an elaborate carelessness he arose and walked around the table—then, turning quickly, pulled open the green door, precipitating Private Rose into the room.

Peter bowed.

'How do you do?' he said.

Private Rose set one foot slightly in front of the other, poised for fight, flight, or compromise.

'How do you do?' repeated Peter politely.

'I'm o'right.'

'Can I offer you a drink?'

Private Rose looked at him searchingly, suspecting possible sarcasm.

'O'right,' he said finally.

Peter indicated a chair.

'Sit down.'

'I got a friend,' said Rose, 'I got a friend in there.' He pointed to the green door.

'By all means let's have him in.'

Peter crossed over, opened the door and welcomed in Private Key, very suspicious and uncertain and guilty. Chairs were found and the three took their seats around the punch bowl. Peter gave them each a highball and offered them a cigarette from his case. They accepted both with some diffidence.

'Now,' continued Peter easily, 'may I ask why you gentlemen prefer to lounge away your leisure hours in a room which is chiefly furnished, as far as I can see, with

scrubbing brushes. And when the human race has pro-
gressed to the stage where seventeen thousand chairs are
manufactured on every day except Sunday—' he paused.
Rose and Key regarded him vacantly. 'Will you tell me,'
went on Peter, 'why you choose to rest yourselves on articles
intended for the transportation of water from one place to
another?'

At this point Rose contributed a grunt to the conversation.

'And lastly,' finished Peter, 'will you tell me why, when
you are in a building beautifully hung with enormous
candelabra, you prefer to spend these evening hours under
one anaemic electric light?'

Rose looked at Key; Key looked at Rose. They laughed;
they laughed uproariously; they found it was impossible
to look at each other without laughing. But they were not
laughing with this man—they were laughing at him. To
them a man who talked after this fashion was either raving
drunk or raving crazy.

'You are Yale men, I presume,' said Peter, finishing his
highball and preparing another.

They laughed again.

'Na-ah.'

'So? I thought perhaps you might be members of that
lowly section of the university known as the Sheffield
Scientific School.'

'Na-ah.'

'Hm. Well, that's too bad. No doubt you are Harvard
men, anxious to preserve your incognito in this—this
paradise of violet blue, as the newspapers say.'

'Na-ah,' said Key scornfully, 'we was just waitin' for
somebody.'

'Ah,' exclaimed Peter, rising and filling their glasses,
'very interestin'. Had a date with a scrublady, eh?'

They both denied this indignantly.

'It's all right,' Peter reassured them, 'don't apologize. A
scrublady's as good as any lady in the world. Kipling says
"Any lady and Judy O'Grady under the skin."'

'Sure,' said Key, winking broadly at Rose.

'My case, for instance,' continued Peter, finishing his glass. 'I got a girl up there that's spoiled. Spoildest darn girl I ever saw. Refused to kiss me; no reason whatsoever. Led me on deliberately to think sure I want to kiss you and then plunk! Threw me over! What's the younger generation comin' to?'

'Say tha's hard luck,' said Key—'that's awful hard luck.'

'Oh boy!' said Rose.

'Have another?' said Peter.

'We got in a sort of fight for a while,' said Key after a pause, 'but it was too far away.'

'A fight?—tha's stuff!' said Peter, seating himself unsteadily. 'Fight 'em all! I was in the army.'

'This was a Bolshevik fella.'

'Tha's stuff!' exclaimed Peter, enthusiastic. 'That's what I say! Kill the Bolshevik! Exterminate 'em!'

'We're Americuns,' said Rose, implying a sturdy, defiant patriotism.

'Sure,' said Peter. 'Greatest race in the world! We're all Americuns! Have another.'

They had another.

VI

At one o'clock a special orchestra, special even in a day of special orchestras, arrived at Delmonico's, and its members, seating themselves arrogantly around the piano, took up the burden of providing music for the Gamma Psi Fraternity. They were headed by a famous flute-player, distinguished throughout New York for his feat of standing on his head and shimmying with his shoulders while he played the latest jazz on his flute. During his performance the lights were extinguished except for the spotlight on the flute-player and another roving beam that threw flickering shadows and changing kaleidoscopic colours over the massed dancers.

Edith had danced herself into that tired, dreamy state habitual only with débutantes, a state equivalent to the glow of a noble soul after several long highballs. Her mind floated vaguely on the bosom of her music; her partners changed with the unreality of phantoms under the colourful shifting dusk, and to her present coma it seemed as if days had passed since the dance began. She had talked on many fragmentary subjects with many men. She had been kissed once and made love to six times. Earlier in the evening different undergraduates had danced with her, but now, like all the more popular girls there, she had her own entourage—that is, half a dozen gallants had singled her out or were alternating her charms with those of some other chosen beauty; they cut in on her in regular, inevitable succession.

Several times she had seen Gordon—he had been sitting a long time on the stairway with his palm to his head, his dull eyes fixed at an infinite speck on the floor before him, very depressed, he looked, and quite drunk—but Edith each time had averted her glance, hurriedly. All that seemed long ago; her mind was passive now, her senses were lulled to trance-like sleep; only her feet danced and her voice talked on in hazy sentimental banter.

But Edith was not nearly so tired as to be incapable of moral indignation when Peter Himmel cut in on her, sublimely and happily drunk. She gasped and looked up at him.

'Why, *Peter* !'

'I'm a li'l' stewed, Edith.'

'Why, Peter, you're a *peach*, you are! Don't you think it's a bum way of doing—when you're with me?'

Then she smiled unwillingly, for he was looking at her with owlish sentimentality varied with a silly spasmodic smile.

'Darlin' Edith,' he began earnestly, 'you know I love you, don't you?'

'You tell it well.'

'I love you—and I mercly wanted you to kiss me,' he added sadly.

His embarrassment, his shame, were both gone. She was a mos' beautiful girl in whole worl'. Mos' beautiful eyes, like stars above. He wanted to 'pologize—firs', for presuming to try to kiss her; second, for drinking—but he'd been so discouraged 'cause he had thought she was mad at him——

The red-fat man cut in, and looking up at Edith smiled radiantly.

'Did you bring any one?' she asked.

No. The red-fat man was a stag.

'Well, would you mind—would it be an awful bother for you to—to take me home to-night?' (this extreme diffidence was a charming affectation on Edith's part—she knew that the red-fat man would immediately dissolve into a paroxysm of delight).

'Bother? Why, good Lord, I'd be darn glad to! You know I'd be darn glad to.'

'Thanks *loads*! You're awfully sweet.'

She glanced at her wrist-watch. It was half-past one. And, as she said 'half-past one' to herself, it floated vaguely into her mind that her brother had told her at luncheon that he worked in the office of his newspaper until after one-thirty every evening.

Edith turned suddenly to her current partner.

'What street is Delmonico's on, anyway?'

'Street? Oh, why Fifth Avenue, of course.'

'I mean, what cross street?'

'Why—let's see—it's on Forty-fourth Street.'

This verified what she had thought. Henry's office must be across the street and just around the corner, and it occurred to her immediately that she might slip over for a moment and surprise him, float in on him, a shimmering marvel in her new crimson opera cloak and 'cheer him up.' It was exactly the sort of thing Edith revelled in doing—an unconventional, jaunty thing. The idea reached out and gripped at her imagination—after an instant's hesitation she had decided.

'My hair is just about to tumble entirely down,' she said pleasantly to her partner; 'would you mind if I go and fix it?'

'Not at all.'

'You're a peach.'

A few minutes later, wrapped in her crimson opera cloak, she flitted down a side-stairs, her cheeks glowing with excitement at her little adventure. She ran by a couple who stood at the door—a weak-chinned waiter and an over-rouged young lady, in hot dispute—and opening the outer door stepped into the warm May night.

VII

The over-rouged young lady followed her with a brief, bitter glance—then turned again to the weak-chinned waiter and took up her argument.

'You better go up and tell him I'm here,' she said defiantly, 'or I'll go up myself.'

'No, you don't!' said George sternly.

The girl smiled sardonically.

'Oh, I don't, don't I? Well, let me tell you I know more college fellas and more of 'em know me, and are glad to take me out on a party, than you ever saw in your whole life.'

'Maybe so——'

'Maybe so,' she interrupted. 'Oh, it's all right for any of 'em like that one that just ran out—God knows where *she* went—it's all right for them that are asked here to come or go as they like—but when I want to see a friend they have some cheap, ham-slinging, bring-me-a-doughnut waiter to stand here and keep me out.'

'See here,' said the elder Key indignantly, 'I can't lose my job. Maybe this fella you're talking about doesn't want to see you.'

'Oh, he wants to see me all right.'

'Anyway, how could I find him in all that crowd?'

'Oh, he'll be there,' she asserted confidently. 'You just ask anybody for Gordon Sterrett and they'll point him out to you. They all know each other, those fellas.'

She produced a mesh bag, and taking out a dollar bill handed it to George.

'Here,' she said, 'here's a bribe. You find him and give

him my message. You tell him if he isn't here in five minutes
I'm coming up.'

George shook his head pessimistically, considered the
question for a moment, wavered violently, and then withdrew.

In less than the allotted time Gordon came downstairs.
He was drunker than he had been earlier in the evening
and in a different way. The liquor seemed to have hardened
on him like a crust. He was heavy and lurching—almost
incoherent when he talked.

''Lo, Jewel,' he said thickly. 'Came right away. Jewel,
I couldn't get that money. Tried my best.'

'Money nothing!' she snapped. 'You haven't been near
me for ten days. What's the matter?'

He shook his head slowly.

'Been very low, Jewel. Been sick.'

'Why didn't you tell me if you were sick. I don't care
about the money that bad. I didn't start bothering you
about it at all until you began neglecting me.'

Again he shook his head.

'Haven't been neglecting you. Not at all.'

'Haven't! You haven't been near me for three weeks,
unless you been so drunk you didn't know what you were
doing.'

'Been sick, Jewel,' he repeated, turning his eyes upon her
wearily.

'You're well enough to come and play with your society
friends here all right. You told me you'd meet me for dinner,
and you said you'd have some money for me. You didn't
even bother to ring me up.'

'I couldn't get any money.'

'Haven't I just been saying that doesn't matter? I wanted to
see *you*, Gordon, but you seem to prefer your somebody else.'

He denied this bitterly.

'Then get your hat and come along', she suggested.

Gordon hesitated—and she came suddenly close to him
and slipped her arms around his neck.

'Come on with me, Gordon,' she said in a half whisper.

'We'll go over to Devineries' and have a drink, and then we can go up to my apartment.'

'I can't, Jewel,——'

'You can,' she said intensely.

'I'm sick as a dog!'

'Well, then, you oughtn't to stay here and dance.'

With a glance around him in which relief and despair were mingled, Gordon hesitated; then she suddenly pulled him to her and kissed him with soft, pulpy lips.

'All right,' he said heavily. 'I'll get my hat.'

VIII

When Edith came out into the clear blue of the May night she found the Avenue deserted. The windows of the big shops were dark; over their doors were drawn great iron masks until they were only shadowy tombs of the late day's splendour. Glancing down towards Forty-second Street she saw a commingled blur of lights from the all-night restaurants. Over on Sixth Avenue the elevated, a flare of fire, roared across the street between the glimmering parallels of light at the station and streaked along into the crisp dark. But at Forty-fourth Street it was very quiet.

Pulling her cloak close about her Edith darted across the Avenue. She started nervously as a solitary man passed her and said in a hoarse whisper—'Where bound, kiddo?' She was reminded of a night in her childhood when she had walked around the block in her pyjamas and a dog had howled at her from a mystery-big back yard.

In a minute she had reached her destination, a two-storey, comparatively old building on Forty-fourth, in the upper windows of which she thankfully detected a wisp of light. It was bright enough outside for her to make out the sign beside the window—the *New York Trumpet*. She stepped inside a dark hall and after a second saw the stairs in the corner.

Then she was in a long, low room furnished with many desks and hung on all sides with file copies of newspapers.

There were only two occupants. They were sitting at different ends of the room, each wearing a green eye-shade and writing by a solitary desk light.

For a moment she stood uncertainly in the doorway, and then both men turned around simultaneously and she recognized her brother.

'Why, Edith!' He rose quickly and approached her in surprise, removing his eye-shade. He was tall, lean, and dark, with black, piercing eyes under very thick glasses. They were far-away eyes that seemed always fixed just over the head of the person to whom he was talking.

He put his hands on her arms and kissed her cheek.

'What is it?' he repeated in some alarm.

'I was at a dance across at Delmonico's, Henry,' she said excitedly, 'and I couldn't resist tearing over to see you.'

'I'm glad you did.' His alertness gave way quickly to a habitual vagueness. 'You oughtn't to be out alone at night though, ought you?'

The man at the other end of the room had been looking at them curiously, but at Henry's beckoning gesture he approached. He was loosely fat with little twinkling eyes, and, having removed his collar and tie, he gave the impression of a Middle-Western farmer on a Sunday afternoon.

'This is my sister,' said Henry. 'She dropped in to see me.'

'How do you do?' said the fat man, smiling. 'My name's Bartholomew, Miss Bradin. I know your brother has forgotten it long ago.'

Edith laughed politely.

'Well,' he continued, 'not exactly gorgeous quarters we have here, are they?'

Edith looked around the room.

'They seem very nice,' she replied. 'Where do you keep the bombs?'

'The bombs?' repeated Bartholomew, laughing. 'That's pretty good—the bombs. Did you hear her, Henry? She wants to know where we keep the bombs. Say, that's pretty good.'

Edith swung herself around onto a vacant desk and sat

dangling her feet over the edge. Her brother took a seat beside her.

'Well,' he asked, absentmindedly, 'how do you like New York this trip?'

'Not bad. I'll be over at the Biltmore with the Hoyts until Sunday. Can't you come to luncheon to-morrow?'

He thought a moment.

'I'm especially busy,' he objected, 'and I hate women in groups.'

'All right,' she agreed, unruffled. 'Let's you and me have luncheon together.'

'Very well.'

'I'll call for you at twelve.'

Bartholomew was obviously anxious to return to his desk, but apparently considered that it would be rude to leave without some parting pleasantry.

'Well'—he began awkwardly.

They both turned to him.

'Well, we—we had an exciting time earlier in the evening.'

The two men exchanged glances.

'You should have come earlier,' continued Bartholomew, somewhat encouraged. 'We had a regular vaudeville.'

'Did you really?'

'A serenade,' said Henry. 'A lot of soldiers gathered down there in the street and began to yell at the sign.'

'Why?' she demanded.

'Just a crowd,' said Henry, abstractedly. 'All crowds have to howl. They didn't have anybody with much initiative in the lead, or they'd probably have forced their way in here and smashed things up.'

'Yes,' said Bartholomew, turning again to Edith, 'you should have been here.'

He seemed to consider this a sufficient cue for withdrawal, for he turned abruptly and went back to his desk.

'Are the soldiers all set against the Socialists?' demanded Edith of her brother. 'I mean do they attack you violently and all that?'

Henry replaced his eye-shade and yawned.

'The human race has come a long way,' he said casually, 'but most of us are throw-backs; the soldiers don't know what they want, or what they hate, or what they like. They're used to acting in large bodies, and they seem to have to make demonstrations. So it happens to be against us. There've been riots all over the city to-night. It's May Day, you see.'

'Was the disturbance here pretty serious?'

'Not a bit,' he said scornfully. 'About twenty-five of them stopped in the street about nine o'clock, and began to bellow at the moon.'

'Oh'—She changed the subject. 'You're glad to see me, Henry?'

'Why, sure.'

'You don't seem to be.'

'I am.'

'I suppose you think I'm a—a waster. Sort of the World's Worst Butterfly.'

Henry laughed.

'Not at all. Have a good time while you're young. Why? Do I seem like the priggish and earnest youth?'

'No—' She paused, '—but somehow I began thinking how absolutely different the party I'm on is from—from all your purposes. It seems sort of—of incongruous, doesn't it?—me being at a party like that, and you over here working for a thing that'll make that sort of party impossible ever any more, if your ideas work.'

'I don't think of it that way. You're young, and you're acting just as you were brought up to act. Go ahead—have a good time.'

Her feet, which had been idly swinging, stopped and her voice dropped a note.

'I wish you'd—you'd come back to Harrisburg and have a good time. Do you feel sure that you're on the right track——'

'You're wearing beautiful stockings,' he interrupted. 'What on earth are they?'

'They're embroidered,' she replied, glancing down.

'Aren't they cunning?' She raised her skirts and uncovered slim, silk-sheathed calves. 'Or do you disapprove of silk stockings?'

He seemed slightly exasperated, bent his dark eyes on her piercingly.

'Are you trying to make me out as criticizing you in any way, Edith?'

'Not at all—'

She paused. Bartholomew had uttered a grunt. She turned and saw that he had left his desk and was standing at the window.

'What is it?' demanded Henry.

'People,' said Bartholomew, and then after an instant: 'Whole jam of them. They're coming from Sixth Avenue.'

'People.'

The fat man pressed his nose to the pane.

'Soldiers, by God!' he said emphatically. 'I had an idea they'd come back.'

Edith jumped to her feet, and running over joined Bartholomew at the window.

'There's a lot of them!' she cried excitedly. 'Come here, Henry!'

Henry readjusted his shade, but kept his seat.

'Hadn't we better turn out the lights?' suggested Bartholomew.

'No. They'll go away in a minute.'

'They're not,' said Edith, peering from the window. 'They're not even thinking of going away. There's more of them coming. Look—there's a whole crowd turning the corner of Sixth Avenue.'

By the yellow glow and blue shadows of the street lamp she could see that the sidewalk was crowded with men. They were mostly in uniform, some sober, some enthusiastically drunk, and over the whole swept an incoherent clamour and shouting.

Henry rose, and going to the window exposed himself as a long silhouette against the office lights. Immediately the shouting became a steady yell, and a rattling fusillade of small missiles, corners of tobacco plugs, cigarette-boxes, and even pennies beat against the window. The sounds of the racket now began floating up the stairs as the folding doors revolved.

'They're coming up!' cried Bartholomew.

Edith turned anxiously to Henry.

'They're coming up, Henry.'

From downstairs in the lower hall their cries were now quite audible.

'—God damn Socialists!'

'Pro-Germans! Boche-lovers!'

'Second floor, front! Come on.'

'We'll get the sons——'

The next five minutes passed in a dream. Edith was conscious that the clamour burst suddenly upon the three of them like a cloud of rain, that there was a thunder of many feet on the stairs, that Henry had seized her arm and drawn her back towards the rear of the office. Then the door opened and an overflow of men were forced into the room—not the leaders, but simply those who happened to be in front.

'Hello, Bo!'

'Up late, ain't you?'

'You an' your girl. Damn *you* !'

She noticed that two very drunken soldiers had been forced to the front, where they wobbled fatuously—one of them was short and dark, the other was tall and weak of chin.

Henry stepped forward and raised his hand.

'Friends!' he said.

The clamour faded into a momentary stillness, punctuated with mutterings.

'Friends!' he repeated, his far-away eyes fixed over the heads of the crowd, 'you're injuring no one but yourselves by breaking in here to-night. Do we look like rich men? Do we look like Germans? I ask you in all fairness——'

'Pipe down!'

'I'll say you do!'

'Say, who's your lady friend, buddy?'

A man in civilian clothes, who had been pawing over a table, suddenly held up a newspaper.

'Here it is!' he shouted. 'They wanted the Germans to win the war!'

A new overflow from the stairs was shouldered in and of a sudden the room was full of men all closing around the pale little group at the back. Edith saw that the tall soldier with the weak chin was still in front. The short dark one had disappeared.

She edged slightly backward, stood close to the open window, through which came a clear breath of cool night air.

Then the room was a riot. She realized that the soldiers were surging forward, glimpsed the fat man swinging a chair over his head—instantly the lights went out, and she felt the push of warm bodies under rough cloth, and her ears were full of shouting and trampling and hard breathing.

A figure flashed by her out of nowhere, tottered, was edged sideways, and of a sudden disappeared helplessly out through the open window with a frightened, fragmentary cry that died staccato on the bosom of the clamour. By the faint light streaming from the building backing on the area Edith had a quick impression that it had been the tall soldier with the weak chin.

Anger rose astonishingly in her. She swung her arms wildly, edged blindly towards the thickest of the scuffling. She heard grunts, curses, the muffled impact of fists.

'Henry!' she called frantically, 'Henry!'

Then, it was minutes later, she felt suddenly that there were other figures in the room. She heard a voice, deep, bullying, authoritative; she saw yellow rays of light sweeping here and there in the fracas. The cries became more scattered. The scuffling increased and then stopped.

Suddenly the lights were on and the room was full of policemen, clubbing left and right. The deep voice boomed out:

'Here now! Here now! Here now!'

And then:

'Quiet down and get out! Here now!'

The room seemed to empty like a wash-bowl. A police-man fast-grappled in the corner released his hold on his soldier antagonist and started him with a shove towards the door. The deep voice continued. Edith perceived now that it came from a bull-necked police captain standing near the door.

'Here now! This is no way! One of your own sojers got shoved out of the back window an' killed hisself!'

'Henry!' called Edith, 'Henry!'

She beat wildly with her fists on the back of the man in front of her; she brushed between two others; fought, shrieked, and beat her way to a very pale figure sitting on the floor close to a desk.

'Henry,' she cried passionately, 'what's the matter? What's the matter? Did they hurt you?'

His eyes were shut. He groaned and then looking up said disgustedly——

'They broke my leg. My God, the fools!'

'Here now!' called the police captain. 'Here now! Here now!'

IX

'Childs', Fifty-ninth Street,' at eight o'clock of any morn-ing differs from its sisters by less than the width of their marble tables or the degree of polish on the frying-pans. You will see there a crowd of poor people with sleep in the corners of their eyes, trying to look straight before them at their food so as not to see the other poor people. But Childs', Fifty-ninth, four hours earlier is quite unlike any Childs' restaurant from Portland, Oregon, to Portland, Maine. Within its pale but sanitary walls one finds a noisy medley of chorus girls, college boys, débutantes, rakes, *filles de joie* —a not unrepresentative mixture of the gayest of Broadway, and even of Fifth Avenue.

In the early morning of May the second it was unusually full. Over the marble-topped tables were bent the excited faces of flappers whose fathers owned individual villages. They were eating buckwheat cakes and scrambled eggs with relish and gusto, an accomplishment that it would have been utterly impossible for them to repeat in the same place four hours later.

Almost the entire crowd were from the Gamma Psi dance at Delmonico's except for several chorus girls from a midnight revue who sat at a side table and wished they'd taken off a little more make-up after the show. Here and there a drab, mouse-like figure, desperately out of place, watched the butterflies with a weary, puzzled curiosity. But the drab figure was the exception. This was the morning after May Day, and celebration was still in the air.

Gus Rose, sober but a little dazed, must be classed as one of the drab figures. How he had got himself from Fortyfourth Street to Fifty-ninth Street after the riot was only a hazy half-memory. He had seen the body of Carrol Key put in an ambulance and driven off, and then he had started up town with two or three soldiers. Somewhere between Forty-fourth Street and Fifty-ninth Street the other soldiers had met some women and disappeared. Rose had wandered to Columbus Circle and chosen the gleaming lights of Childs' to minister to his craving for coffee and doughnuts. He walked in and sat down.

All around him floated airy, inconsequential chatter and high-pitched laughter. At first he failed to understand, but after a puzzled five minutes he realized that this was the aftermath of some gay party. Here and there a restless, hilarious young man wandered fraternally and familiarly between the tables, shaking hands indiscriminately and pausing occasionally for a facetious chat, while excited waiters, bearing cakes and eggs aloft, swore at him silently, and bumped him out of the way. To Rose, seated at the most inconspicuous and least crowded table, the whole scene was a colourful circus of beauty and riotous pleasure.

He became gradually aware, after a few moments, that the couple seated diagonally across from him, with their backs to the crowd, were not the least interesting pair in the room. The man was drunk. He wore a dinner coat with a dishevelled tie and shirt swollen by spillings of water and wine. His eyes, dim and bloodshot, roved unnaturally from side to side. His breath came short between his lips.

'He's been on a spree!' thought Rose.

The woman was almost if not quite sober. She was pretty, with dark eyes and feverish high colour, and she kept her active eyes fixed on her companion with the alertness of a hawk. From time to time she would lean and whisper intently to him, and he would answer by inclining his head heavily or by a particularly ghoulish and repellent wink.

Rose scrutinized them dumbly for some minutes, until the woman gave him a quick, resentful look; then he shifted his gaze to two of the most conspicuously hilarious of the promenaders who were on a protracted circuit of the tables. To his surprise he recognized in one of them the young man by whom he had been so ludicrously entertained at Delmonico's. This started him thinking of Key with a vague sentimentality, not unmixed with awe. Key was dead. He had fallen thirty-five feet and split his skull like a cracked coconut.

'He was a darn good guy,' thought Rose mournfully. 'He was a darn good guy, o'right. That was awful hard luck about him.'

The two promenaders approached and started down between Rose's table and the next, addressing friends and strangers alike with jovial familiarity. Suddenly Rose saw the fair-haired one with the prominent teeth stop, look unsteadily at the man and girl opposite, and then begin to move his head disapprovingly from side to side.

The man with the blood-shot eyes looked up.

'Gordy,' said the promenader with the prominent teeth, 'Gordy.'

'Hello,' said the man with the stained shirt thickly.

Prominent Teeth shook his finger pessimistically at the pair, giving the woman a glance of aloof condemnation.

'What'd I tell you Gordy?'

Gordon stirred in his seat.

'Go to hell!' he said.

Dean continued to stand there shaking his finger. The woman began to get angry.

'You go away!' she cried fiercely. 'You're drunk, that's what you are!'

'So's he,' suggested Dean, staying the motion of his finger and pointing it at Gordon.

Peter Himmel ambled up, owlish now and oratorically inclined.

'Here now,' he began, as if called upon to deal with some petty dispute between children. 'Wha's all trouble?'

'You take your friend away,' said Jewel tartly. 'He's bothering us.'

'What's 'at?'

'You heard me!' she said shrilly. 'I said to take your drunken friend away.'

Her rising voice rang out above the clatter of the restaurant and a waiter came hurrying up.

'You gotta be more quiet!'

'That fella's drunk,' she cried. 'He's insulting us.'

'Ah-ha, Gordy,' persisted the accused. 'What'd I tell you.' He turned to the waiter. 'Gordy an' I friends. Been tryin' help him, haven't I, Gordy?'

Gordy looked up.

'Help me? Hell, no!'

Jewel rose suddenly, and seizing Gordon's arm assisted him to his feet.

'Come on, Gordy!' she said, leaning towards him and speaking in a half whisper. 'Let's get out of here. This fella's got a mean drunk on.'

Gordon allowed himself to be urged to his feet and started towards the door. Jewel turned for a second and addressed the provoker of their flight.

'I know all about you!' she said fiercely. 'Nice friend, you are, I'll say. He told me about you.'

Then she seized Gordon's arm, and together they made

their way through the curious crowd, paid their check, and went out.

'You'll have to sit down,' said the waiter to Peter after they had gone.

'What's 'at? Sit down?'

'Yes—or get out.'

Peter turned to Dean.

'Come on,' he suggested. 'Let's beat up this waiter.'

'All right.'

They advanced towards him, their faces grown stern. The waiter retreated.

Peter suddenly reached over to a plate on the table beside him and picking up a handful of hash tossed it into the air. It descended as a languid parabola in snowflake effect on the heads of those near by.

'Hey! Ease up!'

'Put him out!'

'Sit down, Peter!'

'Cut out that stuff!'

Peter laughed and bowed.

'Thank you for your kind applause, ladies and gents. If someone will lend me some more hash and a tall hat we will go on with the act.'

The bouncer hustled up.

'You've gotta get out!' he said to Peter.

'Hell, no!'

'He's my friend!' put in Dean indignantly.

A crowd of waiters were gathering. 'Put him out!'

'Better go, Peter.'

There was a short struggle and the two were edged and pushed towards the door.

'I got a hat and a coat here!' cried Peter.

'Well, go get 'em and be spry about it!'

The bouncer released his hold on Peter, who, adopting a ludicrous air of extreme cunning, rushed immediately around to the other table, where he burst into derisive laughter and thumbed his nose at the exasperated waiters.

'Think I just better wait a l'il' longer,' he announced.

The chase began. Four waiters were sent around one way and four another. Dean caught hold of two of them by the coat, and another struggle took place before the pursuit of Peter could be resumed; he was finally pinioned after over-turning a sugar-bowl and several cups of coffee. A fresh argument ensued at the cashier's desk, where Peter attempted to buy another dish of hash to take with him and throw at policemen.

But the commotion upon his exit proper was dwarfed by another phenomenon which drew admiring glances and a prolonged involuntary ' Oh-h-h!' from every person in the restaurant.

The great plate-glass front had turned to a deep creamy blue, the colour of a Maxfield Parrish moonlight—a blue that seemed to press close upon the pane as if to crowd its way into the restaurant. Dawn had come up in Columbus Circle, magical, breathless dawn, silhouetting the great statue of the immortal Christopher, and mingling in a curious and uncanny manner with the fading yellow electric light inside.

X

Mr In and Mr Out are not listed by the census-taker. You will search for them in vain through the social register or the births, marriages, and deaths, or the grocer's credit list. Oblivion has swallowed them and the testimony that they ever existed at all is vague and shadowy, and inadmis-sible in a court of law. Yet I have it upon the best authority that for a brief space Mr In and Mr Out lived, breathed, answered to their names and radiated vivid personalities of their own.

During the brief span of their lives they walked in their native garments down the great highway of a great nation; were laughed at, sworn at, chased, and fled from. Then they passed and were heard of no more.

They were already taking form dimly, when a taxicab with

the top open breezed down Broadway in the faintest glim-
mer of May dawn. In this car sat the souls of Mr In and
Mr Out discussing with amazement the blue light that had
so precipitately coloured the sky behind the statue of
Christopher Columbus, discussing with bewilderment the
old, grey faces of the early risers which skimmed palely
along the street like blown bits of paper on a grey lake. They
were agreed on all things, from the absurdity of the bouncer
in Childs' to the absurdity of the business of life. They were
dizzy with the extreme maudlin happiness that the morning
had awakened in their glowing souls. Indeed, so fresh and
vigorous was their pleasure in living that they felt it should
be expressed by loud cries.

'Ye-ow-ow!' hooted Peter, making a megaphone with
his hands—and Dean joined in with a call that, though
equally significant and symbolic, derived its resonance from
its very inarticulateness.

'Yo-ho! Yea! Yoho! Yo-buba!'

Fifty-third Street was a bus with a dark, bobbed-hair
beauty atop; Fifty-second was a street cleaner who dodged,
escaped, and sent up a yell of, 'Look where you're aimin'!'
in a pained and grieved voice. At Fiftieth Street a group of
men on a very white sidewalk in front of a very white building turned to stare after them, and shouted:

'Some party, boys!'

At Forty-ninth Street Peter turned to Dean. 'Beautiful
morning,' he said gravely, squinting up his owlish eyes.

'Probably is.'

'Go get some breakfast, hey?'

Dean agreed—with additions.

'Breakfast and liquor.'

'Breakfast and liquor,' repeated Peter, and they looked
at each other, nodding. 'That's logical.'

Then they both burst into loud laughter.

'Breakfast and liquor! Oh, gosh!'

'No such thing,' announced Peter.

'Don't serve it? Ne'mind. We force 'em serve it. Bring
pressure bear.'

'Bring logic bear.'

The taxi cut suddenly off Broadway, sailed along a cross street, and stopped in front of a heavy tomb-like building in Fifth Avenue.

'What's idea?'

The taxi-driver informed them that this was Delmonico's.

This was somewhat puzzling. They were forced to devote several minutes to intense concentration, for if such an order had been given there must have been a reason for it.

'Somep'm 'bouta coat,' suggested the taxi-man.

That was it. Peter's overcoat and hat. He had left them at Delmonico's. Having decided this, they disembarked from the taxi and strolled towards the entrance arm in arm.

'Hey!' said the taxi-driver.

'Huh?'

'You better pay me.'

They shook their heads in shocked negation.

'Later, not now—we give orders, you wait.'

The taxi-driver objected; he wanted his money now. With the scornful condescension of men exercising tremendous self-control they paid him.

Inside Peter groped in vain through a dim, deserted check-room in search of his coat and derby.

'Gone, I guess. Somebody stole it.'

'Some Sheff student.'

'All probability.'

'Never mind,' said Dean, nobly. 'I'll leave mine here too —then we'll both be dressed the same.'

He removed his overcoat and hat and was hanging them up when his roving glance was caught and held magnetically by two large squares of cardboard tacked to the two coat-room doors. The one on the left-hand bore the word 'In' in big black letters, and the one on the right-hand door flaunted the equally emphatic word 'Out.'

'Look!' he exclaimed happily——

Peter's eyes followed his pointing finger.

'What?'

'Look at the signs. Let's take 'em.'

'Good idea.'

'Probably pair very rare an' valuable signs. Probably come in handy.'

Peter removed the left-hand sign from the door and endeavoured to conceal it about his person. The sign being of considerable proportions, this was a matter of some difficulty. An idea flung itself at him, and with an air of dignified mystery he turned his back. After an instant he wheeled dramatically around, and stretching out his arms displayed himself to the admiring Dean. He had inserted the sign in his vest, completely covering his shirt front. In effect, the word 'In' had been painted upon his shirt in large black letters.

'Yoho!' cheered Dean. 'Mister In.'

He inserted his own sign in like manner.

'Mister Out!' he announced triumphantly. 'Mr In meet Mr Out.'

They advanced and shook hands. Again laughter overcame them and they rocked in a shaken spasm of mirth.

'Yoho!'

'We probably get a flock of breakfast.'

'We'll go—go to the Commodore.'

Arm in arm they sallied out the door, and turning east in Forty-fourth Street set out for the Commodore.

As they came out a short dark soldier, very pale and tired, who had been wandering listlessly along the sidewalk, turned to look at them.

He started over as though to address them, but as they immediately bent on him glances of withering unrecognition, he waited until they had started unsteadily down the street, and then followed at about forty paces, chuckling to himself and saying, 'Oh, boy!' over and over under his breath, in delighted, anticipatory tones.

Mr In and Mr Out were meanwhile exchanging pleasantries concerning their future plans.

'We want liquor; we want breakfast. Neither without the other. One and indivisible.'

'We want both 'em!'

'Both 'em!'

It was quite light now, and passers-by began to bend curious eyes on the pair. Obviously they were engaged in a discussion, which afforded each of them intense amusement, for occasionally a fit of laughter would seize upon them so violently that, still with their arms interlocked, they would bend nearly double.

Reaching the Commodore, they exchanged a few spicy epigrams with the sleepy-eyed doorman, navigated the revolving door with some difficulty, and then made their way through a thinly populated but startled lobby to the dining-room, where a puzzled waiter showed them an obscure table in a corner. They studied the bill of fare help-lessly, telling over the items to each other in puzzled mumbles.

'Don't see any liquor here,' said Peter reproachfully.

The waiter became audible but unintelligible.

'Repeat,' continued Peter, with patient tolerance, 'that there seems to be unexplained and quite distasteful lack of liquor upon bill of fare.'

'Here!' said Dean confidently, 'let me handle him.' He turned to the waiter—'Bring us—bring us—' he scanned the bill of fare anxiously. 'Bring us a quart of champagne and a—a—probably ham sandwich.'

The waiter looked doubtful.

'Bring it!' roared Mr In and Mr Out in chorus.

The waiter coughed and disappeared. There was a short wait during which they were subjected without their know-ledge to a careful scrutiny by the head waiter. Then the champagne arrived, and at the sight of it Mr In and Mr Out became jubilant.

'Imagine their objecting to us having champagne for breakfast—jus' imagine.'

They both concentrated upon the vision of such an awe-some possibility, but the feat was too much for them. It was impossible for their joint imaginations to conjure up a world where anyone might object to anyone else having

7+s.f.

champagne for breakfast. The waiter drew the cork with an enormous *pop*—and their glasses immediately foamed with pale yellow froth.

'Here's health, Mr In.'

'Here's the same to you, Mr Out.'

The waiter withdrew; the minutes passed; the champagne became low in the bottle.

'It's—it's mortifying,' said Dean suddenly.

'Wha's mortifying?'

'The idea their objecting us having champagne breakfast.'

'Mortifying?' Peter considered. 'Yes, tha's word—mortifying.'

Again they collapsed into laughter, howled, swayed, rocked back and forth in their chairs, repeating the word 'mortifying' over and over to each other—each repetition seeming to make it only more brilliantly absurd.

After a few more gorgeous minutes they decided on another quart. Their anxious waiter consulted his immediate superior, and this discreet person gave implicit instructions that no more champagne should be served. Their check was brought.

Five minutes later, arm in arm, they left the Commodore and made their way through a curious, staring crowd along Forty-second Street, and up Vanderbilt Avenue to the Biltmore. There, with sudden cunning, they rose to the occasion and traversed the lobby, walking fast and standing unnaturally erect.

Once in the dining-room they repeated their performance. They were torn between intermittent convulsive laughter and sudden spasmodic discussions of politics, college, and the sunny state of their dispositions. Their watches told them it was now nine o'clock, and a dim idea was born in them that they were on a memorable party, something that they would remember always. They lingered over the second bottle. Either of them had only to mention the word 'mortifying' to send them both into riotous gasps. The dining-room was whirring and shifting now; a curious lightness permeated and rarefied the heavy air.

They paid their check and walked out into the lobby.

It was at this moment that the exterior doors revolved for the thousandth time that morning, and admitted into the lobby a very pale young beauty with dark circles under her eyes, attired in a much-rumpled evening dress. She was accompanied by a plain stout man, obviously not an appropriate escort.

At the top of the stairs this couple encountered Mr In and Mr Out.

'Edith,' began Mr In, stepping towards her hilariously and making a sweeping bow, 'darling, good morning.'

The stout man glanced questioningly at Edith, as if merely asking her permission to throw this man summarily out of the way.

''Scuse familiarity,' added Peter, as an afterthought. 'Edith, good-morning.'

He seized Dean's elbow and impelled him into the foreground.

'Meet Mr Out, Edith, my bes' frien'. Inseparable. Mr In and Mr Out.'

Mr Out advanced and bowed; in fact, he advanced so far and bowed so low that he tipped slightly forward and only kept his balance by placing a hand lightly on Edith's shoulder.

'I'm Mr Out, Edith,' he mumbled pleasantly, 'S'misterin Misterout.'

''Smisterinanout,' said Peter proudly.

But Edith stared straight by them, her eyes fixed on some infinite speck in the gallery above her. She nodded slightly to the stout man, who advanced bull-like and with a sturdy brisk gesture pushed Mr In and Mr Out to either side. Through this alley he and Edith walked.

But ten paces farther on Edith stopped again—stopped and pointed to a short, dark soldier who was eyeing the crowd in general, and the tableau of Mr In and Mr Out in particular, with a sort of puzzled, spell-bound awe.

'There,' cried Edith. 'See there!'

Her voice rose, became somewhat shrill. Her pointing finger shook slightly.

'There's the soldier who broke my brother's leg.'

There were a dozen exclamations; a man in a cutaway coat left his place near the desk and advanced alertly; the stout person made a sort of lightning-like spring towards the short, dark soldier, and then the lobby closed around the little group and blotted them from the sight of Mr In and Mr Out.

But to Mr In and Mr Out this event was merely a particoloured iridescent segment of a whirring, spinning world.

They heard loud voices; they saw the stout man spring; the picture suddenly blurred.

Then they were in an elevator bound skyward.

'What floor, please?' said the elevator man.

'Any floor,' said Mr In.

'Top floor,' said Mr Out.

'This is the top floor,' said the elevator man.

'Have another floor put on,' said Mr Out.

'Higher,' said Mr In.

'Heaven,' said Mr Out.

XI

In a bedroom of a small hotel just off Sixth Avenue Gordon Sterrett awoke with a pain in the back of his head and a sick throbbing in all his veins. He looked at the dusky grey shadows in the corners of the room and at a raw place on a large leather chair in the corner where it had long been in use. He saw clothes, dishevelled, rumpled clothes on the floor and he smelt stale cigarette smoke and stale liquor. The windows were tight shut. Outside the bright sunlight had thrown a dust-filled beam across the sill—a beam broken by the head of the wide wooden bed in which he had slept. He lay very quiet—comatose, drugged, his eyes wide, his mind clicking wildly like an unoiled machine.

It must have been thirty seconds after he perceived the

sunbeam with the dust on it and the rip on the large leather chair that he had the sense of life close beside him, and it was another thirty seconds after that before he realized he was irrevocably married to Jewel Hudson.

He went out half an hour later and bought a revolver at a sporting goods store. Then he took a taxi to the room where he had been living on East Twenty-seventh Street, and, leaning across the table that held his drawing materials, fired a cartridge into his head just behind the temple.

THE JELLY-BEAN
[1920]

JIM POWELL was a Jelly-bean. Much as I desire to make him an appealing character, I feel that it would be unscrupulous to deceive you on that point. He was a bred-in-the-bone, dyed-in-the-wool, ninety-nine and three-quarters per cent Jelly-bean and he grew lazily all during Jelly-bean season, which is every season, down in the land of the Jelly-beans well below the Mason-Dixon line.

Now if you call a Memphis man a Jelly-bean he will quite possibly pull a long sinewy rope from his hip pocket and hang you to a convenient telegraph pole. If you call a New Orleans man a Jelly-bean he will probably grin and ask you who is taking your girl to the Mardi Gras ball. The particular Jelly-bean patch which produced the protagonist of this history lies somewhere between the two— a little city of forty thousand that has dozed sleepily for forty thousand years in southern Georgia, occasionally stirring in its slumbers and muttering something about a war that took place sometime, somewhere, and that everyone else has forgotten long ago.

Jim was a Jelly-bean. I write that again because it has such a pleasant sound—rather like the beginning of a fairy story—as if Jim were nice. It somehow gives me a picture of him with a round, appetizing face and all sorts of leaves and vegetables growing out of his cap. But Jim was long and thin and bent at the waist from stooping over pool-tables, and he was what might have been known in the indiscriminating North as a corner loafer. 'Jelly-bean' is the name throughout the undissolved Confederacy for one who spends his life conjugating the verb to idle in the first person singular—I am idling, I have idled, I will idle.

Jim was born in a white house on a green corner. It had four weather-beaten pillars in front and a great amount of lattice-work in the rear that made a cheerful criss-cross background for a flowery sun-drenched lawn. Originally the dwellers in the white house had owned the ground next door and next door to that and next door to that, but this had been so long ago that even Jim's father scarcely remembered it. He had, in fact, thought it a matter of so little moment that when he was dying from a pistol wound got in a brawl he neglected even to tell little Jim, who was five years old and miserably frightened. The white house became a boarding-house run by a tight-lipped lady from Macon, whom Jim called Aunt Mamie and detested with all his soul.

He became fifteen, went to high school, wore his hair in black snarls, and was afraid of girls. He hated his home where four women and one old man prolonged an interminable chatter from summer to summer about what lots the Powell place had originally included and what sort of flowers would be out next. Sometimes the parents of little girls in town, remembering Jim's mother and fancying a resemblance in the dark eyes and hair, invited him to parties, but parties made him shy and he much preferred sitting on a disconnected axle in Tilly's Garage, rolling the bones or exploring his mouth endlessly with a long straw. For pocket money, he picked up odd jobs, and it was due to this that he stopped going to parties. At his third party little Marjorie Haight had whispered indiscreetly and within hearing distance that he was a boy who brought the groceries sometimes. So instead of the two-step and polka, Jim had learned to throw any number he desired on the dice and had listened to spicy tales of all the shootings that had occurred in the surrounding country during the past fifty years.

He became eighteen. The war broke out and he enlisted as a gob and polished brass in the Charleston Navy-yard for a year. Then, by way of variety, he went North and polished brass in the Brooklyn Navy-yard for a year.

When the war was over he came home. He was twenty-one, his trousers were too short and too tight. His buttoned shoes were long and narrow. His tie was an alarming conspiracy of purple and pink marvellously scrolled, and over it were two blue eyes faded like a piece of very good old cloth long exposed to the sun.

In the twilight of one April evening when a soft grey had drifted down along the cottonfields and over the sultry town, he was a vague figure leaning against a board fence, whistling and gazing at the moon's rim above the lights of Jackson Street. His mind was working persistently on a problem that had held his attention for an hour. The Jelly-bean had been invited to a party.

Back in the days when all the boys had detested all the girls, Clark Darrow and Jim had sat side by side in school. But, while Jim's social aspirations had died in the oily air of the garage, Clark had alternately fallen in and out of love, gone to college, taken to drink, given it up, and, in short, become one of the best beaux of the town. Nevertheless Clark and Jim had retained a friendship that, though casual, was perfectly definite. That afternoon Clark's ancient Ford had slowed up beside Jim, who was on the sidewalk and, out of a clear sky, Clark had invited him to a party at the country club. The impulse that made him do this was no stranger than the impulse which made Jim accept. The latter was probably an unconscious ennui, a half-frightened sense of adventure. And now Jim was soberly thinking it over.

He began to sing, drumming his long foot idly on a stone block in the sidewalk till it wobbled up and down in time to the low throaty tune:

> 'One mile from Home in Jelly-bean town,
> Lives Jeanne, the Jelly-bean Queen.
> She loves her dice and treats 'em nice;
> No dice would treat her mean.'

He broke off and agitated the sidewalk to a bumpy gallop.

'Doggone!' he muttered, half aloud.

They would all be there—the old crowd, the crowd to which, by right of the white house, sold long since, and the portrait of the officer in grey over the mantel, Jim should have belonged. But that crowd had grown up to-gether into a tight little set as gradually as the girls' dresses had lengthened inch by inch, as definitely as the boys' trousers had dropped suddenly to their ankles. And to that society of first names and dead puppy-loves Jim was an outsider—a running mate of poor whites. Most of the men knew him, condescendingly; he tipped his hat to three or four girls. That was all.

When the dusk had thickened into a blue setting for the moon, he walked through the hot, pleasantly pungent town to Jackson Street. The stores were closing and the last shoppers were drifting homeward, as if borne on the dreamy revolution of a slow merry-go-round. A street fair farther down made a brilliant alley of vari-coloured booths and contributed a blend of music to the night—an oriental dance on a calliope, a melancholy bugle in front of a freak show, a cheerful rendition of 'Back Home in Tennessee' on a hand-organ.

The Jelly-bean stopped in a store and bought a collar. Then he sauntered along towards Soda Sam's, where he found the usual three or four cars of a summer evening parked in front and the little darkies running back and forth with sundaes and lemonades.

'Hello, Jim.'

It was a voice at his elbow—Joe Ewing sitting in an automobile with Marylyn Wade. Nancy Lamar and a strange man were in the back seat.

The Jelly-bean tipped his hat quickly.

'Hi, Joe——' then, after an almost imperceptible pause —'How y' all?'

Passing, he ambled on towards the garage where he had

7*

a room uptairs. His 'How y' all' had been said to Nancy
Lamar, to whom he had not spoken in fifteen years.

Nancy had a mouth like a remembered kiss and shadowy
eyes and blue-black hair inherited from her mother, who
had been born in Budapest. Jim passed her often in the
street, walking small-boy fashion with her hands in her
pockets, and he knew that with her inseparable Sally
Carrol Happer she had left a trail of broken hearts from
Atlanta to New Orleans.

For a few fleeting moments Jim wished he could dance.
Then he laughed and as he reached his door began to
sing softly to himself:

> 'Her Jelly Roll can twist your soul,
> Her eyes are big and brown,
> She's the Queen of the Queens of the Jelly-beans—
> My Jeanne of Jelly-bean Town.'

II

At nine-thirty Jim and Clark met in front of Soda Sam's
and started for the Country Club in Clark's Ford.

'Jim,' asked Clark casually, as they rattled through the
jasmine-scented night, 'how do you keep alive?'

The Jelly-bean paused, considered.

'Well,' he said finally, 'I got a room over Tilly's garage.
I help him some with the cars in the afternoon an' he gives
it to me free. Sometimes I drive one of his taxis and pick
up a little thataway. I get fed up doin' that regular though.'

'That all?'

'Well, when there's a lot of work I help him by the day
—Saturdays usually—and then there's one main source of
revenue I don't generally mention. Maybe you don't recol-
lect I'm about the champion crap-shooter of this town.
They make me shoot from a cup now because once I
get the feel of a pair of dice they just roll for me.'

Clark grinned appreciatively.

'I never could learn to set 'em so's they'd do what I
wanted. Wish you'd shoot with Nancy Lamar some day

and take all her money away from her. She will roll 'em with the boys and she loses more than her daddy can afford to give her. I happen to know she sold a good ring last month to pay a debt.'

The Jelly-bean was noncommittal.

'The white house on Elm Street still belong to you?'

Jim shook his head.

'Sold. Got a pretty good price, seein' it wasn't in a good part of town no more. Lawyer told me to put it into Liberty bonds. But Aunt Mamie got so she didn't have no sense, so it takes all the interest to keep her up at Great Farms Sanatorium.'

'Hm.'

'I got an old uncle up-state an' I reckon I kin go up there if ever I get sure enough pore. Nice farm, but not enough niggers around to work it. He's asked me to come up and help him, but I don't guess I'd take much to it. Too doggone lonesome——' He broke off suddenly. 'Clark, I want to tell you I'm much obliged to you for askin' me out, but I'd be a lot happier if you'd just stop the car right here an' let me walk back into town.'

'Shucks!' Clark grunted. 'Do you good to step out. You don't have to dance—just get out there on the floor and shake.'

'Hold on,' exclaimed Jim uneasily, 'Don't you go leadin' me up to any girls and leavin' me there so I'll have to dance with 'em.'

Clark laughed.

' 'Cause,' continued Jim desperately, 'without you swear you won't do that I'm agoin' to get out right here an' my good legs goin' carry me back to Jackson Street.'

They agreed after some argument that Jim, unmolested by females, was to view the spectacle from a secluded settee in the corner, where Clark would join him whenever he wasn't dancing.

So ten o'clock found the Jelly-bean with his legs crossed and his arms conservatively folded, trying to look casually at home and politely uninterested in the dancers. At heart he was torn between overwhelming self-consciousness and an intense curiosity as to all that went on around him. He saw the girls emerge one by one from the dressing-room, stretching and pluming themselves like bright birds, smiling over their powdered shoulders at the chaperones, casting a quick glance around to take in the room and, simultaneously, the room's reaction to their entrance— and then, again like birds, alighting and nestling in the sober arms of their waiting escorts. Sally Carrol Happer, blonde and lazy-eyed, appeared clad in her favourite pink and blinking like an awakened rose. Marjorie Haight, Marylyn Wade, Harriet Cary, all the girls he had seen loitering down Jackson Street by noon, now, curled and brilliantined and delicately tinted for the overhead lights, were miraculously strange Dresden figures of pink and blue and red and gold, fresh from the shop and not yet fully dried.

He had been there half an hour, totally uncheered by Clark's jovial visits, which were each one accompanied by a 'Hello, old boy, how you making out?' and a slap at his knee. A dozen males had spoken to him or stopped for a moment beside him, but he knew that they were each one surprised at finding him there and fancied that one or two were even slightly resentful. But at half past ten his embarrassment suddenly left him and a pull of breathless interest took him completely out of himself—Nancy Lamar had come out of the dressing-room.

She was dressed in yellow organdie, a costume of a hundred cool corners, with three tiers of ruffles and a big bow in back until she shed black and yellow around her in a sort of phosphorescent lustre. The Jelly-bean's eyes opened wide and a lump arose in his throat. For a minute she stood beside the door until her partner hurried up. Jim recognized him as the stranger who had been with her in Joe Ewing's car that afternoon. He saw her arms set akimbo and say something in a low voice, and laugh. The man laughed too and Jim experienced the quick pang of a weird new kind of pain. Some ray had passed between the pair, a shaft of beauty from that sun that had warmed him a moment since. The Jelly-bean felt suddenly like a weed in a shadow.

A minute later Clark approached him, bright-eyed and glowing.

'Hi, old man,' he cried with some lack of originality. 'How you making out?'

Jim replied that he was making out as well as could be expected.

'You come along with me,' commanded Clark. 'I've got something that'll put an edge on the evening.'

Jim followed him awkwardly across the floor and up the stairs to the locker-room where Clark produced a flask of nameless yellow liquid.

'Good old corn.'

Ginger ale arrived on a tray. Such potent nectar as 'good old corn' needed some disguise beyond seltzer.

'Say, boy,' exclaimed Clark breathlessly, 'doesn't Nancy Lamar look beautiful?'

Jim nodded.

'Mighty beautiful,' he agreed.

'She's all dolled up to a fare-you-well to-night,' continued Clark. 'Notice that fellow she's with?'

'Big fella? White pants?'

'Yeah. Well, that's Ogden Merritt from Savannah. Old man Merritt makes the Merritt safety razors. This fella's crazy about her. Been chasing after her all year.'

'She's a wild baby,' continued Clark, 'but I like her. So does everybody. But she sure does do crazy stunts. She usually gets out alive, but she's got scars all over her reputation from one thing or another she's done.'

'That so?' Jim passed over his glass. 'That's good corn.'

'Not so bad. Oh, she's a wild one. Shoots craps, say boy! And she do like her high-balls. Promised I'd give her one later on.'

'She in love with this—Merritt?'

'Damned if I know. Seems like all the best girls around here marry fellas and go off somewhere.'

He poured himself one more drink and carefully corked the bottle.

'Listen, Jim, I got to go dance and I'd be much obliged if you just stick this corn right on your hip as long as you're not dancing. If a man notices I've had a drink he'll come up and ask me and before I know it it's all gone and somebody else is having my good time.'

So Nancy Lamar was going to marry. This toast of a town was to become the private property of an individual in white trousers—and all because white trousers' father had made a better razor than his neighbour. As they descended the stairs Jim found the idea inexplicably depressing. For the first time in his life he felt a vague and romantic yearning. A picture of her began to form in his imagination—Nancy walking boy-like and debonnaire along the street, taking an orange as tithe from a worshipful fruit dealer, charging a dope on a mythical account at Soda Sam's, assembling a convoy of beaux and then driving off in triumphal state for an afternoon of splashing and singing.

The Jelly-bean walked out on the porch to a deserted corner, dark between the moon on the lawn and the single lighted door of the ballroom. There he found a chair and, lighting a cigarette, drifted into the thoughtless reverie that was his usual mood. Yet now it was a reverie made sensuous by the night and by the hot smell of damp powder puffs, tucked in the fronts of low dresses and distilling a thousand rich scents to float out through the open door. The music itself, blurred by a loud trombone, became hot and shadowy, a languorous overtone to the scraping of many shoes and slippers.

Suddenly the square of yellow light that fell through the door was obscured by a dark figure. A girl had come out of the dressing-room and was standing on the porch not more than ten feet away. Jim heard a low-breathed 'doggone' and then she turned and saw him. It was Nancy Lamar.

Jim rose to his feet.

'Howdy?'

'Hello—' She paused, hesitated and then approached. 'Oh, it's—Jim Powell.'

He bowed slightly, tried to think of a casual remark.

'Do you suppose,' she began quickly, 'I mean—do you know anything about gum?'

'What?'

'I've got gum on my shoe. Some utter ass left his or her gum on the floor and of course I stepped in it.'

Jim blushed, inappropriately.

'Do you know how to get it off?' she demanded petulantly. 'I've tried a knife. I've tried every damn thing in the dressing-room. I've tried soap and water—and even perfume and I've ruined my powder-puff trying to make it stick to that.'

Jim considered the question in some agitation.

'Why—I think maybe gasoline——'

The words had scarcely left his lips when she grasped his hand and pulled him at a run off the low veranda, over a flower bed and at a gallop towards a group of cars parked in the moonlight by the first hole of the golf course.

'Turn on the gasoline,' she commanded breathlessly.

'What?'

'For the gum of course. I've got to get it off. I can't dance with gum on.'

Obediently Jim turned to the cars and began inspecting them with a view to obtaining the desired solvent. Had she demanded a cylinder he would have done his best to wrench one out.

'Here,' he said after a moment's search. 'Here's one that's easy. Got a handkerchief?'

'It's up-stairs wet. I used it for the soap and water.'

Jim laboriously explored his pockets.

'Don't believe I've got one either.'

'Doggone it! Well, we can turn it on and let it run on the ground.'

He turned the spout; a dripping began.

'More!'

He turned it on fuller. The dripping became a flow and formed an oily pool that glistened brightly, reflecting a dozen tremulous moons on its quivering bosom.

'Ah,' she sighed contentedly, 'let it all out. The only thing to do is to wade in it.'

In desperation he turned on the tap full and the pool suddenly widened sending tiny rivers and trickles in all directions.

'That's fine. That's something like.'

Raising her skirts she stepped gracefully in.

'I know this'll take it off,' she murmured.

Jim smiled.

'There's lots more cars.'

She stepped daintily out of the gasoline and began scraping her slippers, side and bottom, on the running-board of the automobile. The Jelly-bean contained himself no longer. He bent double with explosive laughter and after a second she joined in.

'You're here with Clark Darrow, aren't you?' she asked as they walked back towards the veranda.

'Yes.'

'You know where he is now?'

'Out dancin', I reckon.'

'The deuce. He promised me a highball.'

'Well,' said Jim, 'I guess that'll be all right. I got his bottle right here in my pocket.'

She smiled at him radiantly.

'I guess maybe you'll need ginger ale though,' he added.

'Not me. Just the bottle.'

'Sure enough?'

She laughed scornfully.

'Try me. I can drink anything any man can. Let's sit down.'

She perched herself on the side of a table and he dropped into one of the wicker chairs beside her. Taking out the cork she held the flask to her lips and took a long drink. He watched her fascinated.

'Like it?'

She shook her head breathlessly.

'No, but I like the way it makes me feel. I think most people are that way.'

Jim agreed.

'My daddy liked it too well. It got him.'

'American men,' said Nancy gravely, 'don't know how to drink.'

'What?' Jim was startled.

'In fact,' she went on carelessly, 'they don't know how to do anything very well. The one thing I regret in my life is that I wasn't born in England.'

'In England?'

'Yes. It's the one regret of my life that I wasn't.'

'Do you like it over there.'

'Yes. Immensely. I've never been there in person, but I've met a lot of Englishmen who were over here in the army, Oxford and Cambridge men—you know, that's like Sewanee and University of Georgia are here—and of course I've read a lot of English novels.'

Jim was interested, amazed.

'D' you ever hear of Lady Diana Manners?' she asked earnestly.

No, Jim had not.

'Well, she's what I'd like to be. Dark, you know, like me, and wild as sin. She's the girl who rode her horse up the steps of some cathedral or church or something and all the novelists made their heroines do it afterwards.'

Jim nodded politely. He was out of his depths.

'Pass the bottle,' suggested Nancy. 'I'm going to take another little one. A little drink wouldn't hurt a baby.'

'You see,' she continued, again breathless after a draught. 'People over there have style. Nobody has style here. I mean the boys here aren't really worth dressing up for or doing sensational things for. Don't you know?'

'I suppose so—I mean I suppose not,' murmured Jim.

'And I'd like to do 'em an' all. I'm really the only girl in town that has style.'

She stretched out her arms and yawned pleasantly.

'Pretty evening.'

'Sure is,' agreed Jim.

'Like to have boat,' she suggested dreamily. 'Like to sail out on a silver lake, say the Thames for instance. Have champagne and caviare sandwiches along. Have about eight people. And one of the men would jump overboard to amuse the party and get drowned like a man did with Lady Diana Manners once.'

'Did he do it to please her?'

'Didn't mean drown himself to please her. He just meant to jump overboard and make everybody laugh.'

'I reckin they just died laughin' when he drowned.'

'Oh, I suppose they laughed a little,' she admitted. 'I imagine she did, anyway. She's pretty hard, I guess—like I am.'

'You hard?'

'Like nails.' She yawned again and added, 'Give me a little more from that bottle.'

Jim hesitated but she held out her hand defiantly.

'Don't treat me like a girl,' she warned him. 'I'm not like any girl *you* ever saw.' She considered. 'Still, perhaps you're right. You got—you got old head on young shoulders.'

She jumped to her feet and moved towards the door. The Jelly-bean rose also.

'Good-bye,' she said politely, 'good-bye. Thanks, Jelly-bean.'

Then she stepped inside and left him wide-eyed upon the porch.

III

At twelve o'clock a procession of cloaks issued single file from the women's dressing-room and, each one pairing with a coated beau like dancers meeting in a cotillion figure, drifted through the door with sleepy happy laughter—through the door into the dark where autos backed and snorted and parties called to one another and gathered around the water-cooler.

Jim, sitting in his corner, rose to look for Clark. They had met at eleven; then Clark had gone in to dance. So, seeking him, Jim wandered into the soft-drink stand that had once been a bar. The room was deserted except for a sleepy Negro dozing behind the counter and two boys lazily fingering a pair of dice at one of the tables. Jim was about to leave when he saw Clark coming in. At the same moment Clark looked up.

'Hi, Jim!' he commanded. 'C'mon over, and help us with this bottle. I guess there's not much left, but there's one all around.'

Nancy, the man from Savannah, Marylyn Wade, and Joe Ewing were lolling and laughing in the doorway. Nancy caught Jim's eye and winked at him humorously.

They drifted over to a table and arranging themselves around it waited for the waiter to bring ginger ale. Jim, faintly ill at ease, turned his eyes on Nancy, who had drifted into a nickel crap game with the two boys at the next table.

'Bring them over here,' suggested Clark.

Joe looked around.

'We don't want to draw a crowd. It's against club rules.'

'Nobody's around,' insisted Clark, 'except Mr. Taylor. He's walking up and down like a wild man trying to find out who let all the gasoline out of his car.'

There was a general laugh.

'I bet a million Nancy got something on her shoe again. You can't park when she's around.'

'O Nancy, Mr Taylor's looking for you!'

Nancy's cheeks were glowing with excitement over the game. 'I haven't seen his silly little flivver in two weeks.'

Jim felt a sudden silence. He turned and saw an individual of uncertain age standing in the doorway.

Clark's voice punctuated the embarrassment.

'Won't you join us, Mr Taylor?'

'Thanks.'

Mr Taylor spread his unwelcome presence over a chair. 'Have to, I guess. I'm waiting till they dig me up some gasoline. Somebody got funny with my car.'

His eyes narrowed and he looked quickly from one to the other. Jim wondered what he had heard from the doorway—tried to remember what had been said.

'I'm right to-night,' Nancy sang out, 'and my four bits is in the ring.'

'Faded!' snapped Taylor suddenly.

'Why, Mr Taylor, I didn't know you shot craps!' Nancy was overjoyed to find that he had seated himself and instantly covered her bet. They had openly disliked each other since the night she had definitely discouraged a series of rather pointed advances.

'All right, babies, do it for your mamma. Just one little seven.' Nancy was *cooing* to the dice. She rattled them with a brave underhand flourish, and rolled them out on the table.

'Ah-h! I suspected it. And now again with the dollar up.'

Five passes to her credit found Taylor a bad loser. She was making it personal, and after each success Jim watched triumph flutter across her face. She was doubling with each throw—such luck could scarcely last.

'Better go easy,' he cautioned her timidly.

'Ah, but watch this one,' she whispered. It was eight on the dice and she called her number.

'Little Ada, this time we're going South.'

Ada from Decatur rolled over the table. Nancy was flushed and half-hysterical, but her luck was holding. She drove the pot up and up, refusing to drag. Taylor was drumming with his fingers on the table, but he was in to stay.

Then Nancy tried for a ten and lost the dice. Taylor seized them avidly. He shot in silence, and in the hush of excitement the clatter of one pass after another on the table was the only sound.

Now Nancy had the dice again, but her luck had broken.

An hour passed. Back and forth it went. Taylor had been at it again—and again and again. They were even at last —Nancy lost her ultimate five dollars.

'Will you take my cheque,' she said quickly, 'for fifty, and we'll shoot it all?' Her voice was a little unsteady and her hand shook as she reached to the money.

Clark exchanged an uncertain but alarmed glance with Joe Ewing. Taylor shot again. He had Nancy's cheque.

'How 'bout another?' she said wildly. 'Jes' any bank'll do—money everywhere as a matter of fact.'

Jim understood—the 'good old corn' he had given her —the 'good old corn' she had taken since. He wished he dared interfere—a girl of that age and position would hardly have two bank accounts. When the clock struck two he contained himself no longer.

'May I—can't you let me roll 'em for you?' he suggested, his low, lazy voice a little strained.

Suddenly sleepy and listless, Nancy flung the dice down before him.

'All right—old boy! As Lady Diana Manners says, "Shoot 'em, Jelly-bean"—My luck's gone.'

'Mr Taylor,' said Jim, carelessly, 'we'll shoot for one of those there cheques against the cash.'

Half an hour later Nancy swayed forward and clapped him on the back.

'Stole my luck, you did.' She was nodding her head sagely.

Jim swept up the last cheque and putting it with the others tore them into confetti and scattered them on the floor. Someone started singing, and Nancy kicking her chair backwards rose to her feet.

'Ladies and gentlemen,' she announced. 'Ladies—that's you Marylyn. I want to tell the world that Mr Jim Powell, who is a well-known Jelly-bean of this city, is an exception to a great rule—"lucky in dice—unlucky in love." He's lucky in dice, and as matter fact I—I *love* him. Ladies and gentlemen, Nancy Lamar, famous dark-haired beauty often featured in the *Herald* as one th' most popular members of younger set as other girls are often featured in this particular case. Wish to announce—wish to announce, anyway, Gentlemen——' She tipped suddenly. Clark caught her and restored her balance.

'My error,' she laughed, 'she stoops to—stoops to—anyways——We'll drink to Jelly-bean . . . Mr Jim Powell, King of the Jelly-beans.'

And a few minutes later as Jim waited hat in hand for Clark in the darkness of that same corner of the porch where she had come searching for gasoline, she appeared suddenly beside him.

'Jelly-bean,' she said, 'are you here, Jelly-bean? I think —' and her slight unsteadiness seemed part of an enchanted dream—'I think you deserve one of my sweetest kisses for that, Jelly-bean.'

For an instant her arms were around his neck—her lips were pressed to his.

'I'm a wild part of the world, Jelly-bean, but you did me a good turn.'

Then she was gone, down the porch, over the cricket-loud lawn. Jim saw Merritt come out the front door and say something to her angrily—saw her laugh and, turning away, walk with averted eyes to his car. Marylyn and Joe followed, singing a drowsy song, about a Jazz baby.

Clark came out and joined Jim on the steps. 'All pretty lit, I guess,' he yawned. 'Merritt's in a mean mood. He's certainly off Nancy.'

Over east along the golf course a faint rug of grey spread itself across the feet of the night. The party in the car began to chant a chorus as the engine warmed up.

'Good-night everybody,' called Clark.

'Good-night, Clark.'

'Good-night.'

There was a pause, and then a soft, happy voice added, 'Good-night, Jelly-bean.'

The car drove off to a burst of singing. A rooster on a farm across the way took up a solitary mournful crow, and behind them a last Negro waiter turned out the porch

light. Jim and Clark strolled over towards the Ford, their
shoes crunching raucously on the gravel drive.

'Oh boy!' sighed Clark softly, 'how you can set those
dice!'

It was still too dark for him to see the flush on Jim's
thin cheeks—or to know that it was a flush of unfamiliar
shame.

IV

Over Tilly's garage a bleak room echoed all day to the
rumble and snorting down-stairs and the singing of the
Negro washers as they turned the hose on the cars outside.
It was a cheerless square of a room, punctuated with a
bed and a battered table on which lay half a dozen books
—Joe Miller's 'Slow Train thru Arkansas,' 'Lucille,' in
an old edition very much annotated in an old-fashioned
hand; 'The Eyes of the World,' by Harold Bell Wright,
and an ancient prayer-book of the Church of England
with the name Alice Powell and the date 1831 written on
the fly-leaf.

The East, grey when the Jelly-bean entered the garage,
became a rich and vivid blue as he turned on his solitary
electric light. He snapped it out again, and going to the
window rested his elbows on the sill and stared into the
deepening morning. With the awakening of his emotions,
his first perception was a sense of futility, a dull ache at the
utter greyness of his life. A wall had sprung up suddenly
around him hedging him in, a wall as definite and tangible
as the white wall of his bare room. And with his perception
of this wall all that had been the romance of his existence,
the casualness, the light-hearted improvidence, the miracu-
lous open-handedness of life, faded out. The Jelly-bean
strolling up Jackson Street humming a lazy song, known
at every shop and street stand, cropful of easy greeting
and local wit, sad sometimes for only the sake of sadness
and the flight of time—that Jelly-bean was suddenly

vanished. The very name was a reproach, a triviality. With a flood of insight he knew that Merritt must despise him, that even Nancy's kiss in the dawn would have awakened not jealousy but only a contempt for Nancy's so lowering herself. And on his part the Jelly-bean had used for her a dingy subterfuge learned from the garage. He had been her moral laundry; the stains were his.

As the grey became blue, brightened and filled the room, he crossed to his bed and threw himself down on it, gripping the edges fiercely.

'I love her,' he cried aloud, 'God!'

As he said this something gave way within him like a lump melting in his throat. The air cleared and became radiant with dawn, and turning over on his face he began to sob dully into the pillow.

In the sunshine of three o'clock Clark Darrow chugging painfully along Jackson Street was hailed by the Jelly-bean, who stood on the curb with his fingers in his vest pockets.

'Hi!' called Clark, bringing his Ford to an astonishing stop alongside. 'Just get up?'

The Jelly-bean shook his head.

'Never did go to bed. Felt sorta restless, so I took a long walk this morning out in the country. Just got into town this minute.'

'Should think you *would* feel restless. I been feeling thataway all day——'

'I'm thinkin' of leavin' town,' continued the Jelly-bean, absorbed by his own thoughts. 'Been thinkin' of goin' up on the farm, and takin' a little that work off Uncle Dun. Reckin I been bummin' too long.'

Clark was silent and the Jelly-bean continued:

'I reckin maybe after Aunt Mamie dies I could sink that money of mine in the farm and make somethin' out of it. All my people originally came from that part up there. Had a big place.'

Clark looked at him curiously.

'That's funny,' he said. 'This—this sort of affected me the same way.'

The Jelly-bean hesitated.

'I don't know,' he began slowly, 'somethin' about—about that girl last night talkin' about a lady named Diana Manners—an English lady, sorta got me thinkin'!' He drew himself up and looked oddly at Clark, 'I had a family once,' he said defiantly.

Clark nodded.

'I know.'

'And I'm the last of 'em,' continued the Jelly-bean, his voice rising slightly, 'and I ain't worth shucks. Name they call me by means jelly—weak and wobbly like. People who weren't nothin' when my folks was a lot turn up their noses when they pass me on the street.'

Again Clark was silent.

'So I'm through. I'm goin' to-day. And when I come back to this town it's going to be like a gentleman.'

Clark took out his handkerchief and wiped his damp brow.

'Reckon you're not the only one it shook up,' he admitted gloomily. 'All this thing of girls going round like they do is going to stop right quick. Too bad, too, but everybody'll have to see it thataway.'

'Do you mean,' demanded Jim in surprise, 'that all that's leaked out?'

'Leaked out? How on earth could they keep it secret. It'll be announced in the papers to-night. Doctor Lamar's got to save his name somehow.'

Jim put his hands on the sides of the car and tightened his long fingers on the metal.

'Do you mean Taylor investigated those cheques?'

It was Clark's turn to be surprised.

'Haven't you heard what happened?'

Jim's startled eyes were answer enough.

'Why,' announced Clark dramatically, 'those four got

another bottle of corn, got tight and decided to shock the town—so Nancy and that fella Merritt were married in Rockville at seven o'clock this morning.'

A tiny indentation appeared in the metal under the Jelly-Bean's fingers.

'Married?'

'Sure enough. Nancy sobered up and rushed back into town, crying and frightened to death—claimed it'd all been a mistake. First Doctor Lamar went wild and was going to kill Merritt, but finally they got it patched up some way, and Nancy and Merritt went to Savannah on the two-thirty train.'

Jim closed his eyes and with an effort overcame a sudden sickness.

'It's too bad,' said Clark philosophically. 'I don't mean the wedding—reckon that's all right, though I don't guess Nancy cared a darn about him. But it's a crime for a nice girl like that to hurt her family that way.'

The Jelly-bean let go the car and turned away. Again something was going on inside him, some inexplicable but almost chemical change.

'Where you going?' asked Clark.

The Jelly-bean turned and looked dully back over his shoulder.

'Got to go,' he muttered. 'Been up too long; feelin' right sick.'

'Oh.'

The street was hot at three and hotter still at four, the April dust seeming to enmesh the sun and give it forth again as a world-old joke forever played on an eternity of afternoons. But at half-past four a first layer of quiet fell and the shades lengthened under the awnings and heavy foliaged trees. In this heat nothing mattered. All life was weather, a waiting through the hot where events had no significance for the cool that was soft and caressing like a woman's hand on a tired forehead. Down in Georgia there is a feeling—perhaps inarticulate—that this is the greatest wisdom of the South—so after a while the Jelly-bean turned into a pool-hall on Jackson Street where he was sure to find a congenial crowd who would make all the old jokes—the ones he knew.

WINTER DREAMS

[1922]

SOME of the caddies were poor as sin and lived in one-room houses with a neurasthenic cow in the front yard, but Dexter Green's father owned the second best grocery-store in Black Bear—the best one was 'The Hub,' patronized by the wealthy people from Sherry Island—and Dexter caddied only for pocket-money.

In the fall when the days became crisp and grey, and the long Minnesota winter shut down like the white lid of a box, Dexter's skis moved over the snow that hid the fairways of the golf course. At these times the country gave him a feeling of profound melancholy—it offended him that the links should lie in enforced fallowness, haunted by ragged sparrows for the long season. It was dreary, too, that on the trees where the gay colours fluttered in summer there were now only the desolate sand-boxes knee-deep in crusted ice. When he crossed the hills the wind blew cold as misery, and if the sun was out he tramped with his eyes squinted up against the hard dimensionless glare.

In April the winter ceased abruptly. The snow ran down into Black Bear Lake scarcely tarrying for the early golfers to brave the season with red and black balls. Without elation, without an interval of moist glory, the cold was gone.

Dexter knew that there was something dismal about this Northern spring, just as he knew there was something gorgeous about the fall. Fall made him clench his hands and tremble and repeat idiotic sentences to himself, and make brisk abrupt gestures of command to imaginary audiences and armies. October filled him with hope which

November raised to a sort of ecstatic triumph, and in this mood the fleeting brilliant impressions of the summer at Sherry Island were ready grist to his mill. He became golf champion and defeated Mr T. A. Hedrick in a marvellous match played a hundred times over the fairways of his imagination, a match each detail of which he changed about untiringly—sometimes he won with almost laughable ease, sometimes he came up magnificently from behind. Again, stepping from a Pierce-Arrow automobile, like Mr Mortimer Jones, he strolled frigidly into the lounge of the Sherry Island Golf Club—or perhaps, surrounded by an admiring crowd, he gave an exhibition of fancy diving from the spring-board of the club raft. . . . Among those who watched in open-mouthed wonder was Mr Mortimer Jones.

And one day it came to pass that Mr Jones—himself and not his ghost—came up to Dexter with tears in his eyes and said that Dexter was the —— best caddy in the club, and wouldn't he decide not to quit if Mr Jones made it worth his while, because every other —— caddy in the club lost one ball a hole for him—regularly——

'No, sir,' said Dexter decisively, 'I don't want to caddy any more.' Then, after a pause: 'I'm too old.'

'You're not more than fourteen. Why the devil did you decide just this morning that you wanted to quit? You promised that next week you'd go over to the state tournament with me.'

'I decided I was too old.'

Dexter handed in his 'A Class' badge, collected what money was due him from the caddy-master, and walked home to Black Bear Village.

'The best —— caddy I ever saw,' shouted Mr Mortimer Jones over a drink that afternoon. 'Never lost a ball! Willing! Intelligent! Quiet! Honest! Grateful!'

The little girl who had done this was eleven—beautifully ugly as little girls are apt to be who are destined after a few years to be inexpressibly lovely and bring no end of misery to a great number of men. The spark however was perceptible. There was a general ungodliness in the way her lips twisted down at the corners when she smiled, and in the—Heaven help us!—in the almost passionate quality of her eyes. Vitality is born early in such women. It was utterly in evidence now, shining through her thin frame in a sort of glow.

She had come eagerly out on to the course at nine o'clock with a white linen nurse and five small new golf-clubs in a white canvas bag which the nurse was carrying. When Dexter first saw her she was standing by the caddy house, rather ill at ease and trying to conceal the fact by engaging her nurse in an obviously unnatural conversation graced by startling and irrelevant grimaces from herself.

'Well, it's certainly a nice day, Hilda,' Dexter heard her say. She drew down the corners of her mouth, smiled, and glanced furtively around, her eyes in transit falling for an instant on Dexter.

Then to the nurse:

'Well, I guess there aren't many people out here this morning, are there?'

The smile again—radiant, blatantly artificial—convincing.

'I don't know what we're supposed to do now,' said the nurse looking nowhere in particular.

'Oh, that's all right. I'll fix it up.'

Dexter stood perfectly still, his mouth slightly ajar. He knew that if he moved forward a step his stare would be in her line of vision—if he moved backward he would lose his full view of her face. For a moment he had not realized how young she was. Now he remembered having seen her several times the year before—in bloomers.

Suddenly, involuntarily, he laughed, a short abrupt laugh—then, startled by himself, he turned and began to walk quickly away.

'Boy!'

Dexter stopped.

'Boy——'

Beyond question he was addressed. Not only that, but he was treated to that absurd smile, that preposterous smile —the memory of which at least a dozen men were to carry into middle age.

'Boy, do you know where the golf teacher is?'

'He's giving a lesson.'

'Well, do you know where the caddy-master is?'

'He isn't here yet this morning.'

'Oh.' For a moment this baffled her. She stood alternately on her right and left foot.

'We'd like to get a caddy,' said the nurse. 'Mrs Mortimer Jones sent us out to play golf, and we don't know how without we get a caddy.'

Here she was stopped by an ominous glance from Miss Jones, followed immediately by the smile.

'There aren't any caddies here except me,' said Dexter to the nurse, 'and I got to stay here in charge until the caddy-master gets here.'

'Oh.'

Miss Jones and her retinue now withdrew, and at a proper distance from Dexter became involved in a heated conversation, which was concluded by Miss Jones taking one of the clubs and hitting it on the ground with violence. For further emphasis she raised it again and was about to bring it down smartly upon the nurse's bosom, when the nurse seized the club and twisted it from her hands.

'You damn little mean old thing!' cried Miss Jones wildly.

Another argument ensued. Realizing that the elements of the comedy were implied in the scene, Dexter several times began to laugh, but each time restrained the laugh before it reached audibility. He could not resist the monstrous conviction that the little girl was justified in beating the nurse.

The situation was resolved by the fortuitous appearance of the caddy-master, who was appealed to immediately by the nurse.

'Miss Jones is to have a little caddy, and this one says he can't go.'

'Mr McKenna said I was to wait here till you came,' said Dexter quickly.

'Well, he's here now.' Miss Jones smiled cheerfully at the caddy-master. Then she dropped her bag and set off at a haughty mince towards the first tee.

'Well?' The caddy-master turned to Dexter. 'What you standing there like a dummy for? Go pick up the young lady's clubs.'

'I don't think I'll go out to-day,' said Dexter.

'You don't——'

'I think I'll quit.'

The enormity of his decision frightened him. He was a favourite caddy, and the thirty dollars a month he earned through the summer were not to be made elsewhere around the lake. But he had received a strong emotional shock, and his perturbation required a violent and immediate outlet.

It is not so simple as that, either. As so frequently would be the case in the future, Dexter was unconsciously dictated to by his winter dreams.

II

Now, of course, the quality and the seasonability of these winter dreams varied, but the stuff of them remained. They persuaded Dexter several years later to pass up a business course at the State University—his father, prospering now, would have paid his way—for the precarious advantage of attending an older and more famous university in the East, where he was bothered by his scanty funds. But do not get the impression, because his winter dreams happened to be concerned at first with musings on the rich, that there was anything merely snobbish in the boy. He wanted not association with glittering things and glittering people—he wanted the glittering things themselves. Often he reached out for the best without knowing why he wanted it—and sometimes he ran up against the mysterious denials and prohibitions in which life indulges. It is with one of those denials and not with his career as a whole that this story deals.

He made money. It was rather amazing. After college he went to the city from which Black Bear Lake draws its wealthy patrons. When he was only twenty-three and had been there not quite two years, there were already people who liked to say: 'Now *there's* a boy——' All about him rich men's sons were peddling bonds precariously, or investing patrimonies precariously, or plodding through the two dozen volumes of the 'George Washington Commercial Course,' but Dexter borrowed a thousand dollars on his college degree and his confident mouth, and bought a partnership in a laundry.

It was a small laundry when he went into it, but Dexter made a speciality of learning how the English washed fine woollen golf-stockings without shrinking them, and within a year he was catering to the trade that wore knickerbockers. Men were insisting that their Shetland hose and sweaters go to his laundry, just as they had insisted on a caddy who could find golf-balls. A little later he was doing their wives' lingerie as well—and running five branches in different parts of the city. Before he was twenty-seven he owned the largest string of laundries in his section of the country. It was then that he sold out and went to New York. But the part of his story that concerns us goes back to the days when he was making his first big success.

When he was twenty-three Mr Hart—one of the grey-haired men who like to say 'Now there's a boy'—gave him a guest card to the Sherry Island Golf Club for a week-end. So he signed his name one day on the register, and that afternoon played golf in a foursome with Mr Hart and Mr Sandwood and Mr T. A. Hedrick. He did not consider it necessary to remark that he had once carried Mr Hart's bag over this same links, and that he knew every trap and gully with his eyes shut—but he found himself glancing at the four caddies who trailed them, trying to catch a gleam or gesture that would remind him of himself, that would lessen the gap which lay between his present and his past.

It was a curious day, slashed abruptly with fleeting, familiar impressions. One minute he had the sense of being a trespasser—in the next he was impressed by the tremendous superiority he felt towards Mr T. A. Hedrick, who was a bore and not even a good golfer any more.

Then, because of a ball Mr Hart lost near the fifteenth green, an enormous thing happened. While they were searching the stiff grasses of the rough there was a clear call of 'Fore!' from behind a hill in their rear. And as they all turned abruptly from their search a bright new ball sliced abruptly over the hill and caught Mr T. A. Hedrick in the abdomen.

'By Gad!' cried Mr T. A. Hedrick, 'they ought to put some of these crazy women off the course. It's getting to be outrageous.'

A head and a voice came up together over the hill:

'Do you mind if we go through?'

'You hit me in the stomach!' declared Mr Hedrick wildly.

'Did I?' The girl approached the group of men. 'I'm sorry. I yelled "Fore!" '

Her glance fell casually on each of the men—then scanned the fairway for her ball.

'Did I bounce into the rough?'

It was impossible to determine whether this question was ingenuous or malicious. In a moment, however, she left no doubt, for as her partner came up over the hill she called cheerfully:

'Here I am! I'd have gone on the green except that I hit something.'

As she took her stance for a short mashie shot, Dexter looked at her closely. She wore a blue gingham dress, rimmed at throat and shoulders with a white edging that accentuated her tan. The quality of exaggeration, of thinness, which had made her passionate eyes and down-turning mouth absurd at eleven, was gone now. She was arrestingly beautiful. The colour in her cheeks was centred like the colour in a picture—it was not a 'high' colour, but a sort of fluctuating and feverish warmth, so shaded that it seemed at any moment it would recede and disappear. This colour and the mobility of her mouth gave a continual impression of flux, of intense life, of passionate vitality—balanced only partially by the sad luxury of her eyes.

She swung her mashie impatiently and without interest, pitching the ball into a sand-pit on the other side of the green. With a quick, insincere smile and a careless 'Thank you!' she went on after it.

'That Judy Jones!' remarked Mr Hedrick on the next tee, as they waited—some moments—for her to play on ahead. 'All she needs is to be turned up and spanked for six months and then to be married off to an old-fashioned cavalry captain.'

'My God, she's good-looking!' said Mr Sandwood, who was just over thirty.

'Good-looking!' cried Mr Hedrick contemptuously, 'she always looks as if she wanted to be kissed! Turning those big cow-eyes on every calf in town!'

It was doubtful if Mr Hedrick intended a reference to the maternal instinct.

'She'd play pretty good golf if she'd try,' said Mr Sandwood.

'She has no form,' said Mr Hedrick solemnly.

'She has a nice figure,' said Mr Sandwood.

'Better thank the Lord she doesn't drive a swifter ball,' said Mr Hart, winking at Dexter.

Later in the afternoon the sun went down with a riotous swirl of gold and varying blues and scarlets, and left the dry, rustling night of Western summer. Dexter watched from the veranda of the Golf Club, watched the even overlap of the waters in the little wind, silver molasses under the harvest-moon. Then the moon held a finger to her lips and the lake became a clear pool, pale and quiet.

Dexter put on his bathing-suit and swam out to the farthest raft, where he stretched dripping on the wet canvas of the springboard.

There was a fish jumping and a star shining and the lights around the lake were gleaming. Over on a dark peninsula a piano was playing the songs of last summer and of summers before that—songs from 'Chin-Chin' and 'The Count of Luxemburg' and 'The Chocolate Soldier'— and because the sound of a piano over a stretch of water had always seemed beautiful to Dexter he lay perfectly quiet and listened.

The tune the piano was playing at that moment had been gay and new five years before when Dexter was a sophomore at college. They had played it at a prom once when he could not afford the luxury of proms, and he had stood outside the gymnasium and listened. The sound of the tune precipitated in him a sort of ecstasy and it was with that ecstasy he viewed what happened to him now. It was a mood of intense appreciation, a sense that, for once, he was magnificently attuned to life and that everything about him was radiating a brightness and a glamour he might never know again.

A low, pale oblong detached itself suddenly from the darkness of the Island, spitting forth the reverberate sound of a racing motor-boat. Two white streamers of cleft water rolled themselves out behind it and almost immediately the boat was beside him, drowning out the hot tinkle of the piano in the drone of its spray. Dexter raising himself on his arms was aware of a figure standing at the wheel, of two dark eyes regarding him over the lengthening space of water—then the boat had gone by and was sweeping in an immense and purposeless circle of spray round and round in the middle of the lake. With equal eccentricity one of the circles flattened out and headed back towards the raft.

'Who's that?' she called, shutting off her motor. She was so near now that Dexter could see her bathing-suit, which consisted apparently of pink rompers.

The nose of the boat bumped the raft, and as the latter tilted rakishly he was precipitated toward her. With different degrees of interest they recognized each other.

'Aren't you one of those men we played through this afternoon,' she demanded.

He was.

'Well, do you know how to drive a motor-boat? Because if you do I wish you'd drive this one so I can ride on the surf-board behind. My name is Judy Jones'—she favoured him with an absurd smirk—rather, what tried to be a smirk, for, twist her mouth as she might, it was not grotesque, it was merely beautiful—'and I live in a house over there on the Island, and in that house there is a man waiting for me. When he drove up at the door I drove out of the dock because he says I'm his ideal.'

There was a fish jumping and a star shining and the lights around the lake were gleaming. Dexter sat beside Judy Jones and she explained how her boat was driven. Then she was in the water, swimming to the floating surf-board with a sinuous crawl. Watching her was without effort to the eye, watching a branch waving or a sea-gull flying. Her arms, burned to butternut, moved sinuously among the dull platinum ripples, elbow appearing first, casting the forearm back with a cadence of falling water, then reaching out and down, stabbing a path ahead.

They moved out into the lake; turning, Dexter saw that she was kneeling on the low rear of the now up-tilted surf-board.

'Go faster,' she called, 'fast as it'll go.'

Obediently he jammed the lever forward and the white spray mounted at the bow. When he looked around again the girl was standing up on the rushing board, her arms spread wide, her eyes lifted towards the moon.

'It's awful cold,' she shouted. 'What's your name?'

He told her.

'Well, why don't you come to dinner to-morrow night?'

His heart turned over like the fly-wheel of the boat, and,

for the second time, her casual whim gave a new direction to his life.

III

Next evening while he waited for her to come downstairs, Dexter peopled the soft deep summer room and the sun-porch that opened from it with the men who had already loved Judy Jones. He knew the sort of men they were— the men who when he first went to college had entered from the great prep schools with graceful clothes and the deep tan of healthy summers. He had seen that, in one sense, he was better than these men. He was newer and stronger. Yet in acknowledging to himself that he wished his children to be like them he was admitting that he was but the rough, strong stuff from which they eternally sprang.

When the time had come for him to wear good clothes, he had known who were the best tailors in America, and the best tailors in America had made him the suit he wore this evening. He had acquired that particular reserve peculiar to his university, that set it off from other universities. He recognized the value to him of such a mannerism and he had adopted it; he knew that to be careless in dress and manner required more confidence than to be careful. But carelessness was for his children. His mother's name had been Krimslich. She was a Bohemian of the peasant class and she had talked broken English to the end of her days. Her son must keep to the set patterns.

At a little after seven Judy Jones came downstairs. She wore a blue silk afternoon dress, and he was disappointed at first that she had not put on something more elaborate. This feeling was accentuated when, after a brief greeting, she went to the door of a butler's pantry and pushing it open called: 'You can serve dinner, Martha.' He had rather expected that a butler would announce dinner, that there would be a cocktail. Then he put these thoughts behind him as they sat down side by side on a lounge and looked at each other.

'Father and mother won't be here,' she said thoughtfully.

He remembered the last time he had seen her father, and he was glad the parents were not to be here to-night— they might wonder who he was. He had been born in Keeble, a Minnesota village fifty miles farther north, and he always gave Keeble as his home instead of Black Bear Village. Country towns were well enough to come from if they weren't inconveniently in sight and used as foot-stools by fashionable lakes.

They talked of his university, which she had visited frequently during the past two years, and of the nearby city which supplied Sherry Island with its patrons, and whither Dexter would return next day to his prospering laundries.

During dinner she slipped into a moody depression which gave Dexter a feeling of uneasiness. Whatever petu-lance she uttered in her throaty voice worried him. What-ever she smiled at, at him, at a chicken liver, at nothing— it disturbed him that her smile could have no root in mirth, or even in amusement. When the scarlet corners of her lips turned down, it was less a smile than an invitation to a kiss.

Then, after dinner, she led him out on the dark sun-porch and deliberately changed the atmosphere.

'Do you mind if I weep a little?' she said.

'I'm afraid I'm boring you,' he responded quickly.

'You're not. I like you. But I've just had a terrible after-noon. There was a man I cared about, and this afternoon he told me out of a clear sky that he was poor as a church-mouse. He'd never even hinted it before. Does this sound horribly mundane?'

'Perhaps he was afraid to tell you.'

'Suppose he was,' she answered. 'He didn't start right. You see, if I'd thought of him as poor—well, I've been mad about loads of poor men, and fully intended to marry them all. But in this case, I hadn't thought of him that way, and my interest in him wasn't strong enough to survive the shock. As if a girl calmly informed her fiancé that she was a widow. He might not object to widows, but——

'Let's start right,' she interrupted herself suddenly. 'Who are you, anyhow?'

For a moment Dexter hesitated. Then:

'I'm nobody,' he announced. 'My career is largely a matter of futures.'

'Are you poor?'

'No,' he said frankly, 'I'm probably making more money than any man my age in the Northwest. I know that's an obnoxious remark, but you advised me to start right.'

There was a pause. Then she smiled and the corners of her mouth drooped and an almost imperceptible sway brought her closer to him, looking up into his eyes. A lump rose in Dexter's throat, and he waited breathless for the experiment, facing the unpredictable compound that would form mysteriously from the elements of their lips. Then he saw—she communicated her excitement to him, lavishly, deeply, with kisses that were not a promise but a fulfilment. They aroused in him not hunger demanding renewal but surfeit that would demand more surfeit ... kisses that were like charity, creating want by holding back nothing at all.

It did not take him many hours to decide that he had wanted Judy Jones ever since he was a proud, desirous little boy.

IV

It began like that—and continued, with varying shades of intensity, on such a note right up to the dénouement. Dexter surrendered a part of himself to the most direct and unprincipled personality with which he had ever come in contact. Whatever Judy wanted, she went after with the full pressure of her charm. There was no divergence of method, no jockeying for position or premeditation of effects—there was a very little mental side to any of her affairs. She simply made men conscious to the highest degree of her physical loveliness. Dexter had no desire to change her. Her deficiencies were knit up with a passionate energy that transcended and justified them.

When, as Judy's head lay against his shoulder that first night, she whispered, 'I don't know what's the matter with me. Last night I thought I was in love with a man and to-night I think I'm in love with you——'—it seemed to him a beautiful and romantic thing to say. It was the exquisite excitability that for the moment he controlled and owned. But a week later he was compelled to view this same quality in a different light. She took him in her roadster to a picnic supper, and after supper she disappeared, likewise in her roadster, with another man. Dexter became enormously upset and was scarcely able to be decently civil to the other people present. When she assured him that she had not kissed the other man, he knew she was lying—yet he was glad that she had taken the trouble to lie to him.

He was, as he found before the summer ended, one of a varying dozen who circulated about her. Each of them had at one time been favoured above all others—about half of them still basked in the solace of occasional sentimental revivals. Whenever one showed signs of dropping out through long neglect, she granted him a brief honeyed hour; which encouraged him to tag along for a year or so longer. Judy made these forays upon the helpless and defeated without malice, indeed half unconscious that there was anything mischievous in what she did.

When a new man came to town everyone dropped out —dates were automatically cancelled.

The helpless part of trying to do anything about it was that she did it all herself. She was not a girl who could be 'won' in the kinetic sense—she was proof against cleverness, she was proof against charm; if any of these assailed her too strongly she would immediately resolve the affair to a physical basis, and under the magic of her physical splendour the strong as well as the brilliant played her game and not their own. She was entertained only by the

8*

gratification of her desires and by the direct exercise of her own charm. Perhaps from so much youthful love, so many youthful lovers, she had come, in self-defence, to nourish herself wholly from within.

Succeeding Dexter's first exhilaration came restlessness and dissatisfaction. The helpless ecstasy of losing himself in her was opiate rather than tonic. It was fortunate for his work during the winter that those moments of ecstasy came infrequently. Early in their acquaintance it had seemed for a while that there was a deep and spontaneous mutual attraction—that first August, for example, three days of long evenings on her dusky veranda, of strange wan kisses through the late afternoon, in shadowy alcoves or behind the protecting trellises of the garden arbours, of mornings when she was fresh as a dream and almost shy at meeting him in the clarity of the rising day. There was all the ecstasy of an engagement about it, sharpened by his realization that there was no engagement. It was during those three days that, for the first time, he had asked her to marry him. She said 'maybe some day,' she said 'kiss me,' she said 'I'd like to marry you,' she said 'I love you'—she said—nothing.

The three days were interrupted by the arrival of a New York man who visited at her house for half September. To Dexter's agony, rumour engaged them. The man was the son of the president of a great trust company. But at the end of a month it was reported that Judy was yawning. At a dance one night she sat all evening in a motor-boat with a local beau, while the New Yorker searched the club for her frantically. She told the local beau that she was bored with her visitor, and two days later he left. She was seen with him at the station, and it was reported that he looked very mournful indeed.

On this note the summer ended. Dexter was twenty-four, and he found himself increasingly in a position to do as he wished. He joined two clubs in the city and lived at one of them. Though he was by no means an integral part of the stag-lines at these clubs, he managed to be on hand at dances where Judy Jones was likely to appear. He could have gone out socially as much as he liked—he was an eligible young man, now, and popular with down-town fathers. His confessed devotion to Judy Jones had rather solidified his position. But he had no social aspirations and rather despised the dancing men who were always on tap for the Thursday or Saturday parties and who filled in at dinners with the younger married set. Already he was playing with the idea of going East to New York. He wanted to take Judy Jones with him. No disillusion as to the world in which she had grown up could cure his illusion as to her desirability.

Remember that—for only in the light of it can what he did for her be understood.

Eighteen months after he first met Judy Jones he became engaged to another girl. Her name was Irene Scheerer, and her father was one of the men who had always believed in Dexter. Irene was light-haired and sweet and honourable, and a little stout, and she had two suitors whom she pleasantly relinquished when Dexter formally asked her to marry him.

Summer, fall, winter, spring, another summer, another fall—so much he had given of his active life to the incorrigible lips of Judy Jones. She had treated him with interest, with encouragement, with malice, with indifference, with contempt. She had inflicted on him the innumerable little slights and indignities possible in such a case—as if in revenge for having ever cared for him at all. She had beckoned him and yawned at him and beckoned him again and he had responded often with bitterness and narrowed eyes. She had brought him ecstatic happiness and intolerable agony of spirit. She had caused him untold inconvenience and not a little trouble. She had insulted him, and she had ridden over him, and she had played his interest in her against his interest in his work—for fun. She had done everything to him except to criticise him—this she had not done—it seemed to him only because it might have sullied the utter indifference she manifested and sincerely felt towards him.

When autumn had come and gone again it occurred to him that he could not have Judy Jones. He had to beat this into his mind but he convinced himself at last. He lay awake at night for a while and argued it over. He told himself the trouble and the pain she had caused him, he enumerated her glaring deficiencies as a wife. Then he said to himself that he loved her, and after a while he fell asleep. For a week, lest he imagined her husky voice over the telephone or her eyes opposite him at lunch, he worked hard and late, and at night he went to his office and plotted out his years.

At the end of a week he went to a dance and cut in on her once. For almost the first time since they had met he did not ask her to sit out with him or tell her that she was lovely. It hurt him that she did not miss these things—that was all. He was not jealous when he saw that there was a new man to-night. He had been hardened against jealousy long before.

He stayed late at the dance. He sat for an hour with Irene Scheerer and talked about books and about music. He knew very little about either. But he was beginning to be master of his own time now, and he had a rather priggish notion that he—the young and already fabulously successful Dexter Green—should know more about such things.

That was in October, when he was twenty-five. In January, Dexter and Irene became engaged. It was to be announced in June, and they were to be married three months later.

The Minnesota winter prolonged itself interminably, and it was almost May when the winds came soft and the snow ran down into Black Bear Lake at last. For the first time in over a year Dexter was enjoying a certain tranquillity of spirit. Judy Jones had been in Florida, and afterwards in Hot Springs, and somewhere she had been engaged, and somewhere she had broken it off. At first, when Dexter had definitely given her up, it had made him sad that people still linked them together and asked for news of her, but when he began to be placed at dinner next to Irene Scheerer people didn't ask him about her any more—they told him about her. He ceased to be an authority on her.

May at last. Dexter walked the streets at night when the darkness was damp as rain, wondering that so soon, with so little done, so much of ecstasy had gone from him. May one year back had been marked by Judy's poignant, unforgivable, yet forgiven turbulence—it had been one of those rare times when he fancied she had grown to care for him. That old penny's worth of happiness he had spent for this bushel of content. He knew that Irene would be no more than a curtain spread behind him, a hand moving among gleaming teacups, a voice calling to children ... fire and loveliness were gone, the magic of nights and the wonder of the varying hours and seasons ... slender lips, down-turning, dropping to his lips and bearing him up into a heaven of eyes. . . . The thing was deep in him. He was too strong and alive for it to die lightly.

In the middle of May when the weather balanced for a few days on the thin bridge that led to deep summer he turned in one night at Irene's house. Their engagement was to be announced in a week now—no one would be surprised at it. And to-night they would sit together on the lounge at the University Club and look on for an hour at the dancers. It gave him a sense of solidity to go with her—she was so sturdily popular, so intensely 'great.'

He mounted the steps of the brownstone house and stepped inside.

'Irene,' he called.

Mrs Scheerer came out of the living-room to meet him.

'Dexter,' she said, 'Irene's gone upstairs with a splitting headache. She wanted to go with you but I made her go to bed.'

'Nothing serious, I——'

'Oh, no. She's going to play golf with you in the morning. You can spare her for just one night, can't you, Dexter?'

Her smile was kind. She and Dexter liked each other. In the living-room he talked for a moment before he said good-night.

Returning to the University Club, where he had rooms, he stood in the doorway for a moment and watched the dancers. He leaned against the door-post, nodded at a man or two—yawned.

'Hello, darling.'

The familiar voice at his elbow startled him. Judy Jones had left a man and crossed the room to him—Judy Jones, a slender enamelled doll in cloth of gold: gold in a band at her head, gold in two slipper points at her dress's hem. The fragile glow of her face seemed to blossom as she smiled at him. A breeze of warmth and light blew through the room. His hands in the pockets of his dinner-jacket tightened spasmodically. He was filled with a sudden excitement.

'When did you get back?' he asked casually.

'Come here and I'll tell you about it.'

She turned and he followed her. She had been away—he could have wept at the wonder of her return. She had passed through enchanted streets, doing things that were like provocative music. All mysterious happenings, all fresh and quickening hopes, had gone away with her, come back with her now.

She turned in the doorway.

'Have you a car here? If you haven't, I have.'

'I have a coupé.'

In then, with a rustle of golden cloth. He slammed the door. Into so many cars she had stepped—like this—like that—her back against the leather, so—her elbow resting on the door—waiting. She would have been soiled long since had there been anything to soil her—except herself—but this was her own self outpouring.

With an effort he forced himself to start the car and back into the street. This was nothing, he must remember. She had done this before, and he had put her behind him, as he would have crossed a bad account from his books.

He drove slowly down-town and, affecting abstraction, traversed the deserted streets of the business section, peopled here and there where a movie was giving out its crowd or where consumptive or pugilistic youth lounged in front of pool halls. The clink of glasses and the slap of hands on the bars issued from saloons, cloisters of glazed glass and dirty yellow light.

She was watching him closely and the silence was embarrassing, yet in this crisis he could find no casual word with which to profane the hour. At a convenient turning he began to zigzag back towards the University Club.

'Have you missed me?' she asked suddenly.

'Everybody missed you.'

He wondered if she knew of Irene Scheerer. She had been back only a day—her absence had been almost contemporaneous with his engagement.

'What a remark!' Judy laughed sadly—without sadness. She looked at him searchingly. He became absorbed in the dashboard.

'You're handsomer than you used to be,' she said thoughtfully. 'Dexter, you have the most rememberable eyes.'

He could have laughed at this, but he did not laugh. It was the sort of thing that was said to sophomores. Yet it stabbed at him.

'I'm awfully tired of everything, darling.' She called every one darling, endowing the endearment with careless, individual cameraderie. 'I wish you'd marry me.'

The directness of this confused him. He should have told her now that he was going to marry another girl, but he could not tell her. He could as easily have sworn that he had never loved her.

'I think we'd get along,' she continued, on the same

note, 'unless probably you've forgotten me and fallen in love with another girl.'

Her confidence was obviously enormous. She had said, in effect, that she found such a thing impossible to believe, that if it were true he had merely committed a childish indiscretion—and probably to show off. She would forgive him, because it was not a matter of any moment but rather something to be brushed aside lightly.

'Of course you could never love anybody but me,' she continued, 'I like the way you love me. Oh, Dexter, have you forgotten last year?'

'No, I haven't forgotten.'

'Neither have I!'

Was she sincerely moved—or was she carried along by the wave of her own acting?

'I wish we could be like that again,' she said, and he forced himself to answer:

'I don't think we can.'

'I suppose not. . . . I hear you're giving Irene Scheerer a violent rush.'

There was not the faintest emphasis on the name, yet Dexter was suddenly ashamed.

'Oh, take me home,' cried Judy suddenly; 'I don't want to go back to that idiotic dance—with those children.'

Then, as he turned up the street that led to the residence district, Judy began to cry quietly to herself. He had never seen her cry before.

The dark street lightened, the dwellings of the rich loomed up around them, he stopped his coupé in front of the great white bulk of the Mortimer Joneses' house, somnolent, gorgeous, drenched with the splendour of the damp moonlight. Its solidity startled him. The strong walls, the steel of the girders, the breadth and beam and pomp of it were there only to bring out the contrast with the young beauty beside him. It was sturdy to accentuate her slightness—as if to show what a breeze could be generated by a butterfly's wing.

He sat perfectly quiet, his nerves in wild clamour, afraid

that if he moved he would find her irresistibly in his arms. Two tears had rolled down her wet face and trembled on her upper lip.

'I'm more beautiful than anybody else,' she said brokenly, 'why can't I be happy?' Her moist eyes tore at his stability—her mouth turned slowly downwards with an exquisite sadness: 'I'd like to marry you if you'll have me, Dexter. I suppose you think I'm not worth having, but I'll be so beautiful for you, Dexter.'

A million phrases of anger, pride, passion, hatred, tenderness fought on his lips. Then a perfect wave of emotion washed over him, carrying off with it a sediment of wisdom, of convention, of doubt, of honour. This was his girl who was speaking, his own, his beautiful, his pride.

'Won't you come in?' He heard her draw in her breath sharply.

Waiting.

'All right,' his voice was trembling, 'I'll come in.'

V

It was strange that neither when it was over nor a long time afterwards did he regret that night. Looking at it from the perspective of ten years, the fact that Judy's flare for him endured just one month seemed of little importance. Nor did it matter that by his yielding he subjected himself to a deeper agony in the end and gave serious hurt to Irene Scheerer and to Irene's parents, who had befriended him. There was nothing sufficiently pictorial about Irene's grief to stamp itself on his mind.

Dexter was at bottom hard-minded. The attitude of the city on his action was of no importance to him, not because he was going to leave the city, but because any outside attitude on the situation seemed superficial. He was completely indifferent to popular opinion. Nor, when he had seen that it was no use, that he did not possess in himself the power to move fundamentally or to hold

Judy Jones, did he bear any malice towards her. He loved her, and he would love her until the day he was too old for loving—but he could not have her. So he tasted the deep pain that is reserved only for the strong, just as he had tasted for a little while the deep happiness.

Even the ultimate falsity of the grounds upon which Judy terminated the engagement that she did not want to 'take him away' from Irene—Judy who had wanted nothing else—did not revolt him. He was beyond any revulsion or any amusement.

He went East in February with the intention of selling out his laundries and settling in New York—but the war came to America in March and changed his plans. He returned to the West, handed over the management of the business to his partner, and went into the first officers' training-camp in late April. He was one of those young thousands who greeted the war with a certain amount of relief, welcoming the liberation from webs of tangled emotion.

VI

This story is not his biography, remember, although things creep into it which have nothing to do with those dreams he had when he was young. We are almost done with them and with him now. There is only one more incident to be related here, and it happens seven years farther on.

It took place in New York, where he had done well— so well that there were no barriers too high for him. He was thirty-two years old, and, except for one flying trip immediately after the war, he had not been West in seven years. A man named Devlin from Detroit came into his office to see him in a business way, and then and there this incident occurred, and closed out, so to speak, this particular side of his life.

'So you're from the Middle West,' said the man Devlin with careless curiosity. 'That's funny—I thought men like you were probably born and raised on Wall Street. You know—wife of one of my best friends in Detroit came from your city. I was an usher at the wedding.'

Dexter waited with no apprehension of what was coming.

'Judy Simms,' said Devlin with no particular interest; 'Judy Jones she was once.'

'Yes, I knew her.' A dull impatience spread over him. He had heard, of course, that she was married—perhaps deliberately he had heard no more.

'Awfully nice girl,' brooded Devlin meaninglessly, 'I'm sort of sorry for her.'

'Why?' Something in Dexter was alert, receptive, at once.

'Oh, Lud Simms has gone to pieces in a way. I don't mean he ill-uses her, but he drinks and runs around——'

'Doesn't she run around?'

'No. Stays at home with her kids.'

'Oh.'

'She's a little too old for him,' said Devlin.

'Too old!' cried Dexter. 'Why, man, she's only twenty-seven.'

He was possessed with a wild notion of rushing out into the streets and taking a train to Detroit. He rose to his feet spasmodically.

'I guess you're busy,' Devlin apologized quickly. 'I didn't realize——'

'No, I'm not busy,' said Dexter, steadying his voice. 'I'm not busy at all. Not busy at all. Did you say she was —twenty-seven? No, I said she was twenty-seven.'

'Yes, you did,' agreed Devlin dryly.

'Go on, then. Go on.'

'What do you mean?'

'About Judy Jones.'

Devlin looked at him helplessly.

'Well, that's—I told you all there is to it. He treats her like the devil. Oh, they're not going to get divorced or anything. When he's particularly outrageous she forgives him. In fact, I'm inclined to think she loves him. She was a pretty girl when she first came to Detroit.'

A pretty girl! The phrase struck Dexter as ludicrous.

'Isn't she—a pretty girl, any more?'

'Oh, she's all right.'

'Look here,' said Dexter, sitting down suddenly. 'I don't understand. You say she was a "pretty girl" and now you say she's "all right." I don't understand what you mean—Judy Jones wasn't a pretty girl, at all. She was a great beauty. Why, I knew her, I knew her. She was——'

Devlin laughed pleasantly.

'I'm not trying to start a row,' he said. 'I think Judy's a nice girl and I like her. I can't understand how a man like Lud Simms could fall madly in love with her, but he did.' Then he added: 'Most of the women like her.'

Dexter looked closely at Devlin, thinking wildly that there must be a reason for this, some insensitivity in the man or some private malice.

'Lots of women fade just like *that*,' Devlin snapped his fingers. 'You must have seen it happen. Perhaps I've forgotten how pretty she was at her wedding. I've seen her so much since then, you see. She has nice eyes.'

A sort of dullness settled down upon Dexter. For the first time in his life he felt like getting very drunk. He knew that he was laughing loudly at something Devlin had said, but he did not know what it was or why it was funny. When, in a few minutes, Devlin went he lay down on his lounge and looked out of the window at the New York sky-line into which the sun was sinking in dull lovely shades of pink and gold.

He had thought that having nothing else to lose he was invulnerable at last—but he knew that he had just lost something more, as surely as if he had married Judy Jones and seen her fade away before his eyes.

The dream was gone. Something had been taken from him. In a sort of panic he pushed the palms of his hands into his eyes and tried to bring up a picture of the waters lapping on Sherry Island and the moonlit veranda, and gingham on the golf-links and the dry sun and the gold colour of her neck's soft down. And her mouth damp to his kisses and her eyes plaintive with melancholy and her freshness like new fine linen in the morning. Why, these things were no longer in the world! They had existed and they existed no longer.

For the first time in years the tears were streaming down his face. But they were for himself now. He did not care about mouth and eyes and moving hands. He wanted to care, and he could not care. For he had gone away and he could never go back any more. The gates were closed, the sun was gone down, and there was no beauty but the grey beauty of steel that withstands all time. Even the grief he could have borne was left behind in the country of illusion, of youth, of the richness of life, where his winter dreams had flourished.

'Long ago,' he said, 'long ago, there was something in me, but now that thing is gone. Now that thing is gone, that thing is gone. I cannot cry. I cannot care. That thing will come back no more.'

'THE SENSIBLE THING'

[1924]

AT THE Great American Lunch Hour young George O'Kelly straightened his desk deliberately and with an assumed air of interest. No one in the office must know that he was in a hurry, for success is a matter of atmosphere, and it is not well to advertise the fact that your mind is separated from your work by a distance of seven hundred miles.

But once out of the building he set his teeth and began to run, glancing now and then at the gay noon of early spring which filled Times Square and loitered less than twenty feet over the heads of the crowd. The crowd all looked slightly upward and took deep March breaths, and the sun dazzled their eyes so that scarcely any one saw any one else but only their own reflection on the sky.

George O'Kelly, whose mind was over seven hundred miles away, thought that all outdoors was horrible. He rushed into the subway, and for ninety-five blocks bent a frenzied glance on a car-card which showed vividly how he had only one chance in five of keeping his teeth for ten years. At 137th Street he broke off his study of commercial art, left the subway, and began to run again, a tireless, anxious run that brought him this time to his home—one room in a high, horrible apartment-house in the middle of nowhere.

There it was on the bureau, the letter—in sacred ink, on blessed paper—all over the city, people, if they listened, could hear the beating of George O'Kelly's heart. He read the commas, the blots, and the thumb-smudge on the margin—then he threw himself hopelessly upon his bed.

He was in a mess, one of those terrific messes which are ordinary incidents in the life of the poor, which follow poverty like birds of prey. The poor go under or go up or go wrong or even go on, somehow, in a way the poor have—but George O'Kelly was so new to poverty that had any one denied the uniqueness of his case he would have been astounded.

Less than two years ago he had been graduated with honours from The Massachusetts Institute of Technology and had taken a position with a firm of construction engineers in southern Tennessee. All his life he had thought in terms of tunnels and skyscrapers and great squat dams and tall, three-towered bridges, that were like dancers holding hands in a row, with heads as tall as cities and skirts of cable strand. It had seemed romantic to George O'Kelly to change the sweep of rivers and the shape of mountains so that life could flourish in the old bad lands of the world where it had never taken root before. He loved steel, and there was always steel near him in his dreams, liquid steel, steel in bars, and blocks and beams and formless plastic masses, waiting for him, as paint and canvas to his hand. Steel inexhaustible, to be made lovely and austere in his imaginative fire . . .

At present he was an insurance clerk at forty dollars a week with his dream slipping fast behind him. The dark little girl who had made this mess, this terrible and intolerable mess, was waiting to be sent for in a town in Tennessee.

In fifteen minutes the woman from whom he sublet his room knocked and asked him with maddening kindness if, since he was home, he would have some lunch. He shook his head, but the interruption aroused him, and getting up from the bed he wrote a telegram.

'Letter depressed me have you lost your nerve you are foolish and just upset to think of breaking off why not marry me immediately sure we can make it all right——'

He hesitated for a wild minute, and then added in a

hand that could scarcely be recognized as his own: 'In any case I will arrive to-morrow at six o'clock.'

When he finished he ran out of the apartment and down to the telegraph office near the subway stop. He possessed in this world not quite one hundred dollars, but the letter showed that she was 'nervous' and this left him no choice. He knew what 'nervous' meant—that she was emotionally depressed, that the prospect of marrying into a life of poverty and struggle was putting too much strain upon her love.

George O'Kelly reached the insurance company at his usual run, the run that had become almost second nature to him, that seemed best to express the tension under which he lived. He went straight to the manager's office.

'I want to see you, Mr Chambers,' he announced breathlessly.

'Well?' Two eyes, eyes like winter windows, glared at him with ruthless impersonality.

'I want to get four days' vacation.'

'Why, you had a vacation just two weeks ago!' said Mr Chambers in surprise.

'That's true,' admitted the distraught young man, 'but now I've got to have another.'

'Where'd you go last time? To your home?'

'No, I went to—a place in Tennessee.'

'Well, where do you want to go this time?'

'Well, this time I want to go to—a place in Tennessee.'

'You're consistent, anyhow,' said the manager dryly. 'But I didn't realize you were employed here as a travelling salesman.'

'I'm not,' cried George desperately, 'but I've got to go.'

'All right,' agreed Mr Chambers, 'but you don't have to come back. So don't!'

'I won't.' And to his own astonishment as well as Mr Chambers' George's face grew pink with pleasure. He felt happy, exultant—for the first time in six months he was absolutely free. Tears of gratitude stood in his eyes, and he seized Mr Chambers warmly by the hand.

'I want to thank you,' he said with a rush of emotion, 'I don't want to come back. I think I'd have gone crazy if you'd said that I could come back. Only I couldn't quit myself, you see, and I want to thank you for—for quitting for me.'

He waved his hand magnanimously, shouted aloud, 'You owe me three days' salary but you can keep it!' and rushed from the office. Mr Chambers rang for his stenographer to ask if O'Kelly had seemed queer lately. He had fired many men in the course of his career, and they had taken it in many different ways, but none of them had thanked him—ever before.

II

Jonquil Cary was her name, and to George O'Kelly nothing had ever looked so fresh and pale as her face when she saw him and fled to him eagerly along the station platform. Her arms were raised to him, her mouth was half parted for his kiss, when she held him off suddenly and lightly and, with a touch of embarrassment, looked around. Two boys, somewhat younger than George, were standing in the background.

'This is Mr Craddock and Mr Holt,' she announced cheerfully. 'You met them when you were here before.'

Disturbed by the transition of a kiss into an introduction and suspecting some hidden significance, George was more confused when he found that the automobile which was to carry them to Jonquil's house belonged to one of the two young men. It seemed to put him at a disadvantage. On the way Jonquil chattered between the front and back seats, and when he tried to slip his arm around her under cover of the twilight she compelled him with a quick movement to take her hand instead.

'Is this street on the way to your house?' he whispered. 'I don't recognize it.'

'It's the new boulevard. Jerry just got this car to-day, and he wants to show it to me before he takes us home.'

When, after twenty minutes, they were deposited at Jonquil's house, George felt that the first happiness of the meeting, the joy he had recognized so surely in her eyes back in the station, had been dissipated by the intrusion of the ride. Something that he had looked forward to had been rather casually lost, and he was brooding on this as he said goodnight stiffly to the two young men. Then his ill-humour faded as Jonquil drew him into a familiar embrace under the dim light of the front hall and told him in a dozen ways, of which the best was without words, how she had missed him. Her emotion reassured him, promised his anxious heart that everything would be all right.

They sat together on the sofa, overcome by each other's presence, beyond all except fragmentary endearments. At the supper hour Jonquil's father and mother appeared and were glad to see George. They liked him, and had been interested in his engineering career when he had first come to Tennessee over a year before. They had been sorry when he had given it up and gone to New York to look for something more immediately profitable, but while they deplored the curtailment of his career they sympathized with him and were ready to recognize the engagement. During dinner they asked about his progress in New York.

'Everything's going fine,' he told them with enthusiasm. 'I've been promoted—better salary.'

He was miserable as he said this—but they were all *so* glad.

'They must like you,' said Mrs Cary, 'that's certain—or they wouldn't let you off twice in three weeks to come down here.'

'I told them they had to,' explained George hastily; 'I told them if they didn't I wouldn't work for them any more.'

'But you ought to save your money,' Mrs Cary reproached him gently. 'Not spend it all on this expensive trip.'

Dinner was over—he and Jonquil were alone and she came back into his arms.

'So glad you're here,' she sighed. 'Wish you never were going away again, darling.'

'Do you miss me?'

'Oh, so much, so much.'

'Do you—do other men come to see you often? Like those two kids?'

The question surprised her. The dark velvet eyes stared at him.

'Why, of course they do. All the time. Why—I've told you in letters that they did, dearest.'

This was true—when he had first come to the city there had been already a dozen boys around her, responding to her picturesque fragility with adolescent worship, and a few of them perceiving that her beautiful eyes were also sane and kind.

'Do you expect me never to go anywhere'—Jonquil demanded, leaning back against the sofa-pillows until she seemed to look at him from many miles away—'and just fold my hands and sit still—forever?'

'What do you mean?' he blurted out in a panic. 'Do you mean you think I'll never have enough money to marry you?'

'Oh, don't jump at conclusions so, George.'

'I'm not jumping at conclusions. That's what you said.'

George decided suddenly that he was on dangerous grounds. He had not intended to let anything spoil this night. He tried to take her again in his arms, but she resisted unexpectedly, saying:

'It's hot. I'm going to get the electric fan.'

When the fan was adjusted they sat down again, but he was in a supersensitive mood and involuntarily he plunged into the specific world he had intended to avoid.

'When will you marry me?'

'Are you ready for me to marry you?'

All at once his nerves gave way, and he sprang to his feet.

'Let's shut off that damned fan,' he cried, 'it drives me wild. It's like a clock ticking away all the time I'll be with you. I came here to be happy and forget everything about New York and time——'

He sank down on the sofa as suddenly as he had risen. Jonquil turned off the fan, and drawing his head down into her lap began stroking his hair.

'Let's sit like this,' she said softly, 'just sit quiet like this, and I'll put you to sleep. You're all tired and nervous and your sweetheart'll take care of you.'

'But I don't want to sit like this,' he complained, jerking up suddenly, 'I don't want to sit like this at all. I want you to kiss me. That's the only thing that makes me rest. And anyways I'm not nervous—it's you that's nervous. I'm not nervous at all.'

To prove that he wasn't nervous he left the couch and plumped himself into a rocking-chair across the room.

'Just when I'm ready to marry you you write me the most nervous letters, as if you're going to back out, and I have to come rushing down here——'

'You don't have to come if you don't want to.'

'But I *do* want to!' insisted George.

It seemed to him that he was being very cool and logical and that she was putting him deliberately in the wrong. With every word they were drawing farther and farther apart—and he was unable to stop himself or to keep worry and pain out of his voice.

But in a minute Jonquil began to cry sorrowfully and he came back to the sofa and put his arm around her. He was the comforter now, drawing her head close to his shoulder, murmuring old familiar things until she grew calmer and only trembled a little, spasmodically, in his arms. For over an hour they sat there, while the evening pianos thumped their last cadences into the street outside. George did not move, or think, or hope, lulled into numbness by the premonition of disaster. The clock would tick on, past eleven, past twelve, and then Mrs

Cary would call down gently over the banister—beyond that he saw only to-morrow and despair.

III

In the heat of the next day the breaking-point came. They had each guessed the truth about the other, but of the two she was the more ready to admit the situation.

'There's no use going on,' she said miserably, 'you know you hate the insurance business, and you'll never do well in it.'

'That's not it,' he insisted stubbornly; 'I hate going on alone. If you'll marry me and come with me and take a chance with me, I can make good at anything, but not while I'm worrying about you down here.'

She was silent a long time before she answered, not thinking—for she had seen the end—but only waiting, because she knew that every word would seem more cruel than the last. Finally she spoke:

'George, I love you with all my heart, and I don't see how I can ever love anyone else but you. If you'd been ready for me two months ago I'd have married you—now I can't because it doesn't seem to be the sensible thing.'

He made wild accusations—there was someone else—she was keeping something from him!

'No, there's no one else.'

This was true. But reacting from the strain of this affair she had found relief in the company of young boys like Jerry Holt, who had the merit of meaning absolutely nothing in her life.

George didn't take the situation well, at all. He seized her in his arms and tried literally to kiss her into marrying him at once. When this failed, he broke into a long monologue of self-pity, and ceased only when he saw that he was making himself despicable in her sight. He threatened to leave when he had no intention of leaving, and refused to go when she told him that, after all, it was best that he should.

For a while she was sorry, then for another while she was merely kind.

'You'd better go now,' she cried at last, so loud that Mrs Cary came downstairs in alarm.

'Is something the matter?'

'I'm going away, Mrs Cary,' said George brokenly. Jonquil had left the room.

'Don't feel so badly, George.' Mrs Cary blinked at him in helpless sympathy—sorry and, in the same breath, glad that the little tragedy was almost done. 'If I were you I'd go home to your mother for a week or so. Perhaps after all this is the sensible thing——'

'Please don't talk,' he cried. 'Please don't say anything to me now!'

Jonquil came into the room again, her sorrow and her nervousness alike tucked under powder and rouge and hat.

'I've ordered a taxicab,' she said impersonally. 'We can drive around until your train leaves.'

She walked out on the front porch. George put on his coat and hat and stood for a minute exhausted in the hall—he had eaten scarcely a bite since he had left New York. Mrs Cary came over, drew his head down and kissed him on the cheek, and he felt very ridiculous and weak in his knowledge that the scene had been ridiculous and weak at the end. If he had only gone the night before —left her for the last time with a decent pride.

The taxi had come, and for an hour these two that had been lovers rode along the less-frequented streets. He held her hand and grew calmer in the sunshine, seeing too late that there had been nothing all along to do or say.

'I'll come back,' he told her.

'I know you will,' she answered, trying to put a cheery faith into her voice. 'And we'll write each other—sometimes.'

'No,' he said, 'we won't write. I couldn't stand that. Some day I'll come back.'

'I'll never forget you, George.'

They reached the station, and she went with him while he bought his ticket. . . .

'Why, George O'Kelly and Jonquil Cary!'

It was a man and a girl whom George had known when he had worked in town, and Jonquil seemed to greet their presence with relief. For an interminable five minutes they all stood there talking; then the train roared into the station, and with ill-concealed agony in his face George held out his arms towards Jonquil. She took an uncertain step towards him, faltered, and then pressed his hand quickly as if she were taking leave of a chance friend.

'Good-bye, George,' she was saying, 'I hope you have a pleasant trip.

'Good-bye, George. Come back and see us all again.'

Dumb, almost blind with pain, he seized his suitcase, and in some dazed way got himself aboard the train.

Past clanging street-crossings, gathering speed through wide suburban spaces towards the sunset. Perhaps she too would see the sunset and pause for a moment, turning, remembering, before he faded with her sleep into the past. This night's dusk would cover up forever the sun and the trees and the flowers and laughter of his young world.

IV

On a damp afternoon in September of the following year a young man with his face burned to a deep copper glow got off a train at a city in Tennessee. He looked around anxiously, and seemed relieved when he found that there was no one in the station to meet him. He taxied to the best hotel in the city where he registered with some satisfaction as George O'Kelly, Cuzco, Peru.

Up in his room he sat for a few minutes at the window looking down into the familiar street below. Then with his hand trembling faintly he took off the telephone receiver and called a number.

'Is Miss Jonquil in?'

'This is she.'

'Oh—' His voice after overcoming a faint tendency to waver went on with friendly formality.

'This is George O'Kelly. Did you get my letter?'

'Yes. I thought you'd be in to-day.'

Her voice, cool and unmoved, disturbed him, but not as he had expected. This was the voice of a stranger, unexcited, pleasantly glad to see him—that was all. He wanted to put down the telephone and catch his breath.

'I haven't seen you for—a long time.' He succeeded in making this sound offhand. 'Over a year.'

He knew how long it had been—to the day.

'It'll be awfully nice to talk to you again.'

'I'll be there in about an hour.'

He hung up. For four long seasons every minute of his leisure had been crowded with anticipation of this hour, and now this hour was here. He had thought of finding her married, engaged, in love—he had not thought she would be unstirred at his return.

There would never again in his life, he felt, be another ten months like these he had just gone through. He had made an admittedly remarkable showing for a young engineer—stumbled into two unusual opportunities, one in Peru, whence he had just returned, and another consequent upon it, in New York, whither he was bound. In his short time he had risen from poverty into a position of unlimited opportunity.

He looked at himself in the dressing-table mirror. He was almost black with tan, but it was a romantic black, and in the last week, since he had had time to think it, it had given him considerable pleasure. The hardiness of his frame, too, he appraised with a sort of fascination. He had lost part of an eyebrow somewhere, and he still wore an elastic bandage on his knee, but he was too young not to realize that on the steamer many women had looked at him with unusual tributary interest.

His clothes, of course, were frightful. They had been made for him by a Greek tailor in Lima—in two days. He was young enough, too, to have explained this sartorial deficiency to Jonquil in his otherwise laconic note. The only further detail it contained was a request that he should *not* be met at the station.

George O'Kelly, of Cuzco, Peru, waited an hour and a half in the hotel, until, to be exact, the sun had reached a midway position in the sky. Then, freshly shaven and talcum-powdered towards a somewhat more Caucasian hue, for vanity at the last minute had overcome romance, he engaged a taxicab and set out for the house he knew so well.

He was breathing hard—he noticed this but he told himself that it was excitement, not emotion. He was here; she was not married—that was enough. He was not even sure what he had to say to her. But this was the moment of his life that he felt he could least easily have dispensed with. There was no triumph, after all, without a girl concerned, and if he did not lay his spoils at her feet he could at least hold them for a passing moment before her eyes.

The house loomed up suddenly beside him, and his first thought was that it had assumed a strange unreality. There was nothing changed—only everything was changed. It was smaller and it seemed shabbier than before—there was no cloud of magic hovering over its roof and issuing from the windows of the upper floor. He rang the door-bell and an unfamiliar coloured maid appeared. Miss Jonquil would be down in a moment. He wet his lips nervously and walked into the sitting-room—and the feeling of unreality increased. After all, he saw, this was only a room, and not the enchanted chamber where he had passed those poignant hours. He sat in a chair, amazed to find it a chair, realizing that his imagination had distorted and coloured all these simple familiar things.

Then the door opened and Jonquil came into the room —and it was as though everything in it suddenly blurred before his eyes. He had not remembered how beautiful she was, and he felt his face grow pale and his voice diminish to a poor sigh in his throat.

She was dressed in pale green, and a gold ribbon bound back her dark, straight hair like a crown. The familiar velvet eyes caught his as she came through the door, and a spasm of fright went through him at her beauty's power of inflicting pain.

He said 'Hello,' and they each took a few steps forward and shook hands. Then they sat in chairs quite far apart and gazed at each other across the room.

'You've come back,' she said, and he answered just as tritely: 'I wanted to stop in and see you as I came through.'

He tried to neutralize the tremor in his voice by looking anywhere but at her face. The obligation to speak was on him, but, unless he immediately began to boast, it seemed that there was nothing to say. There had never been anything casual in their previous relations—it didn't seem possible that people in this position would talk about the weather.

'This is ridiculous,' he broke out in sudden embarrassment. 'I don't know exactly what to do. Does my being here bother you?'

'No.' The answer was both reticent and impersonally sad. It depressed him.

'Are you engaged?' he demanded.

'No.'

'Are you in love with someone?'

She shook her head.

'Oh.' He leaned back in his chair. Another subject seemed exhausted—the interview was not taking the course he had intended.

'Jonquil,' he began, this time on a softer key, 'after all that's happened between us, I wanted to come back and see you. Whatever I do in the future I'll never love another girl as I've loved you.'

This was one of the speeches he had rehearsed. On the steamer it had seemed to have just the right note— a reference to the tenderness he would always feel for her combined with a non-committal attitude towards his present state of mind. Here with the past around him, beside him, growing minute by minute more heavy on the air, it seemed theatrical and stale.

She made no comment, sat without moving, her eyes fixed on him with an expression that might have meant everything or nothing.

'You don't love me any more, do you?' he asked her in a level voice.

'No.'

When Mrs Cary came in a minute later, and spoke to him about his success—there had been a half-column about him in the local paper—he was a mixture of emotions. He knew now that he still wanted this girl, and he knew that the past sometimes comes back—that was all. For the rest he must be strong and watchful and he would see.

'And now,' Mrs Cary was saying, 'I want you two to go and see the lady who has the chrysanthemums. She particularly told me she wanted to see you because she'd read about you in the paper.'

They went to see the lady with the chrysanthemums. They walked along the street, and he recognized with a sort of excitement just how her shorter footsteps always fell in between his own. The lady turned out to be nice, and the chrysanthemums were enormous and extraordinarily beautiful. The lady's gardens were full of them, white and pink and yellow, so that to be among them was a trip back into the heart of summer. There were two gardens full, and a gate between them; when they strolled towards the second garden the lady went first through the gate.

And then a curious thing happened. George stepped aside to let Jonquil pass, but instead of going through she stood still and stared at him for a minute. It was not so much the look, which was not a smile, as it was the moment of silence. They saw each other's eyes, and both took a short, faintly accelerated breath, and then they went on into the second garden. That was all.

The afternoon waned. They thanked the lady and walked home slowly, thoughtfully, side by side. Through dinner, too, they were silent. George told Mr Cary something of what had happened in South America, and managed to let it be known that everything would be plain sailing for him in the future.

Then dinner was over, and he and Jonquil were alone in the room which had seen the beginning of their love affair and the end. It seemed to him long ago and inexpressibly sad. On the sofa he had felt agony and grief such as he would never feel again. He would never be so weak or so tired and miserable and poor. Yet he knew that that boy of fifteen months before had had something, a trust, a warmth that was gone forever. The sensible thing—they had done the sensible thing. He had traded his youth for strength and carved success out of despair. But with his youth, life had carried away the freshness of his love.

'You won't marry me, will you?' he said quietly.

Jonquil shook her dark head.

'I'm never going to marry,' she answered.

He nodded.

'I'm going on to Washington in the morning,' he said.

'Oh——'

'I have to go. I've got to be in New York by the first, and meanwhile I want to stop off in Washington.'

'Business!'

'No-o,' he said as if reluctantly. 'There's someone there I must see who was very kind to me when I was so—down and out.'

This was invented. There was no one in Washington for him to see—but he was watching Jonquil narrowly, and he was sure that she winced a little, that her eyes closed and then opened wide again.

'But before I go I want to tell you the things that happened to me since I saw you, and, as maybe we won't meet again, I wonder if—if just this once you'd sit in my lap like you used to. I wouldn't ask except since there's no one else—yet—perhaps it doesn't matter.'

She nodded, and in a moment was sitting in his lap as she had sat so often in that vanished spring. The feel of her head against his shoulder, of her familiar body, sent a shock of emotion over him. His arms holding her had a tendency to tighten around her, so he leaned back and began to talk thoughtfully into the air.

He told her of a despairing two weeks in New York which had terminated with an attractive if not very profitable job in a construction plant in Jersey City. When the Peru business had first presented itself it had not seemed an extraordinary opportunity. He was to be third assistant engineer on the expedition, but only ten of the American party, including eight rodmen and surveyors, had ever reached Cuzco. Ten days later the chief of the expedition was dead of yellow fever. That had been his chance, a chance for anybody but a fool, a marvellous chance——

'A chance for anybody but a fool?' she interrupted innocently.

'Even for a fool,' he continued. 'It was wonderful. Well, I wired New York——'

'And so,' she interrupted again, 'they wired that you ought to take a chance?'

'Ought to!' he exclaimed, still leaning back. 'That I *had* to. There was no time to lose——'

'Not a minute?'

'Not a minute.'

'Not even time for——' she paused.

'For what?'

'Look.'

He bent his head forward suddenly, and she drew

herself to him in the same moment, her lips half open like a flower.

'Yes,' he whispered into her lips. 'There's all the time in the world. . . .'

All the time in the world—his life and hers. But for an instant as he kissed her he knew that though he search through eternity he could never recapture those lost April hours. He might press her close now till the muscles knotted on his arms—she was something desirable and rare that he had fought for and made his own—but never again an intangible whisper in the dusk, or on the breeze of night. . . .

Well, let it pass, he thought; April is over, April is over. There are all kinds of love in the world, but never the same love twice.

ABSOLUTION

[1924]

THERE was once a priest with cold, watery eyes, who, in the still of the night, wept cold tears. He wept because the afternoons were warm and long, and he was unable to attain a complete mystical union with our Lord. Sometimes, near four o'clock, there was a rustle of Swede girls along the path by his window, and in their shrill laughter he found a terrible dissonance that made him pray aloud for the twilight to come. At twilight the laughter and the voices were quieter, but several times he had walked past Romberg's Drug Store when it was dusk and the yellow lights shone inside and the nickel taps of the soda-fountain were gleaming, and he had found the scent of cheap toilet soap desperately sweet on the air. He passed that way when he returned from hearing confessions on Saturday nights, and he grew careful to walk on the other side of the street so that the smell of the soap would float upward before it reached his nostrils as it drifted, rather like incense, towards the summer moon.

But there was no escape from the hot madness of four o'clock. From his window, as far as he could see, the Dakota wheat thronged the valley of the Red River. The wheat was terrible to look upon and the carpet pattern to which in agony he bent his eyes sent his thought brooding through grotesque labyrinths, open always to the unavoidable sun.

One afternoon when he had reached the point where the mind runs down like an old clock, his housekeeper brought into his study a beautiful, intense little boy of eleven named Rudolph Miller. The little boy sat down in a patch of sunshine, and the priest, at his walnut desk, pretended to be very busy. This was to conceal his relief that some one had come into his haunted room.

Presently he turned around and found himself staring into two enormous, staccato eyes, lit with gleaming points of cobalt light. For a moment their expression startled him —then he saw that his visitor was in a state of abject fear.

'Your mouth is trembling,' said Father Schwartz, in a haggard voice.

The little boy covered his quivering mouth with his hand.

'Are you in trouble?' asked Father Schwartz, sharply. 'Take your hand away from your mouth and tell me what's the matter.'

The boy—Father Schwartz recognized him now as the son of a parishioner, Mr Miller, the freight-agent—moved his hand reluctantly off his mouth and became articulate in a despairing whisper.

'Father Schwartz—I've committed a terrible sin.'

'A sin against purity?'

'No, Father . . . worse.'

Father Schwartz's body jerked sharply.

'Have you killed somebody?'

'No—but I'm afraid——' the voice rose to a shrill whimper.

'Do you want to go to confession?'

The little boy shook his head miserably. Father Schwartz cleared his throat so that he could make his voice soft and say some quiet, kind thing. In this moment he should forget his own agony, and try to act like God. He repeated to himself a devotional phrase, hoping that in return God would help him to act correctly.

'Tell me what you've done,' said his new soft voice.

The little boy looked at him through his tears, and was reassured by the impression of moral resiliency which the distraught priest had created. Abandoning as much of himself as he was able to this man, Rudolph Miller began to tell his story.

'On Saturday, three days ago, my father he said I had

to go to confession, because I hadn't been for a month, and the family they go every week, and I hadn't been. So I just as leave go, I didn't care. So I put it off till after supper because I was playing with a bunch of kids and father asked me if I went, and I said "no," and he took me by the neck and he said "You go now," so I said "All right," so I went over to church. And he yelled after me: "Don't come back till you go." . . . '

II

"On Saturday, Three Days Ago"

The plush curtain of the confessional rearranged its dismal creases, leaving exposed only the bottom of an old man's shoe. Behind the curtain an immortal soul was alone with God and the Reverend Adolphus Schwartz, priest of the parish. Sound began, a laboured whispering, sibilant and discreet, broken at intervals by the voice of the priest in audible question.

Rudolph Miller knelt in the pew beside the confessional and waited, straining nervously to hear, and yet not to hear what was being said within. The fact that the priest was audible alarmed him. His own turn came next, and the three or four others who waited might listen unscrupulously while he admitted his violations of the Sixth and Ninth Commandments.

Rudolph had never committed adultery, nor even coveted his neighbour's wife—but it was the confession of the associate sins that was particularly hard to contemplate. In comparison he relished the less shameful fallings away— they formed a greyish background which relieved the ebony mark of sexual offences upon his soul.

He had been covering his ears with his hands, hoping that his refusal to hear would be noticed, and a like courtesy rendered to him in turn, when a sharp movement of the penitent in the confessional made him sink his face precipitately into the crook of his elbow. Fear assumed solid form, and pressed out a lodging between his heart

9*

and his lungs. He must try now with all his might to be sorry for his sins—not because he was afraid, but because he had offended God. He must convince God that he was sorry and to do so he must first convince himself. After a tense emotional struggle he achieved a tremulous self-pity, and decided that he was now ready. If, by allowing no other thought to enter his head, he could preserve this state of emotion unimpaired until he went into that large coffin set on end, he would have survived another crisis in his religious life.

For some time, however, a demoniac notion had partially possessed him. He could go home now, before his turn came, and tell his mother that he had arrived too late, and found the priest gone. This, unfortunately, involved the risk of being caught in a lie. As an alternative he could say that he *had* gone to confession, but this meant that he must avoid communion next day, for communion taken upon an uncleansed soul would turn to poison in his mouth, and he would crumple limp and damned from the altar-rail.

Again Father Schwartz's voice became audible.

'And for your——'

The words blurred to a husky mumble, and Rudolph got excitedly to his feet. He felt that it was impossible to go to confession this afternoon. He hesitated tensely. Then from the confessional came a tap, a creak, and a sustained rustle. The slide had fallen and the plush curtain trembled. Temptation had come to him too late. . . .

'Bless me, Father, for I have sinned. . . . I confess to Almighty God and to you, Father, that I have sinned. . . . Since my last confession it has been one month and three days. . . . I accuse myself of—taking the Name of the Lord in vain. . . .'

This was an easy sin. His curses had been but bravado—telling of them was little less than a brag.

'. . . of being mean to an old lady.'

The wan shadow moved a little on the latticed slat.

'How, my child?'

'Old lady Swenson,' Rudolph's murmur soared jubilantly. 'She got our baseball that we knocked in her window, and she wouldn't give it back, so we yelled "Twenty-three, Skidoo," at her all afternoon. Then about five o'clock she had a fit, and they had to have the doctor.'

'Go on, my child.'

'Of—of not believing I was the son of my parents.'

'What?' The interrogation was distinctly startled.

'Of not believing that I was the son of my parents.'

'Why not?'

'Oh, just pride,' answered the penitent airily.

'You mean you thought yourself too good to be the son of your parents?'

'Yes, Father.' On a less jubilant note.

'Go on.'

'Of being disobedient and calling my mother names. Of slandering people behind their back. Of smoking——'

Rudolph had now exhausted the minor offences, and was approaching the sins it was agony to tell. He held his fingers against his face like bars as if to press out between them the shame in his heart.

'Of dirty words and immodest thoughts and desires,' he whispered very low.

'How often?'

'I don't know.'

'Once a week? Twice a week?'

'Twice a week.'

'Did you yield to these desires?'

'No, Father.'

'Were you alone when you had them?'

'No Father. I was with two boys and a girl.'

'Don't you know, my child, that you should avoid the occasions of sin as well as the sin itself? Evil companionship leads to evil desires and evil desires to evil actions. Where were you when this happened?'

'In a barn back of——'

'I don't want to hear any names,' interrupted the priest sharply.

'Well, it was up in the loft of this barn and this girl and —a fella, they were saying things—saying immodest things, and I stayed.'

'You should have gone—you should have told the girl to go.'

He should have gone! He could not tell Father Schwartz how his pulse had bumped in his wrist, how a strange, romantic excitement had possessed him when those curious things had been said. Perhaps, in the houses of delinquency among the dull and hard-eyed incorrigible girls can be found those for whom has burned the whitest fire.

'Have you anything else to tell me?'

'I don't think so, Father.'

Rudolph felt a great relief. Perspiration had broken out under his tight-pressed fingers.

'Have you told any lies?'

The question startled him. Like all those who habitually and instinctively lie, he had an enormous respect and awe for the truth. Something almost exterior to himself dictated a quick, hurt answer. 'Oh no, Father, I never tell lies.'

For a moment, like the commoner in the king's chair, he tasted the pride of the situation. Then as the priest began to murmur conventional admonitions he realized that in heroically denying he had told lies, he had committed a terrible sin—he had told a lie in confession.

In automatic response to Father Schwartz's 'Make an act of contrition,' he began to repeat aloud meaninglessly:

'Oh, my God, I am heartily sorry for having offended Thee. . . .'

He must fix this now—it was a bad mistake—but as his teeth shut on the last words of his prayer there was a sharp sound, and the slat was closed.

A minute later when he emerged into the twilight the relief in coming from the muggy church into an open world of wheat and sky postponed the full realization of what he had done. Instead of worrying he took a deep breath of the crisp air and began to say over and over to himself the words 'Blatchford Sarnemington, Blatchford Sarne-mington!'

Blatchford Sarnemington was himself, and these words were in effect a lyric. When he became Blatchford Sarne-mington a suave nobility flowed from him. Blatchford Sarnemington lived in great sweeping triumphs. When Rudolph half closed his eyes it meant that Blatchford had established dominance over him and, as he went by, there were envious mutters in the air: 'Blatchford Sarneming-ton! There goes Blatchford Sarnemington.'

He was Blatchford now for a while as he strutted home-ward along the staggering road, but when the road braced itself in macadam in order to become the main street of Ludwig, Rudolph's exhilaration faded out and his mind cooled, and he felt the horror of his lie. God, of course, already knew of it—but Rudolph reserved a corner of his mind where he was safe from God, where he prepared the subterfuges with which he often tricked God. Hiding now in this corner he considered how he could best avoid the consequences of his mis-statement.

At all costs he must avoid communion next day. The risk of angering God to such an extent was too great. He would have to drink water 'by accident' in the morning, and thus, in accordance with a church law, render himself unfit to receive communion that day. In spite of its flimsi-ness this subterfuge was the most feasible that occurred to him. He accepted its risks and was concentrating on how best to put it into effect, as he turned the corner by Romberg's Drug Store and came in sight of his father's house.

III

Rudolph's father, the local freight-agent, had floated with the second wave of German and Irish stock to the Minne-sota-Dakota country. Theoretically, great opportunities lay ahead of a young man of energy in that day and place, but Carl Miller had been incapable of establishing either with his superiors or his subordinates the reputation for approximate immutability which is essential to success in a hierarchic industry. Somewhat gross, he was, nevertheless, insufficiently hard-headed and unable to take fundamental relationships for granted, and this inability made him suspicious, unrestful, and continually dismayed.

His two bonds with the colourful life were his faith in the Roman Catholic Church and his mystical worship of the Empire Builder, James J. Hill. Hill was the apotheosis of that quality in which Miller himself was deficient—the sense of things, the feel of things, the hint of rain in the wind on the cheek. Miller's mind worked late on the old decisions of other men, and he had never in his life felt the balance of any single thing in his hands. His weary, sprightly, undersized body was growing old in Hill's gigantic shadow. For twenty years he had lived alone with Hill's name and God.

On Sunday morning Carl Miller awoke in the dustless quiet of six o'clock. Kneeling by the side of the bed he bent his yellow-grey hair and the full dapple bangs of his moustache into the pillow, and prayed for several minutes. Then he drew off his night-shirt—like the rest of his generation he had never been able to endure pyjamas —and clothed his thin, white, hairless body in woollen underwear.

He shaved. Silence in the other bedroom where his wife lay nervously asleep. Silence from the screened-off corner of the hall where his son's cot stood, and his son slept among his Alger books, his collection of cigar-bands, his mothy pennants—'Cornell,' 'Hamlin,' and 'Greetings from Pueblo, New Mexico'—and the other possessions of his private life. From outside Miller could hear the shrill birds and the whirring movement of the poultry, and, as an undertone, the low, swelling click-a-click of the six-fifteen through train for Montana and the green coast beyond. Then as the cold water dripped from the wash-rag in his hand he raised his head suddenly—he had heard a furtive sound from the kitchen below.

He dried his razor hastily, slipped his dangling suspenders to his shoulder, and listened. Some one was walking in the kitchen, and he knew by the light footfall that it was not his wife. With his mouth faintly ajar he ran quickly down the stairs and opened the kitchen door.

Standing by the sink, with one hand on the still dripping faucet and the other clutching a full glass of water, stood his son. The boy's eyes, still heavy with sleep, met his father's with a frightened, reproachful beauty. He was barefooted, and his pyjamas were rolled up at the knees and sleeves.

For a moment they both remained motionless—Carl Miller's brow went down and his son's went up, as though they were striking a balance between the extremes of emotion which filled them. Then the bangs of the parent's moustache descended portentously until they obscured his mouth, and he gave a short glance around to see if anything had been disturbed.

The kitchen was garnished with sunlight which beat on the pans and made the smooth boards of the floor and table yellow and clean as wheat. It was the centre of the house where the fire burned and the tins fitted into tins like toys, and the steam whistled all day on a thin pastel note. Nothing was moved, nothing touched—except the faucet where beads of water still formed and dripped with a white flash into the sink below.

'What are you doing?'

'I got awful thirsty, so I thought I'd just come down and get——'

'I thought you were going to communion.'

A look of vehement astonishment spread over his son's face.

'I forgot all about it.'

'Have you drunk any water?'

'No——'

As the word left his mouth Rudolph knew it was the wrong answer, but the faded indignant eyes facing him had signalled up the truth before the boy's will could act.

He realized, too, that he should never have come downstairs; some vague necessity for verisimilitude had made him want to leave a wet glass as evidence by the sink; the honesty of his imagination had betrayed him.

'Pour it out,' commanded his father, 'that water!'

Rudolph despairingly inverted the tumbler.

'What's the matter with you, anyways?' demanded Miller angrily.

'Nothing.'

'Did you go to confession yesterday?'

'Yes.'

'Then why were you going to drink water?'

'I don't know—I forgot.'

'Maybe you care more about being a little thirsty than you do about your religion.'

'I forgot.' Rudolph could feel the tears straining in his eyes.

'That's no answer.'

'Well, I did.'

'You better look out!' His father held to a high, persistent inquisitory note: 'If you're so forgetful that you can't remember your religion something better be done about it.'

Rudolph filled a sharp pause with:

'I can remember it all right.'

'First you begin to neglect your religion,' cried his father, fanning his own fierceness, 'the next thing you'll begin to lie and steal, and the *next* thing is the *reform* school!'

Not even this familiar threat could deepen the abyss that Rudolph saw before him. He must either tell all now, offering his body for what he knew would be a ferocious beating or else tempt the thunderbolts by receiving the Body and Blood of Christ with sacrilege upon his soul. And of the two the former seemed more terrible—it was not so much the beating he dreaded as the savage ferocity, outlet of the ineffectual man, which would lie behind it.

'Put down that glass and go upstairs and dress!' his

father ordered, 'and when we get to church, before you go to communion, you better kneel down and ask God to forgive you for your carelessness.'

Some accidental emphasis in the phrasing of this command acted like a catalytic agent on the confusion and terror of Rudolph's mind. A wild, proud anger rose in him, and he dashed the tumbler passionately into the sink.

His father uttered a strained, husky sound, and sprang for him. Rudolph dodged to the side, tipped over a chair, and tried to get beyond the kitchen table. He cried out sharply when a hand grasped his pyjama shoulder, then he felt the dull impact of a fist against the side of his head, and glancing blows on the upper part of his body. As he slipped here and there in his father's grasp, dragged or lifted when he clung instinctively to an arm, aware of sharp smarts and strains, he made no sound except that he laughed hysterically several times. Then in less than a minute the blows abruptly ceased. After a lull during which Rudolph was tightly held, and during which they both trembled violently and uttered strange, truncated words, Carl Miller half dragged, half threatened his son upstairs.

'Put on your clothes!'

Rudolph was now both hysterical and cold. His head hurt him, and there was a long, shallow scratch on his neck from his father's fingernail, and he sobbed and trembled as he dressed. He was aware of his mother standing at the doorway in a wrapper, her wrinkled face compressing and squeezing and opening out into new series of wrinkles which floated and eddied from neck to brow. Despising her nervous ineffectuality and avoiding her rudely when she tried to touch his neck with witch-hazel, he made a hasty, choking toilet. Then he followed his father out of the house and along the road towards the Catholic church.

IV

They walked without speaking except when Carl Miller acknowledged automatically the existence of passers-by.

Rudolph's uneven breathing alone ruffled the hot Sunday silence.

His father stopped decisively at the door of the church.

'I've decided you'd better go to confession again. Go and tell Father Schwartz what you did and ask God's pardon.'

'You lost your temper, too!' said Rudolph quickly.

Carl Miller took a step towards his son, who moved cautiously backward.

'All right, I'll go.'

'Are you going to do what I say?' cried his father in a hoarse whisper.

'All right.'

Rudolph walked into the church, and for the second time in two days entered the confessional and knelt down. The slat went up almost at once.

'I accuse myself of missing my morning prayers.'

'Is that all?'

'That's all.'

A maudlin exultation filled him. Not easily ever again would he be able to put an abstraction before the necessities of his ease and pride. An invisible line had been crossed, and he had become aware of his isolation—aware that it applied not only to those moments when he was Blatchford Sarnemington but that it applied to all his inner life. Hitherto such phenomena as 'crazy' ambitions and petty shames and fears had been but private reservations, unacknowledged before the throne of his official soul. Now he realized unconsciously that his private reservations were himself—and all the rest a garnished front and a conventional flag. The pressure of his environment had driven him into the lonely secret road of adolescence.

He knelt in the pew beside his father. Mass began. Rudolph knelt up—when he was alone he slumped his posterior back against the seat—and tasted the consciousness of a sharp, subtle revenge. Beside him his father prayed that God would forgive Rudolph, and asked also that his own outbreak of temper would be pardoned. He glanced sidewise at this son, and was relieved to see that the strained, wild look had gone from his face and that he had ceased sobbing. The Grace of God, inherent in the Sacrament, would do the rest, and perhaps after Mass everything would be better. He was proud of Rudolph in his heart, and beginning to be truly as well as formally sorry for what he had done.

Usually, the passing of the collection box was the significant point for Rudolph in the services. If, as was often the case, he had no money to drop in he would be furiously ashamed and bow his head and pretend not to see the box, lest Jeanne Brady in the pew behind should take notice and suspect an acute family poverty. But to-day he glanced coldly into it as it skimmed under his eyes, noting with casual interest the large number of pennies it contained.

When the bell rang for communion, however, he quivered. There was no reason why God should not stop his heart. During the past twelve hours he had committed a series of mortal sins increasing in gravity, and he was now to crown them all with a blasphemous sacrilege.

'*Domine, non sum dignus; ut intres sub tectum meum; sed tantum dic verbo, et sanabitur anima mea. . . .*'

There was a rustle in the pews, and the communicants worked their ways into the aisle with downcast eyes and joined hands. Those of larger piety pressed together their finger-tips to form steeples. Among these latter was Carl Miller. Rudolph followed him towards the altar-rail and knelt down, automatically taking up the napkin under his chin. The bell rang sharply, and the priest turned from the altar with the white Host held above the chalice:

'*Corpus Domini nostri Jesu Christi custodiat animam tuam in vitam æternam.*'

A cold sweat broke out on Rudolph's forehead as the communion began. Along the line Father Schwartz moved, and with gathering nausea Rudolph felt his heart-valves weakening at the will of God. It seemed to him that the church was darker and that a great quiet had fallen, broken only by the inarticulate mumble which announced the approach of the Creator of Heaven and Earth. He dropped his head down between his shoulders and waited for the blow.

Then he felt a sharp nudge in his side. His father was poking him to sit up, not to slump against the rail; the priest was only two places away.

'*Corpus Domini nostri Jesus Christi custodiat animam tuam in vitam æternam.*'

Rudolph opened his mouth. He felt the sticky wax taste of the wafer on his tongue. He remained motionless for what seemed an interminable period of time, his head still raised, the wafer undissolved in his mouth. Then again he started at the pressure of his father's elbow, and saw that the people were falling away from the altar like leaves and turning with blind downcast eyes to their pews, alone with God.

Rudolph was alone with himself, drenched with perspiration and deep in mortal sin. As he walked back to his pew the sharp taps of his cloven hoofs were loud upon the floor, and he knew that it was a dark poison he carried in his heart.

V

'*Sagitta Volante in Dei*'

The beautiful little boy with eyes like blue stones, and lashes that sprayed open from them like flower-petals had finished telling his sin to Father Schwartz—and the square of sunshine in which he sat had moved forward an hour into the room. Rudolph had become less frightened now; once eased of the story a reaction had set in. He knew that as long as he was in the room with this priest God would not stop his heart, so he sighed and sat quietly, waiting for the priest to speak.

Father Schwartz's cold watery eyes were fixed upon the carpet pattern on which the sun had brought out the swastikas and the flat bloomless vines and the pale echoes of flowers. The hall-clock ticked insistently towards sunset, and from the ugly room and from the afternoon outside the window arose a stiff monotony, shattered now and then by the reverberate clapping of a far-away hammer on the dry air. The priest's nerves were strung thin and the beads of his rosary were crawling and squirming like snakes upon the green felt of his table top. He could not remember now what it was he should say.

Of all the things in this lost Swede town he was most aware of this little boy's eyes—the beautiful eyes, with lashes that left them reluctantly and curved back as though to meet them once more.

For a moment longer the silence persisted while Rudolph waited, and the priest struggled to remember something that was slipping farther and farther away from him, and the clock ticked in the broken house. Then Father Schwartz stared hard at the little boy and remarked in a peculiar voice:

'When a lot of people get together in the best places things go glimmering.'

Rudolph started and looked quickly at Father Schwartz's face.

'I said——' began the priest, and paused, listening. 'Do you hear the hammer and the clock ticking and the bees? Well, that's no good. The thing is to have a lot of people in the centre of the world, wherever that happens to be. Then'—his watery eyes widened knowingly—'things go glimmering.'

'Yes, Father,' agreed Rudolph, feeling a little frightened.

'What are you going to be when you grow up?'

'Well, I was going to be a baseball-player for a while,' answered Rudolph nervously, 'but I don't think that is a very good ambition, so I think I'll be an actor or a Navy officer.'

Again the priest stared at him.

'I see *exactly* what you mean,' he said, with a fierce air.

Rudolph had not meant anything in particular, and at the implication that he had, he became more uneasy.

'This man is crazy,' he thought, 'and I'm scared of him. He wants me to help him out some way, and I don't want to.'

'You look as if things went glimmering,' cried Father Schwartz wildly. 'Did you ever go to a party?'

'Yes, Father.'

'And did you notice that everybody was properly dressed? That's what I mean. Just as you went into the party there was a moment when everybody was properly dressed. Maybe two little girls were standing by the door and some boys were leaning over the banisters, and there were bowls around full of flowers.'

'I've been to a lot of parties,' said Rudolph, rather relieved that the conversation had taken this turn.

'Of course,' continued Father Schwartz triumphantly, 'I knew you'd agree with me. But my theory is that when a whole lot of people get together in the best places things go glimmering all the time.'

Rudolph found himself thinking of Blatchford Sarnemington.

'Please listen to me!' commanded the priest impatiently. 'Stop worrying about last Saturday. Apostasy implies an absolute damnation only on the supposition of a previous perfect faith. Does that fix it?'

Rudolph had not the faintest idea what Father Schwartz was talking about, but he nodded and the priest nodded back at him and returned to his mysterious preoccupation.

'Why,' he cried, 'they have lights now as big as stars— do you realize that? I heard of one light they had in Paris or somewhere that was as big as a star. A lot of people had it—a lot of gay people. They have all sorts of things now that you never dreamed of.'

'Look here——' He came nearer to Rudolph, but the boy drew away, so Father Schwartz went back and sat down in his chair, his eyes dried out and hot. 'Did you ever see an amusement park?'

'No, Father.'

'Well, go and see an amusement park.' The priest waved his hand vaguely. 'It's a thing like a fair, only much more glittering. Go to one at night and stand a little way off from it in a dark place—under dark trees. You'll see a big wheel made of lights turning in the air, and a long slide shooting boats down into the water. A band playing somewhere, and a smell of peanuts—and everything will twinkle. But it won't remind you of anything, you see. It will all just hang out there in the night like a coloured balloon—like a big yellow lantern on a pole.'

Father Schwartz frowned as he suddenly thought of something.

'But don't get up close,' he warned Rudolph, 'because if you do you'll only feel the heat and the sweat and the life.'

All this talking seemed particularly strange and awful to Rudolph, because this man was a priest. He sat there, half terrified, his beautiful eyes open wide and staring at Father Schwartz. But underneath his terror he felt that his own inner convictions were confirmed. There was something ineffably gorgeous somewhere that had nothing to do with God. He no longer thought that God was angry at him about the original lie, because He must have understood that Rudolph had done it to make things finer in the confessional, brightening up the dinginess of his admissions by saying a thing radiant and proud. At the moment when he had affirmed immaculate honour a silver pennon had flapped out into the breeze somewhere and there had been the crunch of leather and the shine of silver spurs and a troop of horsemen waiting for dawn on a low green hill. The sun had made stars of light on their breastplates like the picture at home of the German cuirassiers at Sedan.

But now the priest was muttering inarticulate and heartbroken words, and the boy became wildly afraid. Horror entered suddenly in at the open window, and the atmosphere of the room changed. Father Schwartz collapsed precipitously down on his knees, and let his body settle back against a chair.

'Oh, my God!' he cried out, in a strange voice, and wilted to the floor.

Then a human oppression rose from the priest's worn clothes, and mingled with the faint smell of old food in the corners. Rudolph gave a sharp cry and ran in panic

from the house—while the collapsed man lay there quite
still, filling his room, filling it with voices and faces until
it was crowded with echolalia, and rang loud with a steady,
shrill note of laughter.

Outside the window the blue sirocco trembled over the
wheat, and girls with yellow hair walked sensuously along
roads that bounded the fields, calling innocent, exciting
things to the young men who were working in the lines
between the grain. Legs were shaped under starchless
gingham, and rims of the necks of dresses were warm and
damp. For five hours now hot fertile life had burned in
the afternoon. It would be night in three hours, and all
along the land there would be these blonde Northern girls
and the tall young men from the farms lying out beside the
wheat, under the moon.

II
GLAMOUR AND
DISILLUSIONMENT

EDITOR'S NOTE

This second group consists of nine stories written between 1924, the year when Fitzgerald was working on *The Great Gatsby*, and 1929, when he and Zelda were quarrelling in Paris under the shadow of her approaching breakdown. During those years he was devoting most of his energies to magazine stories and the stories continued to improve, after taking a leap forward at the time of *Gatsby*; but already the author was suffering from a form of neglect. The situation was in some ways preposterous. Here was a greatly talented author doing some of his nearly best work, which was being featured in the most popular American magazines, and here were the critics wondering what had become of him after his early success. The critics didn't read the *Saturday Evening Post* or expect to find serious fiction there. Fitzgerald was so much influenced by their attitude that he never reprinted some of his most effective stories.

Four of the stories that he disowned—or, in his own phrase, 'junked and dismantled'—are included in the present group. 'The Bowl' (1928) is partly Fitzgerald's early dream of becoming a football player, idol of his college, but it also expresses his later admiration for what he called the 'final people' in any profession. All these had an authority and, he believed, a sense of kinship that was based on their common respect for disciplined effort. 'Why, I'm Dolly Harlan,' the football hero says, in the same spirit that the author would like to have said, 'Why, I'm Scott Fitzgerald.'... He had made a first visit to Hollywood in 1927, under contract to write a script for Constance Talmadge. Besides being the life of several wild parties, he had worked hard on the script, but the producer turned it down. One story, 'Magnetism' (1928), was the only fruit of his visit. It is a serious study of the movie colony, even if it deals with the farcical dilemma of a good man and faithful husband who can't keep other women from falling in love with him. . . . 'Outside the Cabinet-Maker's' (1928) is a story-teller's lament for the sense of mystery he could still awaken in his little daughter, 'but whose lustre and texture he could never see or touch any more himself.'. . . 'The Rough Crossing' (1929), with its hint of disasters to come, was the souvenir of a stormy voyage from New York to Genoa, during which Scott and Zelda had flirted with strangers and nagged at each other. The first two paragraphs of this 'junked and dismantled' story went into Fitzgerald's notebook and were afterwards re-written into Book II, Chapter XIX, of *Tender is the Night*.

Two other stories in the present group were reprinted in *All the Sad Young Men*. 'The Rich Boy' (1926) was the first serious work that Fitzgerald undertook after finishing *Gatsby*. Like the novel it reveals his complicated attitude towards the very rich, with its mixture of distrust, admiration, and above all curiosity about how their minds work. Anson Hunter's central trait, in the story, is the sense of superiority that he feeds by captivating others. In revealing the trait, Fitzgerald shows how much he has learned about irony and understatement. . . . 'The Baby Party' (1925) goes back to a somewhat earlier period. After spending a year among the rich on the north shore of Long Island, where he entertained mobs of week-end guests, Fitzgerald was $5,000 in debt and had to stop work on *Gatsby*. He wrote himself out of debt by rapidly producing eleven stories, which he sold for more than $17,000. 'I really worked hard as hell last winter,' he said in a letter to Edmund Wilson—'but it was all trash and it nearly broke my heart as well as my iron constitution.' Although 'The Baby Party' was written in a single all-night session, it is far from trash, and it is Fitzgerald's one excursion into the field of domestic comedy.

The other three stories in the group are reprinted from *Taps at Reveille*, the last and best of the collections published during his lifetime. Among them 'A Short Trip Home' (1927) is a ghost story that is curiously Japanese

in spirit; there are many Japanese legends of re-embodied
spirits who try to seduce the living and carry them off to
a shadow world. In this case, however, the ghost has a
social meaning. The living-dead man in high button shoes
represents the lower order of humanity that offers a
mysterious threat to the standards and the daughters of
the rich people whose mansions rise above them on the
hill. . . . 'Majesty' (1929) is Fitzgerald's coronation of the
Jazz Age flapper; the spoiled brat and beauty ends as a
spoiled but legitimate queen. . . . 'The Last of the Belles'
(1929) is also the last of Tarleton, Georgia, which had
been the scene of some earlier stories. The city seems to
resemble Montgomery, Alabama, where Zelda herself had
been a wartime belle. As for the story, it is one of those
filled with regret for a vanished emotion, but the regret is
seasoned with self-ridicule—as when the hero goes stumbling through knee-deep underbrush, 'looking,' as he said
to himself, 'for my youth in a clapboard or a strip of
roofing or a rusty tomato can.'

THE RICH BOY

[1926]

BEGIN WITH an individual, and before you know it you find
that you have created a type; begin with a type, and you
find that you have created – nothing. That is because we are
all queer fish, queerer behind our faces and voices than we
want any one to know or than we know ourselves. When I
hear a man proclaiming himself an 'average, honest, open
fellow,' I feel pretty sure that he has some definite and perhaps terrible abnormality which he has agreed to conceal –
and his protestation of being average and honest and open is
his way of reminding himself of his misprision.

There are no types, no plurals. There is a rich boy, and
this is his and not his brothers' story. All my life I have lived
among his brothers but this one has been my friend. Besides,
if I wrote about his brothers I should have to begin by
attacking all the lies that the poor have told about the rich
and the rich have told about themselves – such a wild
structure they have erected that when we pick up a book
about the rich, some instinct prepares us for unreality. Even
the intelligent and impassioned reporters of life have made
the country of the rich as unreal as fairy-land.

Let me tell you about the very rich. They are different
from you and me. They possess and enjoy early, and it does
something to them, makes them soft where we are hard, and
cynical where we are trustful, in a way that, unless you were
born rich, it is very difficult to understand. They think, deep
in their hearts, that they are better than we are because we
had to discover the compensations and refuges of life for
ourselves. Even when they enter deep into our world or sink
below us, they still think that they are better than we are.

286

They are different. The only way I can describe young Anson Hunter is to approach him as if he were a foreigner and cling stubbornly to my point of view. If I accept his for a moment I am lost – I have nothing to show but a preposterous movie.

II

Anson was the eldest of six children who would some day divide a fortune of fifteen million dollars, and he reached the age of reason – is it seven ? – at the beginning of the century when daring young women were already gliding along Fifth Avenue in electric 'mobiles.' In those days he and his brother had an English governess who spoke the language very clearly and crisply and well, so that the two boys grew to speak as she did – their words and sentences were all crisp and clear and not run together as ours are. They didn't talk exactly like English children but acquired an accent that is peculiar to fashionable people in the city of New York.

In the summer the six children were moved from the house on 71st Street to a big estate in northern Connecticut. It was not a fashionable locality – Anson's father wanted to delay as long as possible his children's knowledge of that side of life. He was a man somewhat superior to his class, which composed New York society, and to his period, which was the snobbish and formalized vulgarity of the Gilded Age, and he wanted his sons to learn habits of concentration and have sound constitutions and grow up into right-living and successful men. He and his wife kept an eye on them as well as they were able until the two older boys went away to school, but in huge establishments this is difficult – it was much simpler in the series of small and medium-sized houses in which my own youth was spent – I was never far out of the reach of my mother's voice, of the sense of her presence, her approval or disapproval.

Anson's first sense of his superiority came to him when he realized the half-grudging American deference that was paid to him in the Connecticut village. The parents of the boys he played with always inquired after his father and mother, and were vaguely excited when their own children were asked to the Hunters' house. He accepted this as the natural state of things, and a sort of impatience with all groups of which he was not the centre – in money, in position, in authority – remained with him for the rest of his life. He disdained to struggle with other boys for precedence – he expected it to be given him freely, and when it wasn't he withdrew into his family. His family was sufficient, for in the East money is still a somewhat feudal thing, a clan-forming thing. In the snobbish West, money separates families to form 'sets.'

At eighteen, when he went to New Haven, Anson was tall and thick-set, with a clear complexion and a healthy colour from the ordered life he had led in school. His hair was yellow and grew in a funny way on his head, his nose was beaked – these two things kept him from being handsome – but he had a confident charm and a certain brusque style, and the upper-class men who passed him on the street knew without being told that he was a rich boy and had gone to one of the best schools. Nevertheless, his very superiority kept him from being a success in college – the independence was mistaken for egotism, and the refusal to accept Yale standards with the proper awe seemed to belittle all those who had. So, long before he graduated, he began to shift the centre of his life to New York.

He was at home in New York – there was his own house with 'the kind of servants you can't get any more' – and his own family, of which, because of his good humour and a certain ability to make things go, he was rapidly becoming the centre, and the débutante parties, and the correct manly world of the men's clubs, and the occasional wild spree with the gallant girls whom New Haven only knew from the fifth row. His aspirations were conventional enough – they included even the irreproachable shadow he would some day marry, but they differed from the aspirations of the majority of young men in that there was no mist over them, none of that quality which is variously known as 'idealism' or 'illusion.' Anson accepted without reservation the world of high finance and high extravagance, of divorce and dissipation, of snobbery and of privilege. Most of our lives end as a compromise – it was as a compromise that his life began.

He and I first met in the late summer of 1917 when he was just out of Yale, and, like the rest of us, was swept up into the systematized hysteria of the war. In the blue-green uniform of the naval aviation he came down to Pensacola, where the hotel orchestras played 'I'm sorry, dear,' and we young officers danced with the girls. Every one liked him, and though he ran with the drinkers and wasn't an especially good pilot, even the instructors treated him with a certain respect. He was always having long talks with them in his confident, logical voice – talks which ended by his getting himself, or, more frequently, another officer, out of some impending trouble. He was convivial, bawdy, robustly avid for pleasure, and we were all surprised when he fell in love with a conservative and rather proper girl.

Her name was Paula Legendre, a dark, serious beauty from somewhere in California. Her family kept a winter residence just outside of town, and in spite of her primness she was enormously popular; there is a large class of men whose egotism can't endure humour in a woman. But Anson wasn't that sort, and I couldn't understand the attraction of her 'sincerity' – that was the thing to say about her – for his keen and somewhat sardonic mind.

Nevertheless, they fell in love – and on her terms. He no longer joined the twilight gathering at the De Soto bar, and whenever they were seen together they were engaged in a long, serious dialogue, which must have gone on several weeks. Long afterwards he told me that it was not about anything in particular but was composed on both sides of immature and even meaningless statements – the emotional content that gradually came to fill it grew up not out of the words but out of its enormous seriousness. It was a sort of hypnosis. Often it was interrupted, giving way to that emasculated humour we call fun; when they were alone it was resumed again, solemn, low-keyed, and pitched so as to give each other a sense of unity in feeling and thought. They came to resent any interruptions of it, to be unresponsive to facetiousness about life, even to the mild cynicism of their contemporaries. They were only happy when the dialogue was going on, and its seriousness bathed them like the amber glow of an open fire. Toward the end there came an interruption they did not resent – it began to be interrupted by passion.

Oddly enough, Anson was as engrossed in the dialogue as she was and as profoundly affected by it, yet at the same time aware that on his side much was insincere, and on hers much was merely simple. At first, too, he despised her emotional simplicity as well, but with his love her nature deepened and blossomed, and he could despise it no longer. He felt that if he could enter into Paula's warm safe life he would be happy. The long preparation of the dialogue removed any constraint – he taught her some of what he had learned from more adventurous women, and she responded with a rapt holy intensity. One evening after a dance they agreed to marry, and he wrote a long letter about her to his mother. The next day Paula told him that she was rich, that she had a personal fortune of nearly a million dollars.

III

It was exactly as if they could say 'Neither of us has anything: we shall be poor together' – just as delightful that they should be rich instead. It gave them the same communion of adventure. Yet when Anson got leave in April, and Paula and her mother accompanied him North, she was impressed with the standing of his family in New York and with the scale on which they lived. Alone with Anson for the first time in the rooms where he had played as a boy, she was filled with a comfortable emotion, as though she were pre-eminently safe and taken care of. The pictures of Anson in a skull cap at his first school, of Anson on horseback with the sweetheart of a mysterious forgotten summer, of Anson in a gay group of ushers and bridesmaid at a wedding, made her jealous of his life apart from her in the past, and so complete-ly did his authoritative person seem to sum up and typify these possessions of his that she was inspired with the idea of being married immediately and returning to Pensacola as his wife.

But an immediate marriage wasn't discussed – even the engagement was to be secret until after the war. When she realized that only two days of his leave remained, her dis-satisfaction crystallized in the intention of making him as unwilling to wait as she was. They were driving to the country for dinner and she determined to force the issue that night.

Now a cousin of Paula's was staying with them at the Ritz, a severe, bitter girl who loved Paula but was somewhat jealous of her impressive engagement, and as Paula was late in dressing, the cousin, who wasn't going to the party, re-ceived Anson in the parlour of the suite.

Anson had met friends at five o'clock and drunk freely and indiscreetly with them for an hour. He left the Yale Club at a proper time, and his mother's chauffeur drove him to the Ritz, but his usual capacity was not in evidence, and the im-pact of the steam-heated sitting-room made him suddenly dizzy. He knew it, and he was both amused and sorry.

Paula's cousin was twenty-five, but she was exceptionally naïve, and at first failed to realize what was up. She had never met Anson before, and she was surprised when he mumbled strange information and nearly fell off his chair, but until Paula appeared it didn't occur to her that what she had taken for the odour of a dry-cleaned uniform was really whisky. But Paula understood as soon as she appeared; her only thought was to get Anson away before her mother saw him, and at the look in her eyes the cousin understood too.

When Paula and Anson descended to the limousine they

found two men inside, both asleep; they were the men with whom he had been drinking at the Yale Club, and they were also going to the party. He had entirely forgotten their presence in the car. On the way to Hempstead they awoke and sang. Some of the songs were rough, and though Paula tried to reconcile herself to the fact that Anson had few verbal inhibitions, her lips tightened with shame and distaste.

Back at the hotel the cousin, confused and agitated, considered the incident, and then walked into Mrs Legendre's bedroom, saying: 'Isn't he funny?'

'Who is funny?'

'Why – Mr Hunter. He seemed so funny.'

Mrs Legendre looked at her sharply.

'How is he funny?'

'Why, he said he was French. I didn't know he was French.'

'That's absurd. You must have misunderstood.' She smiled: 'It was a joke.'

The cousin shook her head stubbornly.

'No. He said he was brought up in France. He said he couldn't speak any English, and that's why he couldn't talk to me. And he couldn't!'

Mrs Legendre looked away with impatience just as the cousin added thoughtfully, 'Perhaps it was because he was so drunk,' and walked out of the room.

This curious report was true. Anson, finding his voice thick and uncontrollable, had taken the unusual refuge of announcing that he spoke no English. Years afterwards he used to tell that part of the story, and he invariably communicated the uproarious laughter which the memory aroused in him.

Five times in the next hour Mrs Legendre tried to get Hempstead on the phone. When she succeeded, there was a ten-minute delay before she heard Paula's voice on the wire.

'Cousin Jo told me Anson was intoxicated.'

'Oh, no. . . .'

'Oh, yes. Cousin Jo says he was intoxicated. He told her he was French, and fell off his chair and behaved as if he was very intoxicated. I don't want you to come home with him.'

'Mother, he's all right! Please don't worry about——'

'But I do worry. I think it's dreadful. I want you to promise me not to come home with him.'

'I'll take care of it, mother. . . .'

'I don't want you to come home with him.'

'All right, mother. Good-bye.'

'Be sure now, Paula. Ask some one to bring you.'

Deliberately Paula took the receiver from her ear and hung it up. Her face was flushed with helpless annoyance. Anson was stretched out asleep in a bedroom upstairs, while the dinner-party below was proceeding lamely toward conclusion.

The hour's drive had sobered him somewhat – his arrival was merely hilarious – and Paula hoped that the evening was not spoiled, after all, but two imprudent cocktails before dinner completed the disaster. He talked boisterously and somewhat offensively to the party at large for fifteen minutes, and then slid silently under the table; like a man in an old print – but, unlike an old print, it was rather horrible without being at all quaint. None of the young girls present remarked upon the incident – it seemed to merit only silence. His uncle and two other men carried him upstairs, and it was just after this that Paula was called to the phone.

An hour later Anson awoke in a fog of nervous agony, through which he perceived after a moment the figure of his uncle Robert standing by the door.

'. . . I said are you better?'

'What?'

'Do you feel better, old man?'

'Terrible,' said Anson.

'I'm going to try you on another bromo-seltzer. If you can hold it down, it'll do you good to sleep.'

With an effort Anson slid his legs from the bed and stood up.

'I'm all right,' he said dully.

'Take it easy.'

'I thin' if you gave me a glassbrandy I could go down-stairs.'

'Oh, no——'

'Yes, that's the only thin'. I'm all right now. . . . I suppose I'm in Dutch dow' there.'

'They know you're a little under the weather,' said his uncle deprecatingly. 'But don't worry about it. Schuyler didn't even get here. He passed away in the locker-room over at the Links.'

Indifferent to any opinion, except Paula's, Anson was nevertheless determined to save the débris of the evening, but when after a cold bath he made his appearance most of the party had already left. Paula got up immediately to go home.

In the limousine the old serious dialogue began. She had known that he drank, she admitted, but she had never ex-pected anything like this – it seemed to her that perhaps they were not suited to each other, after all. Their ideas about life were too different, and so forth. When she finished speaking, Anson spoke in turn, very soberly. Then Paula said she'd have to think it over; she wouldn't decide to-night; she was not angry but she was terribly sorry. Nor would she let him come into the hotel with her, but just before she got out of the car she leaned and kissed him un-happily on the cheek.

The next afternoon Anson had a long talk with Mrs Legendre while Paula sat listening in silence. It was agreed that Paula was to brood over the incident for a proper period and then, if mother and daughter thought it best, they would follow Anson to Pensacola. On his part he apologized with sincerity and dignity – that was all; with every card in her hand Mrs Legendre was unable to establish any advantage over him. He made no promises, showed no humility, only delivered a few serious comments on life which brought him off with rather a moral superiority at the end. When they came South three weeks later, neither Anson in his satisfaction nor Paula in her relief at the reunion realized that the psychological moment had passed forever.

IV

He dominated and attracted her, and at the same time filled her with anxiety. Confused by his mixture of solidity and self-indulgence, of sentiment and cynicism – incongruities which her gentle mind was unable to resolve – Paula grew to think of him as two alternating personalities. When she saw him alone, or at a formal party, or with his casual inferiors, she felt a tremendous pride in his strong, attractive presence, the paternal, understanding stature of his mind. In other company she became uneasy when what had been a fine imperviousness to mere gentility showed its other face. The other face was gross, humorous, reckless of everything but pleasure. It startled her mind temporarily away from him, even led her into a short covert experiment with an old beau, but it was no use – after four months of Anson's enveloping vitality there was an anæmic pallor in all other men.

In July he was ordered abroad, and their tenderness and desire reached a crescendo. Paula considered a last-minute marriage – decided against it only because there were always cocktails on his breath now, but the parting itself made her physically ill with grief. After his departure she wrote him long letters of regret for the days of love they had missed by waiting. In August Anson's plane slipped down into the North Sea. He was pulled on to a destroyer after a night in the water and sent to hospital with pneumonia; the armistice was signed before he was finally sent home.

Then, with every opportunity given back to them, with no material obstacle to overcome, the secret weavings of their temperaments came between them, drying up their kisses and their tears, making their voices less loud to one another, muffling the intimate chatter of their hearts until the old communication was only possible by letters, from far away. One afternoon a society reporter waited for two hours in the Hunters' house for a confirmation of their engagement. Anson denied it; nevertheless an early issue carried the report as a leading paragraph – they were 'constantly seen together at Southampton, Hot Springs, and Tuxedo Park.' But the serioudialogue had turned a corner into a long-sustained quarrel, and the affair was almost played out. Anson got drunk flagrantly and missed an engagement with her, whereupon Paula made certain behavioristic demands. His despair was helpless before his pride and his knowledge of himself: the engagement was definitely broken.

'Dearest,' said their letters now, 'Dearest, Dearest, when I wake up in the middle of the night and realize that after all it was not to be, I feel that I want to die. I can't go on living any more. Perhaps when we meet this summer we may talk things over and decide differently – we were so excited and sad that day, and I don't feel that I can live all my life without you. You speak of other people. Don't you know there are no other people for me, but only you. . . .'

But as Paula drifted here and there around the East she would sometimes mention her gaieties to make him wonder. Anson was too acute to wonder. When he saw a man's name in her letters he felt more sure of her and a little disdainful – he was always superior to such things. But he still hoped that they would some day marry.

Meanwhile he plunged vigorously into all the movement and glitter of post-bellum New York, entering a brokerage house, joining half a dozen clubs, dancing late, and moving in three worlds – his own world, the world of young Yale graduates, and that section of the half-world which rests one end on Broadway. But there was always a thorough and infrangible eight hours devoted to his work in Wall Street, where the combination of his influential family connection, his sharp intelligence, and his abundance of sheer physical energy brought him almost immediately forward. He had one of those invaluable minds with partitions in it; sometimes he appeared at his office refreshed by less than an hour's sleep, but such occurrences were rare. So early as 1920 his income in salary and commissions exceeded twelve thousand dollars.

As the Yale tradition slipped into the past he became more and more of a popular figure among his classmates in New York, more popular than he had ever been in college. He lived in a great house, and had the means of introducing young men into other great houses. Moreover, his life already seemed secure, while theirs, for the most part, had arrived again at precarious beginnings. They commenced to turn to him for amusement and escape, and Anson responded readily, taking pleasure in helping people and arranging their affairs.

There were no men in Paula's letters now, but a note of tenderness ran through them that had not been there before. From several sources he heard that she had 'a heavy beau,' Lowell Thayer, a Bostonian of wealth and position, and though he was sure she still loved him, it made him uneasy to think that he might lose her, after all. Save for one unsatisfactory day she had not been in New York for almost five months, and as the rumours multiplied he became increasingly anxious to see her. In February he took his vacation and went down to Florida.

Palm Beach sprawled plump and opulent between the sparkling sapphire of Lake Worth, flawed here and there by house-boats at anchor, and the great turquoise bar of the Atlantic Ocean. The huge bulks of the Breakers and the Royal Poinciana rose as twin paunches from the bright level of the sand, and around them clustered the Dancing Glade, Bradley's House of Chance, and a dozen modistes and milliners with goods at triple prices from New York. Upon the trellised veranda of the Breakers two hundred women stepped right, stepped left, wheeled, and slid in that then celebrated calisthenic known as the double-shuffle, while in half-time to the music two thousand bracelets clicked up and down on two hundred arms.

10*

At the Everglades Club after dark Paula and Lowell Thayer and Anson and a casual fourth played bridge with hot cards. It seemed to Anson that her kind, serious face was wan and tired – she had been around now for four, five, years. He had known her for three.

'Two spades.'

'Cigarette? . . . Oh, I beg your pardon. By me.'

'By.'

'I'll double three spades.'

There were a dozen tables of bridge in the room, which was filling up with smoke. Anson's eyes met Paula's, held them persistently even when Thayer's glance fell between them. . . .

'What was bid?' he asked abstractedly.

'*Rose of Washington Square*'

sang the young people in the corners:

'*I'm withering there
In basement air——*'

The smoke banked like fog, and the opening of a door filled the room with blown swirls of ectoplasm. Little Bright Eyes streaked past the tables seeking Mr Conan Doyle among the Englishmen who were posing as Englishmen about the lobby.

'You could cut it with a knife.'

'. . . cut it with a knife.'

'. . . a knife.'

At the end of the rubber Paula suddenly got up and spoke to Anson in a tense, low voice. With scarcely a glance at Lowell Thayer, they walked out of the door and descended a long flight of stone steps – in a moment they were walking hand in hand along the moonlit beach.

'Darling, darling. . . .' They embraced recklessly, passionately, in a shadow. . . . Then Paula drew back her face to let his lips say what she wanted to hear – she could feel the words forming as they kissed again. . . . Again she broke away, listening, but as he pulled her close once more she realized that he had said nothing – only *'Darling ! Darling !'* in that deep, sad whisper that always made her cry. Humbly, obediently, her emotions yielded to him and the tears streamed down her face, but her heart kept on crying: 'Ask me – oh, Anson, dearest, ask me!'

'Paula. . . . *Paula !'*

The words wrung her heart like hands, and Anson, feeling her tremble, knew that emotion was enough. He need say no more, commit their destinies to no practical enigma. Why should he, when he might hold her so, biding his own time, for another year – forever ? He was considering them both, her more than himself. For a moment, when she said suddenly that she must go back to her hotel, he hesitated, thinking first, 'This is the moment, after all,' and then: 'No, let it wait – she is mine. . . .'

He had forgotten that Paula too was worn away inside with the strain of three years. Her mood passed forever in the night.

He went back to New York next morning filled with a certain restless dissatisfaction. Late in April, without warning, he received a telegram from Bar Harbor in which Paula told him that she was engaged to Lowell Thayer, and that they would be married immediately in Boston. What he never really believed could happen had happened at last.

Anson filled himself with whisky that morning, and going to the office, carried on his work without a break – rather with a fear of what would happen if he stopped. In the evening he went out as usual, saying nothing of what had occurred; he was cordial, humorous, unabstracted. But one thing he could not help – for three days, in any place, in any company, he would suddenly bend his head into his hands and cry like a child.

V

In 1922 when Anson went abroad with the junior partner to investigate some London loans, the journey intimated that he was to be taken into the firm. He was twenty-seven now, a little heavy without being definitely stout, and with a manner older than his years. Old people and young people liked him and trusted him, and mothers felt safe when their daughters were in his charge, for he had a way, when he came into a room, of putting himself on a footing with the oldest and most conservative people there. 'You and I,' he seemed to say, 'we're solid. We understand.'

He had an instinctive and rather charitable knowledge of the weaknesses of men and women, and, like a priest, it made him the more concerned for the maintenance of outward forms. It was typical of him that every Sunday morning he taught in a fashionable Episcopal Sunday-school – even though a cold shower and a quick change into a cutaway coat were all that separated him from the wild night before.

After his father's death he was the practical head of his family, and, in effect, guided the destinies of the younger children. Through a complication his authority did not extend to his father's estate, which was administrated by his Uncle Robert, who was the horsey member of the family, a good-natured, hard-drinking member of that set which centres about Wheatley Hills.

Uncle Robert and his wife, Edna, had been great friends of Anson's youth, and the former was disappointed when his nephew's superiority failed to take a horsey form. He backed him for a city club which was the most difficult in America to enter – one could only join if one's family had 'helped to build up New York' (or, in other words, were rich before 1880) – and when Anson, after his election, neglected it for the Yale Club, Uncle Robert gave him a little talk on the subject. But when on top of that Anson declined to enter

Robert Hunter's own conservative and somewhat neglected brokerage house, his manner grew cooler. Like a primary teacher who has taught all he knew, he slipped out of Anson's life.

There were so many friends in Anson's life – scarcely one for whom he had not done some unusual kindness and scarcely one whom he did not occasionally embarrass by his bursts of rough conversation or his habit of getting drunk whenever and however he liked. It annoyed him when any one else blundered in that regard – about his own lapses he was always humorous. Odd things happened to him and he told them with infectious laughter.

I was working in New York that spring, and I used to lunch with him at the Yale Club, which my university was sharing until the completion of our own. I had read of Paula's marriage, and one afternoon, when I asked him about her, something moved him to tell me the story. After that he frequently invited me to family dinners at his house and behaved as though there was a special relation between us, as though with his confidence a little of that consuming memory had passed into me.

I found that despite the trusting mothers, his attitude toward girls was not indiscriminately protective. It was up to the girl – if she showed an inclination toward looseness, she must take care of herself, even with him.

'Life,' he would explain sometimes, 'has made a cynic of me.'

By life he meant Paula. Sometimes, especially when he was drinking, it became a little twisted in his mind, and he thought that she had callously thrown him over.

This 'cynicism,' or rather his realization that naturally fast girls were not worth sparing, led to his affair with Dolly Karger. It wasn't his only affair in those years, but it came nearest to touching him deeply, and it had a profound effect upon his attitude toward life.

Dolly was the daughter of a notorious 'publicist' who had married into society. She herself grew up into the Junior League, came out at the Plaza, and went to the Assembly;

and only a few old families like the Hunters could question whether or not she 'belonged,' for her picture was often in the papers, and she had more enviable attention than many girls who undoubtedly did. She was dark-haired, with carmine lips and a high, lovely colour, which she concealed under pinkish-grey powder all through the first year out, because high colour was unfashionable – Victorian-pale was the thing to be. She wore black, severe suits and stood with her hands in her pockets leaning a little forward, with a humorous restraint on her face. She danced exquisitely – better than anything she liked to dance – better than anything except making love. Since she was ten she had always been in love, and, usually, with some boy who didn't respond to her. Those who did – and there were many – bored her after a brief encounter, but for her failures she reserved the warmest spot in her heart. When she met them she would always try once more – sometimes she succeeded, more often she failed.

It never occurred to this gypsy of the unattainable that there was a certain resemblance in those who refused to love her – they shared a hard intuition that saw through to her weakness, not a weakness of emotion but a weakness of rudder. Anson perceived this when he first met her, less than a month after Paula's marriage. He was drinking rather heavily, and he pretended for a week that he was falling in love with her. Then he dropped her abruptly and forgot – immediately he took up the commanding position in her heart.

Like so many girls of that day Dolly was slackly and indiscreetly wild. The unconventionality of a slightly older generation had been simply one facet of a post-war movement to discredit obsolete manners – Dolly's was both older and shabbier, and she saw in Anson the two extremes which the emotionally shiftless woman seeks, an abandon to indulgence alternating with a protective strength. In his character she felt both the sybarite and the solid rock, and these two satisfied every need of her nature.

She felt that it was going to be difficult, but she mistook

the reason – she thought that Anson and his family expected a more spectacular marriage, but she guessed immediately that her advantage lay in his tendency to drink.

They met at the large débutante dances, but as her infatuation increased they managed to be more and more together. Like most mothers, Mrs Karger believed that Anson was exceptionally reliable, so she allowed Dolly to go with him to distant country clubs and suburban houses without inquiring closely into their activities or questioning her explanations when they came in late. At first these explanations might have been accurate, but Dolly's worldly ideas of capturing Anson were soon engulfed in the rising sweep of her emotion. Kisses in the back of taxis and motor-cars were no longer enough; they did a curious thing:

They dropped out of their world for a while and made another world just beneath it where Anson's tippling and Dolly's irregular hours would be less noticed and commented on. It was composed, this world, of varying elements – several of Anson's Yale friends and their wives, two or three young brokers and bond salesmen and a handful of unattached men, fresh from college, with money and a propensity to dissipation. What this world lacked in spaciousness and scale it made up for by allowing them a liberty that it scarcely permitted itself. Moreover, it centred around them and permitted Dolly the pleasure of a faint condescension – a pleasure which Anson, whose whole life was a condescension from the certitudes of his childhood, was unable to share.

He was not in love with her, and in the long feverish winter of their affair he frequently told her so. In the spring he was weary – he wanted to renew his life at some other source – moreover, he saw that either he must break with her now or accept the responsibility of a definite seduction. Her family's encouraging attitude precipitated his decision – one evening when Mr Karger knocked discreetly at the library door to announce that he had left a bottle of old brandy in the dining-room, Anson felt that life was hemming him in. That night he wrote her a short letter in which he told her that he was going on his vacation, and that in view of all the circumstances they had better meet no more.

It was June. His family had closed up the house and gone to the country, so he was living temporarily at the Yale Club. I had heard about his affair with Dolly as it developed – accounts salted with humour, for he despised unstable women, and granted them no place in the social edifice in which he believed – and when he told me that night that he was definitely breaking with her I was glad. I had seen Dolly here and there, and each time with a feeling of pity at the hopelessness of her struggle, and of shame at knowing so much about her that I had no right to know. She was what is known as 'a pretty little thing,' but there was a certain recklessness which rather fascinated me. Her dedication to the goddess of waste would have been less obvious had she been less spirited – she would most certainly throw herself away, but I was glad when I heard that the sacrifice would not be consummated in my sight.

Anson was going to leave the letter of farewell at her house next morning. It was one of the few houses left open in the Fifth Avenue district, and he knew that the Kargers, acting upon erroneous information from Dolly, had forgone a trip abroad to give their daughter her chance. As he stepped out of the door of the Yale Club into Madison Avenue the postman passed him, and he followed back inside. The first letter that caught his eye was in Dolly's hand.

He knew what it would be – a lonely and tragic monologue, full of the reproaches he knew, the invoked memories, the 'I wonder if's' – all the immemorial intimacies that he had communicated to Paula Legendre in what seemed another age. Thumbing over some bills, he brought it on top again and opened it. To his surprise it was a short, somewhat formal note, which said that Dolly would be unable to go to the country with him for the week-end, because Perry Hull from Chicago had unexpectedly come to town. It added that Anson had brought this on himself: '— if I felt that you loved me as I love you I would go with you at any time, any place, but Perry is *so* nice, and he so much wants me to marry him——'

Anson smiled contemptuously – he had had experience with such decoy epistles. Moreover, he knew how Dolly had laboured over this plan, probably sent for the faithful Perry and calculated the time of his arrival – even laboured over the note so that it would make him jealous without driving him away. Like most compromises, it had neither force nor vitality but only a timorous despair.

Suddenly he was angry. He sat down in the lobby and read it again. Then he went to the phone, called Dolly and told her in his clear, compelling voice that he had received her note and would call for her at five o'clock as they had previously planned. Scarcely waiting for the pretended uncertainty of her 'Perhaps I can see you for an hour,' he hung up the receiver and went down to his office. On the way he tore his own letter into bits and dropped it in the street.

He was not jealous – she meant nothing to him – but at her pathetic ruse everything stubborn and self-indulgent in him came to the surface. It was a presumption from a mental inferior and it could not be overlooked. If she wanted to know to whom she belonged she would see.

He was on the door-step at quarter past five. Dolly was dressed for the street, and he listened in silence to the paragraph of 'I can only see you for an hour,' which she had begun on the phone.

'Put on your hat, Dolly,' he said, 'we'll take a walk.'

They strolled up Madison Avenue and over to Fifth while Anson's shirt dampened upon his portly body in the deep heat. He talked little, scolding her, making no love to her, but before they had walked six blocks she was his again, apologizing for the note, offering not to see Perry at all as an atonement, offering anything. She thought that he had come because he was beginning to love her.

'I'm hot,' he said when they reached 71st Street. 'This is a winter suit. If I stop by the house and change, would you mind waiting for me downstairs ? I'll only be a minute.'

She was happy; the intimacy of his being hot, of any

physical fact about him, thrilled her. When they came to the iron-grated door and Anson took out his key she experienced a sort of delight.

Downstairs it was dark, and after he ascended in the lift Dolly raised a curtain and looked out through opaque lace at the houses over the way. She heard the lift machinery stop, and with the notion of teasing him pressed the button that brought it down. Then on what was more than an impulse she got into it and sent it up to what she guessed was his floor.

'Anson,' she called, laughing a little.

'Just a minute,' he answered from his bedroom . . . then after a brief delay: 'Now you can come in.'

He had changed and was buttoning his vest.

'This is my room,' he said lightly. 'How do you like it?'

She caught sight of Paula's picture on the wall and stared at it in fascination, just as Paula had stared at the pictures of Anson's childish sweethearts five years before. She knew something about Paula – sometimes she tortured herself with fragments of the story.

Suddenly she came close to Anson, raising her arms. They embraced. Outside the area window a soft artificial twilight already hovered, though the sun was still bright on a back roof across the way. In half an hour the room would be quite dark. The uncalculated opportunity overwhelmed them, made them both breathless, and they clung more closely. It was imminent, inevitable. Still holding one another, they raised their heads – their eyes fell together upon Paula's picture, staring down at them from the wall.

Suddenly Anson dropped his arms, and sitting down at his desk tried the drawer with a bunch of keys.

'Like a drink?' he asked in a gruff voice.

'No, Anson.'

He poured himself half a tumbler of whisky, swallowed it, and then opened the door into the hall.

'Come on,' he said.

Dolly hesitated.

'Anson – I'm going to the country with you tonight, after all. You understand that, don't you?'

'Of course,' he answered brusquely.

In Dolly's car they rode on to Long Island, closer in their emotions than they had ever been before. They knew what would happen – not with Paula's face to remind them that something was lacking, but when they were alone in the still, hot Long Island night they did not care.

The estate in Port Washington where they were to spend the week-end belonged to a cousin of Anson's who had married a Montana copper operator. An interminable drive began at the lodge and twisted under imported poplar saplings toward a huge, pink Spanish house. Anson had often visited there before.

After dinner they danced at the Linx Club. About midnight Anson assured himself that his cousins would not leave before two – then he explained that Dolly was tired; he would take her home and return to the dance later. Trembling a little with excitement, they got into a borrowed car together and drove to Port Washington. As they reached the lodge he stopped and spoke to the night-watchman.

'When are you making a round, Carl?'

'Right away.'

'Then you'll be here till everybody's in?'

'Yes, sir.'

'All right. Listen: if any automobile, no matter whose it is, turns in at this gate, I want you to phone the house immediately.' He put a five-dollar bill into Carl's hand. 'Is that clear?'

'Yes, Mr Anson.' Being of the Old World, he neither winked nor smiled. Yet Dolly sat with her face turned slightly away.

Anson had a key. Once inside he poured a drink for both of them – Dolly left hers untouched – then he ascertained definitely the location of the phone, and found that it was within easy hearing distance of their rooms, both of which were on the first floor.

Five minutes later he knocked at the door of Dolly's room.

'Anson?' He went in, closing the door behind him. She

was in bed, leaning up anxiously with elbows on the pillow; sitting beside her he took her in his arms.

'Anson, darling.'

He didn't answer.

'Anson. . . . Anson! I love you. . . . Say you love me. Say it now – can't you say it now ? Even if you don't mean it ?'

He did not listen. Over her head he perceived that the picture of Paula was hanging here upon this wall.

He got up and went close to it. The frame gleamed faintly with thrice-reflected moonlight – within was a blurred shadow of a face that he saw he did not know. Almost sobbing, he turned around and stared with abomination at the little figure on the bed.

'This is all foolishness,' he said thickly. 'I don't know what I was thinking about. I don't love you and you'd better wait for somebody that loves you. I don't love you a bit, can't you understand ?'

His voice broke, and he went hurriedly out. Back in the salon he was pouring himself a drink with uneasy fingers, when the front door opened suddenly, and his cousin came in.

'Why, Anson, I hear Dolly's sick,' she began solicitously. 'I hear she's sick. . . .'

'It was nothing,' he interrupted, raising his voice so that it would carry into Dolly's room. 'She was a little tired. She went to bed.'

For a long time afterwards Anson believed that a protective God sometimes interfered in human affairs. But Dolly Karger, lying awake and staring at the ceiling, never again believed in anything at all.

VI

When Dolly married during the following autumn, Anson was in London on business. Like Paula's marriage, it was sudden, but it affected him in a different way. At first he felt that it was funny, and had an inclination to laugh when he thought of it. Later it depressed him – it made him feel old.

There was something repetitive about it – why, Paula and Dolly had belonged to different generations. He had a fore-taste of the sensation of a man of forty who hears that the daughter of an old flame has married. He wired congratula-tions and, as was not the case with Paula, they were sincere – he had never really hoped that Paula would be happy.

When he returned to New York, he was made a partner in the firm, and, as his responsibilities increased, he had less time on his hands. The refusal of a life-insurance company to issue him a policy made such an impression on him that he stopped drinking for a year, and claimed that he felt better physically, though I think he missed the convivial re-counting of those Celliniesque adventures which, in his early twenties, had played such a part in his life. But he never abandoned the Yale Club. He was a figure there, a personality, and the tendency of his class, who were now seven years out of college, to drift away to more sober haunts was checked by his presence.

His day was never too full nor his mind too weary to give any sort of aid to any one who asked it. What had been done at first through pride and superiority had become a habit and passion. And there was always something – a younger brother in trouble at New Haven, a quarrel to be patched up between a friend and his wife, a position to be found for this man, an investment for that. But his speciality was the solv-ing of problems for young married people. Young married people fascinated him and their apartments were almost sacred to him – he knew the story of their love-affair, ad-vised them where to live and how, and remembered their babies' names. Toward young wives his attitude was circum-spect: he never abused the trust which their husbands – strangely enough in view of his unconcealed irregularities – invariably reposed in him.

He came to take a vicarious pleasure in happy marriages, and to be inspired to an almost equally pleasant melancholy by those that went astray. Not a season passed that he did not witness the collapse of an affair that perhaps he himself had fathered. When Paula was divorced and almost immediately remarried to another Bostonian, he talked about her to me all one afternoon. He would never love any one as he had loved Paula, but he insisted that he no longer cared.

'I'll never marry,' he came to say; 'I've seen too much of it, and I know a happy marriage is a very rare thing. Besides, I'm too old.'

But he did believe in marriage. Like all men who spring from a happy and successful marriage, he believed in it passionately – nothing he had seen would change his belief, his cynicism dissolved upon it like air. But he did really believe he was too old. At twenty-eight he began to accept with equanimity the prospect of marrying without romantic love; he resolutely chose a New York girl of his own class, pretty, intelligent, congenial, above reproach – and set about falling in love with her. The things he had said to Paula with sincerity, to other girls with grace, he could no longer say at all without smiling, or with the force necessary to convince.

'When I'm forty,' he told his friends, 'I'll be ripe. I'll fall for some chorus girl like the rest.'

Nevertheless, he persisted in his attempt. His mother wanted to see him married, and he could now well afford it – he had a seat on the Stock Exchange, and his earned income came to twenty-five thousand a year. The idea was agreeable: when his friends – he spent most of his time with the set he and Dolly had evolved – closed themselves in behind domestic doors at night, he no longer rejoiced in his freedom. He even wondered if he should have married Dolly. Not even Paula had loved him more, and he was learning the rarity, in a single life, of encountering true emotion.

Just as this mood began to creep over him a disquieting story reached his ear. His Aunt Edna, a woman just this side of forty, was carrying on an open intrigue with a dissolute, hard-drinking young man named Cary Sloane. Every one knew of it except Anson's Uncle Robert, who for fifteen years had talked long in clubs and taken his wife for granted.

Anson heard the story again and again with increasing annoyance. Something of his old feeling for his uncle came back to him, a feeling that was more than personal, a reversion toward that family solidarity on which he had based his pride. His intuition singled out the essential point of the affair, which was that his uncle shouldn't be hurt. It was his first experiment in unsolicited meddling, but with his knowledge of Edna's character he felt that he could handle the matter better than a district judge or his uncle.

His uncle was in Hot Springs. Anson traced down the sources of the scandal so that there should be no possibility of mistake and then he called Edna and asked her to lunch with him at the Plaza next day. Something in his tone must have frightened her, for she was reluctant, but he insisted, putting off the date until she had no excuse for refusing.

She met him at the appointed time in the Plaza lobby, a lovely, faded, grey-eyed blonde in a coat of Russian sable. Five great rings, cold with diamonds and emeralds, sparkled on her slender hands. It occurred to Anson that it was his father's intelligence and not his uncle's that had earned the fur and the stones, the rich brilliance that buoyed up her passing beauty.

Though Edna scented his hostility, she was unprepared for the directness of his approach.

'Edna, I'm astonished at the way you've been acting,' he said in a strong, frank voice. 'At first I couldn't believe it.'

'Believe what?' she demanded sharply.

'You needn't pretend with me, Edna. I'm talking about Cary Sloane. Aside from any other consideration, I didn't think you could treat Uncle Robert——'

'Now look here, Anson——' she began angrily, but his peremptory voice broke through hers:

'——and your children in such a way. You've been married eighteen years, and you're old enough to know better.'

'You can't talk to me like that! You——'

'Yes, I can. Uncle Robert has always been my best friend.' He was tremendously moved. He felt a real distress about his uncle, about his three young cousins.

Edna stood up, leaving her crab-flake cocktail untasted.

'This is the silliest thing——'

'Very well, if you won't listen to me I'll go to Uncle Robert and tell him the whole story – he's bound to hear it sooner or later. And afterwards I'll go to old Moses Sloane.'

Edna faltered back into her chair.

'Don't talk so loud,' she begged him. Her eyes blurred with tears. 'You have no idea how your voice carries. You might have chosen a less public place to make all these crazy accusations.'

He didn't answer.

'Oh, you never liked me, I know,' she went on. 'You're just taking advantage of some silly gossip to try and break up the only interesting friendship I've ever had. What did I ever do to make you hate me so?'

Still Anson waited. There would be the appeal to his chivalry, then to his pity, finally to his superior sophistication – when he had shouldered his way through all these there would be admissions, and he could come to grips with her. By being silent, by being impervious, by returning constantly to his main weapon, which was his own true emotion, he bullied her into frantic despair as the luncheon hour slipped away. At two o'clock she took out a mirror and a handkerchief, shined away the marks of her tears and powdered the slight hollows where they had lain. She had agreed to meet him at her own house at five.

When he arrived she was stretched on a chaise-longue which was covered with cretonne for the summer, and the tears he had called up at luncheon seemed still to be standing in her eyes. Then he was aware of Cary Sloane's dark anxious presence upon the cold hearth.

'What's this idea of yours?' broke out Sloane immediately. 'I understand you invited Edna to lunch and then threatened her on the basis of some cheap scandal.'

Anson sat down.

'I have no reason to think it's only scandal.'

'I hear you're going to take it to Robert Hunter, and to my father.'

Anson nodded.

'Either you break it off – or I will,' he said.

'What God-damned business is it of yours, Hunter?'

'Don't lose your temper, Cary,' said Edna nervously. 'It's only a question of showing him how absurd——'

'For one thing, it's my name that's being handed around,' interrupted Anson. 'That's all that concerns you, Cary.'

'Edna isn't a member of your family.'

'She most certainly is!' His anger mounted. 'Why – she owes this house and the rings on her fingers to my father's brains. When Uncle Robert married her she didn't have a penny.'

They all looked at the rings as if they had a significant bearing on the situation. Edna made a gesture to take them from her hand.

'I guess they're not the only rings in the world,' said Sloane.

'Oh, this is absurd,' cried Edna. 'Anson, will you listen to me? I've found out how the silly story started. It was a maid I discharged who went right to the Chilicheffs – all these Russians pump things out of their servants and then put a false meaning on them.' She brought down her fist angrily on the table: 'And after Robert lent them the limousine for a whole month when we were South last winter——'

'Do you see?' demanded Sloane eagerly. 'This maid got hold of the wrong end of the thing. She knew that Edna and I were friends, and she carried it to the Chilicheffs. In Russia they assume that if a man and a woman——'

He enlarged the theme to a disquisition upon social relations in the Caucasus.

'If that's the case it better be explained to Uncle Robert,' said Anson dryly, 'so that when the rumours do reach him he'll know they're not true.'

Adopting the method he had followed with Edna at luncheon he let them explain it all away. He knew that they were guilty and that presently they would cross the line from explanation into justification and convict themselves more definitely than he could ever do. By seven they had taken the desperate step of telling him the truth – Robert Hunter's neglect, Edna's empty life, the casual dalliance that had flamed up into passion – but like so many true stories it had the misfortune of being old, and its enfeebled body beat helplessly against the armour of Anson's will. The threat to go to Sloane's father sealed their helplessness, for the latter, a retired cotton broker out of Alabama, was a notorious fundamentalist who controlled his son by a rigid allowance and the promise that at his next vagary the allowance would stop forever.

They dined at a small French restaurant, and the discussion continued – at one time Sloane resorted to physical threats, a little later they were both imploring him to give them time. But Anson was obdurate. He saw that Edna was breaking up, and that her spirit must not be refreshed by any renewal of their passion.

At two o'clock in a small night-club on 53rd Street, Edna's nerves suddenly collapsed, and she cried to go home. Sloane had been drinking heavily all evening, and he was faintly maudlin, leaning on the table and weeping a little with his face in his hands. Quickly Anson gave them his terms. Sloane was to leave town for six months, and he must be gone within forty-eight hours. When he returned there was to be no resumption of the affair, but at the end of a year Edna might, if she wished, tell Robert Hunter that she wanted a divorce and go about it in the usual way.

He paused, gaining confidence from their faces for his final word.

'Or there's another thing you can do,' he said slowly, 'if Edna wants to leave her children, there's nothing I can do to prevent your running off together.'

'I want to go home!' cried Edna again. 'Oh, haven't you done enough to us for one day?'

Outside it was dark, save for a blurred glow from Sixth Avenue down the street. In that light those two who had been lovers looked for the last time into each other's tragic faces, realizing that between them there was not enough youth and strength to avert their eternal parting. Sloane walked suddenly off down the street and Anson tapped a dozing taxi-driver on the arm.

It was almost four; there was a patient flow of cleaning water along the ghostly pavement of Fifth Avenue, and the shadows of two night women flitted over the dark façade of St Thomas's church. Then the desolate shrubbery of Central Park where Anson had often played as a child, and the mounting numbers, significant as names, of the marching streets. This was his city, he thought, where his name had flourished through five generations. No change could alter the permanence of its place here, for change itself was the essential substratum by which he and those of his name identified themselves with the spirit of New York. Resourcefulness and a powerful will – for his threats in weaker hands would have been less than nothing – had beaten the gathering dust from his uncle's name, from the name of his family, from even this shivering figure that sat beside him in the car.

Cary Sloane's body was found next morning on the lower shelf of a pillar of Queensboro Bridge. In the darkness and in his excitement he had thought that it was the water flowing black beneath him, but in less than a second it made no possible difference – unless he had planned to think one last thought of Edna, and call out her name as he struggled feebly in the water.

VII

Anson never blamed himself for his part in this affair – the situation which brought it about had not been of his making. But the just suffer with the unjust, and he found that his oldest and somehow his most precious friendship was over. He never knew what distorted story Edna told, but he was welcome in his uncle's house no longer.

Just before Christmas Mrs Hunter retired to a select

Episcopal heaven, and Anson became the responsible head of his family. An unmarried aunt who had lived with them for years ran the house, and attempted with helpless inefficiency to chaperone the younger girls. All the children were less self-reliant than Anson, more conventional both in their virtues and in their shortcomings. Mrs Hunter's death had postponed the début of one daughter and the wedding of another. Also it had taken something deeply material from all of them, for with her passing the quiet, expensive superiority of the Hunters came to an end.

For one thing, the estate, considerably diminished by two inheritance taxes and soon to be divided among six children, was not a notable fortune any more. Anson saw a tendency in his youngest sisters to speak rather respectfully of families that hadn't 'existed' twenty years ago. His own feeling of precedence was not echoed in them – sometimes they were conventionally snobbish, that was all. For another thing, this was the last summer they would spend on the Connecticut estate; the clamour against it was too loud: 'Who wants to waste the best months of the year shut up in that dead old town ?' Reluctantly he yielded – the house would go into the market in the fall, and next summer they would rent a smaller place in Westchester County. It was a step down from the expensive simplicity of his father's idea, and, while he sympathized with the revolt, it also annoyed him; during his mother's lifetime he had gone up there at least every other week-end – even in the gayest summers.

Yet he himself was part of this change, and his strong instinct for life had turned him in his twenties from the hollow obsequies of that abortive leisure class. He did not see this clearly – he still felt that there was a norm, a standard of society. But there was no norm, it was doubtful if there ever had been a true norm in New York. The few who still paid and fought to enter a particular set succeeded only to find that as a society it scarcely functioned – or, what was more alarming, that the Bohemia from which they fled sat above them at table.

At twenty-nine Anson's chief concern was his own growing loneliness. He was sure now that he would never marry. The number of weddings at which he had officiated as best man or usher was past all counting – there was a drawer at home that bulged with the official neckties of this or that wedding-party, neckties standing for romances that had not endured a year, for couples who had passed completely from his life. Scarf-pins, gold pencils, cuff-buttons, presents from a generation of grooms had passed through his jewel-box and been lost – and with every ceremony he was less and less able to imagine himself in the groom's place. Under his hearty good-will toward all those marriages there was despair about his own.

And as he neared thirty he became not a little depressed at the inroads that marriage, especially lately, had made upon his friendships. Groups of people had a disconcerting tendency to dissolve and disappear. The men from his own college – and it was upon them he had expended the most time and affection – were the most elusive of all. Most of them were drawn deep into domesticity, two were dead, one lived abroad, one was in Hollywood writing continuities for pictures that Anson went faithfully to see.

Most of them, however, were permanent commuters with an intricate family life centring around some suburban country club, and it was from these that he felt his estrangement most keenly.

In the early days of their married life they had all needed him; he gave them advice about their slim finances, he exorcised their doubts about the advisability of bringing a baby into two rooms and a bath, especially he stood for the great world outside. But now their financial troubles were in the past and the fearfully expected child had evolved into an absorbing family. They were always glad to see old Anson, but they dressed up for him and tried to impress him with their present importance, and kept their troubles to themselves. They needed him no longer.

A few weeks before his thirtieth birthday the last of his early and intimate friends was married. Anson acted in his usual rôle of best man, gave his usual silver tea-service, and

went down to the usual *Homeric* to say good-bye. It was a hot
Friday afternoon in May, and as he walked from the pier he
realized that Saturday closing had begun and he was free
until Monday morning.

'Go where ?' he asked himself.

The Yale Club, of course; bridge until dinner, then four
or five raw cocktails in somebody's room and a pleasant confused evening. He regretted that this afternoon's groom
wouldn't be along – they had always been able to cram so
much into such nights: they knew how to attach women and
how to get rid of them, how much consideration any girl
deserved from their intelligent hedonism. A party was an
adjusted thing – you took certain girls to certain places and
spent just so much on their amusement; you drank a little,
not much, more than you ought to drink, and at a certain
time in the morning you stood up and said you were going
home. You avoided college boys, sponges, future engagements, fights, sentiment, and indiscretions. That was the
way it was done. All the rest was dissipation.

In the morning you were never violently sorry – you made
no resolutions, but if you had overdone it and your heart
was slightly out of order, you went on the wagon for a few
days without saying anything about it, and waited until an
accumulation of nervous boredom projected you into another
party.

The lobby of the Yale Club was unpopulated. In the bar
three very young alumni looked up at him, momentarily and
without curiosity.

'Hello, there, Oscar,' he said to the bartender. 'Mr Cahill
been around this afternoon ?'

'Mr Cahill's gone to New Haven.'

'Oh . . . that so ?'

'Gone to the ball game. Lot of men gone up.'

Anson looked once again into the lobby, considered for a
moment, and then walked out and over to Fifth Avenue.
From the broad window of one of his clubs – one that he had
scarcely visited in five years – a grey man with watery eyes
stared down at him. Anson looked quickly away – that figure

sitting in vacant resignation, in supercilious solitude, depressed him. He stopped and, retracing his steps, started over 47th Street toward Teak Warden's apartment. Teak and his wife had once been his most familiar friends – it was a household where he and Dolly Karger had been used to go in the days of their affair. But Teak had taken to drink, and his wife had remarked publicly that Anson was a bad influence on him. The remark reached Anson in an exaggerated form – when it was finally cleared up, the delicate spell of intimacy was broken, never to be renewed.

'Is Mr Warden at home?' he inquired.

'They've gone to the country.'

The fact unexpectedly cut at him. They were gone to the country and he hadn't known. Two years before he would have known the date, the hour, come up at the last moment for a final drink, and planned his first visit to them. Now they had gone without a word.

Anson looked at his watch and considered a week-end with his family, but the only train was a local that would jolt through the aggressive heat for three hours. And to-morrow in the country, and Sunday – he was in no mood for porch-bridge with polite undergraduates, and dancing after dinner at a rural roadhouse, a diminutive of gaiety which his father had estimated too well.

'Oh, no,' he said to himself. . . . 'No.'

He was a dignified, impressive young man, rather stout now, but otherwise unmarked by dissipation. He could have been cast for a pillar of something – at times you were sure it was not society, at others nothing else – for the law, for the church. He stood for a few minutes motionless on the sidewalk in front of a 47th Street apartment-house; for almost the first time in his life he had nothing whatever to do.

Then he began to walk briskly up Fifth Avenue, as if he had just been reminded of an important engagement there. The necessity of dissimulation is one of the few characteristics that we share with dogs, and I think of Anson on that day as some well-bred specimen who had been disappointed at a familiar back door. He was going to see Nick, once a fashionable bartender in demand at all private dances, and now employed in cooling non-alcoholic champagne among the labyrinthine cellars of the Plaza Hotel.

'Nick,' he said, 'what's happened to everything?'

'Dead,' Nick said.

'Make me a whisky sour.' Anson handed a pint bottle over the counter. 'Nick, the girls are different; I had a little girl in Brooklyn and she got married last week without letting me know.'

'That a fact? Ha-ha-ha,' responded Nick diplomatically. 'Slipped it over on you.'

'Absolutely,' said Anson. 'And I was out with her the night before.'

'Ha-ha-ha,' said Nick, 'ha-ha-ha!'

'Do you remember the wedding, Nick, in Hot Springs where I had the waiters and the musicians singing "God save the King"?'

'Now where was that, Mr Hunter?' Nick concentrated doubtfully. 'Seems to me that was——'

'Next time they were back for more, and I began to wonder how much I'd paid them,' continued Anson.

'—seems to me that was at Mr Trenholm's wedding.'

'Don't know him,' said Anson decisively. He was offended that a strange name should intrude upon his reminiscences; Nick perceived this.

'Na – aw—' he admitted, 'I ought to know that. It was one of *your* crowd – Brakins . . . Baker——'

'Bicker Baker,' said Anson responsively. 'They put me in a hearse after it was over and covered me up with flowers and drove me away.'

'Ha-ha-ha,' said Nick. 'Ha-ha-ha.'

Nick's simulation of the old family servant paled presently and Anson went upstairs to the lobby. He looked around – his eyes met the glance of an unfamiliar clerk at the desk, then fell upon a flower from the morning's marriage hesitating in the mouth of a brass cuspidor. He went out and walked slowly toward the blood-red sun over Columbus

Circle. Suddenly he turned around and, retracing his steps to the Plaza, immured himself in a telephone-booth.

Later he said that he tried to get me three times that afternoon, that he tried every one who might be in New York – men and girls he had not seen for years, an artist's model of his college days whose faded number was still in his address book – Central told him that even the exchange existed no longer. At length his quest roved into the country, and he held brief disappointing conversations with emphatic butlers and maids. So-and-so was out, riding, swimming, playing golf, sailed to Europe last week. Who shall I say phoned?

It was intolerable that he should pass the evening alone – the private reckonings which one plans for a moment of leisure lose every charm when the solitude is enforced. There were always women of a sort, but the ones he knew had temporarily vanished, and to pass a New York evening in the hired company of a stranger never occurred to him – he would have considered that that was something shameful and secret, the diversion of a travelling salesman in a strange town.

Anson paid the telephone bill – the girl tried unsuccessfully to joke with him about its size – and for the second time that afternoon started to leave the Plaza and go he knew not where. Near the revolving door the figure of a woman, obviously with child, stood sideways to the light – a sheer beige cape fluttered at her shoulders when the door turned and, each time, she looked impatiently toward it as if she were weary of waiting. At the first sight of her a strong nervous thrill of familiarity went over him, but not until he was within five feet of her did he realize that it was Paula.

'Why, Anson Hunter!'

His heart turned over

'Why, Paula——'

'Why, this is wonderful. I can't believe it, *Anson!*'

She took both his hands, and he saw in the freedom of the gesture that the memory of him had lost poignancy to her.

11 + s.f.

But not to him – he felt that old mood that she evoked in him stealing over his brain, that gentleness with which he had always met her optimism as if afraid to mar its surface.

'We're at Rye for the summer. Pete had to come East on business – you know of course I'm Mrs Peter Hagerty now – so we brought the children and took a house. You've got to come out and see us.'

'Can I?' he asked directly. 'When?'

'When you like. Here's Pete.' The revolving door functioned, giving up a fine tall man of thirty with a tanned face and a trim moustache. His immaculate fitness made a sharp contrast with Anson's increasing bulk, which was obvious under the faintly tight cut-away coat.

'You oughtn't to be standing,' said Hagerty to his wife. 'Let's sit down here.' He indicated lobby chairs, but Paula hesitated.

'I've got to go right home,' she said. 'Anson, why don't you – why don't you come out and have dinner with us to-night! We're just getting settled, but if you can stand that——'

Hagerty confirmed the invitation cordially.

'Come out for the night.'

Their car waited in front of the hotel, and Paula with a tired gesture sank back against silk cushions in the corner.

'There's so much I want to talk to you about,' she said, 'it seems hopeless.'

'I want to hear about you.'

'Well' – she smiled at Hagerty – 'that would take a long time too. I have three children – by my first marriage. The oldest is five, then four, then three.' She smiled again. 'I didn't waste much time having them, did I?'

'Boys?'

'A boy and two girls. Then – oh, a lot of things happened, and I got a divorce in Paris a year ago and married Pete. That's all – except that I'm awfully happy.'

In Rye they drove up to a large house near the Beach Club, from which there issued presently three dark, slim children who broke from an English governess and approached them with an esoteric cry. Abstractedly and with difficulty, Paula took each one into her arms, a caress which they accepted stiffly, as they had evidently been told not to bump into Mummy. Even against their fresh faces Paula's skin showed scarcely any weariness – for all her physical languor she seemed younger than when he had last seen her at Palm Beach seven years ago.

At dinner she was preoccupied, and afterwards, during the homage to the radio, she lay with closed eyes on the sofa, until Anson wondered if his presence at this time were not an intrusion. But at nine o'clock, when Hagerty rose and said pleasantly that he was going to leave them by themselves for a while, she began to talk slowly about herself and the past.

'My first baby,' she said – 'the one we call Darling, the biggest little girl – I wanted to die when I knew I was going to have her, because Lowell was like a stranger to me. It didn't seem as though she could be my own. I wrote you a letter and tore it up. Oh, you were *so* bad to me, Anson.'

It was the dialogue again, rising and falling, Anson felt a sudden quickening of memory.

'Weren't you engaged once?' she asked – 'a girl named Dolly something?'

'I wasn't ever engaged. I tried to be engaged, but I never loved anybody but you, Paula.'

'Oh,' she said. Then after a moment: 'This baby is the first one I ever really wanted. You see, I'm in love now – at last.'

He didn't answer, shocked at the treachery of her remembrance. She must have seen that the 'at last' bruised him, for she continued:

'I was infatuated with you, Anson – you could make me do anything you liked. But we wouldn't have been happy. I'm not smart enough for you. I don't like things to be complicated like you do.' She paused. 'You'll never settle down,' she said.

The phrase struck at him from behind – it was an accusation that of all accusations he had never merited.

'I could settle down if women were different,' he said. 'If I didn't understand so much about them, if women didn't spoil you for other women, if they had only a little pride. If I could go to sleep for a while and wake up into a home that was really mine – why, that's what I'm made for, Paula, that's what women have seen in me and liked in me. It's only that I can't get through the preliminaries any more.'

Hagerty came in a little before eleven; after a whisky Paula stood up and announced that she was going to bed. She went over and stood by her husband.

'Where did you go, dearest?' she demanded.

'I had a drink with Ed Saunders.'

'I was worried. I thought maybe you'd run away.'

She rested her head against his coat.

'He's sweet, isn't he, Anson?' she demanded.

'Absolutely,' said Anson, laughing.

She raised her face to her husband.

'Well, I'm ready,' she said. She turned to Anson: 'Do you want to see our family gymnastic stunt?'

'Yes,' he said in an interested voice.

'All right. Here we go!'

Hagerty picked her up easily in his arms.

'This is called the family acrobatic stunt,' said Paula. 'He carries me upstairs. Isn't it sweet of him?'

'Yes,' said Anson.

Hagerty bent his head slightly until his face touched Paula's.

'And I love him,' she said. 'I've just been telling you, haven't I, Anson?'

'Yes,' he said.

'He's the dearest thing that ever lived in this world; aren't you, darling? . . . Well, good night. Here we go. Isn't he strong?'

'Yes,' Anson said.

'You'll find a pair of Pete's pyjamas laid out for you. Sweet dreams – see you at breakfast.'

'Yes,' Anson said.

VIII

The older members of the firm insisted that Anson should go abroad for the summer. He had scarcely had a vacation in seven years, they said. He was stale and needed a change. Anson resisted.

'If I go,' he declared, 'I won't come back any more.'

'That's absurd, old man. You'll be back in three months with all this depression gone. Fit as ever.'

'No.' He shook his head stubbornly. 'If I stop, I won't go back to work. If I stop, that means I've given up – I'm through.'

'We'll take a chance on that. Stay six months if you like – we're not afraid you'll leave us. Why, you'd be miserable if you didn't work.'

They arranged his passage for him. They liked Anson – every one liked Anson – and the change that had been coming over him cast a sort of pall over the office. The enthusiasm that had invariably signalled up business, the consideration toward his equals and his inferiors, the lift of his vital presence – within the past four months his intense nervousness had melted down these qualities into the fussy pessimism of a man of forty. On every transaction in which he was involved he acted as a drag and a strain.

'If I go I'll never come back,' he said.

Three days before he sailed Paula Legendre Hagerty died in childbirth. I was with him a great deal then, for we were crossing together, but for the first time in our friendship he told me not a word of how he felt, nor did I see the slightest sign of emotion. His chief preoccupation was with the fact that he was thirty years old – he would turn the conversation to the point where he could remind you of it and then fall silent, as if he assumed that the statement would start a chain of thought sufficient to itself. Like his partners, I was amazed at the change in him, and I was glad when the *Paris* moved off into the wet space between the worlds, leaving his principality behind.

'How about a drink?' he suggested.

We walked into the bar with that defiant feeling that characterizes the day of departure and ordered four Martinis. After one cocktail a change came over him – he suddenly reached across and slapped my knee with the first joviality I had seen him exhibit for months.

'Did you see that girl in the red tam?' he demanded, 'the one with the high colour who had the two police dogs down to bid her good-bye.'

'She's pretty,' I agreed.

'I looked her up in the purser's office and found out that she's alone. I'm going down to see the steward in a few minutes. We'll have dinner with her to-night.'

After a while he left me, and within an hour he was walking up and down the deck with her, talking to her in his strong, clear voice. Her red tam was a bright spot of colour against the steel-grey sea, and from time to time she looked up with a flashing bob of her head, and smiled with amusement and interest, and anticipation. At dinner we had champagne, and were very joyous – afterwards Anson ran the pool with infectious gusto, and several people who had seen me with him asked me his name. He and the girl were talking and laughing together on a lounge in the bar when I went to bed.

I saw less of him on the trip than I had hoped. He wanted to arrange a foursome, but there was no one available, so I saw him only at meals. Sometimes, though, he would have a cocktail in the bar, and he told me about the girl in the red tam, and his adventures with her, making them all bizarre and amusing, as he had a way of doing, and I was glad that he was himself again, or at least the self that I knew, and with which I felt at home. I don't think he was ever happy unless some one was in love with him, responding to him like filings to a magnet, helping him to explain himself, promising him something. What it was I do not know. Perhaps they promised that there would always be women in the world who would spend their brightest, freshest, rarest hours to nurse and protect that superiority he cherished in his heart.

THE BABY PARTY

[1925]

When John Andros felt old he found solace in the thought of life continuing through his child. The dark trumpets of oblivion were less loud at the patter of his child's feet or at the sound of his child's voice babbling mad non sequiturs to him over the telephone. The latter incident occurred every afternoon at three when his wife called the office from the country, and he came to look forward to it as one of the vivid minutes of his day.

He was not physically old, but his life had been a series of struggles up a series of rugged hills, and here at thirty-eight having won his battles against ill-health and poverty he cherished less than the usual number of illusions. Even his feeling about his little girl was qualified. She had interrupted his rather intense love-affair with his wife, and she was the reason for their living in a suburban town, where they paid for country air with endless servant troubles and the weary merry-go-round of the commuting train.

It was little Ede as a definite piece of youth that chiefly interested him. He liked to take her on his lap and examine minutely her fragrant, downy scalp and her eyes with their irises of morning blue. Having paid this homage John was content that the nurse should take her away. After ten minutes the very vitality of the child irritated him; he was inclined to lose his temper when things were broken, and one Sunday afternoon when she had disrupted a bridge game by permanently hiding up the ace of spades, he had made a scene that had reduced his wife to tears.

This was absurd and John was ashamed of himself. It was inevitable that such things would happen, and it was impossible that little Ede should spend all her indoor

328

hours in the nursery upstairs when she was becoming, as her mother said, more nearly a 'real person' every day.

She was two and a half, and this afternoon, for instance, she was going to a baby-party. Grown-up Edith, her mother, had telephoned the information to the office, and little Ede had confirmed the business by shouting 'I yam going to a *pantry*!' into John's unsuspecting left ear.

'Drop in at the Markeys' when you get home, won't you, dear?' resumed her mother. 'It'll be funny. Ede's going to be all dressed up in her new pink dress——'

The conversation terminated abruptly with a squawk which indicated that the telephone had been pulled violently to the floor. John laughed and decided to get an early train out; the prospect of a baby party in some one else's house amused him.

'What a peach of a mess!' he thought humorously. 'A dozen mothers, and each one looking at nothing but her own child. All the babies breaking things and grabbing at the cake, and each mama going home thinking about the subtle superiority of her own child to every other child there.

He was in a good humour to-day—all the things in his life were going better than they had ever gone before. When he got off the train at his station he shook his head at an importunate taxi man, and began to walk up the long hill towards his house through the crisp December twilight. It was only six o'clock but the moon was out, shining with proud brilliance on the thin sugary snow that lay over the lawns.

As he walked along drawing his lungs full of cold air his happiness increased, and the idea of a baby party appealed to him more and more. He began to wonder how Ede compared to other children of her own age, and if the pink dress she was to wear was something radical and mature. Increasing his gait he came in sight of his own house, where the lights of a defunct Christmas-tree still blossomed in the window, but he continued on past the walk. The party was at the Markeys' next door.

11*

As he mounted the brick step and rang the bell he became aware of voices inside, and he was glad he was not too late. Then he raised his head and listened—the voices were not children's voices, but they were loud and pitched high with anger; there were at least three of them and one, which rose as he listened to a hysterical sob, he recognized immediately as his wife's.

'There's been some trouble,' he thought quickly.

Trying the door, he found it unlocked and pushed it open.

The baby party started at half past four, but Edith Andros, calculating shrewdly that the new dress would stand out more sensationally against vestments already rumpled, planned the arrival of herself and little Ede for five. When they appeared it was already a flourishing affair. Four baby girls and nine baby boys, each one curled and washed and dressed with all the care of a proud and jealous heart, were dancing to the music of a phonograph. Never more than two or three were dancing at once, but as all were continually in motion running to and from their mothers for encouragement, the general effect was the same.

As Edith and her daughter entered, the music was temporarily drowned out by a sustained chorus, consisting largely of the word *cute* and directed towards little Ede, who stood looking timidly about and fingering the edges of her pink dress. She was not kissed—this is the sanitary age—but she was passed along a row of mamas each one of whom said 'cu-u-ute' to her and held her pink little hand before passing her on to the next. After some encouragement and a few mild pushes she was absorbed into the dance, and became an active member of the party.

Edith stood near the door talking to Mrs Markey, and keeping one eye on the tiny figure in the pink dress. She did not care for Mrs Markey; she considered her both snippy and common, but John and Joe Markey were congenial and went in together on the commuting train every morning, so the two women kept up an elaborate pretence of warm amity. They were always reproaching each other for 'not coming to see me,' and they were always planning the kind of parties that began with 'You'll have to come to dinner with us soon, and we'll go to the theatre,' but never matured further.

'Little Ede looks perfectly darling,' said Mrs Markey, smiling and moistening her lips in a way that Edith found particularly repulsive. 'So *grown-up*—I can't *believe* it!'

Edith wondered if 'little Ede' referred to the fact that Billy Markey, though several months younger, weighed almost five pounds more. Accepting a cup of tea she took a seat with two other ladies on a divan and launched into the real business of the afternoon, which of course lay in relating the recent accomplishments and insouciances of her child.

An hour passed. Dancing palled and the babies took to sterner sport. The ran into the dining-room, rounded the big table, and essayed the kitchen door, from which they were rescued by an expeditionary force of mothers. Having been rounded up they immediately broke loose, and rushing back to the dining-room tried the familiar swinging door again. The word 'overheated' began to bc uscd, and small white brows were dried with small white handkerchiefs. A general attempt to make the babies sit down began, but the babies squirmed off laps with peremptory cries of 'Down! Down!' and the rush into the fascinating dining-room began anew.

This phase of the party came to an end with the arrival of refreshments, a large cake with two candles, and saucers of vanilla ice-cream. Billy Markey, a stout laughing baby with red hair and legs somewhat bowed, blew out the candles, and placed an experimental thumb on the white frosting. The refreshments were distributed, and the children ate, greedily but without confusion—they had behaved remarkably well all afternoon. They were modern babies who ate and slept at regular hours, so their dispositions were good, and their faces healthy and pink—

such a peaceful party would not have been possible thirty years ago.

After the refreshments a gradual exodus began. Edith glanced anxiously at her watch—it was almost six, and John had not arrived. She wanted him to see Ede with the other children—to see how dignified and polite and intelligent she was, and how the only ice-cream spot on her dress was some that had dropped from her chin when she was joggled from behind.

'You're a darling,' she whispered to her child, drawing her suddenly against her knee. 'Do you know you're a darling? Do you *know* you're a darling?'

Ede laughed. 'Bow-wow,' she said suddenly.

'Bow-wow?' Edith looked around. 'There isn't any bow-wow.'

'Bow-wow,' repeated Ede. 'I want a bow-bow.'

Edith followed the small pointing finger.

'That isn't a bow-wow, dearest, that's a teddy-bear.'

'Bear?'

'Yes, that's a teddy-bear, and it belongs to Billy Markey. You don't want Billy Markey's teddy-bear, do you?'

Ede did want it.

She broke away from her mother and approached Billy Markey, who held the toy closely in his arms. Ede stood regarding him with inscrutable eyes, and Billy laughed.

Grown-up Edith looked at her watch again, this time impatiently.

The party had dwindled until, besides Ede and Billy, there were only two babies remaining—and one of the two remained only by virtue of having hidden himself under the dining-room table. It was selfish of John not to come. It showed so little pride in the child. Other fathers had come, half a dozen of them, to call for their wives, and they had stayed for a while and looked on.

There was a sudden wail. Ede had obtained Billy's teddy-bear by pulling it forcibly from his arms, and on Billy's attempt to recover it, she had pushed him casually to the floor.

'Why, Ede!' cried her mother, repressing an inclination to laugh.

Joe Markey, a handsome, broad-shouldered man of thirty-five, picked up his son and set him on his feet. 'You're a fine fellow,' he said jovially. 'Let a girl knock you over! You're a fine fellow.'

'Did he bump his head?' Mrs Markey returned anxiously from bowing the next to last remaining mother out of the door.

'No-o-o-o,' exclaimed Markey. 'He bumped something else, didn't you, Billy? He bumped something else.'

Billy had so far forgotten the bump that he was already making an attempt to recover his property. He seized a leg of the bear which projected from Ede's enveloping arms and tugged at it but without success.

'No,' said Ede emphatically.

Suddenly, encouraged by the success of her former half-accidental manœuvre, Ede dropped the teddy-bear, placed her hands on Billy's shoulders and pushed him backward off his feet.

This time he landed less harmlessly; his head hit the bare floor just off the rug with a dull hollow sound, whereupon he drew in his breath and delivered an agonized yell.

Immediately the room was in confusion. With an exclamation Markey hurried to his son, but his wife was first to reach the injured baby and catch him up into her arms.

'Oh, *Billy*,' she cried, 'what a terrible bump! She ought to be spanked.'

Edith, who had rushed immediately to her daughter, heard this remark, and her lips came sharply together.

'Why, Ede,' she whispered perfunctorily, 'you bad girl!'

Ede put back her little head suddenly and laughed. It was a loud laugh, a triumphant laugh with victory in it and challenge and contempt. Unfortunately it was also an infectious laugh. Before her mother realized the delicacy of the situation, she too had laughed, an audible, distinct laugh not unlike the baby's, and partaking of the same overtones.

Then, as suddenly, she stopped.

Mrs Markey's face had grown red with anger, and Markey, who had been feeling the back of the baby's head with one finger, looked at her, frowning.

'It's swollen already,' he said with a note of reproof in his voice. 'I'll get some witch-hazel.'

But Mrs Markey had lost her temper. 'I don't see anything funny about a child being hurt!' she said in a trembling voice.

Little Ede meanwhile had been looking at her mother curiously. She noted that her own laugh had produced her mother's and she wondered if the same cause would always produce the same effect. So she chose this moment to throw back her head and laugh again.

To her mother the additional mirth added the final touch of hysteria to the situation. Pressing her handkerchief to her mouth she giggled irrepressibly. It was more than nervousness—she felt that in a peculiar way she was laughing with her child—they were laughing together.

It was in a way a defiance—those two against the world.

While Markey rushed upstairs to the bathroom for ointment, his wife was walking up and down rocking the yelling boy in her arms.

'Please go home!' she broke out suddenly. 'The child's badly hurt, and if you haven't the decency to be quiet, you'd better go home.'

'Very well,' said Edith, her own temper rising. 'I've never seen any one make such a mountain out of——'

'Get out!' cried Mrs Markey frantically. 'There's the door, get out—I never want to see you in our house again. You or your brat either!'

Edith had taken her daughter's hand and was moving quickly towards the door, but at this remark she stopped and turned around, her face contracting with indignation.

'Don't you dare call her that!'

Mrs Markey did not answer but continued walking up

and down, muttering to herself and to Billy in an inaudible
voice.

Edith began to cry.

'I will get out!' she sobbed, 'I've never heard anybody
so rude and c-common in my life. I'm glad your baby did
get pushed down—he's nothing but a f-fat little fool
anyhow.'

Joe Markey reached the foot of the stairs just in time
to hear this remark.

'Why, Mrs Andros,' he said sharply, 'can't you see the
child's hurt. You really ought to control yourself.'

'Control m-myself!' exclaimed Edith brokenly. 'You
better ask her to c-control herself. I've never heard anybody
so c-common in my life.'

'She's insulting me!' Mrs Markey was now livid with
rage. 'Did you hear what she said, Joe? I wish you'd put
her out. If she won't go, just take her by the shoulders
and put her out!'

'Don't you dare touch me!' cried Edith. 'I'm going just
as quick as I can find my c-coat!'

Blind with tears she took a step towards the hall. It was
just at this moment that the door opened and John Andros
walked anxiously in.

'John!' cried Edith, and fled to him wildly.

'What's the matter? Why, what's the matter?'

'They're—they're putting me out!' she wailed, col-
lapsing against him. 'He'd just started to take me by the
shoulders and put me out. I want my coat!'

'That's not true,' objected Markey hurriedly. 'Nobody's
going to put you out.' He turned to John. 'Nobody's going
to put her out,' he repeated. 'She's——'

'What do you mean "put her out"?' demanded John
abruptly. 'What's all this talk, anyhow?'

'Oh, let's go!' cried Edith. 'I want to go. They're so
common, John!'

'Look here!' Markey's face darkened. 'You've said that
about enough. You're acting sort of crazy.'

'They called Ede a brat!'

For the second time that afternoon little Ede expressed emotion at an inopportune moment. Confused and frightened at the shouting voices, she began to cry, and her tears had the effect of conveying that she felt the insult in her heart.

'What's the idea of this?' broke out John. 'Do you insult your guests in your own house?'

'It seems to me it's your wife that's done the insulting!' answered Markey crisply. 'In fact, your baby there started all the trouble.'

John gave a contemptuous snort. 'Are you calling names at a little baby?' he inquired. 'That's a fine manly business!'

'Don't talk to him, John,' insisted Edith. 'Find my coat!'

'You must be in a bad way,' went on John angrily, 'if you have to take out your temper on a helpless little baby.'

'I never heard anything so damn twisted in my life,' shouted Markey. 'If that wife of yours would shut her mouth for a minute——'

'Wait a minute! You're not talking to a woman and child now——'

There was an incidental interruption. Edith had been fumbling on a chair for her coat, and Mrs Markey had been watching her with hot, angry eyes. Suddenly she laid Billy down on the sofa, where he immediately stopped crying and pulled himself upright, and coming into the hall she quickly found Edith's coat and handed it to her without a word. Then she went back to the sofa, picked up Billy, and rocking him in her arms looked again at Edith with hot, angry eyes. The interruption had taken less than half a minute.

'Your wife comes in here and begins shouting around about how common we are!' burst out Markey violently. 'Well, if we're so damn common, you'd better stay away! And what's more, you'd better get out now!'

Again John gave a short, contemptuous laugh.

'You're not only common,' he returned, 'you're evidently an awful bully—when there's any helpless women and children around.' He felt for the knob and swung the door open. 'Come on, Edith.'

Taking up her daughter in her arms, his wife stepped outside and John, still looking contemptuously at Markey, started to follow.

'Wait a minute!' Markey took a step forward; he was trembling slightly, and two large veins on his temple were suddenly full of blood. 'You don't think you can get away with that, do you? With me?'

Without a word John walked out the door, leaving it open.

Edith, still weeping, had started for home. After following her with his eyes until she reached her own walk, John turned back towards the lighted doorway where Markey was slowly coming down the slippery steps. He took off his overcoat and hat, tossed them off the path onto the snow. Then, sliding a little on the iced walk, he took a step forward.

At the first blow, they both slipped and fell heavily to the sidewalk, half rising then, and again pulling each other to the ground. They found a better foothold in the thin snow to the side of the walk and rushed at each other, both swinging wildly and pressing out the snow into a pasty mud underfoot.

The street was deserted, and except for their short tired gasps and the padded sound as one or the other slipped down into the slushy mud, they fought in silence, clearly defined to each other by the full moonlight as well as by the amber glow that shone out of the open door. Several times they both slipped down together, and then for a while the conflict threshed about wildly on the lawn.

For ten, fifteen, twenty minutes they fought there senselessly in the moonlight. They had both taken off coats and vests at some silently agreed upon interval and now their shirts dripped from their backs in wet pulpy shreds. Both were torn and bleeding and so exhausted that they could stand only when by their position they mutually supported each other—the impact, the mere effort of a blow, would send them both to their hands and knees.

But it was not weariness that ended the business, and the very meaninglessness of the fight was a reason for not stopping. They stopped because once when they were straining at each other on the ground, they heard a man's footsteps coming along the sidewalk. They had rolled somehow into the shadow, and when they heard these footsteps they stopped fighting, stopped moving, stopped breathing, lay huddled together like two boys playing Indian until the footsteps had passed. Then, staggering to their feet, they looked at each other like two drunken men.

'I'll be damned if I'm going on with this thing any more,' cried Markey thickly.

'I'm not going on any more either,' said John Andros. 'I've had enough of this thing.'

Again they looked at each other, sulkily this time, as if each suspected the other of urging him to a renewal of the fight. Markey spat out a mouthful of blood from a cut lip; then he cursed softly, and picking up his coat and vest, shook off the snow from them in a surprised way, as if their comparative dampness was his only worry in the world.

'Want to come in and wash up?' he asked suddenly.

'No, thanks,' said John. 'I ought to be going home—my wife'll be worried.'

He too picked up his coat and vest and then his overcoat and hat. Soaking wet and dripping with perspiration, it seemed absurd that less than half an hour ago he had been wearing all these clothes.

'Well—good night,' he said hesitantly.

Suddenly they walked towards each other and shook hands. It was no perfunctory hand-shake: John Andros's arm went around Markey's shoulder, and he patted him softly on the back for a little while.

'No harm done,' he said brokenly.

'No—you?'

'No, no harm done.'

'Well,' said John Andros after a minute, 'I guess I'll say good night.'

Limping slightly and with his clothes over his arm, John Andros turned away. The moonlight was still bright as he left the dark patch of trampled ground and walked over the intervening lawn. Down at the station, half a mile away, he could hear the rumble of the seven o'clock train.

'But you must have been crazy,' cried Edith brokenly. 'I thought you were going to fix it all up there and shake hands. That's why I went away.'

'Did you want us to fix it up?'

'Of course not, I never want to see them again. But I thought of course that was what you were going to do.' She was touching the bruises on his neck and back with iodine as he sat placidly in a hot bath. 'I'm going to get the doctor,' she said insistently. 'You may be hurt internally.'

He shook his head. 'Not a chance,' he answered. 'I don't want this to get all over the town.'

'I don't understand yet how it all happened.'

'Neither do I.' He smiled grimly. 'I guess these baby parties are pretty rough affairs.'

'Well, one thing——' suggested Edith hopefully, 'I'm certainly glad we have beef steak in the house for tomorrow's dinner.'

'Why?'

'For your eye, of course. Do you know I came within an ace of ordering veal? Wasn't that the luckiest thing?'

Half an hour later, dressed except that his neck would accommodate no collar, John moved his limbs experimentally before the glass. 'I believe I'll get myself in better shape,' he said thoughtfully. 'I must be getting old.'

'You mean so that next time you can beat him?'

'I did beat him,' he announced. 'At least, I beat him as much as he beat me. And there isn't going to be any next time. Don't you go calling people common any more.

If you get in any trouble, you just take your coat and go home. Understand?'

'Yes, dear,' she said meekly. 'I was very foolish and now I understand.'

Out in the hall, he paused abruptly by the baby's door.

'Is she asleep?'

'Sound asleep. But you can go in and peek at her—just to say good night.'

They tiptoed in and bent together over the bed. Little Ede, her cheeks flushed with health, her pink hands clasped tight together, was sleeping soundly in the cool, dark room. John reached over the railing of the bed and passed his hand lightly over the silken hair.

'She's asleep,' he murmured in a puzzled way.

'Naturally, after such an afternoon.'

'Miz Andros,' the coloured maid's stage whisper floated in from the hall. 'Mr and Miz Markey downstairs an' want to see you. Mr Markey he's all cut up in pieces, mam'n. His face look like a roast beef. An' Miz Markey she 'pear mighty mad.'

'Why, what incomparable nerve!' exclaimed Edith. 'Just tell them we're not home. I wouldn't go down for anything in the world.'

'You most certainly will.' John's voice was hard and set.

'What?'

'You'll go down right now, and, what's more, whatever that other woman does, you'll apologize for what you said this afternoon. After that you don't ever have to see her again.'

'Why—John, I can't.'

'You've got to. And just remember that she probably hated to come over here twice as much as you hate to go downstairs.'

'Aren't you coming? Do I have to go alone?'

'I'll be down—in just a minute.'

John Andros waited until she had closed the door behind her; then he reached over into the bed, and picking up his daughter, blankets and all, sat down in the rocking-chair holding her tightly in his arms. She moved a little, and he held his breath, but she was sleeping soundly, and in a moment she was resting quietly in the hollow of his elbow. Slowly he bent his head until his cheek was against her bright hair. 'Dear little girl,' he whispered. 'Dear little girl, dear little girl.'

John Andros knew at length what it was he had fought for so savagely that evening. He had it now, he possessed it forever, and for some time he sat there rocking very slowly to and fro in the darkness.

A SHORT TRIP HOME*

[1927]

I was near her, for I had lingered behind in order to get the short walk with her from the living-room to the front door. That was a lot, for she had flowered suddenly and I, being a man and only a year older, hadn't flowered at all, had scarcely dared to come near her in the week we'd been home. Nor was I going to say anything in that walk of ten feet, or touch her; but I had a vague hope she'd do something, give a gay little performance of some sort, personal only in so far as were alone together.

She had bewitchment suddenly in the twinkle of short hairs on her neck, in the sure, clear confidence that at about eighteen begins to deepen and sing in attractive American girls. The lamplight shopped in the yellow strands of her hair.

Already she was sliding into another world—the world of Joe Jelke and Jim Cathcart waiting for us now in the car. In another year she would pass beyond me forever.

As I waited, feeling the others outside in the snowy night, feeling the excitement of Christmas week and the excitement of Ellen here, blooming away, filling the room with 'sex appeal'—a wretched phrase to express a quality that isn't like that at all—a maid came in from the dining-room, spoke to Ellen quietly and handed her a note. Ellen read it and her eyes faded down, as when the current grows weak on rural circuits, and smouldered off into space. Then she gave me an odd look—in which I prob-

* In a moment of hasty misjudgement a whole paragraph of description was lifted out of this tale where it originated, and properly belongs, and applied to quite a different character in a novel of mine. I have ventured none the less to leave it here, even at the risk of seeming to serve warmed-over fare.—F.S.F.

ably didn't show—and without a word, followed the
maid into the dining-room and beyond. I sat turning
over the pages of a magazine for a quarter of an hour.

Joe Jelke came in, red-faced from the cold, his white
silk muffler gleaming at the neck of his fur coat. He was
a senior at New Haven, I was a sophomore. He was
prominent, a member of Scroll and Keys, and, in my eyes,
very distinguished and handsome.

'Isn't Ellen coming?'

'I don't know,' I answered discreetly. 'She was all ready.'

'Ellen!' he called. 'Ellen!'

He had left the front door open behind him and a great
cloud of frosty air rolled in from outside. He went half-
way up the stairs—he was a familiar in the house—and
called again, till Mrs Baker came to the banister and said
that Ellen was below. Then the maid, a little excited,
appeared in the dining-room door.

'Mr Jelke,' she called in a low voice.

Joe's face fell as he turned towards her, sensing bad
news.

'Miss Ellen says for you to go to the party. She'll come
later.'

'What's the matter?'

'She can't come now. She'll come later.'

He hesitated, confused. It was the last big dance of
vacation, and he was mad about Ellen. He had tried to
give her a ring for Christmas, and failing that, got her
to accept a gold mesh bag that must have cost two
hundred dollars. He wasn't the only one—there were
three or four in the same wild condition, and all in the
ten days she'd been home—but his chance came first,
for he was rich and gracious and at that moment the
'desirable' boy of St Paul. To me it seemed impossible
that she could prefer another, but the rumour was she'd
described Joe as much too perfect. I suppose he lacked
mystery for her, and when a man is up against that with
a young girl who isn't thinking of the practical side of
marriage yet—well——.

'No, she's not.' The maid was defiant and a little scared.

'She is.'

'She went out the back way, Mr Jelke.'

'I'm going to see.'

I followed him. The Swedish servants washing dishes looked up sideways at our approach and an interested crashing of pans marked our passage through. The storm door, unbolted, was flapping in the wind, and as we walked out into the snowy yard we saw the tail light of a car turn the corner at the end of the back alley.

'I'm going after her,' Joe said slowly. 'I don't understand this at all.'

I was too awed by the calamity to argue. We hurried to his car and drove in a fruitless, despairing zigzag all over the residence section, peering into every machine on the streets. It was half an hour before the futility of the affair began to dawn upon him—St Paul is a city of almost three hundred thousand people—and Jim Cathcart reminded him that we had another girl to stop for. Like a wounded animal he sank into a melancholy mass of fur in the corner, from which position he jerked upright every few minutes and waved himself backward and forward a little in protest and despair.

Jim's girl was ready and impatient, but after what had happened her impatience didn't seem important. She looked lovely though. That's one thing about Christmas vacation—the excitement of growth and change and adventure in foreign parts transforming the people you've known all your life. Joe Jelke was polite to her in a daze—he indulged in one burst of short, loud, harsh laughter by way of conversation—and we drove to the hotel.

The chauffeur approached it on the wrong side—the side on which the line of cars was not putting forth guests—and because of that we came suddenly upon Ellen Baker just getting out of a small coupé. Even before we came to a stop, Joe Jelke had jumped excitedly from the car.

Ellen turned towards us, a faintly distracted look—

perhaps of surprise, but certainly not of alarm—in her face; in fact, she didn't seem very aware of us. Joe approached her with a stern, dignified, injured and, I thought, just exactly correct reproof in his expression. I followed.

Seated in the coupé—he had not dismounted to help Ellen out—was a hard thin-faced man of about thirty-five with an air of being scarred, and a slight sinister smile. His eyes were a sort of taunt to the whole human family —they were the eyes of an animal, sleepy and quiescent in the presence of another species. They were helpless yet brutal, unhopeful yet confident. It was as if they felt themselves powerless to originate activity, but infinitely capable of profiting by a single gesture of weakness in another.

Vaguely I placed him as one of the sort of men whom I had been conscious of from my earliest youth as 'hanging around'—leaning with one elbow on the counters of tobacco stores, watching, through heaven knows what small chink of the mind, the people who hurried in and out. Intimate to garages, where he had vague business conducted in undertones, to barber shops and to the lobbies of theatres—in such places, anyhow, I placed the type, if type it was, that he reminded me of. Sometimes his face bobbed up in one of Tad's more savage cartoons, and I had always from earliest boyhood thrown a nervous glance towards the dim borderland where he stood, and seen him watching me and despising me. Once, in a dream, he had taken a few steps towards me, jerking his head back and muttering 'Say, kid' in what was intended to be a reassuring voice, and I had broken for the door in terror. This was that sort of man.

Joe and Ellen faced each other silently; she seemed, as I have said, to be in a daze. It was cold, but she didn't notice that her coat had blown open; Joe reached out and pulled it together, and automatically she clutched it with her hand.

Suddenly the man in the coupé, who had been watching them silently, laughed. It was a bare laugh, done with the breath—just a noisy jerk of the head—but it was an insult if I had ever heard one; definite and not to be passed over. I wasn't surprised when Joe, who was quick tempered, turned to him angrily and said:

'What's your trouble?'

The man waited a moment, his eyes shifting and yet staring, and always seeing. Then he laughed again in the same way. Ellen stirred uneasily.

'Who is this—this—' Joe's voice trembled with annoyance.

'Look out now,' said the man slowly.

Joe turned to me.

'Eddie, take Ellen and Catherine in, will you?' he said quickly. . . . 'Ellen, go with Eddie.'

'Look out now,' the man repeated.

Ellen made a little sound with her tongue and teeth, but she didn't resist when I took her arm and moved her towards the side door of the hotel. It struck me as odd that she should be so helpless, even to the point of acquiescing by her silence in this imminent trouble.

'Let it go, Joe!' I called back over my shoulder. 'Come inside!'

Ellen, pulling against my arm, hurried us on. As we were caught up into the swinging doors I had the impression that the man was getting out of his coupé.

Ten minutes later, as I waited for the girls outside the women's dressing-room, Joe Jelke and Jim Cathcart stepped out of the elevator. Joe was very white, his eyes were heavy and glazed, there was a trickle of dark blood on his forehead and on his white muffler. Jim had both their hats in his hand.

'He hit Joe with brass knuckles,' Jim said in a low voice. 'Joe was out cold for a minute or so. I wish you'd send a bell boy for some witch-hazel and court-plaster.'

It was late and the hall was deserted; brassy fragments of the dance below reached us as if heavy curtains were being blown aside and dropping back into place. When Ellen came out I took her directly downstairs. We avoided the receiving line and went into a dim room set with scraggly hotel palms where couples sometimes sat out during the dance; there I told her what had happened.

'It was Joe's own fault,' she said, surprisingly. 'I told him not to interfere.'

This wasn't true. She had said nothing, only uttered one curious little click of impatience.

'You ran out the back door and disappeared for almost an hour,' I protested. 'Then you turned up with a hard-looking customer who laughed in Joe's face.'

'A hard-looking customer,' she repeated, as if tasting the sound of the words.

'Well, wasn't he? Where on earth did you get hold of him, Ellen?'

'On the train,' she answered. Immediately she seemed to regret this admission. 'You'd better stay out of things that aren't your business, Eddie. You see what happened to Joe.'

Literally I gasped. To watch her, seated beside me, immaculately glowing, her body giving off wave after wave of freshness and delicacy—and to hear her talk like that.

'But that man's a thug!' I cried. 'No girl could be safe with him. He used brass knuckles on Joe—brass knuckles!'

'Is that pretty bad?'

She asked this as she might have asked such a question a few years ago. She looked at me at last and really wanted an answer; for a moment it was as if she were trying to recapture an attitude that had almost departed; then she hardened again. I say 'hardened,' for I began to notice that when she was concerned with this man her eyelids fell a little, shutting other things—everything else—out of view.

That was a moment I might have said something, I suppose, but in spite of everything, I couldn't light into her. I was too much under the spell of her beauty and its success. I even began to find excuses for her—perhaps that man wasn't what he appeared to be; or perhaps—

more romantically—she was involved with him against her will to shield some one else. At this point people began to drift into the room and come up to speak to us. We couldn't talk any more, so we went in and bowed to the chaperones. Then I gave her up to the bright restless sea of the dance, where she moved in an eddy of her own among the pleasant islands of coloured favours set out on tables and the south winds from the brasses moaning across the hall. After a while I saw Joe Jelke sitting in a corner with a strip of court-plaster on his forehead watching Ellen as if she herself had struck him down, but I didn't go up to him. I felt queer myself—like I feel when I wake up after sleeping through an afternoon, strange and portentous, as if something had gone on in the interval that changed the values of everything and that I didn't see.

The night slipped on through successive phases of cardboard horns, amateur tableaux and flashlights for the morning papers. Then was the grand march and supper, and about two o'clock some of the committee dressed up as revenue agents pinched the party, and a facetious newspaper was distributed, burlesquing the events of the evening. And all the time out of the corner of my eye I watched the shining orchid on Ellen's shoulder as it moved like Stuart's plume about the room. I watched it with a definite foreboding until the last sleepy groups had crowded into the elevators, and then, bundled to the eyes in great shapeless fur coats, drifted out into the clear dry Minnesota night.

II

There is a sloping mid-section of our city which lies between the residence quarter on the hill and the business district on the level of the river. It is a vague part of town, broken by its climb into triangles and odd shapes —there are names like Seven Corners—and I don't believe a dozen people could draw an accurate map of it, though every one traversed it by trolley, auto or shoe leather twice a day. And though it was a busy section, it would be hard for me to name the business that comprised its activity. There were always long lines of trolley cars waiting to start somewhere; there was a big movie theatre and many small ones with posters of Hoot Gibson and Wonder Dogs and Wonder Horses outside; there were small stores with 'Old King Brady' and 'The Liberty Boys of '76' in the windows, and marbles, cigarettes and candy inside; and—one definite place at least—a fancy costumer whom we all visited at least once a year. Some time during boyhood I became aware that on one side of a certain obscure street there were bawdy houses, and all through the district were pawnshops, cheap jewellers, small athletic clubs and gymnasiums and somewhat too blatantly run-down saloons.

The morning after the Cotillion Club party, I woke up late and lazy, with the happy feeling that for a day or two more there was no chapel, no classes—nothing to do but wait for another party to-night. It was crisp and bright—one of those days when you forget how cold it is until your cheek freezes—and the events of the evening before seemed dim and far away. After luncheon I started down-town on foot through a light, pleasant snow of small flakes that would probably fall all afternoon, and I was about half through that halfway section of town—so far as I know, there's no inclusive name for it—when suddenly whatever idle thought was in my mind blew away like a hat and I began thinking hard of Ellen Baker. I began worrying about her as I'd never worried about anything outside myself before. I began to loiter, with an instinct to go up on the hill again and find her and talk to her; then I remembered that she was at a tea, and I went on again, but still thinking of her, and harder than ever. Right then the affair opened up again.

It was snowing, I said, and it was four o'clock on a December afternoon, when there is a promise of darkness in the air and the street lamps are just going on. I passed a combination pool parlour and restaurant, with a stove loaded with hot-dogs in the window, and a few loungers hanging around the door. The lights were on inside—not bright lights but just a few pale yellow high up on the ceiling—and the glow they threw out into the frosty dusk wasn't bright enough to tempt you to stare inside. As I went past, thinking hard of Ellen all this time, I took in the quartet of loafers out of the corner of my eye. I hadn't gone half a dozen steps down the street when one of them called to me, not by name but in a way clearly intended for my ear. I thought it was a tribute to my raccoon coat and paid no attention, but a moment later whoever it was called to me again in a peremptory voice. I was annoyed and turned around. There, standing in the group not ten feet away and looking at me with the half-sneer on his face with which he'd looked at Joe Jelke, was the scarred, thin-faced man of the night before.

He had on a black fancy-cut coat, buttoned up to his neck as if he were cold. His hands were deep in his pockets and he wore a derby and high button shoes. I was startled, and for a moment I hesitated, but I was most of all angry, and knowing that I was quicker with my hands than Joe Jelke, I took a tentative step back towards him. The other men weren't looking at me—I don't think they saw me at all—but I knew that this one recognized me; there was nothing casual about his look, no mistake.

'Here I am. What are you going to do about it?' his eyes seemed to say.

I took another step towards him and he laughed soundlessly, but with active contempt, and drew back into the group. I followed. I was going to speak to him—I wasn't sure what I was going to say—but when I came up he had either changed his mind and backed off, or else he wanted me to follow him inside, for he had slipped off and the three men watched my intent approach without curiosity. They were the same kind—sporty, but, unlike him, smooth rather than truculent; I didn't find any personal malice in their collective glance.

'Did he go inside?' I asked.

They looked at one another in that cagey way; a wink passed between them, and after a perceptible pause, one said:

'Who go inside?'

'I don't know his name.'

There was another wink. Annoyed and determined, I walked past them and into the pool room. There were a few people at a lunch counter along one side and a few more playing billiards, but he was not among them.

Again I hesitated. If his idea was to lead me into any blind part of the establishment—there were some half-open doors farther back—I wanted more support. I went up to the man at the desk.

'What became of the fellow who just walked in here?'

Was he on his guard immediately, or was that my imagination?

'What fellow?'

'Thin face—derby hat.'

'How long ago?'

'Oh—a minute.'

He shook his head again. 'Didn't see him,' he said.

I waited. The three men from outside had come in and were lined up beside me at the counter. I felt that all of them were looking at me in a peculiar way. Feeling helpless and increasingly uneasy, I turned suddenly and went out. A little way down the street I turned again and took a good look at the place, so I'd know it and could find it again. On the next corner I broke impulsively into a run, found a taxicab in front of the hotel and drove back up the hill.

Ellen wasn't home. Mrs Baker came downstairs and talked to me. She seemed entirely cheerful and proud of Ellen's beauty, and ignorant of anything amiss or of anything unusual having taken place the night before. She was glad that vacation was almost over—it was a strain and Ellen wasn't very strong. Then she said something that relieved my mind enormously. She was glad that I had come in, for of course Ellen would want to see me, and the time was so short. She was going back at half-past eight tonight.

'Tonight!' I exclaimed. 'I thought it was the day after to-morrow.'

'She's going to visit the Brokaws in Chicago,' Mrs Baker said. 'They want her for some party. We just decided it to-day. She's leaving with the Ingersoll girls tonight.'

I was so glad I could barely restrain myself from shaking her hand. Ellen was safe. It had been nothing all along but a moment of the most casual adventure. I felt like an idiot, but I realized how much I cared about Ellen and how little I could endure anything terrible happening to her.

'She'll be in soon?'

'Any minute now. She just phoned from the University Club.'

I said I'd be over later—I lived almost next door and I wanted to be alone. Outside I remembered I didn't have a key, so I started up the Bakers' driveway to take the old cut we used in childhood through the intervening yard. It was still snowing, but the flakes were bigger now against the darkness, and trying to locate the buried walk I noticed that the Bakers' back door was ajar.

I scarcely know why I turned and walked into that kitchen. There was a time when I would have known the Bakers' servants by name. That wasn't true now, but they knew me, and I was aware of a sudden suspension as I came in—not only a suspension of talk but of some mood or expectation that had filled them. They began to go to work too quickly; they made unnecessary movements and clamour—those three. The parlour maid looked at me in a frightened way and I suddenly guessed she was waiting to deliver another message. I beckoned her into the pantry.

'I know all about this,' I said. 'It's a very serious

business. Shall I go to Mrs Baker now, or will you shut and lock that back door?'

'Don't tell Mrs Baker, Mr Stinson!'

'Then I don't want Miss Ellen disturbed. If she is— and if she is I'll know of it—' I delivered some outrageous threat about going to all the employment agencies and seeing she never got another job in the city. She was thoroughly intimidated when I went out; it wasn't a minute before the back door was locked and bolted behind me.

Simultaneously I heard a big car drive up in front, chains crunching on the soft snow; it was bringing Ellen home, and I went in to say good-bye.

Joe Jelke and two other boys were along, and none of the three could manage to take his eyes off her, even to say hello to me. She had one of those exquisite rose skins frequent in our part of the country, and beautiful until the little veins begin to break at about forty; now, flushed with the cold, it was a riot of lovely delicate pinks like many carnations. She and Joe had reached some sort of reconciliation, or at least he was too far gone in love to remember last night; but I saw that though she laughed a lot she wasn't really paying any attention to him or any of them. She wanted them to go, so that there'd be a message from the kitchen, but I knew that the message wasn't coming—that she was safe. There was talk of the Pump and Slipper dance at New Haven and of the Princeton Prom, and then, in various moods, we four left and separated quickly outside. I walked home with a certain depression of spirit and lay for an hour in a hot bath thinking that vacation was all over for me now that she was gone; feeling, even more deeply than I had yesterday, that she was out of my life.

And something eluded me, some one more thing to do, something that I had lost amid the events of the afternoon, promising myself to go back and pick it up, only to find that it had escaped me. I associated it vaguely with Mrs Baker, and now I seemed to recall that it had poked up

12 + s.f.

its head somewhere in the stream of conversation with her. In my relief about Ellen I had forgotten to ask her a question regarding something she had said.

The Brokaws—that was it—where Ellen was to visit. I knew Bill Brokaw well; he was in my class at Yale. Then I remembered and sat bolt upright in the tub—the Brokaws weren't in Chicago this Christmas; they were at Palm Beach!

Dripping I sprang out of the tub, threw an insufficient union suit around my shoulders and sprang for the phone in my room. I got the connection quick, but Miss Ellen had already started for the train.

Luckily our car was in, and while I squirmed, still damp, into my clothes, the chauffeur brought it around to the door. The night was cold and dry, and we made good time to the station through the hard, crusty snow. I felt queer and insecure starting out this way, but somehow more confident as the station loomed up bright and new against the dark, cold air. For fifty years my family had owned the land on which it was built and that made my temerity seem all right somehow. There was always a possibility that I was rushing in where angels feared to tread, but that sense of having a solid foothold in the past made me willing to make a fool of myself. This business was all wrong—terribly wrong. Any idea I had entertained that it was harmless dropped away now; between Ellen and some vague overwhelming catastrophe there stood me, or else the police and a scandal. I'm no moralist—there was another element here, dark and frightening, and I didn't want Ellen to go through it alone.

There are three competing trains from St Paul to Chicago that all leave within a few minutes of half-past eight. Hers was the Burlington, and as I ran across the station I saw the grating being pulled over and the light above it go out. I knew, though, that she had a drawing-room with the Ingersoll girls, because her mother had mentioned buying the ticket, so she was, literally speaking, tucked in until to-morrow.

The C., M. & St P. gate was down at the other end and I raced for it and made it. I had forgotten one thing, though, and that was enough to keep me awake and worried half the night. This train got into Chicago ten minutes after the other. Ellen had that much time to disappear into one of the largest cities in the world.

I gave the porter a wire to my family to send from Milwaukee, and at eight o'clock next morning I pushed violently by a whole line of passengers, clamouring over their bags parked in the vestibule, and shot out of the door with a sort of scramble over the porter's back. For a moment the confusion of a great station, the voluminous sounds and echoes and cross-currents of bells and smoke struck me helpless. Then I dashed for the exit and towards the only chance I knew of finding her.

I had guessed right. She was standing at the telegraph counter, sending off heaven knows what black lie to her mother, and her expression when she saw me had a sort of terror mixed up with its surprise. There was cunning in it too. She was thinking quickly—she would have liked to walk away from me as if I weren't there, and go about her own business, but she couldn't. I was too matter-of-fact a thing in her life. So we stood silently watching each other and each thinking hard.

'The Brokaws are in Florida,' I said after a minute.

'It was nice of you to take such a long trip to tell me that.'

'Since you've found it out, don't you think you'd better go on to school?'

'Please let me alone, Eddie,' she said.

'I'll go as far as New York with you. I've decided to go back early myself.'

'You'd better let me alone.' Her lovely eyes narrowed and her face took on a look of dumb-animal resistance. She made a visible effort, the cunning flickered back into it, then both were gone, and in their stead was a cheerful reassuring smile that all but convinced me.

'Eddie, you silly child, don't you think I'm old enough to take care of myself?' I didn't answer. 'I'm going to meet a man, you understand. I just want to see him to-day. I've got my ticket East on the five o'clock train. If you don't believe it, here it is in my bag.'

'I believe you.'

'The man isn't anybody that you know and—frankly, I think you're being awfully fresh and impossible.'

'I know who the man is.'

Again she lost control of her face. The terrible expression came back into it and she spoke with almost a snarl:

'You'd better let me alone.'

I took the blank out of her hand and wrote out an explanatory telegram to her mother. Then I turned to Ellen and said a little roughly:

'We'll take the five o'clock train East together. Meanwhile you're going to spend the day with me.'

The mere sound of my own voice saying this so emphatically encouraged me, and I think it impressed her too; at any rate, she submitted—at least temporarily—and came along without protest while I bought my ticket.

When I start to piece together the fragments of that day a sort of confusion begins, as if my memory didn't want to yield up any of it, or my consciousness let any of it pass through. There was a bright, fierce morning during which we rode about in a taxicab and went to a department store where Ellen said she wanted to buy something and then tried to slip away from me by a back way. I had the feeling, for an hour, that someone was following us along Lake Shore Drive in a taxicab, and I would try to catch them by turning quickly or looking suddenly into the chauffeur's mirror; but I could find no one, and when I turned back I could see that Ellen's face was contorted with mirthless, unnatural laughter.

All morning there was a raw, bleak wind off the lake,

but when we went to the Blackstone for lunch a light snow came down past the windows and we talked almost naturally about our friends, and about casual things. Suddenly her tone changed; she grew serious and looked me in the eye, straight and sincere.

'Eddie, you're the oldest friend I have,' she said, 'and you oughtn't to find it too hard to trust me. If I promise you faithfully on my word of honour to catch that five o'clock train, will you let me alone a few hours this afternoon?'

'Why?'

'Well'—she hesitated and hung her head a little—'I guess everybody has a right to say—good-bye.'

'You want to say good-bye to that——'

'Yes, yes,' she said hastily; 'just a few hours, Eddie, and I promise faithfully that I'll be on that train.'

'Well, I suppose no great harm could be done in two hours. If you really want to say good-bye——'

I looked up suddenly, and surprised a look of such tense cunning in her face that I winced before it. Her lip was curled up and her eyes were slits again; there wasn't the faintest touch of fairness and sincerity in her whole face.

We argued. The argument was vague on her part and somewhat hard and reticent on mine. I wasn't going to be cajoled again into any weakness or be infected with any —and there was a contagion of evil in the air. She kept trying to imply, without any convincing evidence to bring forward, that everything was all right. Yet she was too full of the thing itself—whatever it was—to build up a real story, and she wanted to catch at any credulous and acquiescent train of thought that might start in my head, and work that for all it was worth. After every reassuring suggestion she threw out, she stared at me eagerly, as if she hoped I'd launch into a comfortable moral lecture with the customary sweet at the end—which in this case would be her liberty. But I was wearing her away a little. Two or three times it needed just a touch of pressure to bring her to the point of tears—which, of course, was what I wanted—but I couldn't seem to manage it. Almost I had her—almost possessed her interior attention—then she would slip away.

I bullied her remorselessly into a taxi about four o'clock and started for the station. The wind was raw again, with a sting of snow in it, and the people in the streets, waiting for buses and street cars too small to take them all in, looked cold and disturbed and unhappy. I tried to think how lucky we were to be comfortably off and taken care of, but all the warm, respectable world I had been part of yesterday had dropped away from me. There was something we carried with us now that was the enemy and the opposite of all that; it was in the cabs beside us, the streets we passed through. With a touch of panic, I wondered if I wasn't slipping almost imperceptibly into Ellen's attitude of mind. The column of passengers waiting to go aboard the train were as remote from me as people from another world, but it was I that was drifting away and leaving them behind.

My lower was in the same car with her compartment. It was an old-fashioned car, its lights somewhat dim, its carpets and upholstery full of the dust of another generation. There were half a dozen other travellers, but they made no special impression on me, except that they shared the unreality that I was beginning to feel everywhere around me. We went into Ellen's compartment, shut the door and sat down.

Suddenly I put my arms around her and drew her over to me, just as tenderly as I knew how—as if she were a little girl—as she was. She resisted a little, but after a moment she submitted and lay tense and rigid in my arms.

'Ellen,' I said helplessly. 'you asked me to trust you. You have much more reason to trust me. Wouldn't it help to get rid of all this, if you told me a little?'

'I can't,' she said, very low—'I mean, there's nothing to tell.'

'You met this man on the train coming home and you fell in love with him, isn't that true?'

'I don't know.'

'Tell me, Ellen. You fell in love with him?'

'I don't know. Please let me alone.'

'Call it anything you want,' I went on, 'he has some sort of hold over you. He's trying to use you; he's trying to get something from you. He's not in love with you.'

'What does that matter?' she said in a weak voice.

'It does matter. Instead of trying to fight this—this thing—you're trying to fight me. And I love you, Ellen. Do you hear? I'm telling you all of a sudden, but it isn't new with me. I love you.'

She looked at me with a sneer on her gentle face; it was an expression I had seen on men who were tight and didn't want to be taken home. But it was human. I was reaching her, faintly and from far away, but more than before.

'Ellen, I want you to answer me one question. Is he going to be on this train?'

She hesitated; then, an instant too late, she shook her head.

'Be careful, Ellen. Now I'm going to ask you one thing more, and I wish you'd try very hard to answer. Coming West, when did this man get on the train?'

'I don't know,' she said with an effort.

Just at that moment I became aware, with the unquestionable knowledge reserved for facts, that he was just outside the door. She knew it, too; the blood left her face and that expression of low-animal perspicacity came creeping back. I lowered my face into my hands and tried to think.

We must have sat there, with scarcely a word, for well over an hour. I was conscious that the lights of Chicago, then of Englewood and of endless suburbs, were moving by, and then there were no more lights and we were out on the dark flatness of Illinois. The train seemed to draw in upon itself; it took on the air of being alone. The porter knocked at the door and asked if he could make up the berth, but I said no and he went away.

After a while I convinced myself that the struggle inevitably coming wasn't beyond what remained of my sanity, my faith in the essential all-rightness of things and people. That this person's purpose was what we call 'criminal' I took for granted, but there was no need of ascribing to him an intelligence that belonged to a higher plane of human, or inhuman endeavour. It was still as a man that I considered him, and tried to get at his essence, his self-interest—what took the place in him of a comprehensible heart—but I suppose I more than half knew what I would find when I opened the door.

When I stood up Ellen didn't seem to see me at all. She was hunched into a corner staring straight ahead with a sort of film over her eyes, as if she were in a state of suspended animation of body and mind. I lifted her and put two pillows under her head and threw my fur coat over her knees. Then I knelt beside her and kissed her two hands, opened the door and went out into the hall.

I closed the door behind me and stood with my back against it for a minute. The car was dark save for the corridor lights at each end. There was no sound except the groaning of the couplers, the even click-a-click of the rails and someone's loud sleeping breath farther down the car. I became aware after a moment that the figure of a man was standing by the water cooler just outside the men's smoking-room, his derby hat on his head, his coat collar turned up around his neck as if he were cold, his hands in his coat pockets. When I saw him, he turned and went into the smoking-room, and I followed. He was sitting in the far corner of the long leather bench; I took the single armchair beside the door.

As I went in I nodded to him and he acknowledged my presence with one of those terrible soundless laughs of his. But this time it was prolonged, it seemed to go on forever, and mostly to cut it short, I asked: 'Where are you from?' in a voice I tried to make casual.

He stopped laughing and looked at me narrowly, wondering what my game was. When he decided to answer, his voice was muffled as though he were speaking through a silk scarf, and it seemed to come from a long way off.

'I'm from St Paul, Jack.'

'Been making a trip home?'

He nodded. Then he took a long breath and spoke in a hard, menacing voice:

'You better get off at Fort Wayne, Jack.'

He was dead. He was dead as hell—he had been dead all along, but what force had flowed through him, like blood in his veins, out to St Paul and back, was leaving him now. A new outline—the outline of him dead—was coming through the palpable figure that had knocked down Joe Jelke.

He spoke again, with a sort of jerking effort:

'You get off at Fort Wayne, Jack, or I'm going to wipe you out.' He moved his hand in his coat pocket and showed me the outline of a revolver.

I shook my head. 'You can't touch me,' I answered. 'You see, I know.' His terrible eyes shifted over me quickly, trying to determine whether or not I did know. Then he gave a snarl and made as though he were going to jump to his feet.

'You climb off here or else I'm going to get you, Jack!' he cried hoarsely. The train was slowing up for Fort Wayne and his voice rang loud in the comparative quiet, but he didn't move from his chair—he was too weak, I think—and we sat staring at each other while workmen passed up and down outside the window banging the brakes and wheels, and the engine gave out loud mournful pants up ahead. No one got into our car. After a while the porter closed the vestibule door and passed back along the corridor, and we slid out of the murky yellow station light and into the long darkness.

What I remember next must have extended over a space of five or six hours, though it comes back to me as something without any existence in time—something that

12*

might have taken five minutes or a year. There began a slow, calculated assault on me, wordless and terrible. I felt what I can only call a strangeness stealing over me—akin to the strangeness I had felt all afternoon, but deeper and more intensified. It was like nothing so much as the sensation of drifting away, and I gripped the arms of the chair convulsively, as if to hang onto a piece in the living world. Sometimes I felt myself going out with a rush. There would be almost a warm relief about it, a sense of not caring; then, with a violent wrench of the will, I'd pull myself back into the room.

Suddenly I realized that from a while back I had stopped hating him, stopped feeling violently alien to him, and with the realization, I went cold and sweat broke out all over my head. He was getting around my abhorrence, as he had got around Ellen coming West on the train; and it was just that strength he drew from preying on people that had brought him up to the point of concrete violence in St Paul, and that, fading and flickering out, still kept him fighting now.

He must have seen that faltering in my heart, for he spoke at once, in a low, even, almost gentle voice: 'You better go now.'

'Oh, I'm not going,' I forced myself to say.

'Suit yourself, Jack.'

He was my friend, he implied. He knew how it was with me and he wanted to help. He pitied me. I'd better go away before it was too late. The rhythm of his attack was soothing as a song: I'd better go away—*and let him get at Ellen*. With a little cry I sat bolt upright.

'What do you want of this girl?' I said, my voice shaking. 'To make a sort of walking hell of her.'

His glance held a quality of dumb surprise, as if I were punishing an animal for a fault of which he was not conscious. For an instant I faltered; then I went on blindly:

'You've lost her; she's put her trust in me.'

His countenance went suddenly black with evil, and

he cried: 'You're a liar!' in a voice that was like cold hands.

'She trusts me,' I said. 'You can't touch her. She's safe!'

He controlled himself. His face grew bland, and I felt that curious weakness and indifference begin again inside me. What was the use of all this? What was the use?

'You haven't got much time left,' I forced myself to say, and then, in a flash of intuition, I jumped at the truth. 'You died, or you were killed, not far from here!' —Then I saw what I had not seen before—that his forehead was drilled with a small round hole like a larger picture nail leaves when it's pulled from a plaster wall. 'And now you're sinking. You've only got a few hours. The trip home is over!'

His face contorted, lost all semblance of humanity, living or dead. Simultaneously the room was full of cold air and with a noise that was something between a paroxysm of coughing and a burst of horrible laughter, he was on his feet, reeking of shame and blasphemy.

'Come and look!' he cried. 'I'll show you——'

He took a step towards me, then another and it was exactly as if a door stood open behind him, a door yawning out to an inconceivable abyss of darkness and corruption. There was a scream of mortal agony, from him or from somewhere behind, and abruptly the strength went out of him in a long husky sigh and he wilted to the floor. . . .

How long I sat there, dazed with terror and exhaustion, I don't know. The next thing I remember is the sleepy porter shining shoes across the room from me, and outside the window the steel fires of Pittsburgh breaking the flat perspective of the night. There was something extended on the bench also—something too faint for a man, too heavy for a shadow. Even as I perceived it it faded off and away.

Some minutes later I opened the door of Ellen's compartment. She was asleep where I had left her. Her lovely cheeks were white and wan, but she lay naturally—her hands relaxed and her breathing regular and clear. What had possessed her had gone out of her, leaving her exhausted but her own dear self again.

I made her a little more comfortable, tucked a blanket around her, extinguished the light and went out.

III

When I came home for Easter vacation, almost my first act was to go down to the billiard parlour near Seven Corners. The man at the cash register quite naturally didn't remember my hurried visit of three months before.

'I'm trying to locate a certain party who, I think, came here a lot some time ago.'

I described the man rather accurately, and when I had finished, the cashier called to a little jockeylike fellow who was sitting near with an air of having something very important to do that he couldn't quite remember.

'Hey, Shorty, talk to this guy, will you? I think he's looking for Joe Varland.'

The little man gave me a tribal look of suspicion. I went and sat near him.

'Joe Varland's dead, fella,' he said grudgingly. 'He died last winter.'

I described him again—his overcoat, his laugh, the habitual expression of his eyes.

'That's Joe Varland you're looking for all right, but he's dead.'

'I want to find out something about him.'

'What you want to find out?'

'What did he do, for instance?'

'How should I know?'

'Look here! I'm not a policeman. I just want some kind of information about his habits. He's dead now and it can't hurt him. And it won't go beyond me.'

'Well'—he hesitated, looking me over—'he was a great one for travelling. He got in a row in the station in Pittsburgh and a dick got him.'

I nodded. Broken pieces of the puzzle began to assemble in my head.

'Why was he a lot on trains?'

'How should I know, fella?'

'If you can use ten dollars, I'd like to know anything you may have heard on the subject.'

'Well,' said Shorty reluctantly, 'all I know is they used to say he worked the trains.'

'Worked the trains?'

'He had some racket of his own he'd never loosen up about. He used to work the girls travelling alone on the trains. Nobody ever knew much about it—he was a pretty smooth guy—but sometimes he'd turn up here with a lot of dough and he let 'em know it was the janes he got it off of.'

I thanked him and gave him the ten dollars and went out, very thoughtful, without mentioning that part of Joe Varland had made a last trip home.

Ellen wasn't West for Easter, and even if she had been I wouldn't have gone to her with the information, either —at least I've seen her almost every day this summer and we've managed to talk about everything else. Sometimes, though, she gets silent about nothing and wants to be very close to me, and I know what's in her mind.

Of course she's coming out this fall, and I have two more years at New Haven; still, things don't look so impossible as they did a few months ago. She belongs to me in a way—even if I lose her she belongs to me. Who knows? Anyhow, I'll always be there.

THE BOWL

[1928]

THERE was a man in my class at Princeton who never went to football games. He spent his Saturday afternoons delving for minutiae about Greek athletics and the somewhat fixed battles between Christians and wild beasts under the Antonines. Lately—several years out of college—he has discovered football players and is making etchings of them in the manner of the late George Bellows. But he was once unresponsive to the very spectacle at his door, and I suspect the originality of his judgments on what is beautiful, what is remarkable and what is fun.

I revelled in football, as audience, amateur statistician and foiled participant—for I had played in prep school, and once there was a headline in the school newspaper: 'Deering and Mullins Star Against Taft in Stiff Game Saturday.' When I came in to lunch after the battle the school stood up and clapped and the visiting coach shook hands with me and prophesied—incorrectly—that I was going to be heard from. The episode is laid away in the most pleasant lavender of my past. That year I grew very tall and thin, and when at Princeton the following fall I looked anxiously over the freshman candidates and saw the polite disregard with which they looked back at me, I realized that that particular dream was over. Keene said he might make me into a very fair pole vaulter —and he did—but it was a poor substitute; and my terrible disappointment that I wasn't going to be a great football player was probably the foundation of my friendship with Dolly Harlan. I want to begin this story about Dolly with a little rehashing of the Yale game up at New Haven, sophomore year.

Dolly was started at halfback; this was his first big game. I roomed with him and I had scented something peculiar about his state of mind, so I didn't let him out of the corner of my eye during the whole first half. With field glasses I could see the expression on his face; it was strained and incredulous, as it had been the day of his father's death, and it remained so, long after any nervousness had had time to wear off. I thought he was sick and wondered why Keene didn't see and take him out; it wasn't until later that I learned what was the matter.

It was the Yale Bowl. The size of it or the enclosed shape of it or the height of the sides had begun to get on Dolly's nerves when the team practised there the day before. In that practice he dropped one or two punts, for almost the first time in his life, and he began thinking it was because of the Bowl.

There is a new disease called agoraphobia—afraid of crowds—and another called siderodromophobia—afraid of railroad travelling—and my friend Doctor Glock, the psychoanalyst, would probably account easily for Dolly's state of mind. But here's what Dolly told me afterwards:

'Yale would punt and I'd look up. The minute I looked up, the sides of that damn pan would seem to go shooting up too. Then when the ball started to come down, the sides began leaning forward and bending over me until I could see all the people on the top seats screaming at me and shaking their fists. At the last minute I couldn't see the ball at all, but only the Bowl; every time it was just luck that I was under it and every time I juggled it in my hands.'

To go back to the game. I was in the cheering section with a good seat on the forty-yard line—good, that is, except when a very vague graduate, who had lost his friends and his hat, stood up in front of me at intervals and faltered, 'Stob Ted Coy!' under the impression that we were watching a game played a dozen years before. When he realized finally that he was funny he began performing for the gallery and aroused a chorus of whistles and boos until he was dragged unwillingly under the stand.

It was a good game—what is known in college publications as a historic game. A picture of the team that played it now hangs in every barber shop in Princeton, with Captain Gottlieb in the middle wearing a white sweater, to show that they won a championship. Yale had had a poor season, but they had the breaks in the first quarter, which ended 3 to 0 in their favour.

Between quarters I watched Dolly. He walked around panting and sucking a water bottle and still wearing that strained stunned expression. Afterwards he told me he was saying over and over to himself: 'I'll speak to Roper. I'll tell him between halves. I'll tell him I can't go through this any more.' Several times already he had felt an almost irresistible impulse to shrug his shoulders and trot off the field, for it was not only this unexpected complex about the Bowl; the truth was that Dolly fiercely and bitterly hated the game.

He hated the long, dull period of training, the element of personal conflict, the demand on his time, the monotony of the routine and the nervous apprehension of disaster just before the end. Sometimes he imagined that all the others detested it as much as he did, and fought down their aversion as he did and carried it around inside them like a cancer that they were afraid to recognize. Sometimes he imagined that a man here and there was about to tear off the mask and say, 'Dolly, do you hate this lousy business as much as I do?'

His feeling had begun back at St Regis' School and he had come up to Princeton with the idea that he was through with football for ever. But upper classmen from St Regis kept stopping him on the campus and asking him how much he weighed, and he was nominated for vice president of our class on the strength of his athletic reputation—and it was autumn, with achievement in the air. He wandered down to freshman practice one afternoon, feeling oddly lost and dissatisfied, and smelled the

turf and smelled the thrilling season. In half an hour he
was lacing on a pair of borrowed shoes and two weeks
later he was captain of the freshman team.

Once committed, he saw that he had made a mistake;
he even considered leaving college. For, with his decision
to play, Dolly assumed a moral responsibility, personal
to him, besides. To lose or to let down, or to be let
down, was simply intolerable to him. It offended his
Scotch sense of waste. Why sweat blood for an hour with
only defeat at the end?

Perhaps the worst of it was that he wasn't really a star
player. No team in the country could have spared using
him, but he could do no spectacular thing superlatively
well, neither run, pass nor kick. He was five-feet-eleven
and weighed a little more than a hundred and sixty; he
was a first-rate defensive man, sure in interference, a fair
line plunger and a fair punter. He never fumbled and
he was never inadequate; his presence, his constant cold
sure aggression, had a strong effect on other men. Morally,
he captained any team he played on and that was why
Roper had spent so much time trying to get length in his
kicks all season—he wanted him in the game.

In the second quarter Yale began to crack. It was a
mediocre team composed of flashy material, but un-
co-ordinated because of injuries and impending changes
in the Yale coaching system. The quarterback, Josh Logan,
had been a wonder at Exeter—I could testify to that—
where games can be won by the sheer confidence and spirit
of a single man. But college teams are too highly organized
to respond so simply and boyishly, and they recover less
easily from fumbles and errors of judgment behind the
line.

So, with nothing to spare, with much grunting and
straining, Princeton moved steadily down the field. On the
Yale twenty-yard line things suddenly happened. A Princeton pass was intercepted; the Yale man, excited by his own
opportunity, dropped the ball and it bobbled leisurely in
the general direction of the Yale goal. Jack Devlin and

Dolly Harlan of Princeton and somebody—I forget who—
from Yale were all about the same distance from it. What
Dolly did in that split second was all instinct; it presented
no problem to him. He was a natural athlete and in a
crisis his nervous system thought for him. He might have
raced the two others for the ball; instead, he took out the
Yale man with savage precision while Devlin scooped up
the ball and ran ten yards for a touchdown.

This was when the sports writers still saw games through
the eyes of Ralph Henry Barbour. The press box was
right behind me, and as Princeton lined up to kick goal
I heard the radio man ask:

'Who's Number 22?'

'Harlan.'

'Harlan is going to kick goal. Devlin, who made the
touchdown, comes from Lawrenceville School. He is
twenty years old. The ball went true between the bars.'

Between the halves, as Dolly sat shaking with fatigue
in the locker room, Little, the backfield coach, came and
sat beside him.

'When the ends are right on you, don't be afraid to make
a fair catch,' Little said. 'That big Havemeyer is liable to
jar the ball right out of your hands.'

Now was the time to say it: 'I wish you'd tell Bill——'
But the words twisted themselves into a trivial question
about the wind. His feeling would have to be explained,
gone into, and there wasn't time. His own self seemed
less important in this room, redolent with the tired breath,
the ultimate effort, the exhaustion of ten other men. He
was shamed by a harsh sudden quarrel that broke out
between an end and tackle; he resented the former players
in the room—especially the graduate captain of two years
before, who was a little tight and over-vehement about the
referee's favouritism. It seemed terrible to add one more
jot to all this strain and annoyance. But he might have
come out with it all the same if Little hadn't kept saying
in a low voice: 'What a take-out, Dolly! What a beautiful

take-out!' and if Little's hand hadn't rested there patting his shoulder.

II

In the third quarter Joe Dougherty kicked an easy field goal from the twenty-yard line and we felt safe, until towards twilight a series of desperate forward passes brought Yale close to a score. But Josh Logan had exhausted his personality in sheer bravado and he was outguessed by the defence at the last. As the substitutes came running in, Princeton began a last march down the field. Then abruptly it was over and the crowd poured from the stands, and Gottlieb, grabbing the ball, leaped up in the air. For a while everything was confused and crazy and happy; I saw some freshmen try to carry Dolly, but they were shy and he got away.

We all felt a great personal elation. We hadn't beaten Yale for three years and now everything was going to be all right. It meant a good winter at college, something pleasant and slick to think back upon in the damp cold days after Christmas, when a bleak futility settles over a university town. Down on the field, an improvised and uproarious team ran through plays with a derby, until the snake dance rolled over them and blotted them out. Outside the Bowl, I saw two abysmally gloomy and disgusted Yale men get into a waiting taxi and in a tone of final abnegation tell the driver 'New York.' You couldn't find Yale men; in the manner of the vanquished, they had absolutely melted away.

I begin Dolly's story with my memories of this game because that evening the girl walked into it. She was a friend of Josephine Pickman's and the four of us were going to drive up to the Midnight Frolic in New York. When I suggested to him that he'd be too tired he laughed dryly—he'd have gone anywhere that night to get the feel and rhythm of football out of his head. He walked into the hall of Josephine's house at half-past six, looking as if he'd spent the day in the barber shop save for a small and fetching strip of court plaster over one eye. He was one of the handsomest men I ever knew, anyhow; he appeared tall and slender in street clothes, his hair was dark, his eyes big and sensitive and dark, his nose aquiline and, like all his features, somehow romantic. It didn't occur to me then, but I suppose he was pretty vain—not conceited, but vain —for he always dressed in brown or soft light grey, with black ties, and people don't match themselves so successfully by accident.

He was smiling a little to himself as he came in. He shook my hand buoyantly and said, 'Why, what a surprise to meet you here, Mr Deering,' in a kidding way. Then he saw the girls through the long hall, one dark and shining, like himself, and one with gold hair that was foaming and frothing in the firelight, and said in the happiest voice I've ever heard, 'Which one is mine?'

'Either one you want, I guess.'

'Seriously, which is Pickman?'

'She's light.'

'Then the other one belongs to me. Isn't that the idea?'

'I think I'd better warn them about the state you're in.'

Miss Thorne, small, flushed and lovely, stood beside the fire. Dolly went right up to her.

'You're mine,' he said; 'you belong to me.'

She looked at him coolly, making up her mind; suddenly she liked him and smiled. But Dolly wasn't satisfied. He wanted to do something incredibly silly or startling to express his untold jubilation that he was free.

'I love you,' he said. He took her hand, his brown velvet eyes regarding her tenderly, unseeingly, convincingly. 'I love you.'

For a moment the corners of her lips fell as if in dismay that she had met someone stronger, more confident, more challenging than herself. Then, as she drew herself together visibly, he dropped her hand and the little scene in which he had expended the tension of the afternoon was over.

It was a bright cold November night and the rush of air past the open car brought a vague excitement, a sense that we were hurrying at top speed towards a brilliant destiny. The road were packed with cars that came to long inexplicable halts while police, blinded by the lights, walked up and down the line giving obscure commands. Before we had been gone an hour New York began to be a distant hazy glow against the sky.

Miss Thorne, Josephine told me, was from Washington, and had just come down from a visit in Boston.

'For the game?' I said.

'No; she didn't go to the game.'

'That's too bad. If you'd let me know I could have picked up a seat——'

'She wouldn't have gone. Vienna never goes to games.'

I remembered now that she hadn't even murmured the conventional congratulations to Dolly.

'She hates football. Her brother was killed in a prep-school game last year. I wouldn't have brought her to-night, but when we got home from the game I saw she'd been sitting there holding a book open at the same page all afternoon. You see, he was this wonderful kid and her family saw it happen and naturally never got over it.'

'But does she mind being with Dolly?'

'Of course not. She just ignores football. If anyone mentions it she simply changes the subject.'

I was glad that it was Dolly and not, say, Jack Devlin who was sitting back there with her. And I felt rather sorry for Dolly. However strongly he felt about the game, he must have waited for some acknowledgment that his effort had existed.

He was probably giving her credit for subtle considera-tion—yet, as the images of the afternoon flashed into his mind he might have welcomed a compliment to which he could respond 'What nonsense!' Neglected entirely, the images would become insistent and obtrusive.

I turned around and was somewhat startled to find that

Miss Thorne was in Dolly's arms; I turned quickly back and decided to let them take care of themselves.

As we waited for a traffic light on upper Broadway, I saw a sporting extra headlined with the score of the game. The green sheet was more real than the afternoon itself—succinct, condensed and clear:

PRINCETON CONQUERS YALE 10–3

SEVENTY THOUSAND WATCH TIGER TRIM

BULLDOG

DEVLIN SCORES ON YALE FUMBLE

There it was—not like the afternoon, muddled, uncertain, patchy and scrappy to the end, but nicely mounted now in the setting of the past:

PRINCETON, 10; YALE, 3.

Achievement was a curious thing, I thought. Dolly was largely responsible for that. I wondered if all things that screamed in the headlines were simply arbitrary accents. As if people should ask, 'What does it look like?'

'It looks most like a cat.'

'Well, then, let's call it a cat.'

My mind, brightened by the lights and the cheerful tumult, suddenly grasped the fact that all achievement was a placing of emphasis—a moulding of the confusion of life into form.

Josephine stopped in front of the New American Theatre, where her chauffeur met us and took the car. We were quite early, but a small buzz of excitement went up from the undergraduates waiting in the lobby—'There's Dolly Harlan'—and as we moved towards the elevator several acquaintances came up to shake his hand. Apparently oblivious to these ceremonies, Miss Thorne caught my eye and smiled. I looked at her with curiosity; Josephine had imparted the rather surprising information that she was just sixteen years old. I suppose my return smile was rather patronizing, but instantly I realized that the fact could not be imposed on. In spite of all the warmth

and delicacy of her face, the figure that somehow reminded me of an exquisite, romanticized little ballerina,
there was a quality in her that was as hard as steel. She
had been brought up in Rome, Vienna and Madrid, with
flashes of Washington; her father was one of those
charming American diplomats who, with fine obstinacy,
try to re-create the Old World in their children by making
their education rather more royal than that of princes.
Miss Thorne was sophisticated. In spite of all the abandon
of American young people, sophistication is still a Continental monopoly.

We walked in upon a number in which a dozen chorus
girls in orange and black were racing wooden horses
against another dozen dressed in Yale blue. When the
lights went on, Dolly was recognized and some Princeton
students set up a clatter of approval with the little wooden
hammers given out for applause; he moved his chair un-
ostentatiously into a shadow.

Almost immediately a flushed and very miserable young
man appeared beside our table. In better form he would
have been extremely prepossessing; indeed, he flashed a
charming and dazzling smile at Dolly, as if requesting his
permission to speak to Miss Thorne.

Then he said: 'I thought you weren't coming to New
York to-night?'

'Hello, Carl.' She looked up at him coolly.

'Hullo, Vienna. That's just it; "Hello Vienna—Hello
Carl." But why? I thought you weren't coming to New
York to-night.'

Miss Thorne made no move to introduce the man, but
we were conscious of his somewhat raised voice.

'I thought you promised me you weren't coming.'

'I didn't expect to, child. I just left Boston this morning.'

'And who did you meet in Boston—the fascinating
Tunti?' he demanded.

'I didn't meet anyone, child.'

'Oh, yes, you did! You met the fascinating Tunti and

you discussed living on the Riviera.' She didn't answer. 'Why are you so dishonest, Vienna?' he went on. 'Why did you tell me on the phone ——'

'I am not going to be lectured,' she said, her tone changing suddenly. 'I told you if you took another drink I was through with you. I'm a person of my word and I'd be enormously happy if you went away.'

'Vienna!' he cried in a sinking, trembling voice.

At this point I got up and danced with Josephine. When we came back there were people at the table—the men to whom we were to hand over Josephine and Miss Thorne, for I had allowed for Dolly being tired, and several others. One of them was Al Ratoni, the composer, who, it appeared, had been entertained at the embassy in Madrid. Dolly Harlan had drawn his chair aside and was watching the dancers. Just as the lights went down for a new number a man came up out of the darkness and leaning over Miss Thorne whispered in her ear. She started and made a motion to rise, but he put his hand on her shoulder and forced her down. They began to talk together in low excited voices.

The tables were packed close at the old Frolic. There was a man rejoining the party next to us and I couldn't help hearing what he said:

'A young fellow just tried to kill himself down in the wash room. He shot himself through the shoulder, but they got the pistol away before——' A minute later his voice again: 'Carl Sanderson, they said.'

When the number was over I looked around. Vienna Thorne was staring very rigidly at Miss Lillian Lorraine, who was rising towards the ceiling as an enormous telephone doll. The man who had leaned over Vienna was gone and the others were obliviously unaware that anything had happened. I turned to Dolly and suggested that he and I had better go, and after a glance at Vienna in which reluctance, weariness and then resignation were mingled, he consented. On the way to the hotel I told Dolly what had happened.

'Just some souse,' he remarked after a moment's fatigued consideration. 'He probably tried to miss himself and get a little sympathy. I suppose those are the sort of things a really attractive girl is up against all the time.'

This wasn't my attitude. I could see that mussed white shirt front with very young blood pumping over it, but I didn't argue, and after a while Dolly said, 'I suppose that sounds brutal, but it seems a little soft and weak, doesn't it? Perhaps that's just the way I feel to-night.'

When Dolly undressed I saw that he was a mass of bruises, but he assured me that none of them would keep him awake. Then I told him why Miss Thorne hadn't mentioned the game and he woke up suddenly; the familiar glitter came back into his eyes.

'So that was it! I wondered. I thought maybe you'd told her not to say anything about it.'

Later, when the lights had been out half an hour, he suddenly said 'I see' in a loud clear voice. I don't know whether he was awake or asleep.

III

I've put down as well as I can everything I can remember about the first meeting between Dolly and Miss Vienna Thorne. Reading it over, it sounds casual and insignificant, but the evening lay in the shadow of the game and all that happened seemed like that. Vienna went back to Europe almost immediately and for fifteen months passed out of Dolly's life.

It was a good year—it still rings true in my memory as a good year. Sophomore year is the most dramatic at Princeton, just as junior year is at Yale. It's not only the elections to the upper-class clubs but also everyone's destiny begins to work itself out. You can tell pretty well who's going to come through, not only by their immediate success but by the way they survive failure. Life was very full for me. I made the board of the *Princetonian*, and our house burned down in Dayton, and I had a silly half-hour fist fight in the gymnasium with a man who later became one of my closest friends, and in March Dolly and I joined the upper-class club we'd always wanted to be in. I fell in love, too, but it would be an irrelevancy to tell about that here.

April came and the first real Princeton weather, the lazy green-and-gold afternoons and the bright thrilling nights haunted with the hour of senior singing. I was happy, and Dolly would have been happy except for the approach of another football season. He was playing baseball, which excused him from spring practice, but the bands were beginning to play faintly in the distance. They rose to concert pitch during the summer, when he had to answer the question, 'Are you going back early for football?' a dozen times a day. On the fifteenth of September he was down in the dust and heat of late-summer Princeton, crawling over the ground on all fours, trotting through the old routine and turning himself into just the sort of specimen that I'd have given ten years of my life to be.

From first to last, he hated it, and never let down for a minute. He went into the Yale game that fall weighing a hundred and fifty-three pounds, though that wasn't the weight printed in the paper, and he and Joe McDonald were the only men who played all through that disastrous game. He could have been captain by lifting his finger— but that involves some stuff that I know confidentially and can't tell. His only horror was that by some chance he'd have to accept it! Two seasons! He didn't even talk about it now. He left the room or the club when the conversation veered around to football. He stopped announcing to me that he 'wasn't going through that business any more.' This time it took the Christmas holidays to drive that unhappy look from his eyes.

Then at the New Year Miss Vienna Thorne came home from Madrid and in February a man named Case brought her down to the Senior Prom.

IV

She was even prettier than she had been before, softer, externally at least, and a tremendous success. People passing her on the street jerked their heads quickly to look at her—a frightened look, as if they realized that they had almost missed something. She was temporarily tired of European men, she told me, letting me gather that there had been some sort of unfortunate love affair. She was coming out in Washington next fall.

Vienna and Dolly. She disappeared with him for two hours the night of the club dances, and Harold Case was in despair. When they walked in again at midnight I thought they were the handsomest pair I saw. They were both shining with that peculiar luminosity that dark people sometimes have. Harold Case took one look at them and went proudly home.

Vienna came back a week later, solely to see Dolly. Late that evening I had occasion to go up to the deserted club for a book and they called me from the rear terrace, which opens out to the ghostly stadium and to an un-peopled sweep of night. It was an hour of thaw, with spring voices in the warm wind, and wherever there was light enough you could see drops glistening and falling. You could feel the cold melting out of the stars and the bare trees and shrubbery towards Stony Brook turning lush in the darkness.

They were sitting together on a wicker bench, full of themselves and romantic and happy.

'We had to tell someone about it,' they said.

'Now can I go?'

'No, Jeff,' they insisted; 'stay here and envy us. We're in the stage where we want someone to envy us. Do you think we're a good match?'

What could I say?

'Dolly's going to finish at Princeton next year,' Vienna went on, 'but we're going to announce it after the season in Washington in the autumn.'

I was vaguely relieved to find that it was going to be a long engagement.

'I approve of you, Jeff,' Vienna said. 'I want Dolly to have more friends like you. You're stimulating for him —you have ideas. I told Dolly he could probably find others like you if he looked around his class.'

Dolly and I both felt a little uncomfortable.

'She doesn't want me to be a Babbitt,' he said lightly.

'Dolly's perfect,' asserted Vienna. 'He's the most beautiful thing that ever lived, and you'll find I'm very good for him, Jeff. Already I've helped him make up his mind about one important thing.' I guessed what was coming. 'He's going to speak a little piece if they bother him about playing football next autumn, aren't you, child?'

'Oh, they won't bother me,' said Dolly uncomfortably. 'It isn't like that——'

'Well, they'll try to bully you into it, morally.'

'Oh no,' he objected. 'It isn't like that. Don't let's talk about it now, Vienna. It's such a swell night.'

Such a swell night! When I think of my own love passages at Princeton, I always summon up that night of Dolly's as if it had been I and not he who sat there with youth and hope and beauty in his arms.

Dolly's mother took a place on Ram's Point, Long Island, for the summer, and late in August I went East to visit him. Vienna had been there a week when I arrived, and my impressions were: first, that he was very much in love; and, second, that it was Vienna's party. All sorts of curious people used to drop in to see Vienna. I wouldn't mind them now—I'm more sophisticated—but then they seemed rather a blot on the summer. They were all slightly famous in one way or another, and it was up to you to find out how. There was a lot of talk, and especially there was much discussion of Vienna's personality. They thought I was dull, and most of them thought Dolly was dull. He was better in his line than any of them were in theirs, but his was the only speciality that wasn't mentioned. Still, I felt vaguely that I was being improved and I boasted about knowing most of those people in the ensuing year, and was annoyed when people failed to recognize their names.

The day before I left, Dolly turned his ankle playing tennis, and afterwards he joked about it to me rather sombrely.

'If I'd only broken it things would be so much easier. Just a quarter of an inch more bend and one of the bones would have snapped. By the way, look here.'

He tossed me a letter. It was a request that he report at Princeton for practice on September fifteenth and that meanwhile he begin getting himself in good condition.

'You're not going to play this fall?'

He shook his head.

'No. I'm not a child any more. I've played for two years and I want this year free. If I went through it again it'd be a piece of moral cowardice.'

'I'm not arguing, but—would you have taken this stand if it hadn't been for Vienna?'

'Of course I would. If I let myself be bullied into it I'd never be able to look myself in the face again.'

Two weeks later I got the following letter:

DEAR JEFF: When you read this you'll be somewhat surprised. I have, actually, this time, broken my ankle playing tennis. I can't even walk with crutches at present; it's on a chair in front of me swollen up and wrapped up as big as a house as I write. No one, not even Vienna, knows about our conversation on the same subject last summer and so let us both absolutely forget it. One thing, though—an ankle is a darn hard thing to break, though I never knew it before.

I feel happier than I have for years—no early-season practice, no sweat and suffer, a little discomfort and inconvenience, but free. I feel as if I've outwitted a whole lot of people, and it's nobody's business but that of your

Machiavellian (sic) friend,
DOLLY

P.S. You might as well tear up this letter.

It didn't sound like Dolly at all.

V

Once down in Princeton I asked Frank Kane—who sells sporting goods on Nassau Street and can tell you offhand the name of the scrub quarterback in 1901—what was the matter with Bob Tatnall's team senior year.

'Injuries and tough luck,' he said. 'They wouldn't sweat after the hard games. Take Joe McDonald, for instance, All-American tackle the year before; he was slow and stale, and he knew it and didn't care. It's a wonder Bill got that outfit through the season at all.'

I sat in the stands with Dolly and watched them beat Lehigh 3–0 and tie Bucknell by a fluke. The next week we were trimmed 14–0 by Notre Dame. On the day of the Notre Dame game Dolly was in Washington with Vienna, but he was awfully curious about it when he came back next day. He had all the sporting pages of all the papers and he sat reading them and shaking his head. Then he stuffed them suddenly into the wastepaper basket.

'This college is football crazy,' he announced. 'Do you know that English teams don't even train for sports?'

I didn't enjoy Dolly so much in those days. It was curious to see him with nothing to do. For the first time in his life he hung around—around the room, around the club, around casual groups—he who had always been going somewhere with dynamic indolence. His passage along a walk had once created groups—groups of class-mates who wanted to walk with him, of under classmen who followed with their eyes a moving shrine. He became democratic, he mixed around, and it was somehow not appropriate. He explained that he wanted to know more men in his class.

But people wanted their idols a little above them, and Dolly had been a sort of private and special idol. He began to hate to be alone, and that, of course, was most apparent to me. If I got up to go out and he didn't happen to be writing a letter to Vienna, he'd ask 'Where are you going?' in a rather alarmed way and make an excuse to limp along with me.

'Are you glad you did it, Dolly?' I asked him suddenly one day.

He looked at me with reproach behind the defiance in his eyes.

'Of course I'm glad.'

'I wish you were in that back field, all the same.'

'It wouldn't matter a bit. This year's game's in the Bowl. I'd probably be dropping kicks for them.'

The week of the Navy game he suddenly began going to all the practices. He worried; that terrible sense of responsibility was at work. Once he had hated the mention of football; now he thought and talked of nothing else. The night before the Navy game I woke up several times to find the lights burning brightly in his room.

We lost 7 to 3 on Navy's last-minute forward pass over Devlin's head. After the first half Dolly left the stands and sat down with the players on the field. When he joined me afterwards his face was smudgy and dirty as if he had been crying.

The game was in Baltimore that year. Dolly and I were going to spend the night in Washington with Vienna, who was giving a dance. We rode over there in an atmosphere of sullen gloom and it was all I could do to keep him from snapping out at two naval officers who were holding an exultant post mortem in the seat behind.

The dance was what Vienna called her second coming-out party. She was having only the people she liked, this time, and these turned out to be chiefly importations from New York. The musicians, the playwrights, the vague supernumeraries of the arts, who had dropped in at Dolly's house on Ram's Point, were here in force. But Dolly, relieved of his obligations as host, made no clumsy attempt to talk their language that night. He stood moodily against the wall with some of that old air of superiority that had first made me want to know him.

Afterwards, on my way to bed, I passed Vienna's sitting-room and she called me to come in. She and Dolly, both a little white, were sitting across the room from each other and there was tensity in the air.

'Sit down, Jeff,' said Vienna wearily. 'I want you to witness the collapse of a man into a schoolboy.' I sat down reluctantly. 'Dolly's changed his mind,' she said. 'He prefers football to me.'

'That's not it,' said Dolly stubbornly.

'I don't see the point,' I objected. 'Dolly can't possibly play.'

'But he thinks he can. Jeff, just in case you imagine I'm being pig-headed about it, I want to tell you a story. Three years ago, when we first came back to the United States, father put my young brother in school. One afternoon we all went out to see him play football. Just after the game started he was hurt, but father said, 'It's all right. He'll be up in a minute. It happens all the time.' But, Jeff, he never got up. He lay there, and finally they carried him off the field and put a blanket over him. Just as we got to him he died.'

She looked from one to the other of us and began to sob convulsively. Dolly went over, frowning, and put his arm around her shoulder.

'Oh, Dolly,' she cried, 'won't you do this for me—just this one little thing for me?'

He shook his head miserably. 'I tried, but I can't,' he said.

'It's my stuff, don't you understand, Vienna? People have got to do their stuff.'

Vienna had risen and was powdering her tears at a mirror; now she flashed around angrily.

'Then I've been labouring under a misapprehension when I supposed you felt about it much as I did.'

'Let's not go over all that. I'm tired of talking, Vienna; I'm tired of my own voice. It seems to me that no one I know does anything but talk any more.'

'Thanks. I suppose that's meant for me.'

'It seems to me your friends talk a great deal. I've never heard so much jabber as I've listened to to-night. Is the idea of actually doing anything repulsive to you, Vienna?'

'It depends upon whether it's worth doing.'

'Well, this is worth doing—to me.'

'I know your trouble, Dolly,' she said bitterly. 'You're weak and you want to be admired. This year you haven't had a lot of little boys following you around as if you were Jack Dempsey, and it almost breaks your heart. You want to get out in front of them all and make a show of yourself and hear the applause.'

He laughed shortly. 'If that's your idea of how a football player feels——'

'Have you made up your mind to play?' she interrupted.

'If I'm any use to them—yes.'

'Then I think we're both wasting our time.'

Her expression was ruthless, but Dolly refused to see that she was in earnest. When I got away he was still trying to make her 'be rational,' and next day on the train he said that Vienna had been 'a little nervous.' He was deeply in love with her, and he didn't dare think of losing her; but he was still in the grip of the sudden emotion that had decided him to play, and his confusion and exhaustion of mind made him believe vainly that everything was going to be all right. But I had seen that look on Vienna's face the night she talked with Mr Carl Sanderson at the Frolic two years before.

Dolly didn't get off the train at Princeton Junction, but continued on to New York. He went to two orthopaedic specialists and one of them arranged a bandage braced with a whole little fence of whalebones that he was to wear day and night. The probabilities were that it would snap at the first brisk encounter, but he could run on it and stand on it when he kicked. He went out on University Field in uniform the following afternoon.

His appearance was a small sensation. I was sitting in the stands watching practice with Harold Case and young Daisy Cary. She was just beginning to be famous then,

13+s.f.

and I don't know whether she or Dolly attracted the most attention. In those times it was still rather daring to bring down a moving-picture actress; if that same young lady went to Princeton to-day she would probably be met at the station with a band.

Dolly limped around and everyone said, 'He's limping!' He got under a punt and everyone said, 'He did that pretty well!' The first team were laid off after the hard Navy game and everyone watched Dolly all afternoon. After practice I caught his eye and he came over and shook hands. Daisy asked him if he'd like to be in a football picture she was going to make. It was only conversation, but he looked at me with a dry smile.

When he came back to the room his ankle was swollen up as big as a stove pipe, and next day he and Keene fixed up an arrangement by which the bandage would be loosened and tightened to fit its varying size. We called it the balloon. The bone was nearly healed, but the little bruised sinews were stretched out of place again every day. He watched the Swarthmore game from the sidelines and the following Monday he was in scrimmage with the second team against the scrubs.

In the afternoons sometimes he wrote to Vienna. His theory was that they were still engaged, but he tried not to worry about it, and I think the very pain that kept him awake at night was good for that. When the season was over he would go and see.

We played Harvard and lost 7 to 3. Jack Devlin's collar bone was broken and he was out for the season, which made it almost sure that Dolly would play. Amid the rumours and the fears of mid-November the news aroused a spark of hope in an otherwise morbid undergraduate body—hope out of all proportion to Dolly's condition. He came back to the room the Thursday before the game with his face drawn and tired.

'They're going to start me,' he said, 'and I'm going to be back for punts. If they only knew——'

'Couldn't you tell Bill how you feel about that?'

He shook his head and I had a sudden suspicion that he was punishing himself for his 'accident' last August. He lay silently on the couch while I packed his suitcase for the team train.

The actual day of the game was, as usual, like a dream —unreal with its crowds of friends and relatives and the inessential trappings of a gigantic show. The eleven little men who ran out on the field at last were like bewitched figures in another world, strange and infinitely romantic, blurred by a throbbing mist of people and sound. One aches with them intolerably, trembles with their excitement, but they have no traffic with us now, they are beyond help, consecrated and unreachable—vaguely holy.

The field is rich and green, the preliminaries are over and the teams trickle out into position. Head guards are put on; each man claps his hands and breaks into a lonely little dance. People are still talking around you, arranging themselves, but you have fallen silent and your eye wanders from man to man. There's Jack Whitehead, a senior, at end; Joe McDonald, large and reassuring, at tackle; Toole, a sophomore, at guard; Red Hopman, centre; someone you can't identify at the other guard— Bunker probably—he turns and you see his number— Bunker; Bean Gile, looking unnaturally dignified and significant at the other tackle; Poae, another sophomore at end. Back of them is Wash Sampson at quarter—imagine how he feels! But he runs here and there on light feet, speaking to this man and that, trying to communicate his alertness and his confidence of success. Dolly Harlan stands motionless, his hands on his hips, watching the Yale kicker tee up the ball; near him is Captain Bob Tatnall——

There's the whistle! The line of the Yale team sways ponderously forward from its balance and a split second afterwards comes the sound of the ball. The field streams with running figures and the whole Bowl strains forward as if thrown by the current of an electric chair.

Suppose we fumbled right away.

Tatnall catches it, goes back ten yards, is surrounded and blotted out of sight. Spears goes through centre for three. A short pass, Sampson to Tatnall, is completed, but for no gain. Harlan punts to Devereaux, who is downed in his tracks on the Yale forty-yard line.

Now we'll see what they've got.

It developed immediately that they had a great deal. Using an effective crisscross and a short pass over centre, they carried the ball fifty yards to the Princeton six-yard line, where they lost it on a fumble, recovered by Red Hopman. After a trade of punts, they began another push, this time to the fifteen-yard line, where, after four hair-raising forward passes, two of them batted down by Dolly, we got the ball on downs. But Yale was still fresh and strong, and with a third onslaught the weaker Princeton line began to give way. Just after the second quarter began Devereaux took the ball over for a touchdown and the half ended with Yale in possession of the ball on our ten-yard line. Score, Yale, 7; Princeton, 0.

We hadn't a chance. The team was playing above itself, better than it had played all year, but it wasn't enough. Save that it was the Yale game, when anything could happen, anything *had* happened, the atmosphere of gloom would have been deeper than it was, and in the cheering section you could cut it with a knife.

Early in the game Dolly Harlan had fumbled Devereaux's high punt, but recovered without gain; towards the end of the half another kick slipped through his fingers, but he scooped it up and, slipping past the end, went back twelve yards. Between halves he told Roper he couldn't seem to get under the ball, but they kept him there. His own kicks were carrying well and he was essential in the only backfield combination that could hope to score.

After the first play of the game he limped slightly, moving around as little as possible to conceal the fact. But I knew enough about football to see that he was in every play, starting at that rather slow pace of his and finishing with a quick side lunge that almost always took out his man. Not a single Yale forward pass was finished in his territory, but towards the end of the third quarter he dropped another kick—backed around in a confused little circle under it, lost it and recovered on the five-yard line just in time to avert a certain score. That made the third time, and I saw Ed Kimball throw off his blanket and begin to warm up on the sidelines.

Just at that point our luck began to change. From a kick formation, with Dolly set to punt from behind our goal, Howard Bement, who had gone in for Wash Sampson at quarter, took the ball through the centre of the line, got by the secondary defence and ran twenty-six yards before he was pulled down. Captain Tasker, of Yale, had gone out with a twisted knee, and Princeton began to pile plays through his substitute, between Bean Gile and Hopman, with George Spears and sometimes Bob Tatnall carrying the ball. We went up to the Yale forty-yard line, lost the ball on a fumble and recovered it on another as the third quarter ended. A wild ripple of enthusiasm ran through the Princeton stands. For the first time we had the ball in their territory with first down and the possibility of tying the score. You could hear the tenseness growing all around you in the intermission; it was reflected in the excited movements of the cheer leaders and the uncontrollable patches of sound that leaped out of the crowd, catching up voices here and there and swelling to an undisciplined roar.

I saw Kimball dash out on the field and report to the referee and I thought Dolly was through at last, and was glad, but it was Bob Tatnall who came out, sobbing, and brought the Princeton side cheering to its feet.

With the first play pandemonium broke loose and continued to the end of the game. At intervals it would swoon away to a plaintive humming; then it would rise to the intensity of wind and rain and thunder, and beat across the twilight from one side of the Bowl to the other like the agony of lost souls swinging across a gap in space.

The teams lined up on Yale's forty-one-yard line and

Spears immediately dashed off tackle for six yards. Again he carried the ball—he was a wild unpopular Southerner with inspired moments—going through the same hole for five more and a first down. Dolly made two on a cross buck and Spears was held at centre. It was third down, with the ball on Yale's twenty-nine-yard line and eight to go.

There was some confusion immediately behind me, some pushing and some voices; a man was sick or had fainted—I never discovered which. Then my view was blocked for a minute by rising bodies and then everything went definitely crazy. Substitutes were jumping around down on the field, waving their blankets, the air was full of hats, cushions, coats, and a deafening roar. Dolly Harlan, who had scarcely carried the ball a dozen times in his Princeton career, had picked up a long pass from Kimball out of the air and, dragging a tackler, struggled five yards to the Yale goal.

VI

Some time later the game was over. There was a bad moment when Yale began another attack, but there was no scoring and Bob Tatnall's eleven had redeemed a mediocre season by tying a better Yale team. For us there was the feel of victory about it, the exultation if not the jubilance, and the Yale faces issuing from out the Bowl wore the look of defeat. It would be a good year, after all —a good fight at the last, a tradition for next year's team. Our class—those of us who cared—would go out from Princeton without the taste of final defeat. The symbol stood—such as it was; the banners blew proudly in the wind. All that is childish? Find us something to fill the niche of victory.

I waited for Dolly outside the dressing rooms until almost everyone had come out; then, as he still lingered, I went in. Someone had given him a little brandy, and since he never drank much, it was swimming in his head.

'Have a chair, Jeff.' He smiled broadly and happily. 'Rubber! Tony! Get the distinguished guest a chair. He's an intellectual and he wants to interview one of the bone-headed athletes. Tony, this is Mr Deering. They've got everything in this funny Bowl but armchairs. I love this Bowl. I'm going to build here.'

He fell silent, thinking about all things happily. He was content. I persuaded him to dress—there were people waiting for us. Then he insisted on walking out upon the field, dark now, and feeling the crumbled turf with his shoe.

He picked up a divot from a cleat and let it drop, laughed, looked distracted for a minute, and turned away.

With Tad Davis, Daisy Cary and another girl, we drove to New York. He sat beside Daisy and was silly, charming and attractive. For the first time since I'd known him he talked about the game naturally, even with a touch of vanity.

'For two years I was pretty good and I was always mentioned at the bottom of the column as being among those who played. This year I dropped three punts and slowed up every play till Bob Tatnall kept yelling at me, 'I don't see why they won't take you out!' But a pass not even aimed at me fell in my arms and I'll be in the headlines to-morrow.'

He laughed. Somebody touched his foot; he winced and turned white.

'How did you hurt it?' Daisy asked. 'In football?'

'I hurt it last summer,' he said shortly.

'It must have been terrible to play on it.'

'It was.'

'I suppose you had to.'

'That's the way sometimes.'

They understood each other. They were both workers; sick or well, there were things that Daisy also had to do. She spoke of how, with a vile cold, she had had to fall into an open-air lagoon out in Hollywood the winter before.

'Six times—with a fever of a hundred and two. But the production was costing ten thousand dollars a day.'

'Couldn't they use a double?'

'They did whenever they could—I only fell in when it had to be done.'

She was eighteen and I compared her background of courage and independence and achievement, of politeness based upon realities of co-operation, with that of most society girls I had known. There was no way in which she wasn't inestimably their superior—if she had looked for a moment my way—but it was Dolly's shining velvet eyes that signalled to her own.

'Can't you go out with me to-night?' I heard her ask him.

He was sorry, but he had to refuse. Vienna was in New York; she was going to see him. I didn't know, and Dolly didn't know, whether there was to be a reconciliation or a good-bye.

When she dropped Dolly and me at the Ritz there was real regret, that lingering form of it, in both their eyes.

'There's a marvellous girl,' Dolly said. I agreed. 'I'm going up to see Vienna. Will you get a room for us at the Madison?'

So I left him. What happened between him and Vienna I don't know; he has never spoken about it to this day. But what happened later in the evening was brought to my attention by several surprised and even indignant witnesses to the event.

Dolly walked into the Ambassador Hotel about ten o'clock and went to the desk to ask for Miss Cary's room. There was a crowd around the desk, among them some Yale or Princeton undergraduates from the game. Several of them had been celebrating and evidently one of them knew Daisy and had tried to get her room by phone. Dolly was abstracted and he must have made his way through them in a somewhat brusque way and asked to be connected with Miss Cary.

One young man stepped back, looked at him un-

pleasantly and said, 'You seem to be in an awful hurry.
Just who are you?'

There was one of those slight silent pauses and the
people near the desk all turned to look. Something happened inside Dolly; he felt as if life had arranged his
role to make possible this particular question—a question
that now he had no choice but to answer. Still, there was
silence. The small crowd waited.

'Why, I'm Dolly Harlan,' he said deliberately. 'What
do you think of that?'

It was quite outrageous. There was a pause and then
a sudden little flurry and chorus; 'Dolly Harlan! What?
What did he say?'

The clerk had heard the name; he gave it as the phone
was answered from Miss Cary's room.

'Mr Harlan's to go right up, please.'

Dolly turned away, alone with his achievement, taking
it for once to his breast. He found suddenly that he would
not have it long so intimately; the memory would outlive
the triumph and even the triumph would outlive the glow
in his heart that was best of all. Tall and straight, an
image of victory and pride, he moved across the lobby,
oblivious alike to the fate ahead of him or the small
chatter behind.

MAGNETISM

[1928]

THE pleasant, ostentatious boulevard was lined at prosperous intervals with New England Colonial houses—without ship models in the hall. When the inhabitants moved out here the ship models had at last been given to the children. The next street was a complete exhibit of the Spanish-bungalow phase of West Coast architecture; while two streets over, the cylindrical windows and round towers of 1897—melancholy antiques which sheltered swamis, yogis, fortune tellers, dressmakers, dancing teachers, art academies and chiropractors—looked down now upon brisk buses and trolley cars. A little walk around the block could, if you were feeling old that day, be a discouraging affair.

On the green flanks of the modern boulevard children, with their knees marked by the red stains of the mercurochrome era, played with toys with a purpose—beams that taught engineering, soldiers that taught manliness, and dolls that taught motherhood. When the dolls were so banged up that they stopped looking like real babies and began to look like dolls, the children developed affection for them. Everything in the vicinity—even the March sunlight—was new, fresh, hopeful and thin, as you would expect in a city that had tripled its population in fifteen years.

Among the very few domestics in sight that morning was a handsome young maid sweeping the steps of the biggest house on the street. She was a large, simple Mexican girl with the large, simple ambitions of the time and the locality, and she was already conscious of being a luxury—she received one hundred dollars a month in return for her personal liberty. Sweeping, Dolores kept an eye on the stairs inside, for Mr Hannaford's car was waiting and he would soon be coming down to breakfast. The problem came first this morning, however—the problem as to whether it was a duty or a favour when she helped the English nurse down the steps with the perambulator. The English nurse always said 'Please,' and 'Thanks very much,' but Dolores hated her and would have liked, without any special excitement, to beat her insensible. Like most Latins under the stimulus of American life, she had irresistible impulses towards violence.

The nurse escaped, however. Her blue cape faded haughtily into the distance just as Mr Hannaford, who had come quietly downstairs, stepped into the space of the front door.

'Good morning.' He smiled at Dolores; he was young and extraordinarily handsome. Dolores tripped on the broom and fell off the stoop. George Hannaford hurried down the steps, reached her as she was getting to her feet cursing volubly in Mexican, just touched her arm with a helpful gesture and said, 'I hope you didn't hurt yourself.'

'Oh, no.'

'I'm afraid it was my fault; I'm afraid I startled you, coming out like that.'

His voice had real regret in it; his brow was knit with solicitude.

'Are you sure you're all right?'

'Aw, sure.'

'Didn't turn your ankle?'

'Aw, no.'

'I'm terribly sorry about it.'

'Aw, it wasn't your fault.'

He was still frowning as she went inside, and Dolores, who was not hurt and thought quickly, suddenly contemplated having a love affair with him. She looked at herself several times in the pantry mirror and stood close to him as she poured his coffee, but he read the paper and she saw that that was all for the morning.

Hannaford entered his car and drove to Jules Rennard's house. Jules was a French Canadian by birth, and George Hannaford's best friend; they were fond of each other and spent much time together. Both of them were simple and dignified in their tastes and in their way of thinking, instinctively gentle, and in a world of the volatile and the bizzare found in each other a certain quiet solidity.

He found Jules at breakfast.

'I want to fish for barracuda,' said George abruptly. 'When will you be free? I want to take the boat and go down to Lower California.'

Jules had dark circles under his eyes. Yesterday he had closed out the greatest problem of his life by settling with his ex-wife for two hundred thousand dollars. He had married too young, and the former slavey from the Quebec slums had taken to drugs upon her failure to rise with him. Yesterday, in the presence of lawyers, her final gesture had been to smash his finger with the base of a telephone. He was tired of women for a while and welcomed the suggestion of a fishing trip.

'How's the baby?' he asked.

'The baby's fine.'

'And Kay?'

'Kay's not herself, but I don't pay any attention. What did you do to your hand?'

'I'll tell you another time. What's the matter with Kay, George?'

'Jealous.'

'Of who?'

'Helen Avery. It's nothing. She's not herself, that's all.' He got up. 'I'm late,' he said. 'Let me know as soon as you're free. Any time after Monday will suit me.'

George left and drove out by an interminable boulevard which narrowed into a long, winding concrete road and rose into the hilly country behind. Somewhere in the vast emptiness a group of buildings appeared, a barnlike struc-

ture, a row of offices, a large but quick restaurant and
half a dozen small bungalows. The chauffeur dropped
Hannaford at the main entrance. He went in and passed
through various enclosures, each marked off by swinging
gates and inhabited by a stenographer.

'Is anybody with Mr Schroeder?' he asked, in front
of a door lettered with that name.

'No, Mr Hannaford.'

Simultaneously his eye fell on a young lady who was
writing at a desk aside, and he lingered a moment.

'Hello, Margaret,' he said. 'How are you, darling?'

A delicate, pale beauty looked up, frowning a little, still
abstracted in her work. It was Miss Donovan, the script
girl, a friend of many years.

'Hello. Oh, George, I didn't see you come in. Mr
Douglas wants to work on the book sequence this afternoon.'

'All right.'

'These are the changes we decided on Thursday night.'
She smiled up at him and George wondered for the
thousandth time why she had never gone into pictures.

'All right,' he said. 'Will initials do?'

'Your initials look like George Harris's.'

'Very well, darling.'

As he finished, Pete Schroeder opened his door and
beckoned him. 'George, come here!' he said with an air
of excitement. 'I want you to listen to some one on the
phone.'

Hannaford went in.

'Pick up the phone and say "Hello,"' directed Schroeder. 'Don't say who you are.'

'Hello,' said Hannaford obediently.

'Who is this?' asked a girl's voice.

Hannaford put his hand over the mouthpiece. 'What
am I supposed to do?'

Schroeder snickered and Hannaford hesitated, smiling
and suspicious.

'Who do you want to speak to?' he temporized into the phone.

'To George Hannaford, I want to speak to. Is this him?'

'Yes.'

'Oh, George; it's me.'

'Who?'

'Me—Gwen. I had an awful time finding you. They told me——'

'Gwen who?'

'Gwen—can't you hear? From San Francisco—last Thursday night.'

'I'm sorry,' objected George. 'Must be some mistake.'

'Is this George Hannaford?'

'Yes.'

The voice grew slightly tart: 'Well, this is Gwen Becker you spent last Thursday evening with in San Francisco. There's no use pretending you don't know who I am, because you do.'

Schroeder took the apparatus from George and hung up the receiver.

'Somebody has been doubling for me up in Frisco,' said Hannaford.

'So that's where you were Thursday night!'

'Those things aren't funny to me—not since that crazy Zeller girl. You can never convince them they've been sold because the man always looks something like you. What's new, Pete?'

'Let's go over to the stage and see.'

Together they walked out a back entrance, along a muddy walk, and opening a little door in the big blank wall of the studio building entered into its half darkness.

Here and there figures spotted the dim twilight, figures that turned up white faces to George Hannaford, like souls in purgatory watching the passage of a half-god through. Here and there were whispers and soft voices and, apparently from afar, the gentle tremolo of a small organ. Turning the corner made by some flats, they came upon the white crackling glow of a stage with two people motionless upon it.

An actor in evening clothes, his shirt front, collar and cuffs tinted a brilliant pink, made as though to get chairs for them, but they shook their heads and stood watching. For a long while nothing happened on the stage—no one moved. A row of lights went off with a savage hiss, went on again. The plaintive tap of a hammer begged admission to nowhere in the distance; a blue face appeared among the blinding lights above and called something unintelligible into the upper blackness. Then the silence was broken by a low clear voice from the stage:

'If you want to know why I haven't got stockings on, look in my dressing-room. I spoiled four pairs yesterday and two already this morning. . . . This dress weighs six pounds.'

A man stepped out of the group of observers and regarded the girl's brown legs; their lack of covering was scarcely distinguishable, but, in any event, her expression implied that she would do nothing about it. The lady was annoyed, and so intense was her personality that it had taken only a fractional flexing of her eyes to indicate the fact. She was a dark, pretty girl with a figure that would be full-blown sooner than she wished. She was just eighteen.

Had this been the week before, George Hannaford's heart would have stood still. Their relationship had been in just that stage. He hadn't said a word to Helen Avery that Kay could have objected to, but something had begun between them on the second day of this picture that Kay had felt in the air. Perhaps it had begun even earlier, for he had determined, when he saw Helen Avery's first release, that she should play opposite him. Helen Avery's voice and the dropping of her eyes when she finished speaking, like a sort of exercise in control, fascinated him. He had felt that they both tolerated something, that each knew half of some secret about people and life, and that if they rushed towards each other there would be a romantic communion of almost unbelievable intensity. It was this element of promise and possibility that had haunted him for a fortnight and was now dying away.

Hannaford was thirty, and he was a moving-picture actor only through a series of accidents. After a year in a small technical college he had taken a summer job with an electric company, and his first appearance in a studio was in the role of repairing a bank of Klieg lights. In an emergency he played a small part and made good, but for fully a year after that he thought of it as a purely transitory episode in his life. At first much of it had offended him—the almost hysterical egotism and excitability hidden under an extremely thin veil of elaborate good-fellowship. It was only recently, with the advent of such men as Jules Rennard into pictures, that he began to see the possibilities of a decent and secure private life, much as his would have been as a successful engineer. At last his success felt solid beneath his feet.

He met Kay Tompkins at the old Griffith Studios at Mamaroneck and their marriage was a fresh, personal affair, removed from most stage marriages. Afterwards they had possessed each other completely, had been pointed to: 'Look, there's one couple in pictures who manage to stay together.' It would have taken something out of many people's lives—people who enjoyed a vicarious security in the contemplation of their marriage—if they hadn't stayed together, and their love was fortified by a certain effort to live up to that.

He held women off by a polite simplicity that underneath was hard and watchful; when he felt a certain current being turned on he became emotionally stupid. Kay expected and took much more from men, but she, too, had a careful thermometer against her heart. Until the other night, when she reproached him for being interested in Helen Avery, there had been an absolute minimum of jealousy between them.

George Hannaford was still absorbed in the thought of Helen Avery as he left the studio and walked towards his bungalow over the way. There was in his mind, first, a horror that anyone should come between him and Kay, and second, a regret that he no longer carried that possibility in the forefront of his mind. It had given him a tremendous pleasure, like the things that had happened to him during his first big success, before he was so 'made' that there was scarcely anything better ahead; it was something to take out and look at—a new and still mysterious joy. It hadn't been love, for he was critical of Helen Avery as he had never been critical of Kay. But his feeling of last week had been sharply significant and memorable, and he was restless, now that it had passed.

Working that afternoon, they were seldom together, but he was conscious of her and he knew that she was conscious of him.

She stood a long time with her back to him at one point, and when she turned at length, their eyes swept past each other's, brushing like bird wings. Simultaneously he saw they had gone far, in their way; it was well that he had drawn back. He was glad that someone came for her when the work was almost over.

Dressed, he returned to the office wing, stopping in for a moment to see Schroeder. No one answered his knock, and, turning the knob, he went in. Helen Avery was there alone.

Hannaford shut the door and they stared at each other. Her face was young, frightened. In a moment in which neither of them spoke, it was decided that they would have some of this out now. Almost thankfully he felt the warm sap of emotion flow out of his heart and course through his body.

'Helen!'

She murmured 'What?' in an awed voice.

'I feel terribly about this.' His voice was shaking.

Suddenly she began to cry; painful, audible sobs shook her. 'Have you got a handkerchief?' she said.

He gave her a handkerchief. At that moment there were

steps outside. George opened the door halfway just in time to keep Schroeder from entering on the spectacle of her tears.

'Nobody's in,' he said facetiously. For a moment longer he kept his shoulder against the door. Then he let it open slowly.

Outside in his limousine, he wondered how soon Jules would be ready to go fishing.

II

From the age of twelve Kay Tompkins had worn men like rings on every finger. Her face was round, young, pretty and strong; a strength accentuated by the responsive play of brows and lashes around her clear, glossy, hazel eyes. She was the daughter of a senator from a Western state and she hunted unsuccessfully for glamour through a small Western city until she was seventeen, when she ran away from home and went on the stage. She was one of those people who are famous far beyond their actual achievement.

There was that excitement about her that seemed to reflect the excitement of the world. While she was playing small parts in Ziegfeld shows she attended proms at Yale, and during a temporary venture into pictures she met George Hannaford, already a star of the new 'natural' type then just coming into vogue. In him she found what she had been seeking.

She was at present in what is known as a dangerous state. For six months she had been helpless and dependent entirely upon George, and now that her son was the property of a strict and possessive English nurse, Kay, free again, suddenly felt the need of proving herself attractive. She wanted things to be as they had been before the baby was thought of. Also she felt that lately George had taken her too much for granted; she had a strong instinct that he was interested in Helen Avery.

When George Hannaford came home that night he had

minimized to himself their quarrel of the previous evening and was honestly surprised at her perfunctory greeting.

'What's the matter, Kay?' he asked after a minute. 'Is this going to be another night like last night?'

'Do you know we're going out to-night?' she said, avoiding an answer.

'Where?'

'To Katherine Davis'. I didn't know whether you'd want to go——'

'I'd like to go.'

'I didn't know whether you'd want to go. Arthur Busch said he'd stop for me.'

They dined in silence. Without any secret thoughts to dip into like a child into a jam jar, George felt restless, and at the same time was aware that the atmosphere was full of jealousy, suspicion and anger. Until recently they had preserved between them something precious that made their house one of the pleasantest in Hollywood to enter. Now suddenly it might be any house; he felt common and he felt unstable. He had come near to making something bright and precious into something cheap and unkind. With a sudden surge of emotion, he crossed the room and was about to put his arm around her when the doorbell rang. A moment later Dolores announced Mr Arthur Busch.

Busch was an ugly, popular little man, a continuity writer and lately a director. A few years ago they had been hero and heroine to him, and even now, when he was a person of some consequence in the picture world, he accepted with equanimity Kay's use of him for such purposes as to-night's. He had been in love with her for years, but, because his love seemed hopeless, it had never caused him much distress.

They went on to the party. It was a housewarming, with Hawaiian musicians in attendance, and the guests were largely of the old crowd. People who had been in the early Griffith pictures, even though they were scarcely thirty, were considered to be of the old crowd; they were different from those coming along now, and they were conscious of it. They had a dignity and straightforwardness about them from the fact that they had worked in pictures before pictures were bathed in a golden haze of success. They were still rather humble before their amazing triumph, and thus, unlike the new generation, who took it all for granted, they were constantly in touch with reality. Half a dozen or so of the women were especially aware of being unique. No one had come along to fill their places; here and there a pretty face had caught the public imagination for a year, but those of the old crowd were already legends, ageless and disembodied. With all this, they were still young enough to believe that they would go forever.

George and Kay were greeted affectionately; people moved over and made place for them. The Hawaiians performed and the Duncan sisters sang at the piano. From the moment George saw who was here he guessed that Helen Avery would be here, too, and the fact annoyed him. It was not appropriate that she should be part of this gathering through which he and Kay had moved familiarly and tranquilly for years.

He saw her first when someone opened the swinging door to the kitchen, and when, a little later, she came out and their eyes met, he knew absolutely that he didn't love her. He went up to speak to her, and at her first words he saw something had happened to her, too, that had dissipated the mood of the afternoon. She had got a big part.

'And I'm in a daze!' she cried happily. 'I didn't think there was a chance and I've thought of nothing else since I read the book a year ago.'

'It's wonderful. I'm awfully glad.'

He had the feeling, though, that he should look at her with a certain regret; one couldn't jump from such a scene as this afternoon to a plane of casual friendly interest. Suddenly she began to laugh.

'Oh, we're such actors, George—you and I.'

'What do you mean?'

'You know what I mean.'

'I don't.'

'Oh, yes, you do. You did this afternoon. It was a pity we didn't have a camera.'

Short of declaring then and there that he loved her, there was absolutely nothing more to say. He grinned acquiescently. A group formed around them and absorbed them, and George, feeling that the evening had settled something, began to think about going home. An excited and sentimental elderly lady—someone's mother—came up and began telling him how much she believed in him, and he was polite and charming to her, as only he could be, for half an hour. Then he went to Kay, who had been sitting with Arthur Busch all evening, and suggested that they go.

She looked up unwillingly. She had had several high-balls and the fact was mildly apparent. She did not want to go, but she got up after a mild argument and George went upstairs for his coat. When he came down Katherine Davis told him that Kay had already gone out to the car.

The crowd had increased; to avoid a general good-night he went out through the sun-parlour door to the lawn; less than twenty feet away from him he saw the figures of Kay and Arthur Busch against a bright street lamp; they were standing close together and staring into each other's eyes. He saw that they were holding hands.

After the first start of surprise George instinctively turned about, retraced his steps, hurried through the room he had just left, and came noisily out the front door. But Kay and Arthur Busch were still standing close together, and it was lingeringly and with abstracted eyes that they turned around finally and saw him. Then both of them seemed to make an effort; they drew apart as if it was a physical ordeal. George said good-bye to Arthur Busch with special cordiality, and in a moment he and Kay were driving homeward through the clear California night.

He said nothing, Kay said nothing. He was incredulous.

He suspected that Kay had kissed a man here and there, but he had never seen it happen or given it any thought. This was different; there had been an element of tenderness in it and there was something veiled and remote in Kay's eyes that he had never seen there before.

Without having spoken, they entered the house; Kay stopped by the library door and looked in.

'There's someone there,' she said, and she added without interest: 'I'm going upstairs. Good-night.'

As she ran up the stairs the person in the library stepped out into the hall.

'Mr Hannaford——'

He was a pale and hard young man; his face was vaguely familiar, but George didn't remember where he had seen it before.

'Mr Hannaford?' said the young man. 'I recognize you from your pictures.' He looked at George, obviously a little awed.

'What can I do for you?'

'Well, will you come in here?'

'What is it? I don't know who you are.'

'My name is Donovan. I'm Margaret Donovan's brother.' His face toughened a little.

'Is anything the matter?'

Donovan made a motion towards the door. 'Come in here.' His voice was confident now, almost threatening.

George hesitated, then he walked into the library. Donovan followed and stood across the table from him, his legs apart, his hands in his pockets.

'Hannaford,' he said, in the tone of a man trying to whip himself up to anger, 'Margaret wants fifty thousand dollars.'

'What the devil are you talking about?' exclaimed George incredulously.

'Margaret wants fifty thousand dollars,' repeated Donovan.

'You're Margaret Donovan's brother?'

'I am."

'I don't believe it.' But he saw the resemblance now. 'Does Margaret know you're here?'

'She sent me here. She'll hand over those two letters for fifty thousand, and no questions asked.'

'What letters?' George chuckled irresistibly. 'This is some joke of Schroeder's, isn't it?'

'This ain't a joke, Hannaford. I mean the letters you signed your name to this afternoon.'

III

An hour later George went upstairs in a daze. The clumsiness of the affair was at once outrageous and astounding. That a friend of seven years should suddenly request his signature on papers that were not what they were purported to be made all his surroundings seem diaphanous and insecure. Even now the design engrossed him more than a defence against it, and he tried to re-create the steps by which Margaret had arrived as this act of recklessness or despair.

She had served as a script girl in various studios and for various directors for ten years; earning first twenty, now a hundred dollars a week. She was lovely-looking and she was intelligent; at any moment in those years she might have asked for a screen test, but some quality of initiative or ambition had been lacking. Not a few times had her opinion made or broken incipient careers. Still she waited at directors' elbows, increasingly aware that the years were slipping away.

That she had picked George as a victim amazed him most of all. Once, during the year before his marriage, there had been a momentary warmth; he had taken her to a Mayfair ball, and he remembered that he had kissed her going home that night in the car. The flirtation trailed along hesitatingly for a week. Before it could develop into anything serious he had gone East and met Kay.

Young Donovan had shown him a carbon of the letters he had signed. They were written on the typewriter that he kept in his bungalow at the studio, and they were carefully and convincingly worded. They purported to be love letters, asserting that he was Margaret Donovan's lover, that he wanted to marry her, and that for that reason he was about to arrange a divorce. It was incredible. Someone must have seen him sign them that morning; someone must have heard her say: 'Your initials are like Mr Harris's.'

George was tired. He was training for a screen football game to be played next week, with the Southern California varsity as extras, and he was used to regular hours. In the middle of a confused and despairing sequence of thought about Margaret Donovan and Kay, he suddenly yawned. Mechanically he went upstairs, undressed and got into bed.

Just before dawn Kay came to him in the garden. There was a river that flowed past it now, and boats faintly lit with green and yellow lights moved slowly, remotely by. A gentle starlight fell like rain upon the dark, sleeping face of the world, upon the black mysterious bosoms of the trees, the tranquil gleaming water and the farther shore.

The grass was damp, and Kay came to him on hurried feet; her thin slippers were drenched with dew. She stood upon his shoes, nestling close to him, and held up her face as one shows a book open at a page.

'Think how you love me,' she whispered. 'I don't ask you to love me always like this, but I ask you to remember.'

'You'll always be like this to me.'

'Oh, no; but promise me you'll remember.' Her tears were falling. 'I'll be different, but somewhere lost inside me there'll always be the person I am to-night.'

The scene dissolved slowly and George struggled into consciousness. He sat up in bed; it was morning. In the yard outside he heard the nurse instructing his son in the niceties of behaviour for two-month-old babies. From the yard next door a small boy shouted mysteriously: 'Who let that barrier through on me?'

Still in his pyjamas, George went to the phone and called his lawyers. Then he rang for his man, and while he was being shaved a certain order evolved from the chaos of the night before. First, he must deal with Margaret Donovan; second, he must keep the matter from Kay, who in her present state might believe anything; and third, he must fix things up with Kay. The last seemed the most important of all.

As he finished dressing he heard the phone ring downstairs and, with an instinct of danger, picked up the receiver.

'Hello. . . . Oh, yes.' Looking up, he saw that both his doors were closed. 'Good morning, Helen. . . . It's all right, Dolores. I'm taking it up here.' He waited till he heard the receiver click downstairs.

'How are you this morning, Helen?'

'George, I called up about last night. I can't tell you how sorry I am.'

'Sorry? Why are you sorry?'

'For treating you like that. I don't know what was in me, George. I didn't sleep all night thinking how terrible I'd been.'

A new disorder established itself in George's already littered mind.

'Don't be silly,' he said. To his despair he heard his own voice run on: 'For a minute I didn't understand, Helen. Then I thought it was better so.'

'Oh, George,' came her voice after a moment, very low.

Another silence. He began to put in a cuff button.

'I had to call up,' she said after a moment. 'I couldn't leave things like that.'

The cuff button dropped to the floor; he stooped to pick it up, and then said 'Helen!' urgently into the mouthpiece to cover the fact that he had momentarily been away.

'What, George?'

At this moment the hall door opened and Kay, radiating a faint distaste, came into the room. She hesitated.

'Are you busy?'

'It's all right.' He stared into the mouthpiece for a

moment. 'Well, good-bye,' he muttered abruptly and hung up the receiver. He turned to Kay: 'Good morning.'

'I didn't mean to disturb you,' she said distantly.

'You didn't disturb me.' He hesitated. 'That was Helen Avery.'

'It doesn't concern me who it was. I came to ask you if we're going to the Coconut Grove to-night.'

'Sit down, Kay.'

'I don't want to talk.'

'Sit down a minute,' he said impatiently. She sat down. 'How long are you going to keep this up?' he demanded.

'I'm not keeping up anything. We're simply through, George, and you know it as well as I do.'

'That's absurd,' he said. 'Why, a week ago——'

'It doesn't matter. We've been getting nearer to this for months, and now it's over.'

'You mean you don't love me?' He was not particularly alarmed. They had been through scenes like this before.

'I don't know. I suppose I'll always love you in a way.' Suddenly she began to sob. 'Oh, it's all so sad. He's cared for me so long.'

George stared at her. Face to face with what was apparently a real emotion, he had no words of any kind. She was not angry, not threatening or pretending, not thinking about him at all, but concerned entirely with her emotions towards another man.

'What is it?' he cried. 'Are you trying to tell me you're in love with this man?'

'I don't know,' she said helplessly.

He took a step towards her, then went to the bed and lay down on it, staring in misery at the ceiling. After a while a maid knocked to say that Mr Busch and Mr Castle, George's lawyer, were below. The fact carried no meaning to him. Kay went into her room and he got up and followed her.

'Let's send word we're out,' he said. 'We can go away somewhere and talk this over.'

'I don't want to go away.'

She was already away, growing more mysterious and remote with every minute. The things on her dressing-table were the property of a stranger.

He began to speak in a dry, hurried voice. 'If you're still thinking about Helen Avery, it's nonsense. I've never given a damn for anybody but you.'

They went downstairs and into the living-room. It was nearly noon—another bright emotionless California day. George saw that Arthur Busch's ugly face in the sunshine was wan and white; he took a step towards George and then stopped, as if he were waiting for something—a challenge, a reproach, a blow.

In a flash the scene that would presently take place ran itself off in George's mind. He saw himself moving through the scene, saw his part, an infinite choice of parts, but in every one of them Kay would be against him and with Arthur Busch. And suddenly he rejected them all.

'I hope you'll excuse me,' he said quickly to Mr Castle. 'I called you up because a script girl named Margaret Donovan wants fifty thousand dollars for some letters she claims I wrote her. Of course the whole thing is——' He broke off. It didn't matter. 'I'll come to see you to-morrow.' He walked up to Kay and Arthur, so that only they could hear.

'I don't know about you two—what you want to do. But leave me out of it; you haven't any right to inflict any of it on me, for after all it's not my fault. I'm not going to be mixed up in your emotions.'

He turned and went out. His car was before the door and he said 'Go to Santa Monica' because it was the first name that popped into his head. The car drove off into the everlasting hazeless sunlight.

He rode for three hours, past Santa Monica and then along towards Long Beach by another road. As if it were something he saw out of the corner of his eye and with but a fragment of his attention, he imagined Kay and Arthur Busch progressing through the afternoon. Kay would cry a great deal and the situation would seem harsh

and unexpected to them at first, but the tender closing of
the day would draw them together. They would turn inevitably towards each other and he would slip more and
more into the position of the enemy outside.

Kay had wanted him to get down in the dirt and dust
of a scene and scramble for her. Not he; he hated scenes.
Once he stooped to compete with Arthur Busch in pulling
at Kay's heart, he would never be the same to himself. He
would always be a little like Arthur Busch; they would
always have that in common, like a shameful secret. There
was little of the theatre about George; the millions before
whose eyes the moods and changes of his face had flickered
during ten years had not been deceived about that. From
the moment when, as a boy of twenty, his handsome eyes
had gazed off into the imaginary distance of a Griffith
Western, his audience had been really watching the progress of a straightforward, slow-thinking, romantic man
through an accidentally glamorous life.

His fault was that he had felt safe too soon. He realized
suddenly that the two Fairbankses, in sitting side by side
at table, were not keeping up a pose. They were giving
hostages to fate. This was perhaps the most bizarre com-
munity in the rich, wild, bored empire, and for a marriage
to succeed here, you must expect nothing or you must be
always together. For a moment his glance had wavered
from Kay and he stumbled blindly into disaster.

As he was thinking this and wondering where he
would go and what he should do, he passed an apartment
house that jolted his memory. It was on the outskirts of
town, a pink horror built to represent something, somewhere, so cheaply and sketchily that whatever it copied
the architect must have long since forgotten. And suddenly George remembered that he had once called for
Margaret Donovan here the night of a Mayfair dance.

'Stop at this apartment!' he called through the speaking-
tube.

He went in. The negro elevator boy stared open-

mouthed at him as they rose in the cage. Margaret
Donovan herself opened the door.

When she saw him she shrank away with a little cry.
As he entered and closed the door she retreated before him
into the front room. George followed.

It was twilight outside and the apartment was dusky
and sad. The last light fell softly on the standardized
furniture and the great gallery of signed photographs of
moving-picture people that covered one wall. Her face
was white, and as she stared at him she began nervously
wringing her hands.

'What's this nonsense, Margaret?' George said, trying
to keep any reproach out of his voice. 'Do you need money
that bad?'

She shook her head vaguely. Her eyes were still fixed
on him with a sort of terror; George looked at the floor.

'I suppose this was your brother's idea. At least I can't
believe you'd be so stupid.' He looked up, trying to preserve the brusque masterly attitude of one talking to a
naughty child, but at the sight of her face every emotion
except pity left him. 'I'm a little tired. Do you mind if
I sit down?'

'No.'

'I'm a little confused to-day,' said George after a minute.
'People seem to have it in for me to-day.'

'Why, I thought'—her voice became ironic in mid-
sentence—'I thought everybody loved you, George.'

'They don't.'

'Only me?'

'Yes,' he said abstractedly.

'I wish it had been only me. But then, of course, you
wouldn't have been you.'

Suddenly he realized that she meant what she was
saying.

'That's just nonsense.'

'At least you're here,' Margaret went on. 'I suppose
I ought to be glad of that. And I am. I most decidedly am.
I've often thought of you sitting in that chair, just at this

time when it was almost dark. I used to make up little one-act plays about what would happen then. Would you like to hear one of them? I'll have to begin by coming over and sitting on the floor at your feet.'

Annoyed and yet spellbound, George kept trying desperately to seize upon a word or mood that would turn the subject.

'I've seen you sitting there so often that you don't look a bit more real than your ghost. Except that your hat has squashed your beautiful hair down on one side and you've got dark circles or dirt under your eyes. You look white, too, George. Probably you were on a party last night.'

'I was. And I found your brother waiting for me when I got home.'

'He's a good waiter, George. He's just out of San Quentin prison, where he's been waiting the last six years.'

'Then it was his idea?'

'We cooked it up together. I was going to China on my share.'

'Why was I the victim?'

'That seemed to make it realer. Once I thought you were going to fall in love with me five years ago.'

The bravado suddenly melted out of her voice and it was still light enough to see that her mouth was quivering.

'I've loved you for years,' she said—'since the first day you came West and walked into the old Realart Studio. You were so brave about people, George. Whoever it was, you walked right up to them and tore something aside as if it was in your way and began to know them. I tried to make love to you, just like the rest, but it was difficult. You drew people right up close to you and held them there, not able to move either way.'

'This is all entirely imaginary,' said George, frowning uncomfortably, 'and I can't control——'

'No, I know. You can't control charm. It's simply got to be used. You've got to keep your hand in if you have it, and go through life attaching people to you that you don't want. I don't blame you. If you only hadn't kissed me the night of the Mayfair dance. I suppose it was the champagne.'

George felt as if a band which had been playing for a long time in the distance had suddenly moved up and taken a station beneath his window. He had always been conscious that things like this were going on around him. Now that he thought of it, he had always been conscious that Margaret loved him, but the faint music of these emotions in his ear had seemed to bear no relation to actual life. They were phantoms that he had conjured up out of nothing; he had never imagined their actual incarnations. At his wish they should die inconsequently away.

'You can't imagine what it's been like,' Margaret continued after a minute. 'Things you've just said and forgotten, I've put myself asleep night after night remembering—trying to squeeze something more out of them. After that night you took me to the Mayfair other men didn't exist for me any more. And there were others, you know—lots of them. But I'd see you walking along somewhere about the lot, looking at the ground and smiling a little, as if something very amusing had just happened to you, the way you do. And I'd pass you and you'd look up and really smile: "Hello, darling!" "Hello, darling" and my heart would turn over. That would happen four times a day.'

George stood up and she, too, jumped up quickly.

'Oh, I've bored you,' she cried softly. 'I might have known I'd bore you. You want to go home. Let's see—is there anything else? Oh, yes; you might as well have those letters.'

Taking them out of a desk, she took them to a window and identified them by a rift of lamplight.

'They're really beautiful letters. They'd do you credit. I suppose it was pretty stupid, as you say, but it ought to teach you a lesson about—about signing things, or something.' She tore the letters small and threw them in the wastebasket: 'Now go on,' she said.

'Why must I go now?'

For the third time in twenty-four hours sad and un-controllable tears confronted him.

'Please go!' she cried angrily—'or stay if you like. I'm yours for the asking. You know it. You can have any woman you want in the world by just raising your hand. Would I amuse you?'

'Margaret——'

'Oh, go on then.' She sat down and turned her face away. 'After all, you'll begin to look silly in a minute. You wouldn't like that, would you? So get out.'

George stood there helpless, trying to put himself in her place and say something that wouldn't be priggish, but nothing came.

He tried to force down his personal distress, his dis-comfort, his vague feeling of scorn, ignorant of the fact that she was watching him and understanding it all and loving the struggle in his face. Suddenly his own nerves gave way under the strain of the past twenty-four hours and he felt his eyes grow dim and his throat tighten. He shook his head helplessly. Then he turned away—still not knowing that she was watching him and loving him until she thought her heart would burst with it—and went out to the door.

IV

The car stopped before his house, dark save for small lights in the nursery and the lower hall. He heard the telephone ringing, but when he answered it, inside, there was no one on the line. For a few minutes he wandered about in the darkness, moving from chair to chair and going to the window to stare out into the opposite empti-ness of the night.

It was strange to be alone, to feel alone. In his over-wrought condition the fact was not unpleasant. As the trouble of last night had made Helen Avory infinitely re-mote, so his talk with Margaret had acted as a catharsis to his own personal misery. It would swing back upon him presently, he knew, but for a moment his mind was too tired to remember, to imagine or to care.

Half an hour passed. He saw Dolores issue from the kitchen, take the paper from the front steps and carry it back to the kitchen for a preliminary inspection. With a vague idea of packing his grip, he went upstairs. He opened the door of Kay's room and found her lying down.

For a moment he didn't speak, but moved around the bathroom between. Then he went into her room and switched on the lights.

'What's the matter?' he asked casually. 'Aren't you feeling well?'

'I've been trying to get some sleep,' she said. 'George, do you think that girl's gone crazy?'

'What girl?'

'Margaret Donovan. I've never heard of anything so terrible in my life.'

For a moment he thought that there had been some new development.

'Fifty thousand dollars!' she cried indignantly. 'Why, I wouldn't give it to her even if it was true. She ought to be sent to jail.'

'Oh, it's not so terrible as that,' he said. 'She has a brother who's a pretty bad egg and it was his idea.'

'She's capable of anything,' Kay said solemnly. 'And you're just a fool if you don't see it. I've never liked her She has dirty hair.'

'Well, what of it?' he demanded impatiently, and added: 'Where's Arthur Busch?'

'He went home right after lunch. Or rather I sent him home.'

'You decided you were not in love with him?'

She looked up almost in surprise. 'In love with him? Oh, you mean this morning. I was just mad at you; you ought to have known that. I was a little sorry for him last night, but I guess it was the highballs.'

'Well, what did you mean when you——' He broke off.

14+S.F.

Wherever he turned he found a muddle, and he resolutely determined not to think.

'My heavens!' exclaimed Kay. 'Fifty thousand dollars!'

'Oh, drop it. She tore up the letters—she wrote them herself—and everything's all right.'

'George.'

'Yes.'

'Of course Douglas will fire her right away.'

'Of course he won't. He won't know anything about it.'

'You mean to say you're not going to let her go? After this?'

He jumped up. 'Do you suppose she thought that?' he cried.

'Thought what?'

'That I'd have them let her go?'

'You certainly ought to.'

He looked hastily through the phone book for her name.

'Oxford——' he called.

After an unusually long time the switchboard operator answered: 'Bourbon Apartments.'

'Miss Margaret Donovan, please.'

'Why——' The operator's voice broke off. 'If you'll just wait a minute, please.' He held the line; the minute passed, then another. Then the operator's voice: 'I couldn't talk to you then. Miss Donovan has had an accident. She's shot herself. When you called they were taking her through the lobby to St Catherine's Hospital.'

'Is she—is it serious?' George demanded frantically.

'They thought so at first, but now they think she'll be all right. They're going to probe for the bullet.'

'Thank you.'

He got up and turned to Kay.

'She's tried to kill herself,' he said in a strained voice. 'I'll have to go around to the hospital. I was pretty clumsy this afternoon and I think I'm partly responsible for this.'

'George,' said Kay suddenly.

'What?'

'Don't you think it's sort of unwise to get mixed up in this? People might say——'

'I don't give a damn what they say,' he answered roughly.

He went to his room and automatically began to prepare for going out. Catching sight of his face in the mirror, he closed his eyes with a sudden exclamation of distaste, and abandoned the intention of brushing his hair.

'George,' Kay called from the next room, 'I love you.'

'I love you too.'

'Jules Rennard called up. Something about barracuda fishing. Don't you think it would be fun to get up a party? Men and girls both?'

'Somehow the idea doesn't appeal to me. The whole idea of barracuda fishing——'

The phone rang below and he started. Dolores was answering it.

It was a lady who had already called twice to-day.

'Is Mr Hannaford in?'

'No,' said Dolores promptly. She stuck out her tongue and hung up the phone just as George Hannaford came downstairs. She helped him into his coat, standing as close as she could to him, opened the door and followed a little way out on the porch.

'Meester Hannaford,' she said suddenly, 'that Miss Avery she call up five-six times to-day. I tell her you out and say nothing to missus.'

'What?' He stared at her, wondering how much she knew about his affairs.

'She call up just now and I say you out.'

'All right,' he said absently.

'Meester Hannaford.'

'Yes, Dolores.'

'I deedn't hurt myself thees morning when I fell off the porch.'

'That's fine. Good night, Dolores.'

'Good night, Meester Hannaford.'

George smiled at her, faintly, fleetingly, tearing a veil

from between them, unconsciously promising her a possible admission to the thousand delights and wonders that only he knew and could command. Then he went to his waiting car and Dolores, sitting down on the stoop, rubbed her hands together in a gesture that might have expressed either ecstasy or strangulation, and watched the rising of the thin, pale California moon.

OUTSIDE THE
CABINET-MAKER'S
[1928]

THE automobile stopped at the corner of Sixteenth and some dingy-looking street. The lady got out. The man and the little girl stayed in the car.

'I'm going to tell him it can't cost more than twenty dollars,' said the lady.

'All right. Have you the plans?'

'Oh, yes'—she reached for her bag in the back seat—'at least I have now.'

'Dites qu'il ne faut pas avoir des forts placards,' said the man. 'Ni du bon bois.'

'All right.'

'I wish you wouldn't talk French,' said the little girl.

'Et il faut avoir un bon "height." L'un des Murphys était comme ça.'

He held his hand five feet from the ground. The lady went through a door lettered 'Cabinet-Maker' and disappeared up a small stairs.

The man and the little girl looked around unexpectantly. The neighbourhood was red brick, vague, quiet. There were a few darkies doing something or other up the street and an occasional automobile went by. It was a fine November day.

'Listen,' said the man to the little girl, 'I love you.'

'I love you too,' said the little girl, smiling politely.

'Listen,' the man continued. 'Do you see that house over the way?'

The little girl looked. It was a flat in back of a shop. Curtains masked most of its interior, but there was a faint stir behind them. On one window a loose shutter banged from back to forth every few minutes. Neither the man nor the little girl had ever seen the place before.

'There's a Fairy Princess behind those curtains,' said the man. 'You can't see her but she's there, kept concealed by an Ogre. Do you know what an Ogre is?'

'Yes.'

'Well, this Princess is very beautiful with long golden hair.'

They both regarded the house. Part of a yellow dress appeared momentarily in the window.

'That's her,' the man said. 'The people who live there are guarding her for the Ogre. He's keeping the King and Queen prisoner ten thousand miles below the earth. She can't get out until the Prince finds the three——' He hesitated.

'And what, Daddy? The three what?'

'The three—Look! There she is again.'

'The three what?'

'The three—the three stones that will release the King and Queen.'

He yawned.

'And what then?'

'Then he can come and tap three times on each window and that will set her free.'

The lady's head emerged from the upper storey of the cabinet-maker's.

'He's busy,' she called down. 'Gosh, what a nice day!'

'And what, Daddy?' asked the little girl. 'Why does the Ogre want to keep her there?'

'Because he wasn't invited to the christening. The Prince has already found one stone in President Coolidge's collar-box. He's looking for the second in Iceland. Every time he finds a stone the room where the Princess is kept turns blue. *Gosh!*'

'What, Daddy?'

'Just as you turned away I could see the room turn blue. That means he's found the second stone.'

'Gosh!' said the little girl. 'Look! It turned blue again, that means he's found the third stone.'

Aroused by the competition the man looked around cautiously and his voice grew tense.

'Do you see what I see?' he demanded. 'Coming up the street—there's the Ogre himself, disguised—you know: transformed, like Mombi in *The Land of Oz*.'

'I know.'

They both watched. The small boy, extraordinarily small and taking very long steps, went to the door of the flat and knocked; no one answered, but he didn't seem to expect it or to be greatly disappointed. He took some chalk from his pocket and began drawing pictures under the doorbell.

'He's making magic signs,' whispered the man. 'He wants to be sure that the Princess doesn't get out this door. He must know that the Prince has set the King and Queen free and will be along for her pretty soon.'

The small boy lingered for a moment; then he went to a window and called an unintelligible word. After a while a woman threw the window open and made an answer that the crisp wind blew away.

'She says she's got the Princess locked up,' explained the man.

'Look at the Ogre,' said the little girl. 'He's making magic signs under the window too. And on the sidewalk. Why?'

'He wants to keep her from getting out, of course. That's why he's dancing. That's a charm too—it's a magic dance.'

The Ogre went away, taking very big steps. Two men crossed the street ahead and passed out of sight.

'Who are they, Daddy?'

'They're two of the King's soldiers. I think the army must be gathering over on Market Street to surround the house. Do you know what "surround" means?'

'Yes. Are those men soldiers too?'

'Those too. And I believe that the old one just behind is the King himself. He's keeping bent down low like that so that the Ogre's people won't recognize him.'

'Who is the lady?'

'She's a Witch, a friend of the Ogre's.'

The shutter blew closed with a bang and then slowly opened again.

'That's done by the good and bad fairies,' the man explained. 'They're invisible, but the bad fairies want to close the shutter so nobody can see in and the good ones want to open it.'

'The good fairies are winning now.'

'Yes.' He looked at the little girl. 'You're my good fairy.'

'Yes. Look, Daddy! What is that man?'

'He's in the King's army too.' The clerk of Mr Miller, the jeweller, went by with a somewhat unmartial aspect. 'Hear the whistle? That means they're gathering. And listen—there goes the drum.'

'There's the Queen, Daddy. Look at there. Is that the Queen?'

'No, that's a girl called Miss Television.' He yawned. He began to think of something pleasant that had happened yesterday. He went into a trance. Then he looked at the little girl and saw that she was quite happy. She was six and lovely to look at. He kissed her.

'That man carrying the cake of ice is also one of the King's soldiers,' he said. 'He's going to put the ice on the Ogre's head and freeze his brains so he can't do any more harm.'

Her eyes followed the man down street. Other men passed. A darky in a yellow darky's overcoat drove by with a cart marked The Del Upholstery Co. The shutter banged again and then slowly opened.

'See, Daddy, the good fairies are winning again.'

The man was old enough to know that he would look back to that time—the tranquil street and the pleasant weather and the mystery playing before the child's eyes, mystery which he had created, but whose lustre and texture he could never see or touch any more himself. Again, he touched his daughter's cheek instead and in payment fitted another small boy and limping man into the story.

'Oh, I love you,' he said.

'I know, Daddy,' she answered, abstractedly. She was staring at the house. For a moment he closed his eyes and tried to see with her but he couldn't see—those ragged blinds were drawn against him forever. There were only the occasional darkies and the small boys and the weather that reminded him of more glamorous mornings in the past.

The lady came out of the cabinet-maker's shop.

'How did it go?' he asked.

'Good. Il dit qu'il a fait les maisons de poupée pour les Du Ponts. Il va le faire.'

'Combien?'

'Vingt-cinq. I'm sorry I was so long.'

'Look, Daddy, there go a lot more soldiers!'

They drove off. When they had gone a few miles the man turned around and said, 'We saw the most remarkable thing while you were there.' He summarized the episode. 'It's too bad we couldn't wait and see the rescue.'

'But we did,' the child cried. 'They had the rescue in the next street. And there's the Ogre's body in that yard there. The King and Queen and Prince were killed and now the Princess is queen.'

He had liked his King and Queen and felt that they had been too summarily disposed of.

'You had to have a heroine,' he said rather impatiently.

'She'll marry somebody and make him Prince.'

They rode on abstractedly. The lady thought about the doll's house, for she had been poor and had never had one as a child, the man thought how he had almost a million dollars, and the little girl thought about the odd doings on the dingy street that they had left behind.

THE ROUGH CROSSING

[1929]

ONCE on the long, covered piers, you have come into a ghostly country that is no longer Here and not yet There. Especially at night. There is a hazy yellow vault full of shouting, echoing voices. There is the rumble of trucks and the clump of trunks, the strident chatter of a crane and the first salt smell of the sea. You hurry through, even though there's time. The past, the continent, is behind you; the future is that glowing mouth in the side of the ship; this dim turbulent alley is too confusedly the present.

Up the gangplank, and the vision of the world adjusts itself, narrows. One is a citizen of a commonwealth smaller than Andorra. One is no longer so sure of anything. Curiously unmoved the men at the purser's desk, cell-like the cabin, disdainful the eyes of voyagers and their friends, solemn the officer who stands on the deserted promenade deck thinking something of his own as he stares at the crowd below. A last odd idea that one didn't really have to come, then the loud, mournful whistles, and the thing—certainly not the boat, but rather a human idea, a frame of mind—pushes forth into the big dark night.

Adrian Smith, one of the celebrities on board—not a very great celebrity, but important enough to be bathed in flash-light by a photographer who had been given his name, but wasn't sure what his subject " did "—Adrian Smith and his blonde wife, Eva, went up to the promenade deck, passed the melancholy ship's officer, and, finding a quiet aerie, put their elbows on the rail.

'We're going!' he cried presently, and they both laughed in ecstasy. 'We've escaped. They can't get us now.'

426

'Who?'

He waved his hand vaguely at the civic tiara.

'All those people out there. They'll come with their posses and their warrants and list of crimes we've committed, and ring the bell at our door on Park Avenue and ask for the Adrian Smiths, but what ho! the Adrian Smiths and their children and nurse are off for France.'

'You make me think we really have committed crimes.

'They can't have you,' he said frowning. 'That's one thing they're after me about—they know I haven't got any right to a person like you, and they're furious. That's one reason I'm glad to get away.'

'Darling,' said Eva.

She was twenty-six—five years younger than he. She was something precious to everyone who knew her.

'I like this boat better than the *Majestic* or the *Aquitania*,' she remarked, unfaithful to the ships that had served their honeymoon.

'It's much smaller.'

'But it's very slick and it has all those little shops along the corridors. And I think the staterooms are bigger.'

'The people are very formal—did you notice?—as if they thought everyone else was a card sharp. And in about four days half of them will be calling the other half by their first names.'

Four of the people came by now—a quartet of young girls abreast, making a circuit of the deck. Their eight eyes swept momentarily toward Adrian and Eva, and then swept automatically back, save for one pair which lingered for an instant with a little start. They belonged to one of the girls in the middle, who was, indeed, the only passenger of the four. She was not more than eighteen—a dark little beauty with the fine crystal gloss over her that, in brunettes, takes the place of a blonde's bright glow.

'Now, who's that?' wondered Adrian. 'I've seen her before.'

'She's pretty,' said Eva.

'Yes.' He kept wondering, and Eva deferred momentarily

to his distraction; then, smiling up at him, she drew him back into their privacy.

'Tell me more,' she said.

'About what?'

'About us—what a good time we'll have, and how we'll be much better and happier, and very close always.'

'How could we be any closer?' His arm pulled her to him.

'But I mean never even quarrel any more about silly things. You know, I made up my mind when you gave me my birthday present last week'—her fingers caressed the fine seed pearls at her throat—'that I'd try never to say a mean thing to you again.'

'You never have, my precious.'

Yet even as he strained her against his side he knew that the moment of utter isolation had passed almost before it had begun. His antennæ were already out, feeling over this new world.

'Most of the people look rather awful,' he said—'little and swarthy and ugly. Americans didn't use to look like that.'

'They look dreary,' she agreed. 'Let's not get to know anybody, but just stay together.'

A gong was beating now, and stewards were shouting down the decks, 'Visitors ashore, please!' and voices rose to a strident chorus. For a while the gangplanks were thronged; then they were empty, and the jostling crowd behind the barrier waved and called unintelligible things, and kept up a grin of good will. As the stevedores began to work at the ropes a flat-faced, somewhat befuddled young man arrived in a great hurry and was assisted up the gangplank by a porter and a taxi driver. The ship having swallowed him as impassively as though he were a missionary for Beirut, a low, portentous vibration began. The pier with its faces commenced to slide by, and for a moment the boat was just a piece accidentally split off from it; then the faces became remote, voiceless, and the pier was one among many yellow blurs along the water front. Now the harbour flowed swiftly toward the sea.

On a northern parallel of latitude a hurricane was forming and moving south by southeast preceded by a strong west wind. On its course it was destined to swamp the *Peter I. Eudim* of Amsterdam, with a crew of sixty-six, to break a boom on the largest boat in the world, and to bring grief and want to the wives of several hundred seamen. This liner, leaving New York Sunday evening, would enter the zone of the storm Tuesday, and of the hurricane late Wednesday night.

II

Tuesday afternoon Adrian and Eva paid their first visit to the smoking room. This was not in accord with their intentions—they had 'never wanted to see a cocktail again' after leaving America—but they had forgotten the staccato loneliness of ships, and all activity centred about the bar. So they went in for just a minute.

It was full. There were those who had been there since luncheon, and those who would be there until dinner, not to mention a faithful few who had been there since nine this morning. It was a prosperous assembly, taking its recreation at bridge, solitaire, detective stories, alcohol, argument and love. Up to this point you could have matched it in the club or casino life of any country, but over it all played a repressed nervous energy, a barely disguised impatience that extended to old and young alike. The cruise had begun, and they had enjoyed the beginning, but the show was not varied enough to last six days, and already they wanted it to be over.

At a table near them Adrian saw the pretty girl who had stared at him on the deck the first night. Again he was fascinated by her loveliness; there was no mist upon the brilliant gloss that gleamed through the smoky confusion of the room. He and Eva had decided from the passenger list that she was probably 'Miss Elizabeth D'Amido and maid,' and he had heard her called Betsy as he walked past a deck-tennis game. Among the young people with her was the flat-nosed youth who had been 'poured on board,' the night of their departure; yesterday he had walked the deck morosely, but he was apparently reviving. Miss D'Amido whispered something to him, and he looked over at the Smiths with curious eyes. Adrian was new enough at being a celebrity to turn self-consciously away.

'There's a little roll. Do you feel it?' Eva demanded.

'Perhaps we'd better split a pint of champagne.'

While he gave the order a short colloquy was taking place at the other table; presently a young man rose and came over to them.

'Isn't this Mr Adrian Smith?'

'Yes.'

'We wondered if we couldn't put you down for the deck-tennis tournament. We're going to have a deck-tennis tournament.'

'Why——' Adrian hesitated.

'My name's Stacomb,' burst out the young man. 'We all know your—your plays or whatever it is, and all that—and we wondered if you wouldn't like to come over to our table.'

Somewhat overwhelmed, Adrian laughed: Mr Stacomb, glib, soft, slouching, waited; evidently under the impression that he had delivered himself of a graceful compliment.

Adrian, understanding that, too, replied: 'Thanks, but perhaps you'd better come over here.'

'We've got a bigger table.'

'But we're older and more—more settled.'

The young man laughed kindly, as if to say, 'That's all right.'

'Put me down,' said Adrian. 'How much do I owe you?'

'One buck. Call me Stac.'

'Why?' asked Adrian, startled.

'It's shorter.'

When he had gone they smiled broadly.

'Heavens,' Eva gasped, 'I believe they are coming over.'

They were. With a great draining of glasses, calling of waiters, shuffling of chairs, three boys and two girls moved to the Smiths' table. If there was any diffidence, it was confined to the hosts; for the new additions gathered around them eagerly, eyeing Adrian with respect—too much respect —as if to say: 'This was probably a mistake and won't be amusing, but maybe we'll get something out of it to help us in our after life, like at school.'

In a moment Miss D'Amido changed seats with one of the men and placed her radiant self at Adrian's side, looking at him with manifest admiration.

'I fell in love with you the minute I saw you,' she said audibly and without self-consciousness; 'so I'll take all the blame for butting in. I've seen your play four times.'

Adrian called a waiter to take their orders.

'You see,' continued Miss D'Amido, 'we're going into a storm, and you might be prostrated the rest of the trip, so I couldn't take any chances.'

He saw that there was no undertone or innuendo in what she said, nor the need of any. The words themselves were enough, and the deference with which she neglected the young men and bent her politeness on him was somehow very touching. A little glow went over him; he was having rather more than a pleasant time.

Eva was less entertained; but the flat-nosed young man, whose name was Butterworth, knew people that she did, and that seemed to make the affair less careless and casual. She did not like meeting new people unless they had 'something to contribute,' and she was often bored by the great streams of them, of all types and conditions and classes, that passed through Adrian's life. She herself 'had everything'—which is to say that she was well endowed with talents and with charm—and the mere novelty of people did not seem a sufficient reason for eternally offering everything up to them.

Half an hour later when she rose to go and see the children, she was content that the episode was over. It was colder on deck, with a damp that was almost rain, and there was a perceptible motion. Opening the door of her stateroom she was surprised to find the cabin steward sitting languidly on her bed, his head slumped upon the upright pillow. He looked at her listlessly as she came in, but made no move to get up.

'When you've finished your nap you can fetch me a new pillow-case,' she said briskly.

Still the man didn't move. She perceived then that his face was green.

'You can't be seasick in here,' she announced firmly. 'You go and lie down in your own quarters.'

'It's me side,' he said faintly. He tried to rise, gave out a little rasping sound of pain and sank back again. Eva rang for the stewardess.

A steady pitch, toss, roll had begun in earnest and she felt no sympathy for the steward, but only wanted to get him out as quick as possible. It was outrageous for a member of the crew to be seasick. When the stewardess came in Eva tried to explain this, but now her own head was whirring, and throwing herself on the bed, she covered her eyes.

'It's his fault,' she groaned when the man was assisted from the room. 'I was all right and it made me sick to look at him. I wish he'd die.'

In a few minutes Adrian came in.

'Oh, but I'm sick!' she cried.

'Why, you poor baby.' He leaned over and took her in his arms. 'Why didn't you tell me?'

'I was all right upstairs, but there was a steward—— Oh, I'm too sick to talk.'

'You'd better have dinner in bed.'

'Dinner! Oh, my heavens!'

He waited solicitously, but she wanted to hear his voice, to have it drown out the complaining sound of the beams.

'Where've you been?'

'Helping to sign up people for the tournament.'

'Will they have it if it's like this ? Because if they do I'll just lose for you.'

He didn't answer; opening her eyes, she saw that he was frowning.

'I didn't know you were going in the doubles,' he said.

'Why, that's the only fun.'

'I told the D'Amido girl I'd play with her.'

'Oh.'

'I didn't think. You know I'd much rather play with you.'

'Why didn't you, then?' she asked coolly.

'It never occurred to me.'

She remembered that on their honeymoon they had been in the finals and won a prize. Years passed. But Adrian never frowned in this regretful way unless he felt a little guilty. He stumbled about, getting his dinner clothes out of the trunk, and she shut her eyes.

When a particular violent lurch startled her awake again he was dressed and tying his tie. He looked healthy and fresh, and his eyes were bright.

'Well, how about it?' he inquired. 'Can you make it, or no?'

'No.'

'Can I do anything for you before I go?'

'Where are you going?'

'Meeting those kids in the bar. Can I do anything for you?'

'No.'

'Darling, I hate to leave you like this.'

'Don't be silly. I just want to sleep.'

That solicitous frown—when she knew he was crazy to be out and away from the close cabin. She was glad when the door closed. The thing to do was to sleep, sleep.

Up—down—sideways. Hey there, not so far! Pull her round the corner there! Now roll her, right—left—— Crea-eak! Wrench! Swoop!

Some hours later Eva was dimly conscious of Adrian bending over her. She wanted him to put his arms around her and draw her up out of this dizzy lethargy, but by the time she was fully awake the cabin was empty. He had looked in and gone. When she awoke next the cabin was dark and he was in bed.

The morning was fresh and cool, and the sea was just enough calmer to make Eva think she could get up. They breakfasted in the cabin and with Adrian's help she accomplished an unsatisfactory makeshift toilet and they went up on the boat deck. The tennis tournament had already begun and was furnishing action for a dozen amateur movie cameras, but the majority of passengers were represented by lifeless bundles in deck chairs beside untasted trays.

Adrian and Miss D'Amido played their first match. She was deft and graceful; blatantly well. There was even more warmth behind her ivory skin than there had been the day before. The strolling first officer stopped and talked to her; half a dozen men whom she couldn't have known three days ago called her Betsy. She was already the pretty girl of the voyage, the cynosure of starved ship's eyes.

But after a while Eva preferred to watch the gulls in the wireless masts and the slow slide of the roll-top sky. Most of the passengers looked silly with their movie cameras that they had all rushed to get and now didn't know what to use for, but the sailors painting the lifeboat stanchions were quiet and beaten and sympathetic, and probably wished, as she did, that the voyage was over.

Butterworth sat down on the deck beside her chair.

'They're operating on one of the stewards this morning. Must be terrible in this sea.'

'Operating? What for?' she asked listlessly.

'Appendicitis. They have to operate now because we're going into worse weather. That's why they're having the ship's party tonight.'

'Oh, the poor man!' she cried, realizing it must be her steward.

Adrian was showing off now by being very courteous and thoughtful in the game.

'Sorry. Did you hurt yourself? . . . No, it was my fault. . . . You better put on your coat right away, pardner, or you'll catch cold.'

The match was over and they had won. Flushed and hearty, he came up to Eva's chair.

'How do you feel?'

'Terrible.'

'Winners are buying a drink in the bar,' he said apologetically.

'I'm coming, too,' Eva said, but an immediate dizziness made her sink back in her chair.

'You'd better stay here. I'll send you up something.'

She felt that his public manner had hardened toward her slightly.

'You'll come back?'

'Oh, right away.'

She was alone on the boat deck, save for a solitary ship's officer who slanted obliquely as he paced the bridge. When the cocktail arrived she forced herself to drink it, and felt better. Trying to distract her mind with pleasant things, she reached back to the sanguine talks that she and Adrian had had before sailing: There was the little villa in Brittany, the children learning French—that was all she could think of now—the little villa in Brittany, the children learning French—so she repeated the words over and over to herself until they became as meaningless as the wide white sky. The why of their being here had suddenly eluded her; she felt unmotivated, accidental, and she wanted Adrian to come back quick, all responsive and tender, to reassure her. It was in the hope that there was some secret of graceful living, some real compensation for the lost, careless confidence of twenty-one, that they were going to spend a year in France.

The day passed darkly, with fewer people around and a wet sky falling. Suddenly it was five o'clock, and they were all in the bar again, and Mr Butterworth was telling her about his past. She took a good deal of champagne, but she was seasick dimly through it, as if the illness was her soul trying to struggle up through some thickening incrustation of abnormal life.

'You're my idea of a Greek goddess, physically,' Butterworth was saying.

It was pleasant to be Mr Butterworth's idea of a Greek goddess physically, but where was Adrian? He and Miss D'Amido had gone out on a forward deck to feel the spray. Eva heard herself promising to get out her colours and paint the Eiffel Tower on Butterworth's shirt front for the party to-night.

When Adrian and Betsy D'Amido, soaked with spray, opened the door with difficulty against the driving wind and came into the now-covered security of the promenade deck, they stopped and turned toward each other.

'Well?' she said. But he only stood with his back to the rail, looking at her, afraid to speak. She was silent, too, because she wanted him to be first; so for a moment nothing happened. Then she made a step toward him, and he took her in his arms and kissed her forehead.

'You're just sorry for me, that's all.' She began to cry a little. 'You're just being kind.'

'I feel terribly about it.' His voice was taut and trembling.

'Then kiss me.'

The deck was empty. He bent over her swiftly.

'No, really kiss me.'

He could not remember when anything had felt so young and fresh as her lips. The rain lay, like tears shed for him, upon the softly shining porcelain cheeks. She was all new and immaculate, and her eyes were wild.

'I love you,' she whispered. 'I can't help loving you, can I? When I first saw you—oh, not on the boat, but over a year ago—Grace Heally took me to a rehearsal and suddenly you jumped up in the second row and began telling them what to do. I wrote you a letter and tore it up.'

'We've got to go.'

She was weeping as they walked along the deck. Once more, imprudently, she held up her face to him at the door of her cabin. His blood was beating through him in wild tumult as he walked on to the bar.

He was thankful that Eva scarcely seemed to notice him or to know that he had been gone. After a moment he pretended an interest in what she was doing.

'What's that?'

'She's painting the Eiffel Tower on my shirt front for to-night,' explained Butterworth.

'There,' Eva laid away her brush and wiped her hands. 'How's that?'

'A *chef-d'œuvre*.'

Her eyes swept around the watching group, lingered casually upon Adrian.

'You're wet. Go and change.'

'You come too.'

'I want another champagne cocktail.'

'You've had enough. It's time to dress for the party.'

Unwilling she closed her paints and preceded him.

'Stacomb's got a table for nine,' he remarked as they walked along the corridor.

'The younger set,' she said with unnecessary bitterness. 'Oh, the younger set. And you just having the time of your life—with a child.'

They had a long discussion in the cabin, unpleasant on her part and evasive on his, which ended when the ship gave a sudden gigantic heave, and Eva, the edge worn off her champagne, felt ill again. There was nothing to do but to have a cocktail in the cabin, and after that they decided to go to the party—she believed him now, or she didn't care.

Adrian was ready first—he never wore fancy dress.

'I'll go on up. Don't be long.'

'Wait for me, please; it's rocking so.'

He sat down on a bed, concealing his impatience.

'You don't mind waiting, do you? I don't want to parade up there all alone'.

She was taking a tuck in an oriental costume rented from the barber.

'Ships make people feel crazy,' she said. 'I think they're awful.'

'Yes,' he muttered absently.

'When it gets very bad I pretend I'm in the top of a tree, rocking to and fro. But finally I get pretending everything, and finally I have to pretend I'm sane when I know I'm not.'

'If you get thinking that way you will go crazy.'

'Look, Adrian.' She held up the string of pearls before clasping them on. 'Aren't they lovely?'

In Adrian's impatience she seemed to move around the cabin like a figure in a slow-motion picture. After a moment he demanded:

'Are you going to be long? It's stifling in here.'

'You go on!' she fired up.

'I don't want——'

'Go on, please! You just make me nervous trying to hurry me.'

With a show of reluctance he left her. After a moment's hesitation he went down a flight to a deck below and knocked at a door.

'Betsy.'

'Just a minute.'

She came out in the corridor attired in a red pea-jacket and trousers borrowed from the elevator boy.

'Do elevator boys have fleas?' she demanded. 'I've got everything in the world on under this as a precaution.'

'I had to see you,' he said quickly.

'Careful,' she whispered. 'Mrs Worden, who's supposed to be chaperoning me, is across the way. She's sick.'

'I'm sick for you.'

They kissed suddenly, clung close together in the narrow corridor, swaying to and fro with the motion of the ship.

'Don't go away,' she murmured.

'I've got to. I've——'

Her youth seemed to flow into him, bearing him up into a delicate romantic ecstasy that transcended passion. He couldn't relinquish it; he had discovered something that he had thought was lost with his own youth forever. As he walked along the passage he knew that he had stopped thinking, no longer dared to think.

He met Eva going into the bar.

'Where've you been?' she asked with a strained smile.

'To see about the table.'

She was lovely; her cool distinction conquered the trite costume and filled him with a resurgence of approval and pride. They sat down at a table.

The gale was rising hour by hour and the mere traversing

of a passage had become a rough matter. In every stateroom
trunks were lashed to the washstands, and the *Vestris* disaster was being reviewed in detail by nervous ladies,
tossing, ill and wretched, upon their beds. In the smoking-
room a stout gentleman had been hurled backward and
suffered a badly cut head; and now the lighter chairs and
tables were stacked and roped against the wall.

The crowd who had donned fancy dress and were dining
together had swollen to about sixteen. The only remaining
qualification for membership was the ability to reach the
smoking-room. They ranged from a Groton-Harvard lawyer
to an ungrammatical broker they had nicknamed Gyp the
Blood, but distinctions had disappeared; for the moment
they were samurai, chosen from several hundred for their
triumphant resistance to the storm.

The gala dinner, overhung sardonically with lanterns and
streamers, was interrupted by great communal slides across
the room, precipitate retirements and spilled wine, while the
ship roared and complained that under the panoply of a
palace it was a ship after all. Upstairs afterward a dozen
couples tried to dance, shuffling and galloping here and there
in a crazy fandango, thrust around fantastically by a will
alien to their own. In view of the condition of tortured
hundreds below, there grew to be something indecent about
it like a revel in a house of mourning, and presently there was
an egress of the ever-dwindling survivors toward the
bar.

As the evening passed, Eva's feeling of unreality increased. Adrian had disappeared—presumably with Miss
D'Amido—and her mind, distorted by illness and champagne, began to enlarge upon the fact; annoyance changed
slowly to dark and brooding anger, grief to desperation.
She had never tried to bind Adrian, never needed to—for
they were serious people, with all sorts of mutual interests,
and satisfied with each other—but this was a breach of the
contract, this was cruel. How could he think that she
didn't know?

It seemed several hours later that he leaned over her

chair in the bar where she was giving some woman an impassioned lecture upon babies, and said:

'Eva, we'd better turn in.'

Her lip curled. 'So that you can leave me there and then come back to your eighteen-year——'

'Be quiet.'

'I won't come to bed.'

'Very well. Good night.'

More time passed and the people at the table changed. The stewards wanted to close up the room, and thinking of Adrian—her Adrian—off somewhere saying tender things to someone fresh and lovely, Eva began to cry.

'But he's gone to bed,' her last attendants assured her. 'We saw him go.'

She shook her head. She knew better. Adrian was lost. The long seven-year dream was broken. Probably she was punished for something she had done; as this thought occurred to her the shrieking timbers overhead began to mutter that she had guessed at last. This was for the selfishness to her mother, who hadn't wanted her to marry Adrian; for all the sins and omissions of her life. She stood up, saying she must go out and get some air.

The deck was dark and drenched with wind and rain. The ship pounded through valleys, fleeing from black mountains of water that roared toward it. Looking out at the night, Eva saw that there was no chance for them unless she could make atonement, propitiate the storm. It was Adrian's love that was demanded of her. Deliberately she unclasped her pearl necklace, lifted it to her lips—for she knew that with it went the freshest, fairest part of her life— and flung it out into the gale.

III

When Adrian awoke it was lunchtime, but he knew that some heavier sound than the bugle had called him up from his deep sleep. Then he realized that the trunk had broken loose from its lashings and was being thrown back and forth between a wardrobe and Eva's bed. With an exclamation he jumped up, but she was unharmed—still in costume and stretched out in deep sleep. When the steward had helped him secure the trunk, Eva opened a single eye.

'How are you?' he demanded, sitting on the side of her bed.

She closed the eye, opened it again.

'We're in a hurricane now,' he told her. 'The steward says it's the worst he's seen in twenty years.'

'My head,' she muttered. 'Hold my head.'

'How?'

'In front. My eyes are going out. I think I'm dying.'

'Nonsense. Do you want the doctor?'

She gave a funny little gasp that frightened him; he rang and sent the steward for the doctor.

The young doctor was pale and tired. There was a stubble of beard upon his face. He bowed curtly as he came in and, turning to Adrian, said with scant ceremony:

'What's the matter?'

'My wife doesn't feel well.'

'Well, what is it you want—a bromide?'

A little annoyed by his shortness, Adrian said: 'You'd better examine her and see what she needs.'

'She needs a bromide,' said the doctor. 'I've given orders that she is not to have any more to drink on this ship.'

'Why not?' demanded Adrian in astonishment.

'Don't you know what happened last night?'

'Why, no, I was asleep.'

'Mrs Smith wandered around the boat for an hour, not knowing what she was doing. A sailor was set to follow her, and then the medical stewardess tried to get her to bed, and your wife insulted her.'

'Oh, my heavens!' cried Eva faintly.

'The nurse and I had both been up all night with Steward Carton, who died this morning.' He picked up his case. 'I'll send down a bromide for Mrs Smith. Good-bye.'

For a few minutes there was silence in the cabin. Then Adrian put his arm around her quickly.

'Never mind,' he said. 'We'll straighten it out.'

'I remember now.' Her voice was an awed whisper. 'My pearls. I threw them overboard.'

'Threw them overboard!'

'Then I began looking for you.'

'But I was here in bed.'

'I didn't believe it; I thought you were with that girl.'

'She collapsed during dinner. I was taking a nap down here.'

Frowning, he rang the bell and asked the steward for luncheon and a bottle of beer.

'Sorry, but we can't serve any beer to your cabin, sir.'

When he went out Adrian exploded: 'This is an outrage. You were simply crazy from that storm and they can't be so high-handed. I'll see the captain.'

'Isn't that awful?' Eva murmured. 'The poor man died.'

She turned over and began to sob into her pillow. There was a knock at the door.

'Can I come in?'

The assiduous Mr Butterworth, surprisingly healthy and immaculate, came into the crazily tipping cabin.

'Well, how's the mystic?' he demanded of Eva. 'Do you remember praying to the elements in the bar last night?'

'I don't want to remember anything about last night.'

They told him about the stewardess, and with the telling the situation lightened; they all laughed together.

'I'm going to get you some beer to have with your luncheon,' Butterworth said. 'You ought to get up on deck.'

'Don't go,' Eva said. 'You look so cheerful and nice.'

'Just for ten minutes.'

When he had gone, Adrian rang for two baths.

'The thing is to put on our best clothes and walk proudly three times around the deck,' he said.

'Yes.' After a moment she added abstractedly: 'I like that young man. He was awfully nice to me last night when you'd disappeared.'

The bath steward appeared with the information that

bathing was too dangerous today. They were in the midst of the wildest hurricane on the North Atlantic in ten years; there were two broken arms this morning from attempts to take baths. An elderly lady had been thrown down a staircase and was not expected to live. Furthermore, they had received the SOS signal from several boats this morning.

'Will we go to help them?'

'They're all behind us, sir, so we have to leave them to the *Mauretania*. If we tried to turn in this sea the portholes would be smashed.'

This array of calamities minimized their own troubles. Having eaten a sort of luncheon and drunk the beer provided by Butterworth, they dressed and went on deck.

Despite the fact that it was only possible to progress step by step, holding on to rope or rail, more people were abroad than on the day before. Fear had driven them from their cabins, where the trunks bumped and the waves pounded the portholes and they awaited momentarily the call to the boats. Indeed, as Adrian and Eva stood on the transverse deck above the second class, there was a bugle call, followed by a gathering of stewards and stewardesses on the deck below. But the boat was sound; it had outlasted one of its cargo—Steward James Carton was being buried at sea.

It was very British and sad. There were the rows of stiff, disciplined men and women standing in the driving rain, and there was a shape covered by the flag of the Empire that lived by the sea. The chief purser read the service, a hymn was sung, the body slid off into the hurricane. With Eva's burst of wild weeping for this humble end, some last string snapped within her. Now she really didn't care. She responded eagerly when Butterworth suggested that he get some champagne to their cabin. Her mood worried Adrian; she wasn't used to so much drinking and he wondered what he ought to do. At his suggestion that they sleep instead, she merely laughed, and the bromide the doctor had sent stood untouched on the washstand. Pretending to listen to the insipidities of several Mr Stacombs, he watched her; to his surprise and discomfort she seemed on intimate and even sentimental terms with Butterworth and he wondered if this was a form of revenge for his attention to Betsy D'Amido.

The cabin was full of smoke, the voices went on incessantly, the suspension of activity, the waiting for the storm's end, was getting on his nerves. They had been at sea only four days; it was like a year.

The two Mr Stacombs left finally, but Butterworth remained. Eva was urging him to go for another bottle of champagne.

'We've had enough,' objected Adrian. 'We ought to go to bed.'

'I won't go to bed!' she burst out. 'You must be crazy! You play around all you want, and then, when I find somebody I—I like, you want to put me to bed.'

'You're hysterical.'

'On the contrary, I've never been so sane.'

'I think you'd better leave us, Butterworth,' Adrian said. 'Eva doesn't know what she's saying.'

'He won't go. I won't let him go.' She clasped Butterworth's hand passionately. 'He's the only person that's been half decent to me.'

'You'd better go, Butterworth,' repeated Adrian.

The young man looked at him uncertainly.

'It seems to me you're being unjust to your wife,' he ventured.

'My wife isn't herself.'

'That's no reason for bullying her.'

Adrian lost his temper. 'You get out of here!' he cried.

The two men looked at each other for a moment in silence. Then Butterworth turned to Eva, said, 'I'll be back later,' and left the cabin.

'Eva, you've got to pull yourself together,' said Adrian when the door closed.

She didn't answer, looked at him from sullen, half-closed eyes.

'I'll order dinner here for us both and then we'll try to get some sleep.'

'I want to go up and send a wireless.'

'Who to?'

'Some Paris lawyer. I want a divorce.'

In spite of his annoyance, he laughed. 'Don't be silly.'

'Then I want to see the children.'

'Well, go and see them. I'll order dinner.'

He waited for her in the cabin twenty minutes. Then impatiently he opened the door across the corridor; the nurse told him that Mrs Smith had not been there.

With a sudden prescience of disaster he ran upstairs, glanced in the bar, the salons, even knocked at Butterworth's door. Then a quick round of the decks, feeling his way through the black spray and rain. A sailor stopped him at a network of ropes.

'Orders are no one goes by, sir. A wave has gone over the wireless room.'

'Have you seen a lady?'

'There was a young lady here——' He stopped and glanced around. 'Hello, she's gone.'

'She went up the stairs!' Adrian said anxiously. 'Up to the wireless room!'

The sailor ran up to the boat deck; stumbling and slipping, Adrian followed. As he cleared the protected sides of the companionway, a tremendous body struck the boat a staggering blow and, as she keeled over to an angle of forty-five degrees, he was thrown in a helpless roll down the drenched deck, to bring up dizzy and bruised against a stanchion.

'Eva!' he called. His voice was soundless in the black storm. Against the faint light of the wireless-room window he saw the sailor making his way forward.

'Eva!'

The wind blew him like a sail up against a lifeboat. Then there was another shuddering crash, and high over his head, over the very boat, he saw a gigantic, glittering white wave, and in the split second that it balanced there he became conscious of Eva, standing beside a ventilator twenty feet away. Pushing out from the stanchion, he lunged desperately toward her, just as the wave broke with a smashing roar. For a moment the rushing water was five feet deep, sweeping with enormous force toward the side, and then a human body was washed against him, and frantically he clutched it and was swept with it back toward the rail. He felt his body bump against it, but desperately he held on to his burden; then, as the ship rocked slowly back, the two of them, still joined by his fierce grip, were rolled out exhausted on the wet planks. For a moment he knew no more.

IV

Two days later, as the boat train moved tranquilly south toward Paris, Adrian tried to persuade his children to look out the window at the Norman countryside.

'It's beautiful,' he assured them. 'All the little farms like toys. Why, in heaven's name, won't you look?'

'I like the boat better,' said Estelle.

Her parents exchanged an infanticidal glance.

'The boat is still rocking for me,' Eva said with a shiver. 'Is it for you?'

'No. Somehow, it all seems a long way off. Even the passengers looked unfamiliar going through the customs.'

'Most of them hadn't appeared above ground before.'

He hesitated. 'By the way, I cashed Butterworth's cheque for him.'

'You're a fool. You'll never see the money again.'

'He must have needed it pretty badly or he would not have come to me.'

A pale and wan girl, passing along the corridor, recognized them and put her head through the doorway.

'How do you feel?'

'Awful.'

'Me, too,' agreed Miss D'Amido. 'I'm vainly hoping my fiancé will recognize me at the Gare du Nord. Do you know two waves went over the wireless room?'

'So we heard,' Adrian answered dryly.

She passed gracefully along the corridor and out of their life.

'The real truth is that none of it happened,' said Adrian after a moment. 'It was a nightmare—an incredibly awful nightmare.'

'Then, where are my pearls?'

'Darling, there are better pearls in Paris. I'll take the responsibility for those pearls. My real belief is that you saved the boat.'

'Adrian, let's never get to know anyone else, but just stay together always—just we two.'

He tucked her arm under his and they sat close. 'Who do you suppose those Adrian Smiths on the boat were?' he demanded. 'It certainly wasn't me.'

'Nor me.'

'It was two other people,' he said, nodding to himself. 'There are so many Smiths in this world.'

THE extraordinary thing is not that people in a lifetime turn out worse or better than we had prophesied; particularly in America that is to be expected. The extraordinary thing is how people keep their levels, fulfil their promises, seem actually buoyed up by an inevitable destiny.

One of my conceits is that no one has ever disappointed me since I turned eighteen and could tell a real quality from a gift for sleight of hand, and even many of the merely showy people in my past seem to go on being blatantly and successfully showy to the end.

Emily Castleton was born in Harrisburg in a medium-sized house, moved to New York at sixteen to a big house, went to the Brearley School, moved to an enormous house, moved to a mansion at Tuxedo Park, moved abroad, where she did various fashionable things and was in all the papers. Back in her débutante year one of those French artists who are so dogmatic about American beauties, included her with eleven other public and semipublic celebrities as one of America's perfect types. At the time numerous men agreed with him.

She was just faintly tall, with fine, rather large features, eyes with such an expanse of blue in them that you were really aware of it whenever you looked at her, and a good deal of thick blond hair—arresting and bright. Her mother and father did not know very much about the new world they had commandeered, so Emily had to learn everything for herself, and she became involved in various situations and some of the first bloom wore off. However, there was bloom to spare. There were engagements and semi-engagements, short passionate attractions, and then a big

affair at twenty-two that embittered her and sent her
wandering the continents looking for happiness. She became 'artistic,' as most wealthy unmarried girls do at that
age, because artistic people seem to have some secret,
some inner refuge, some escape. But most of her friends
were married now, and her life was a great disappointment to her father; so, at twenty-four, with marriage in
her head if not in her heart, Emily came home.

This was a low point in her career and Emily was
aware of it. She had not done well. She was one of the
most popular, most beautiful girls of her generation, with
charm, money and a sort of fame, but her generation was
moving into new fields. At the first note of condescension
from a former schoolmate, now a young 'matron,' she
went to Newport and was won by William Brevoort Blair.
Immediately she was again the incomparable Emily Castleton. The ghost of the French artist walked once more
in the newspapers; the most-talked-of-leisure-class event
of October was her wedding day.

> Splendour to mark society nuptials. . . . Harold Castle-
> ton sets out a series of five-thousand-dollar pavilions
> arranged like the interconnecting tents of a circus, in
> which the reception, the wedding supper and the ball
> will be held. . . . Nearly a thousand guests, many of
> them leaders in business, will mingle with those who
> dominate the social world. . . . The wedding gifts are
> estimated to be worth a quarter of a million dollars.

An hour before the ceremony, which was to be solem-
nized at St Bartholomew's, Emily sat before a dressing-
table and gazed at her face in the glass. She was a little
tired of her face at that moment and the depressing
thought suddenly assailed her that it would require more
and more looking after in the next fifty years.

'I ought to be happy,' she said aloud, 'but every thought
that comes into my head is sad.'

Her cousin, Olive Mercy, sitting on the side of the
bed, nodded. 'All brides are sad.'

15—S.F.

'It's such a waste,' Emily said.

Olive frowned impatiently.

'Waste of what? Women are incomplete unless they're married and have children.'

For a moment Emily didn't answer. Then she said slowly, 'Yes, but whose children?'

For the first time in her life, Olive, who worshipped Emily, almost hated her. Not a girl in the wedding party but would have been glad of Brevoort Blair—Olive among the others.

'You're lucky,' she said. 'You're so lucky you don't even know it. You ought to be paddled for talking like that.'

'I shall learn to love him,' announced Emily facetiously. 'Love will come with marriage. Now, isn't that a hell of a prospect?'

'Why so deliberately unromantic?'

'On the contrary, I'm the most romantic person I've ever met in my life. Do you know what I think when he puts his arms around me? I think that if I look up I'll see Garland Kane's eyes.'

'But why, then——'

'Getting into his plane the other day I could only remember Captain Marchbanks and the little two-seater we flew over the Channel in, just breaking our hearts for each other and never saying a word about it because of his wife. I don't regret those men; I just regret the part of me that went into caring. There's only the sweepings to hand to Brevoort in a pink wastebasket. There should have been something more; I thought even when I was most carried away that I was saving something for the one. But apparently I wasn't.' She broke off and then added: 'And yet I wonder.'

The situation was no less provoking to Olive for being comprehensible, and save for her position as a poor relation, she would have spoken her mind. Emily was well spoiled—eight years of men had assured her they were not good enough for her and she had accepted the fact as probably true.

'You're nervous.' Olive tried to keep the annoyance out of her voice. 'Why not lie down for an hour?'

'Yes,' answered Emily absently.

Olive went out and downstairs. In the lower hall she ran into Brevoort Blair, attired in a nuptial cutaway even to the white carnation, and in a state of considerable agitation.

'Oh, excuse me,' he blurted out. 'I wanted to see Emily. It's about the rings—which ring, you know. I've got four rings and she never decided and I can't just hold them out in the church and have her take her pick.'

'I happen to know she wants the plain platinum band. If you want to see her anyhow——'

'Oh, thanks very much. I don't want to disturb her.'

They were standing close together, and even at this moment when he was gone, definitely preëmpted, Olive couldn't help thinking how alike she and Brevort were. Hair, colouring, features—they might have been brother and sister—and they shared the same shy serious temperaments, the same simple straightforwardness. All this flashed through her mind in an instant, with the added thought that the blonde, tempestuous Emily, with her vitality and amplitude of scale, was, after all, better for him in every way; and then, beyond this, a perfect wave of tenderness, of pure physical pity and yearning swept over her and it seemed that she must step forward only half a foot to find his arms wide to receive her.

She stepped backward instead, relinquishing him as though she still touched him with the tip of her fingers and then drew the tips away. Perhaps some vibration of her emotion fought its way into his consciousness, for he said suddenly:

'We're going to be good friends, aren't we? Please don't think I'm taking Emily away. I know I can't own her—nobody could—and I don't want to.'

Silently, as he talked, she said good-bye to him, the only man she had ever wanted in her life.

She loved the absorbed hesitancy with which he found

his coat and hat and felt hopefully for the knob on the wrong side of the door.

When he had gone she went into the drawing-room, gorgeous and portentous, with its painted bacchanals and massive chandeliers and the eighteenth-century portraits that might have been Emily's ancestors, but weren't, and by that very fact belonged the more to her. There she rested, as always, in Emily's shadow.

Through the door that led out to the small, priceless patch of grass on Sixtieth Street now inclosed by the pavilions came her uncle, Mr Harold Castleton. He had been sampling his own champagne.

'Olive so sweet and fair.' He cried emotionally, 'Olive, baby, she's done it. She was all right inside, like I knew all the time. The good ones come through, don't they— the real thoroughbreds? I began to think that the Lord and me, between us, had given her too much, that she'd never be satisfied, but now she's come down to earth just like a'—he searched unsuccessfully for a metaphor —'like a thoroughbred, and she'll find it not such a bad place after all.' He came closer. 'You've been crying, little Olive.'

'Not much.'

'It doesn't matter,' he said magnanimously. 'If I wasn't so happy I'd cry too.'

Later, as she embarked with two other bridesmaids for the church, the solemn throbbing of a big wedding seemed to begin with the vibration of the car. At the door the organ took it up, and later it would palpitate in the cellos and bass viols of the dance, to fade off finally with the sound of the car that bore bride and groom away.

The crowd was thick around the church, and ten feet out of it the air was heavy with perfume and faint clean humanity and the fabric smell of new clean clothes. Beyond the massed hats in the van of the church the two families sat in front rows on either side. The Blairs— they were assured a family resemblance by their expression of faint condescension, shared by their in-laws as well as by true Blairs—were represented by the Gardiner Blairs, senior and junior; Lady Mary Bowes Howard, née Blair; Mrs Potter Blair; Mrs Princess Potowski Parr Blair, née Inchbit; Miss Gloria Blair, Master Gardiner Blair III, and the kindred branches, rich and poor, of Smythe, Bickle, Diffendorfer and Hamn. Across the aisle the Castletons made a less impressive showing—Mr Harold Castleton, Mr and Mrs Theodore Castleton and children, Harold Castleton Junior, and, from Harrisburg, Mr Carl Mercy and two little old aunts named O'Keefe hidden off in a corner. Somewhat to their surprise the two aunts had been bundled off in a limousine and dressed from head to foot by a fashionable couturière that morning.

In the vestry, where the bridesmaids fluttered about like birds in their big floppy hats, there was a last lip rouging and adjustment of pins before Emily could arrive. They represented several stages of Emily's life—a schoolmate at Brearley, a last unmarried friend of débutante year, a travelling companion of Europe, and the girl she had visited in Newport when she met Brevoort Blair.

'They've got Wakeman,' this last one said, standing by the door listening to the music. 'He played for my sister, but I shall never have Wakeman.'

'Why not?'

'Why, he's playing the same thing over and over—'At Dawning.' He's played it half a dozen times.'

At this moment another door opened and the solicitous head of a young man appeared around it. 'Almost ready?' he demanded of the nearest bridesmaid. 'Brevoort's having a quiet little fit. He just stands there wilting collar after collar——'

'Be calm,' answered the young lady. 'The bride is always a few minutes late.'

'A few minutes!' protested the best man. 'I don't call it a few minutes. They're beginning to rustle and wriggle like a circuit crowd out there, and the organist has been playing the same tune for half an hour. I'm going to get him to fill in with a little jazz.'

'What time is it?' Olive demanded.

'Quarter of five—ten minutes of five.'

'Maybe there's been a traffic tie-up.' Olive paused as Mr Harold Castleton, followed by an anxious curate, shouldered his way in, demanding a phone.

And now there began a curious dribbling back from the front of the church, one by one, then two by two, until the vestry was crowded with relatives and confusion.

'What's happened?'

'What on earth's the matter?'

A chauffeur came in and reported excitedly. Harold Castleton swore and, his face blazing, fought his way roughly towards the door. There was an attempt to clear the vestry, and then, as if to balance the dribbling, a ripple of conversation commenced at the rear of the church and began to drift up towards the altar, growing louder and faster and more excited, mounting always, bringing people to their feet, rising to a sort of subdued roar. The announcement from the altar that the marriage had been postponed was scarcely heard, for by that time everyone knew that they were participating in a front-page scandal, that Brevoort Blair had been left waiting at the altar and Emily Castleton had run away.

II

There were a dozen reporters outside the Castleton house on Sixteenth Street when Olive arrived, but in her absorption she failed even to hear their questions; she wanted desperately to go and comfort a certain man whom she must not approach, and as a sort of substitute she sought her Uncle Harold. She entered through the interconnecting five-thousand-dollar pavilions, where caterers and servants still stood about in a respectful funereal half-light, waiting for something to happen, amid trays of caviar and turkey's breast and pyramid wedding cake. Upstairs,

Olive found her uncle sitting on a stool before Emily's dressing-table. The articles of make-up spread before him, the repertoire of feminine preparation in evidence about, made his singularly inappropriate presence a symbol of the mad catastrophe.

'Oh, it's you.' His voice was listless; he had aged in two hours. Olive put her arm about his bowed shoulder.

'I'm so terribly sorry, Uncle Harold.'

Suddenly a stream of profanity broke from him, died away, and a single tear welled slowly from one eye.

'I want to get my massage man,' he said. 'Tell McGregor to get him.' He drew a long broken sigh, like a child's breath after crying, and Olive saw that his sleeves were covered with a dust of powder from the dressing-table, as if he had been leaning forward on it, weeping, in the reaction from his proud champagne.

'There was a telegram,' he muttered.

'It's somewhere.'

And he added slowly,

'From now on *you*'re my daughter.'

'Oh, no, you mustn't say that!'

Unrolling the telegram, she read:

I can't make the grade I would feel like a fool either way but this will be over sooner so damn sorry for you.   EMILY

When Olive had summoned the masseur and posted a servant outside her uncle's door, she went to the library, where a confused secretary was trying to say nothing over an inquisitive and persistent telephone.

'I'm so upset, Miss Mercy,' he cried in a despairing treble. 'I do declare I'm so upset I have a frightful headache. I've thought for half an hour I heard dance music from down below.'

Then it occurred to Olive that she, too, was becoming hysterical; in the breaks of the street traffic a melody was drifting up, distinct and clear:

'—*Is she fair*
Is she sweet
I don't care—cause
I can't compete—
Who's the——'

She ran quickly downstairs and through the drawing-room, the tune growing louder in her ears. At the entrance of the first pavilion she stopped in stupefaction.

To the music of a small but undoubtedly professional orchestra a dozen young couples were moving about the canvas floor. At the bar in the corner stood additional young men, and half a dozen of the caterer's assistants were busily shaking cocktails and opening champagne.

'Harold!' she called imperatively to one of the dancers. 'Harold!' A tall young man of eighteen handed his partner to another and came towards her.

'Hello, Olive. How did father take it?'

'Harold, what in the name of——'

'Emily's crazy,' he said consolingly. 'I always told you Emily was crazy. Crazy as a loon. Always was.'

'What's the idea of this?'

'This?' He looked around innocently. 'Oh, these are some fellows that came down from Cambridge with me.'

'But—*dancing*!'

'Well, nobody's dead, are they? I thought we might as well use up some of this——'

'Tell them to go home,' said Olive.

'Why? What on earth's the harm? These fellows came all the way down from Cambridge——'

'It simply isn't dignified.'

'But they don't care, Olive. One fellow's sister did the same thing—only she did it the day after instead of the day before. Lots of people do it nowadays.'

'Send the music home, Harold,' said Olive firmly, 'or I'll go to your father.'

Obviously he felt that no family could be disgraced by an episode on such a magnificent scale, but he re-

luctantly yielded. The abysmally depressed butler saw to
the removal of the champagne, and the young people,
somewhat insulted, moved nonchalantly out into the more
tolerant night. Alone with the shadow—Emily's shadow
—that hung over the house, Olive sat down in the drawing-
room to think. Simultaneously the butler appeared in the
doorway.

'It's Mr Blair, Miss Olive.'

She jumped tensely to her feet.

'Who does he want to see?'

'He didn't say. He just walked in.'

'Tell him I'm in here.'

He entered with an air of abstraction rather than depression, nodded to Olive and sat down on a piano stool.
She wanted to say, 'Come here. Lay your head here, poor
man. Never mind.' But she wanted to cry, too, and so
she said nothing.

'In three hours,' he remarked quietly, 'we'll be able to
get the morning papers. There's a shop on Fifty-ninth
Street.'

'That's foolish——' she began.

'I am not a superficial man'—he interrupted her—
'nevertheless, my chief feeling now is for the morning
papers. Later there will be a politely silent gauntlet of
relatives, friends and business acquaintances. About the
actual affair I surprise myself by not caring at all.'

'I shouldn't care about any of it.'

'I'm rather grateful that she did it in time.'

'Why don't you go away?' Olive leaned forward
earnestly. 'Go to Europe until it all blows over.'

'Blows over.' He laughed. 'Things like this don't ever
blow over. A little snicker is going to follow me around
the rest of my life.' He groaned. 'Uncle Hamilton started
right for Park Row to make the rounds of the newspaper
offices. He's a Virginian and he was unwise enough to
use the old-fashioned word "horsewhip" to one editor.
I can hardly wait to see *that* paper.' He broke off. 'How
is Mr Castleton?'

'He'll appreciate your coming to inquire.'

'I didn't come about that.' He hesitated. 'I came to ask you a question. I want to know if you'll marry me in Greenwich to-morrow morning.'

For a minute Olive fell precipitately through space; she made a strange little sound; her mouth dropped ajar.

'I know you like me,' he went on quickly. 'In fact, I once imagined you loved me a little bit, if you'll excuse the presumption. Anyhow, you're very like a girl that once did love me, so maybe you would—' His face was pink with embarrassment, but he struggled grimly on; 'anyhow, I like you enormously and whatever feeling I may have had for Emily has, I might say, flown.'

The clangour and alarm inside her was so loud that it seemed he must hear it.

'The favour you'll be doing me will be very great,' he continued. 'My heavens, I know it sounds a little crazy, but what could be crazier than the whole afternoon? You see, if you married me the papers would carry quite a different story; they'd think that Emily went off to get out of our way, and the joke would be on her after all.'

Tears of indignation came to Olive's eyes.

'I suppose I ought to allow for your wounded egotism, but do you realize you're making me an insulting proposition?'

His face fell.

'I'm sorry,' he said after a moment. 'I guess I was an awful fool even to think of it, but a man hates to lose the whole dignity of his life for a girl's whim. I see it would be impossible. I'm sorry.'

He got up and picked up his cane.

Now he was moving towards the door, and Olive's heart came into her throat and a great, irresistible wave of self-preservation swept over her—swept over all her scruples and her pride. His steps sounded in the hall.

'Brevoort!' she called. She jumped to her feet and ran to the door. He turned. 'Brevoort, what was the name of that paper—the one your uncle went to?'

'Why?'

'Because it's not too late for them to change their story if I telephone now! I'll say we were married to-night!'

III

There is a society in Paris which is merely a heterogeneous prolongation of American society. People moving in are connected by a hundred threads to the motherland, and their entertainments, eccentricities and ups and downs are an open book to friends and relatives at Southampton, Lake Forest or Back Bay. So during her previous European sojourn Emily's whereabouts, as she followed the shifting Continental season, were publicly advertised; but from the day, one month after the unsolemnized wedding, when she sailed from New York, she dropped completely from sight. There was an occasional letter from her father, an occasional rumour that she was in Cairo, Constantinople or the less frequented Riviera—that was all.

Once, after a year, Mr Castleton saw her in Paris, but, as he told Olive, the meeting only served to make him uncomfortable.

'There was something about her,' he said vaguely, 'as if—well, as if she had a lot of things in the back of her mind I couldn't reach. She was nice enough, but it was all automatic and formal.—She asked about you.'

Despite her solid background of a three-month-old baby and a beautiful apartment on Park Avenue, Olive felt her heart falter uncertainly. 'What did she say?'

'She was delighted about you and Brevoort.' And he added to himself, with a disappointment he could not conceal: 'Even though you picked up the best match in New York when she threw it away.'. . .

. . . It was more than a year after this that his secretary's voice on the telephone asked Olive if Mr Castleton could see them that night. They found the old man walking his library in a state of agitation.

'Well, it's come,' he declared vehemently. 'People won't

stand still; nobody stands still. You go up or down in this world. Emily chose to go down. She seems to be somewhere near the bottom. Did you ever hear of a man described to me as a'—he referred to a letter in his hand —'dissipated ne'er-do-well named Petrocobesco? He calls himself Prince Gabriel Petrocobesco, apparently from— from nowhere. This letter is from Hallam, my European man, and it encloses a clipping from the Paris *Matin*. It seems that this gentleman was invited by the police to leave Paris, and among the small entourage who left with him was an American girl, Miss Castleton, "rumoured to be the daughter of a millionaire." The party was escorted to the station by gendarmes.' He handed clipping and letter to Brevoort Blair with trembling fingers. 'What do you make of it? Emily come to that!'

'It's not so good,' said Brevoort, frowning.

'It's the end. I thought her drafts were big recently, but I never suspected that she was supporting——'

'It may be a mistake,' Olive suggested. 'Perhaps it's another Miss Castleton.'

'It's Emily all right. Hallam looked up the matter. It's Emily, who was afraid ever to dive into the nice clean stream of life and ends up now by swimming around in the sewers.'

Shocked, Olive had a sudden sharp taste of fate in its ultimate diversity. She with a mansion building in West-bury Hills, and Emily was mixed up with a deported adventurer in disgraceful scandal.

'I've got no right to ask you this,' continued Mr Castle-ton. 'Certainly no right to ask Brevoort anything in con-nection with Emily. But I'm seventy-two and Fraser says if I put off the cure another fortnight he won't be respon-sible, and then Emily will be alone for good. I want you to set your trip abroad forward by two months and go over and bring her back.'

'But do you think we'd have the necessary influence?' Brevoort asked. 'I've no reason for thinking that she'd listen to me.'

'There's no one else. If you can't go I'll have to.'

'Oh, no,' said Brevoort quickly. 'We'll do what we can, won't we, Olive?'

'Of course.'

'Bring her back—it doesn't matter how—but bring her back. Go before a court if necessary and swear she's crazy.'

'Very well. We'll do what we can.'

Just ten days after this interview the Brevoort Blairs called on Mr Castleton's agent in Paris to glean what details were available. They were plentiful but unsatisfactory. Hallam had seen Petrocobesco in various restaurants—a fat little fellow with an attractive leer and a quenchless thirst. He was of some obscure nationality and had been moved around Europe for several years, living heaven knew how—probably on Americans, though Hallam understood that of late even the most outlying circles of international society were closed to him. About Emily, Hallam knew very little. They had been reported last week in Berlin and yesterday in Budapest. It was probable that such an undesirable as Petrocobesco was required to register with the police everywhere, and this was the line he recommended the Blairs to follow.

Forty-eight hours later, accompanied by the American vice-consul, they called upon the prefect of police in Budapest. The officer talked in rapid Hungarian to the vice-consul, who presently announced the gist of his remarks—the Blairs were too late.

'Where have they gone?'

'He doesn't know. He received orders to move them on and they left last night.'

Suddenly the prefect wrote something on a piece of paper and handed it, with a terse remark, to the vice-consul.

'He says try there.'

Brevoort looked at the paper.

'Sturmdorp—where's that?'

Another rapid conversation in Hungarian.

'Five hours from here on a local train that leaves Tuesdays and Fridays. This is Saturday.'

'We'll get a car at the hotel,' said Brevoort.

They set out after dinner. It was a rough journey through the night across the still Hungarian plain. Olive awoke once from a worried doze to find Brevoort and the chauffeur changing a tire; then again as they stopped at a muddy little river, beyond which glowed the scattered lights of a town. Two soldiers in an unfamiliar uniform glanced into the car; they crossed a bridge and followed a narrow, warped main street to Sturmdorp's single inn; the roosters were already crowing as they tumbled down on the mean beds.

Olive awoke with a sudden sure feeling that they had caught up with Emily; and with it came that old sense of helplessness in the face of Emily's moods; for a moment the long past, and Emily dominant in it, swept back over her, and it seemed almost a presumption to be here. But Brevoort's singleness of purpose reassured her and confidence had returned when they went downstairs, to find a landlord who spoke fluent American, acquired in Chicago before the war.

'You are not in Hungary now,' he explained. 'You have crossed the border into Czjeck-Hansa. But it is only a little country with two towns, this one and the capital. We don't ask the visa from Americans.'

'That's probably why they came here,' Olive thought.

'Perhaps you could give us some information about strangers?' asked Brevoort. 'We're looking for an American lady—' He described Emily, without mentioning her probable companion; as he proceeded a curious change came over the innkeeper's face.

'Let me see your passports,' he said; then: 'And why you want to see her?'

'This lady is her cousin.'

The innkeeper hesitated momentarily.

'I think perhaps I be able to find her for you,' he said.

He called the porter; there were rapid instructions in an unintelligible patois. Then:

'Follow this boy—he take you there.'

They were conducted through filthy streets to a tumble-down house on the edge of town. A man with a hunting rifle, lounging outside, straightened up and spoke sharply to the porter, but after an exchange of phrases they passed, mounted the stairs and knocked at a door. When it opened a head peered around the corner; the porter spoke again and they went in.

They were in a large dirty room which might have belonged to a poor boarding house in any quarter of the Western world—faded falls, split upholstery, a shapeless bed and an air, despite its bareness, of being overcrowded by the ghostly furniture, indicated by dust rings and worn spots, of the last decade. In the middle of the room stood a small stout man with hammock eyes and a peering nose over a sweet, spoiled little mouth, who stared intently at them as they opened the door, and then with a single disgusted 'Chut!' turned impatiently away. There were several other people in the room, but Brevoort and Olive saw only Emily, who reclined in a chaise-longue with half-closed eyes.

At the sight of them the eyes opened in mild astonishment; she made a move as though to jump up, but instead held out her hand, smiled and spoke their names in a clear polite voice, less as a greeting than as a sort of explanation to the others of their presence here. At their names a grudging amenity replaced the sullenness on the little man's face.

The girls kissed.

'Tutu!' said Emily, as if calling him to attention—'Prince Petrocobesco, let me present my cousin Mrs Blair, and Mr Blair.'

'Plaisir,' said Petrocobesco. He and Emily exchanged a quick glance, whereupon he said, 'Won't you sit down?' and immediately seated himself in the only available chair, as if they were playing Going to Jerusalem.

'*Plaisir,*' he repeated. Olive sat down on the foot of Emily's chaise-longue and Brevoort took a stool from against the wall, meanwhile noting the other occupants of the room. There was a very fierce young man in a cape who stood, with arms folded and teeth gleaming, by the door, and two ragged, bearded men, one holding a revolver, the other with his head sunk dejectedly on his chest, who sat side by side in the corner.

'You come here long?' the prince asked.

'Just arrived this morning.'

For a moment Olive could not resist comparing the two, the tall fair-featured American and the unprepossessing South European, scarcely a likely candidate for Ellis Island. Then she looked at Emily—the same thick bright hair with sunshine in it, the eyes with the hint of vivid seas. Her face was faintly drawn, there were slight new lines around her mouth, but she was the Emily of old —dominant, shining, large of scale. It seemed shameful for all that beauty and personality to have arrived in a cheap boarding house at the world's end.

The man in the cape answered a knock at the door and handed a note to Petrocobesco, who read it, cried '*Chut!*' and passed it to Emily.

'You see, there are no carriages,' he said tragically in French. 'The carriages were destroyed—all except one, which is in a museum. Anyway, I prefer a horse.'

'No,' said Emily.

'Yes, yes, yes!' he cried. 'Whose business is it how I go?'

'Don't let's have a scene, Tutu.'

'Scene!' He fumed. 'Scene!'

Emily turned to Olive: 'You came by automobile?'

'Yes.'

'A big de luxe car? With a back that opens?'

'Yes.'

'There,' said Emily to the prince. 'We can have the arms painted on the side of that.'

'Hold on,' said Brevoort. 'This car belongs to a hotel in Budapest.'

Apparently Emily didn't hear.

'Janierka could do it,' she continued thoughtfully.

At this point there was another interruption. The dejected man in the corner suddenly sprang to his feet and made as though to run to the door, whereupon the other man raised his revolver and brought the butt down on his head. The man faltered and would have collapsed had not his assailant hauled him back to the chair, where he sat comatose, a slow stream of blood trickling over his forehead.

'Dirty townsman! Filthy, dirty spy!' shouted Petrocobesco between clenched teeth.

'Now that's just the kind of remark you're not to make!' said Emily sharply.

'Then why we don't hear?' he cried. 'Are we going to sit here in this pigsty forever?'

Disregarding him, Emily turned to Olive and began to question her conventionally about New York. Was prohibition any more successful? What were the new plays? Olive tried to answer and simultaneously to catch Brevoort's eye. The sooner their purpose was broached, the sooner they could get Emily away.

'Can we see you alone, Emily?' demanded Brevoort abruptly.

'Why, for the moment we haven't got another room.'

Petrocobesco had engaged the man with the cape in agitated conversation, and taking advantage of this, Brevoort spoke hurriedly to Emily in a lowered voice:

'Emily, your father's getting old; he needs you at home. He wants you to give up this crazy life and come back to America. He sent us because he couldn't come himself and no one else knew you well enough——'

She laughed. 'You mean, knew the enormities I was capable of.'

'No,' put in Olive quickly. 'Cared for you as we do. I can't tell you how awful it is to see you wandering over the face of the earth.'

'But we're not wandering now,' explained Emily. 'This is Tutu's native country.'

'Where's your pride, Emily?' said Olive impatiently. 'Do you know that affair in Paris was in the papers? What do you suppose people think back home?'

'That affair in Paris was an outrage.' Emily's blue eyes flashed around her. 'Someone will pay for that affair in Paris.'

'It'll be the same everywhere. Just sinking lower and lower, dragged in the mire, and one day deserted——'

'Stop, please!' Emily's voice was as cold as ice. 'I don't think you quite understand——'

Emily broke off as Petrocobesco came back, threw himself into his chair and buried his face in his hands.

'I can't stand it,' he whispered. 'Would you mind taking my pulse? I think it's bad. Have you got the thermometer in your purse?'

She held his wrist in silence for a moment.

'It's all right, Tutu.' Her voice was soft now, almost crooning. 'Sit up. Be a man.'

'All right.'

He crossed his legs as if nothing had happened and turned abruptly to Brevoort:

'How are financial conditions in New York?' he demanded.

But Brevoort was in no humour to prolong the absurd scene. The memory of a certain terrible hour three years before swept over him. He was no man to be made a fool of twice, and his jaw set as he rose to his feet.

'Emily, get your things together,' he said tersely. 'We're going home.'

Emily did not move; an expression of astonishment, melting to amusement, spread over her face. Olive put her arm around her shoulder.

'Come, dear. Let's get out of this nightmare.' Then:

'We're waiting,' Brevoort said.

Petrocobesco spoke suddenly to the man in the cape,

who approached and seized Brevoort's arm. Brevoort shook him off angrily, whereupon the man stepped back, his hand searching his belt.

'No!' cried Emily imperatively.

Once again there was an interruption. The door opened without a knock and two stout men in frock coats and silk hats rushed in and up to Petrocobesco. They grinned and patted him on the back chattering in a strange language, and presently he grinned and patted them on the back and they kissed all around; then, turning to Emily, Petrocobesco spoke to her in French.

'It's all right,' he said excitedly. 'They did not even argue the matter. I am to have the title of king.'

With a long sigh Emily sank back in her chair and her lips parted in a relaxed, tranquil smile.

'Very well, Tutu. We'll get married.'

'Oh, heavens, how happy!' He clasped his hands and gazed up ecstatically at the faded ceiling. 'How extremely happy!' He fell on his knees beside her and kissed her inside arm.

'What's all this about kings?' Brevoort demanded. 'Is this—is he a king?'

'He's a king. Aren't you, Tutu?' Emily's hand gently stroked his oiled hair and Olive saw that her eyes were unusually bright.

'I am your husband,' cried Tutu weepily. 'The most happy man alive.'

'His uncle was Prince of Czjeck-Hansa before the war,' explained Emily, her voice singing her content. 'Since then there's been a republic, but the peasant party wanted a change and Tutu was next in line. Only I wouldn't marry him unless he insisted on being king instead of prince.'

Brevoort passed his hand over his wet forehead.

'Do you mean that this is actually a fact?'

Emily nodded. 'The assembly voted it this morning. And if you'll lend us this de luxe limousine of yours we'll make our official entrance into the capital this afternoon.'

IV

Over two years later Mr and Mrs Brevoort Blair and their two children stood upon a balcony of the Carlton Hotel in London, a situation recommended by the management for watching royal processions pass. This one began with a fanfare of trumpets down by the Strand, and presently a scarlet line of horse guards came into sight.

'But, mummy,' the little boy demanded, 'is Aunt Emily Queen of England?'

'No, dear; she's queen of a little tiny country, but when she visits here she rides in the queen's carriage.'

'Oh.'

'Thanks to the magnesium deposits,' said Brevoort dryly.

'Was she a princess before she got to be queen?' the little girl asked.

'No, dear; she was an American girl and then she got to be a queen.'

'Why?'

'Because nothing else was good enough for her,' said her father. 'Just think, one time she could have married me. Which would you rather do, baby—marry me or be a queen?'

The little girl hesitated.

'Marry you,' she said politely, but without conviction.

'That'll do, Brevoort,' said her mother. 'Here they come.'

'I see them!' the little boy cried.

The cavalcade swept down the crowded street. There were more horse guards, a company of dragoons, outriders, then Olive found herself holding her breath and squeezing the balcony rail, as between a double line of beefeaters, a pair of great gilt-and-crimson coaches rolled past. In the first were the royal sovereigns, their uniforms gleaming with ribbons, crosses and stars, and in the second their two royal consorts, one old, and the other young. There was about the scene the glamour shed always by the old empire of half the world, by her ships and ceremonies, her pomps and symbols; and the crowd felt it, and a slow murmur rolled along before the carriage, rising to a strong steady cheer. The two ladies bowed to left and right, and though few knew who the second queen was, she was cheered too. In a moment the gorgeous panoply had rolled below the balcony and on out of sight.

When Olive turned away from the window there were tears in her eyes.

'I wonder if she likes it, Brevoort. I wonder if she's really happy with that terrible little man.'

'Well, she got what she wanted, didn't she? And that's something.'

Olive drew a long breath.

'Oh, she's so wonderful,' she cried—'so wonderful! She could always move me like that, even when I was angriest at her.'

'It's all so silly,' Brevoort said.

'I suppose so,' answered Olive's lips. But her heart, winged with helpless adoration, was following her cousin through the palace gates half a mile away.

THE LAST OF THE BELLES

[1929]

I

AFTER Atlanta's elaborate and theatrical rendition of
Southern charm, we all underestimated Tarleton. It was
a little hotter than anywhere we'd been—a dozen rookies
collapsed the first day in that Georgia sun—and when you
saw herds of cows drifting through the business streets,
hi-yaed by coloured drovers, a trance stole down over you
out of the hot light: you wanted to move a hand or foot to be
sure you were alive.

So I stayed out at camp and let Lieutenant Warren tell
me about the girls. This was fifteen years ago, and I've
forgotten how I felt, except that the days went along, one
after another, better than they do now, and I was empty-
hearted, because up North she whose legend I had loved
for three years was getting married. I saw the clippings and
newspaper photographs. It was 'a romantic wartime wedding,' all very rich and sad. I felt vividly the dark radiance of
the sky under which it took place and, as a young snob,
was more envious than sorry.

A day came when I went into Tarleton for a haircut and
ran into a nice fellow named Bill Knowles, who was in my
time at Harvard. He'd been in the National Guard division
that preceded us in camp; at the last moment he had trans-
ferred to aviation and had been left behind.

'I'm glad I met you, Andy,' he said with undue seriousness. 'I'll hand you on all my information before I start for
Texas. You see, there're really only three girls here——'

I was interested; there was something mystical about
there being three girls.

470

'—and here's one of them now.'

We were in front of a drug store and he marched me in and introduced me to a lady I promptly detested.

'The other two are Ailie Calhoun and Sally Carrol Happer.'

I guessed from the way he pronounced her name that he was interested in Ailie Calhoun. It was on his mind what she would be doing while he was gone; he wanted her to have a quiet, uninteresting time.

At my age I don't even hesitate to confess that entirely unchivalrous images of Ailie Calhoun—that lovely name—rushed into my mind. At twenty-three there is no such thing as a preëmpted beauty; though, had Bill asked me, I would doubtless have sworn in all sincerity to care for her like a sister. He didn't; he was just fretting out loud at having to go. Three days later he telephoned me that he was leaving next morning and he'd take me to her house that night.

We met at the hotel and walked uptown through the flowery, hot twilight. The four white pillars of the Calhoun house faced the street, and behind them the veranda was dark as a cave with hanging, weaving, climbing vines.

When we came up the walk a girl in a white dress tumbled out of the front door, crying, 'I'm so sorry I'm late!' and seeing us, added: 'Why, I thought I heard you come ten minutes——'

She broke off as a chair creaked and another man, an aviator from Camp Harry Lee, emerged from the obscurity of the veranda.

'Why, Canby!' she cried. 'How are you?'

He and Bill Knowles waited with the tenseness of open litigants.

'Canby, I want to whisper to you, honey,' she said, after just a second. 'You'll excuse us, Bill.'

They went aside. Presently Lieutenant Canby, immensely displeased, said in a grim voice, 'Then we'll make it Thursday, but that means sure.' Scarcely nodding to us, he went down the walk, the spurs with which he presumably urged on his aeroplane gleaming in the lamplight.

'Come in—I don't just know your name——'

There she was—the Southern type in all its purity. I would have recognized Ailie Calhoun if I'd never heard Ruth Draper or read Marse Chan. She had the adroitness sugar-coated with sweet, voluble simplicity, the suggested background of devoted fathers, brothers and admirers stretching back into the South's heroic age, the unfailing coolness acquired in the endless struggle with the heat. There were notes in her voice that ordered slaves around, that withered up Yankee captains, and then soft, wheedling notes that mingled in unfamiliar loveliness with the night.

I could scarcely see her in the darkness, but when I rose to go—it was plain that I was not to linger—she stood in the orange light from the doorway. She was small and very blonde; there was too much fever-coloured rouge on her face, accentuated by a nose dabbed clownish white, but she shone through that like a star.

'After Bill goes I'll be sitting here all alone night after night. Maybe you'll take me to the country-club dances.' The pathetic prophecy brought a laugh from Bill. 'Wait a minute,' Ailie murmured. 'Your guns are all crooked.'

She straightened my collar pin, looking up at me for a second with something more than curiosity. It was a seeking look, as if she asked, 'Could it be you?' Like Lieutenant Canby, I marched off unwillingly into the suddenly insufficient night.

Two weeks later I sat with her on the same veranda, or rather she half lay in my arms and yet scarcely touched me —how she managed that I don't remember. I was trying unsuccessfully to kiss her, and had been trying for the best part of an hour. We had a sort of joke about my not being sincere. My theory was that if she'd let me kiss her I'd fall in love with her. Her argument was that I was obviously insincere.

In a lull between two of these struggles she told me about her brother who had died in his senior year at Yale. She showed me his picture—it was a handsome, earnest face with a Leyendecker forelock—and told me that when she met someone who measured up to him she'd marry. I found this family idealism discouraging; even my brash confidence couldn't compete with the dead.

The evening and other evenings passed like that, and ended with my going back to camp with the remembered smell of magnolia flowers and a mood of vague dissatisfaction. I never kissed her. We went to the vaudeville and to the country club on Saturday nights, where she seldom took ten consecutive steps with one man, and she took me to barbecues and rowdy watermelon parties, and never thought it was worth while to change what I felt for her into love. I see now that it wouldn't have been hard, but she was a wise nineteen and she must have seen that we were emotionally incompatible. So I became her confidant instead.

We talked about Bill Knowles. She was considering Bill; for, though she wouldn't admit it, a winter at school in New York and a prom at Yale had turned her eyes North. She said she didn't think she'd marry a Southern man. And by degrees I saw that she was consciously and voluntarily different from these other girls who sang nigger songs and shot craps in the country-club bar. That's why Bill and I and others were drawn to her. We recognized her.

June and July, while the rumours reached us faintly, ineffectually, of battle and terror overseas, Ailie's eyes roved here and there about the country-club floor, seeking for something among the tall young officers. She attached several, choosing them with unfailing perspicacity—save in the case of Lieutenant Canby, whom she claimed to despise, but, nevertheless, gave dates to 'because he was so sincere'—and we apportioned her evenings among us all summer.

One day she broke all her dates—Bill Knowles had leave and was coming. We talked of the event with scientific impersonality—would he move her to a decision? Lieutenant Canby, on the contrary, wasn't impersonal at all; made a nuisance of himself. He told her that if she married Knowles he was going to climb up six thousand feet in his aeroplane, shut off the motor and let go. He frightened her—I had to yield him my last date before Bill came.

On Saturday night she and Bill Knowles came to the country club. They were very handome together and once more I felt envious and sad. As they danced out on the floor the three-piece orchestra was playing *After You've Gone*, in a poignant incomplete way that I can hear yet, as if each bar were trickling off a precious minute of that time. I knew then that I had grown to love Tarleton, and I glanced about half in panic to see if some face wouldn't come in for me out of that warm, singing, outer darkness that yielded up couple after couple in organdie and olive drab. It was a time of youth and war, and there was never so much love around.

When I danced with Ailie she suddenly suggested that we go outside to a car. She wanted to know why didn't people cut in on her to-night? Did they think she was already married?

'Are you going to be?'

'I don't know, Andy. Sometimes, when he treats me as if I were sacred, it thrills me.' Her voice was hushed and far away. 'And then——'

She laughed. Her body, so frail and tender, was touching mine, her face was turned up to me, and there, suddenly, with Bill Knowles ten yards off, I could have kissed her at last. Our lips just touched experimentally; then an aviation officer turned a corner of the veranda near us, peered into our darkness and hesitated.

'Ailie.'

'Yes.'

'You heard about this afternoon?'

'What?' She leaned forward, tenseness already in her voice.

'Horace Canby crashed. He was instantly killed.'

She got up slowly and stepped out of the car.

'You mean he was killed?' she said.

'Yes. They don't know what the trouble was. His motor——'

'Oh-h-h!' Her rasping whisper came through the hands suddenly covering her face. We watched her helplessly as she put her head on the side of the car, gagging dry tears. After a minute I went for Bill, who was standing in the stag line, searching anxiously about for her, and told him she wanted to go home.

I sat on the steps outside. I had disliked Canby, but his terrible, pointless death was more real to me then than the day's toll of thousands in France. In a few minutes Ailie and Bill came out. Ailie was whimpering a little, but when she saw me her eyes flexed and she came over swiftly.

'Andy'—she spoke in a quick, low voice—'of course you must never tell anybody what I told you about Canby yesterday. What he said, I mean.'

'Of course not.'

She looked at me a second longer as if to be quite sure. Finally she was sure. Then she sighed in such a quaint little way that I could hardly believe my ears, and her brow went up in what can only be described as mock despair.

'An-dy!'

I looked uncomfortably at the ground, aware that she was calling my attention to her involuntarily disastrous effect on men.

'Good night, Andy!' called Bill as they got into a taxi.

'Good night,' I said, and almost added: 'You poor fool.'

II

Of course I should have made one of those fine moral decisions that people make in books, and despised her. On the contrary, I don't doubt that she could still have had me by raising her hand.

A few days later she made it all right by saying wistfully, 'I know you think it was terrible of me to think of myself at a time like that, but it was such a shocking coincidence.'

At twenty-three I was entirely unconvinced about anything, except that some people were strong and attractive and could do what they wanted, and others were caught and disgraced. I hoped I was of the former. I was sure Ailie was.

I had to revise other ideas about her. In the course of a long discussion with some girl about kissing—in those days people still talked about kissing more than they kissed —I mentioned the fact that Ailie had only kissed two or three men, and only when she thought she was in love. To my considerable disconcertion the girl figuratively just lay on the floor and howled.

'But it is true,' I assured her, suddenly knowing it wasn't. 'She told me herself.'

'Ailie Calhoun! Oh, my heavens! Why, last year at the Tech spring house party——'

This was in September. We were going overseas any week now, and to bring us up to full strength a last batch of officers from the fourth training camp arrived. The fourth camp wasn't like the first three—the candidates were from the ranks; even from the drafted divisions. They had queer names without vowels in them, and save for a few young militiamen, you couldn't take it for granted that they came out of any background at all. The addition to our company was Lieutenant Earl Schoen from New Bedford, Massachusetts; as fine a physical specimen as I have ever seen. He was six-foot-three, with black hair, high colour, and glossy dark-brown eyes. He wasn't very smart and he was definitely illiterate, yet he was a good officer, high-tempered and commanding, and with that becoming touch of vanity that sits well on the military. I had an idea that New Bedford was a country town, and set down his bumptious qualities to that.

We were doubled up in living quarters and he came into my hut. Inside of a week there was a cabinet photograph of some Tarleton girl nailed brutally to the shack wall.

'She's no jane or anything like that. She's a society girl; goes with all the best people here.'

The following Sunday afternoon I met the lady at a semi-private swimming pool in the country. When Ailie and I arrived, there was Schoen's muscular body rippling out of a bathing suit at the far end of the pool.

'Hey, lieutenant!'

When I waved back at him he grinned and winked, jerking his head toward the girl at his side. Then, digging her in the ribs, he jerked his head at me. It was a form of introduction.

'Who's that with Kitty Preston?' Ailie asked, and when I told her she said he looked like a street-car conductor, and pretended to look for her transfer.

A moment later he crawled powerfully and gracefully down the pool and pulled himself up at our side. I introduced him to Ailie.

'How do you like my girl, lieutenant?' he demanded. 'I told you she was all right, didn't I?' He jerked his head toward Ailie; this time to indicate that his girl and Ailie moved in the same circles. 'How about us all having dinner together down at the hotel some night?'

I left them in a moment, amused as I saw Ailie visibly making up her mind that here, anyhow, was not the ideal. But Lieutenant Earl Schoen was not to be dismissed so lightly. He ran his eyes cheerfully and inoffensively over her cute, slight figure, and decided that she would do even better than the other. Then minutes later I saw them in the water together, Ailie swimming away with a grim little stroke she had, and Schoen wallowing riotously around her and ahead of her, sometimes pausing and staring at her, fascinated, as a boy might look at a nautical doll.

While the afternoon passed he remained at her side. Finally Ailie came over to me and whispered, with a laugh: 'He's afollowing me around. He thinks I haven't paid my car-fare.'

She turned quickly. Miss Kitty Preston, her face curiously flustered, stood facing us.

'Ailie Calhoun, I didn't think it of you to go out and delib'ately try to take a man away from another girl.'—

An expression of distress at the impending scene flitted over Ailie's face—'I thought you considered yourself above anything like that.'

Miss Preston's voice was low, but it held that tensity that can be felt farther than it can be heard, and I saw Ailie's clear lovely eyes glance about in panic. Luckily, Earl himself was ambling cheerfully and innocently toward us.

'If you care for him you certainly oughtn't to belittle yourself in front of him,' said Ailie in a flash, her head high.

It was her acquaintance with the traditional way of behaving against Kitty Preston's naïve and fierce possessiveness, or if you prefer it, Ailie's 'breeding' against the other's 'commonness'. She turned away.

'Wait a minute, kid!' cried Earl Schoen. 'How about your address? Maybe I'd like to give you a ring on the phone.'

She looked at him in a way that should have indicated to Kitty her entire lack of interest.

'I'm very busy at the Red Cross this month,' she said, her voice as cool as her slicked-back blond hair. 'Goodbye.'

On the way home she laughed. Her air of having been unwittingly involved in a contemptible business vanished.

'She'll never hold that young man,' she said. 'He wants somebody new.'

'Apparently he wants Ailie Calhoun.'

The idea amused her.

'He could give me his ticket punch to wear, like a fraternity pin. What fun! If Mother ever saw anybody like that come in the house, she'd just lie down and die.'

And to give Ailie credit, it was fully a fortnight before he did come to her house, although he rushed her until she pretended to be annoyed at the next country-club dance.

'He's the biggest tough, Andy,' she whispered to me. 'But he's so sincere.'

She used the word 'tough' without the conviction it would have carried had he been a Southern boy. She only knew it with her mind; her ear couldn't distinguish between one Yankee voice and another. And somehow Mrs. Calhoun didn't expire at his appearance on the threshold. The supposedly ineradicable prejudices of Ailie's parents were a convenient phenomenon that disappeared at her wish. It was her friends who were astonished. Ailie, always a little above Tarleton, whose beaux had been very carefully the 'nicest' men of the camp—Ailie and Lieutenant Schoen! I grew tired of assuring people that she was merely distracting herself—and indeed every week or so there was someone new—an ensign from Pensacola, an old friend from New Orleans—but always, in between times, there was Earl Schoen.

Orders arrived for an advance party of officers and sergeants to proceed to the port of embarkation and take ship to France. My name was on the list. I had been on the range for a week and when I got back to camp, Earl Schoen buttonholed me immediately.

'We're giving a little farewell party in the mess. Just you and I and Captain Craker and three girls.'

Earl and I were to call for the girls. We picked up Sally Carrol Happer and Nancy Lamar, and went on to Ailie's house; to be met at the door by the butler with the announcement that she wasn't home.

'Isn't home?' Earl repeated blankly. 'Where is she?'

'Didn't leave no information about that; just said she wasn't home.'

'But this is a darn funny thing!' he exclaimed. He walked around the familiar dusky veranda while the butler waited at the door. Something occurred to him. 'Say,' he informed me—'say, I think she's sore.'

I waited. He said sternly to the butler, 'You tell her I've got to speak to her a minute.'

'How'm I goin' tell her that when she ain't home?'

Again Earl walked musingly around the porch. Then he nodded several times and said:

'She's sore at something that happened downtown.'

In a few words he sketched out the matter to me.

'Look here; you wait in the car,' I said. 'Maybe I can

fix this.' And when he reluctantly retreated: 'Oliver, you tell Miss Ailie I want to see her alone.'

After some argument he bore this message and in a moment returned with a reply:

'Miss Ailie say she don't want to see that other gentleman about nothing never. She say come in if you like.'

She was in the library. I had expected to see a picture of cool, outraged dignity, but her face was distraught, tumultuous, despairing. Her eyes were red-rimmed, as though she had been crying slowly and painfully, for hours.

'Oh, hello, Andy,' she said brokenly. 'I haven't seen you for so long. Has he gone?'

'Now, Ailie——'

'Now, Ailie!' she cried. 'Now, Ailie! He spoke to me, you see. He lifted his hat. He stood there ten feet from me with that horrible—that horrible woman—holding her arm and talking to her, and then when he saw me he raised his hat. Andy, I didn't know what to do. I had to go in the drug store and ask for a glass of water, and I was so afraid he'd follow in after me that I asked Mr Rich to let me go out the back way. I never want to see him or hear of him again.'

I talked. I said what one says in such cases. I said it for half an hour. I could not move her. Several times she answered by murmuring something about his not being 'sincere', and for the fourth time I wondered what the word meant to her. Certainly not constancy; it was, I half suspected, some special way she wanted to be regarded.

I got up to go. And then, unbelievably, the automobile horn sounded three times impatiently outside. It was stupefying. It said as plainly as if Earl were in the room, 'All right; go to the devil then! I'm not going to wait here all night.'

Ailie looked at me aghast. And suddenly a peculiar look came into her face, spread, flickered, broke into a teary, hysterical smile.

'Isn't he awful?' she cried in helpless despair. 'Isn't he terrible?'

'Hurry up,' I said quickly. 'Get your cape. This is our last night.'

And I can still feel that last night vividly, the candlelight that flickered over the rough boards of the mess shack, over the frayed paper decorations left from the supply company's party, the sad mandolin down a company street that kept picking *My Indiana Home* out of the universal nostalgia of the departing summer. The three girls lost in this mysterious men's city felt something, too—a bewitched impermanence as though they were on a magic carpet that had lighted on the Southern countryside, and any moment the wind would lift it and waft it away. We toasted ourselves and the South. Then we left our napkins and empty glasses and a little of the past on the table, and hand in hand went out into the moonlight itself. Taps had been played; there was no sound but the far-away whinny of a horse, and a loud persistent snore at which we laughed, and the leathery snap of a sentry coming to port over by the guardhouse. Craker was on duty; we others got into a waiting car, motored into Tarleton and left Craker's girl.

Then Ailie and Earl, Sally and I, two and two in the wide back seat, each couple turned from the other, absorbed and whispering, drove away into the wide, flat darkness.

We drove through pinewoods heavy with lichen and Spanish moss, and between the fallow cotton fields along a road white as the rim of the world. We parked under the broken shadow of a mill where there was the sound of running water and restive squawky birds and over everything a brightness that tried to filter in anywhere—into the lost nigger cabins, the automobile, the fastnesses of the heart. The South sang to us—I wonder if they remember. I remember—the cool pale faces, the somnolent amorous eyes and the voices:

'Are you comfortable?'

'Yes; are you?'

'Are you sure you are?'

'Yes.'

Suddenly we knew it was late and there was nothing more. We turned home.

Our detachment started for Camp Mills next day, but I didn't go to France after all. We passed a cold month on Long Island, marched aboard a transport with steel helmets slung at our sides and then marched off again. There wasn't any more war. I had missed the war. When I came back to Tarleton I tried to get out of the Army, but I had a regular commission and it took most of the winter. But Earl Schoen was one of the first to be demobilized. He wanted to find a good job 'while the picking was good.' Ailie was non-committal, but there was an understanding between them that he'd be back.

By January the camps, which for two years had dominated the little city, were already fading. There was only the persistent incinerator smell to remind one of all that activity and bustle. What life remained centred bitterly about divisional headquarters building with the disgruntled regular officers who had also missed the war.

And now the young men of Tarleton began drifting back from the ends of the earth—some with Canadian uniforms, some with crutches or empty sleeves. A returned battalion of the National Guard paraded through the streets with open ranks for their dead, and then stepped down out of romance for ever and sold you things over the counters of local stores. Only a few uniforms mingled with the dinner coats at the country-club dance.

Just before Christmas, Bill Knowles arrived unexpectedly one day and left the next—either he gave Ailie an ultimatum or she had made up her mind at last. I saw her sometimes when she wasn't busy with returned heroes from Savannah and Augusta, but I felt like an outmoded survival—and I was. She was waiting for Earl Schoen with such a vast uncertainty that she didn't like to talk about it. Three days before I got my final discharge he came.

I first happened upon them walking down Market Street together, and I don't think I've ever been so sorry for a couple in my life; though I suppose the same situation was repeating itself in every city where there had been camps. Exteriorly Earl had about everything wrong with him that could be imagined. His hat was green, with a radical feather; his suit was slashed and braided in a grotesque fashion that national advertising and the movies have put an end to. Evidently he had been to his old barber, for his hair bloused neatly on his pink, shaved neck. It wasn't as though he had been shiny and poor, but the background of mill-town dance halls and outing clubs flamed out at you—or rather flamed out at Ailie. For she had never quite imagined the reality; in these clothes even the natural grace of that magnificent body had departed. At first he boasted of his fine job; it would get them along all right until he could 'see some easy money.' But from the moment he came back into her world on its own terms he must have known it was hopeless. I don't know what Ailie said or how much her grief weighed against her stupefaction. She acted quickly —three days after his arrival, Earl and I went North together on the train.

'Well, that's the end of that,' he said moodily. 'She's a wonderful girl, but too much of a highbrow for me. I guess she's got to marry some rich guy that'll give her a great social position. I can't see that stuck-up sort of thing.' And then, later: 'She said to come back and see her in a year, but I'll never go back. This aristocrat stuff is all right if you got the money for it, but——'

'But it wasn't real,' he meant to finish. The provincial society in which he had moved with so much satisfaction for six months already appeared to him as affected, 'dudish' and artificial.

'Say, did you see what I saw getting on the train?' he asked me after a while. 'Two wonderful janes, all alone. What do you say we mosey into the next car and ask them to lunch? I'll take the one in blue.' Halfway down the car he turned around suddenly. 'Say, Andy,' he demanded, frowning; 'one thing—how do you suppose she knew I used to command a street car? I never told her that.'

'Search me.'

III

This narrative arrives now at one of the big gaps that stared me in the face when I began. For six years, while I finished at Harvard Law and built commercial aeroplanes and backed a pavement block that went gritty under trucks, Ailie Calhoun was scarcely more than a name on a Christmas card; something that blew a little in my mind on warm nights when I remembered the magnolia flowers. Occasionally an acquaintance of Army days would ask me, 'What became of that blonde girl who was so popular?' but I didn't know. I ran into Nancy Lamar at the Montmartre in New York one evening and learned that Ailie had become engaged to a man in Cincinatti, had gone North to visit his family and then broken it off. She was lovely as ever and there was always a heavy beau or two. But neither Bill Knowles nor Earl Schoen had ever come back.

And somewhere about that time I heard that Bill Knowles had married a girl he met on a boat. There you are—not much of a patch to mend six years with.

Oddly enough, a girl seen at twilight in a small Indiana station started me thinking about going South. The girl, in stiff pink organdie, threw her arms about a man who got off our train and hurried him to a waiting car, and I felt a sort of pang. It seemed to me that she was bearing him off into the lost midsummer world of my early twenties, where time had stood still and charming girls, dimly seen like the past itself, still loitered along the dusky streets. I suppose that poetry is a Northern man's dream of the South. But it was months later that I sent off a wire to Ailie, and immediately followed it to Tarleton.

It was July. The Jefferson Hotel seemed strangely shabby and stuffy—a boosters' club burst into intermittent song in the dining-room that my memory had long dedicated to officers and girls. I recognized the taxi driver who took me up to Ailie's house, but his 'Sure, I do, Lieutenant,' was unconvincing. I was only one of twenty thousand.

It was a curious three days. I suppose some of Ailie's first young lustre must have gone the way of such mortal shining, but I can't bear witness to it. She was still so physically appealing that you wanted to touch the personality that trembled on her lips. No—the change was more profound than that.

At once I saw she had a different line. The modulations of pride, the vocal hints that she knew the secrets of a brighter, finer ante-bellum day, were gone from her voice; there was no time for them now as it rambled on in the half-laughing, half-desperate banter of the newer South. And everything was swept into this banter in order to make it go on and leave no time for thinking—the present, the future, herself, me. We went to a rowdy party at the house of some young married people, and she was the nervous, glowing centre of it. After all, she wasn't eighteen, and she was as attractive in her role of reckless clown as she had ever been in her life.

'Have you heard anything from Earl Schoen?' I asked her the second night, on our way to the country-club dance.

'No.' She was serious for a moment. 'I often think of him. He was the——' she hesitated.

'Go on.'

'I was going to say the man I loved most, but that wouldn't be true. I never exactly loved him, or I'd have married him any old how, wouldn't I?' She looked at me questioningly. 'At least I wouldn't have treated him like that.'

'It was impossible.'

'Of course,' she agreed uncertainly. Her mood changed; she became flippant: 'How the Yankees did deceive us poor little Southern girls! Ah, me!'

When we reached the country club she melted like a chameleon into the—to me—unfamiliar crowd. There was a new generation upon the floor, with less dignity than the ones I had known, but none of them was more a part of its lazy, feverish essence than Ailie. Possibly she had perceived that in her initial longing to escape from Tarleton's provincialism she had been walking alone, following a generation which was doomed to have no successors. Just where she lost the battle, waged behind the white pillars of her veranda, I don't know. But she had guessed wrong, missed out somewhere. Her wild animation, which even now called enough men around her to rival the entourage of the youngest and freshest, was an admission of defeat.

I left her house, as I had so often left it that vanished June, in a mood of vague dissatisfaction. It was hours later, tossing about my bed in the hotel, that I realized what was the matter, what had always been the matter—I was deeply and incurably in love with her. In spite of every incompatibility, she was still, she would always be to me, the most attractive girl I had ever known. I told her so next afternoon. It was one of those hot days I knew so well, and Ailie sat beside me on a couch in the darkened library.

'Oh, no, I couldn't marry you,' she said, almost frightened; 'I don't love you that way at all. . . . I never did. And you don't love me, I didn't mean to tell you now, but next month I'm going to marry another man. We're not even announcing it, because I've done that twice before.' Suddenly it occurred to her that I might be hurt: 'Andy, you just had a silly idea, didn't you? You know I couldn't ever marry a Northern man.'

'Who is he?' I demanded.

'A man from Savannah.'

'Are you in love with him?'

'Of course I am.' We both smiled. 'Of course I am! What are you trying to make me say?'

There were no doubts, as there had been with other men. She couldn't afford to let herself have doubts. I knew this because she had long ago stopped making any pretensions with me. This very naturalness, I realized, was because she didn't consider me as a suitor. Beneath her mask of an instinctive thoroughbred she had always been on to herself, and she couldn't believe that anyone not taken in to the point of uncritical worship could really love her. That was what she called being 'sincere'; she felt most security with men like

Canby and Earl Schoen, who were incapable of passing judgments on the ostensibly aristocratic heart.

'All right,' I said, as if she had asked my permission to marry. 'Now, would you do something for me?'

'Anything.'

'Ride out to camp.'

'But there's nothing left there, honey.'

'I don't care.'

We walked downtown. The taxi-driver in front of the hotel repeated her objection: 'Nothing there now, Cap.'

'Never mind. Go there anyhow.'

Twenty minutes later he stopped on a wide unfamiliar plain powdered with new cotton fields and marked with isolated clumps of pine.

'Like to drive over yonder where you see the smoke?' asked the driver. 'That's the new state prison.'

'No. Just drive along this road. I want to find where I used to live.'

An old racecourse, inconspicuous in the camp's day of glory, had reared its dilapidated grandstand in the desolation. I tried in vain to orient myself.

'Go along this road past that clump of trees, and then turn right—no, turn left.'

He obeyed, with professional disgust.

'You won't find a single thing, darling,' said Ailie. 'The contractors took it all down.'

We rode slowly along the margin of the fields. It might have been here——

'All right. I want to get out,' I said suddenly.

I left Ailie sitting in the car, looking very beautiful with the warm breeze stirring her long, curly bob.

It might have been here. That would make the company streets down there and the mess shack, where we dined that night, just over the way.

The taxi-driver regarded me indulgently while I stumbled here and there in the knee-deep underbrush, looking for my youth in a clapboard or a strip of roofing or a rusty tomato can. I tried to sight on a vaguely familiar clump of trees, but it was growing darker now and I couldn't be quite sure they were the right trees.

'They're going to fix up the old racecourse,' Ailie called from the car. 'Tarleton's getting quite doggy in its old age.'

No. Upon consideration they didn't look like the right trees. All I could be sure of was this place that had once been so full of life and effort was gone, as if it had never existed, and that in another month Ailie would be gone, and the South would be empty for me for ever.